ALL THE STARS
THAT EVER WERE
ROBERT JOHN JENSON

All The Stars That Ever Were

By Robert John Jenson

First Paperback edition December 2018

Book design and cover art by Robert John Jenson

ISBN 978-0-9600737-0-2 (paperback)

ISBN 978 -0-9600737-1-9 (ebook)

Library of Congress Control Number: 2018914301

https://www.facebook.com/robertjohnjenson

Once again and always,
To my lovely wife and daughters -
Without you, all is lost.

And to all sisters everywhere.
Even sisters-in-law…

All philosophy is founded on two things; an inquisitive mind, and a defective sight...
Bernard le Bovier de Fontenelle
Conversations on the Plurality of Worlds

PART ONE

PART ONE

PART ONE

Prologue

The pencil bobbed and twitched between Carol's fingers, the heavy eraser her see-saw partner, a counterweight against her thumb perpetually batting the dulled graphite. She was careful, however, not to strike the angled rubber against the table surface. Daddy was watching TV, and the tapping would upset him. Byron sat across from her, doing his homework as well. Both of them liked to get it out of the way on a Friday night, with the thought that it made the weekend feel a bit more free. Their sister Cheryl liked to wait until Sunday night. Carol and her brother thought she was crazy. As long as it was *done*, their father had said, then he didn't care when they did it. Byron had taught her the word *magnanimous*. In secret, of course.

Carol glanced up at Byron, and managed not to gasp. Her nervous energy wanted to transfer from her pencil to her leg, but she didn't like displaying such a broad gesture. It might attract attention. Still, her stomach knotted, and she scowled. Byron had a comic book open, his pale blond head twitching in slight jerks from side to side as he hunched over the pages. He shared the poor vision of his sisters. It was an affliction with a long name, and Carol could only remember the astigmatism part of it, but daddy couldn't remember all of it either, so she guessed it wasn't that important to know.

"All it means is you brats can't see worth beans," her father would remark, blaming their mother's side of the family.

She studied the top of her brother's head as it wobbled, wondering how someone so smart could be so *dumb* at times. *Why are you doing this?* she wanted to scream at him. *You know it will make him mad if he catches you!* As if he could hear her thoughts, Byron looked up, the pale bulb hanging above the dining table reflecting in his glasses, his lips pursed in what momma called 'the silent whistle' – something he wouldn't do audibly when daddy was around, but still couldn't help going through the motions to release the tune in his head. And it still annoyed his father.

Carol darted a quick look towards the living room. She suspected their father was asleep in front of the TV again - but he could wake up so *quickly*. She turned back to Byron, set her jaw and widened her eyes as she pushed her face towards him, willing him to put the stupid comic book away. Byron smiled at her.

"It's really cool," he whispered. "It's called *Sandman*, and it's about the aspect of – "

Carol bunched her left hand into a fist and punched the air with it savagely. Loathe to make any noise, she nevertheless darted another look towards daddy and then leaned even closer towards her brother.

"What's wrong with you?" she whispered urgently. "Do you *like* to get in trouble? I don't care what your stupid comic book is about – he'll just take it away from you!"

"He can't," Byron replied with certainty. "It's not mine, I borrowed it from Josh."

"Are you really that stupid?" Carol hissed, and then felt an immediate and raw pang of guilt at the way his head jerked back. Why did he have to make things harder than they needed to be. *Why?* She loved her brother dearly, but she wanted to grab him by his stupid head and shake it until he woke up. "Daddy hates your nerd stuff. Daddy wants you to be big and bad and tough like him," she said. *Like he thinks he is*, a small voice in her head muttered, but Carol clamped down on it. "If you're done with your homework, you should be out in the garage lifting. You *know* that."

Byron leaned back, and Carol felt the quiet stubbornness radiate off him. She closed her eyes, and tried reason.

"Do you think daddy cares if that comic belongs to someone else? He'll trash it anyways. Do you want to lose your friend's comic book?"

12

Byron sat and stared at her, and Carol felt an absurd desire to tattle on him. Getting Byron in trouble might actually draw attention away from her tonight. And that would be okay, wouldn't it? She bet if Byron even knew about it, what daddy did, he would sacrifice himself just for her...

And then Byron closed the comic book and slid it into his Pee Chee folder behind some papers. Carol sighed, relieved. She wanted to apologize for calling him stupid. For wanting to rat him out. For almost hating him for his dumb nerd stuff. Why couldn't he see that he made life harder for them all? Because at some point everyone – mommy, Cheryl, herself – even little Darla – would stick up for Byron and then...well, they never learned, did they?

Carol shut her math book, and tucked the pencil between the spine and dust jacket made from a paper grocery bag. She would finish her homework in her room. She rose from the table without a word, and tread silently past the living room. Her father snored softly on the couch, a can of beer on an end table, just out of reach of his loose fingers. Basketball played silently on the 20-inch Sony, the shifting illumination of the room a cold flickering of the contemporary campfire.

Maybe he'll stay asleep down here tonight, she thought. She climbed the stairs quietly, glancing back at her brother, who sat at the table with his hands folded in front of him.

Carol lay on her side in the dark, her back to her bedroom door, and tried her best to appear deep in sleep. She tried to keep her breathing even and shallow, giving an appearance of angelic slumber - wouldn't anyone just *hate* to disturb that? But she was sure her posture was a tense give away to her wakefulness, and dreamy sleep or not, it never stopped him anyway...

Why? Why does he do it? she thought. *It's not right! I'm too young for this. This isn't supposed to happen until you're married, or at least older and you're boyfriend and girlfriend and you loved each other very much...*

The floorboards creaked, and she expected the tentative, gentle touch – something so far removed from the way he treated her and everyone else the rest of the time – as if...not in apology, never *that*, but perhaps an acknowledgement that what he was doing was wrong, and you only approached such things carefully. No matter how many times they were done.

Another creak, and a touch on her shoulder. She gave an involuntary shudder, and an unfamiliar voice – young, a *boy*? - whispered in her ear.

"You want to go someplace else?"

Before she could react, she felt a pinprick of pain at the base of her skull and she gasped. She felt as if something was tuning up in her head, and her body felt like it was expanding, growing out – or maybe it was only her soul stretching and erupting from her pores and the boy's voice asked, "Ready?"

and then she really was growing expanding it felt like her fingers and toes and hair and eyes reached to the end of time and she was carol but not and she didn't live here but she did and it was so much better yet so much worse and she lived on the street but also lived in luxury a star athlete artist and her dad was here but comforting her bad dreams and yet hadn't her mom killed him and she was in foster care on mars

And then she was just herself, in bed.

"Let's try here," said the voice. "Far enough. But not *too* far."

Carol drew in a deep breath, and her body shook with relief. She found it curious that she thought it was her body – separate from herself – that would feel this way.

"Things will be way different here," said the boy. "But not so different you won't be able to handle it, I think." He sighed, and Carol mustered up the nerve to finally turn away from the wall and face him. He stood in the dark, blond hair a backlit halo ignited by the light of a…fish tank? Where did *that* come from? He turned slightly, and may have smiled, but she couldn't see him very well. And let's face it, she never saw that well anyway. He looked like he was dressed all in black.

They stared at each other for a while, Carol's breath still trying to find the fake rhythm she had maintained before. *I should scream*, she thought. *I should scream about a strange boy in my room. Before daddy sees him.* But she didn't.

He cocked his head, and said, "It *should* be better here – you're gonna be weirded out for sure, but just deal with it and you'll be okay. They'll probably make you see a shrink or something." He paused, took a step closer.

"Remember – this *happened*. Don't let them make *you* think you're crazy, okay? Just play along, and you'll be alright. But you're in a new life now, because..." He pondered that thought for a moment. "I feel bad for us, you know? Those of us where life really *sucks*."

Carol coughed, and tried to find her voice. "Who..." she began, but he put a finger to his lips and whispered, "Remember, just play along – don't let your stubbornness get the best of you. This happened, and you're *not* crazy."

He turned towards the door.

"I gotta go," he said. "But you know what? I bet we will see each other again - if things *finally* come to a head."

And then, instead of leaving by the door, he was gone, like he smeared out of existence, the fish tank giving the room a lavender hue.

"What the heck?" she whispered.

Her eyes roamed the room, and it made no sense. She brought the tips of her index fingers to the outer corners of her eyes to try and tame them for a moment. Sometimes that helped, but her room remained maddeningly off kilter. The dresser was where it should be, but not the *shape* it should be. And there was a desk and a chair, the seat piled with a stalactite of clothes that joined the stalagmite on the floor. The room was messier than she kept it, and her heart began to hammer in her chest because daddy would get mad. She was so much tidier than this!

It occurred to her that she must be dreaming. Either that or she had retreated into the safety of being crazy.

This happened.

She shook her head, and closed her eyes, counted to ten, and opened them. The fish tank still glowed by her closet.

"What the heck?" she whispered again. Her eyelids began to feel heavy, and it was a chore to keep them open. Why was she so tired now?

"What the *heck?*"

She continued to repeat it until she drifted off to sleep.

15

The morning light through the blinds threw bars of shadows across her room, confusing Carol. Gone were the thin drapes sagging from the window frame.

"What the heck?" she muttered, and then drew in a sharp breath as she remembered her nighttime visitor. Her eyes darted over to the far wall, and yes there it was – the fish tank, looking considerably less other-worldly in the morning light. A poster of four young black men hung on the wall above the tank, and she squinted to read who they were, then flushed with a thrill and then alarm: Boyz II Men.

"What the *heck?*" she almost shouted, and sat up. She felt the urge to get up and rip the poster off the wall before daddy saw it, but her head swiveled on her neck, taking in the rest of the room. Nice white desk, cluttered with Lisa Frank school paraphernalia, countless bottles of nail polish, combs, brushes, hair bands and ties, and a boom box with a haphazard pile of CDs. A matching dresser with clothes spilling out of drawers to the floor like foam bubbling out of a cooking pot. Dirty clothes were in a pile by an overturned and empty hamper. Belts, shoes, boots and flip-flops littered the floor wherever they darn well pleased.

"Oh, geeze," she breathed. She was going to be in so much trouble if daddy found her room like... But this wasn't her room. Was it? *Was* it? If not, how the heck did she get here? Was the boy real, and had he brought her here?

She swung her legs out over the edge of the bed, marveling that her feet didn't reach the plush carpeting. The ornate metal bed frame had a leather purse hanging from a corner, and she fought the urge to rifle through it. She was almost certain that she had accidentally wandered, *somehow*, into another girl's room, and didn't want to be caught going through someone else's private stuff.

She still wore her nightshirt – one of her mom's old ones that stretched past her knees. It was a threadbare white tee decorated with a yawning teddy bear and the caption "Beary Tired". So far, other than the general shape of her room, that was the only thing that was familiar to her.

She slid off of the bed, slipped her fingers into her long blond hair and tucked it behind her ears, then cocked her head, listening. The TV downstairs blaring the frenzy of Saturday morning kids programming was muffled through the door. Whoever was watching risked the hungover wrath of daddy, and she felt uneasy. She tip-toed over to the door, and then felt very foolish. Why was she doing that? Still, she felt the need for stealth, not convinced she was in the right house, or even in her right mind. Her heart beat frantically, she could feel it in her ears, and a slow, rising panic filled her chest.

Don't let them make you think you're crazy, okay?

"Don't need anyone's help there," she whispered, and reached out to turn the ornate crystal door knob, then pulled her hand back. Daddy was the only one who would shut her door – had she shut it last night? No. That would have been unacceptable. She could only shut it when changing clothes. He only shut it when... But that hadn't happened.

She gnawed at her lower lip. Should she fling the door open and make a mad dash down the hall, down the stairs, and out the front door? She imagined the shocked looks of strangers as she bolted past them, their mouths round and open with surprise.

Don't mind me, I just sleep-walked into your house! She giggled.

She grabbed the knob, turned it slowly until it stopped, then pushed against the door as she pulled on the knob, hoping to keep it from jerking open with a loud bang. But the door opened smoothly, unlike *hers* where it seemed the paint from the door and frame always stuck to each other like long lost friends, as if they missed the good old days of being mixed in a can together.

This is where she almost lost it. A scream started to build in her gut, and it wanted out desperately. It was rocket-propelled and nothing was going stop it from bursting out of her throat at rock-concert levels. Except the thought of her dad bursting out of his room, with murder in his eyes.

So she settled for a quiet whimper, and pulled the door open all the way.

Hanging on the wall across from her bedroom door was a painting her mother had made when she was a teenager. It was a watercolor of a black cocker spaniel, her mom's dog when she was a kid.

"Okay, good," Carol said with relief. "I know this, I've seen it. Mommy painted it." But she'd never seen it hanging in the house. It was in a box out in the garage, coated in dust. Still, it went a long way in helping calm her nerves, and the pressure she felt in her head seemed to release, and her limbs felt weak and shaky. She managed a soft giggle, then took the time to take several deep breaths and when her legs felt strong she moved down the hall, paused at the top of the landing – the TV louder still – then jogged down the stairs.

Someone was in the downstairs bathroom brushing their teeth. Probably Cheryl – if it was Byron, you probably wouldn't be able to hear his deliberate strokes through the closed door.

She rounded the corner into the family room, and gasped at the TV that dominated the room. *When in the heck did we get that?* she marveled. Darla sat on the couch, a big bowl of Berry Berry Kix between her legs, a plastic sippy cup clutched in her chubby three-year old fist. She stared at Carol, squinted, then raised her arm in a wave that always looked like a salute. Carol grinned – the familiar gesture always cracked her up, and she began to feel a bit better. Her little sister took a long sip of milk from the cup and studied Carol as she negotiated around the end of the couch, folded her legs under her and sat next to the toddler.

Carol plucked a fistful of dry cereal from the bowl, and munched on it while a commercial for Gooey Louie blared from the TV. She could feel Darla staring at her, so she tipped her head to her little sister, wrinkled her nose and asked, "What?"

Darla took a few more drags from the cup, her wide blue eyes darting back and forth, her head wobbling slightly to compensate. She pulled the spout of the cup from her lips with a smack.

"You missed my birthday, Carol," she stated.

"Oh, I'm sorry Darla," Carol began, then frowned. "Wait, what? No I didn't. It was just last month. We all went to Chuck E. Cheese and –"

"You *missed* it, Carol," continued Darla. "We had a bouncy-bounce, and a *mah-jih-shun*, and I got a Big Wheel and Beanie Babies and Sky Dancers but mommy was mad I would put my eye out with 'em and we had kroaky and the whole world was here except *you*." Darla stuck the cup back in her mouth and eyed Carol with a cool certainty that only toddlers and God on judgement day could pull off.

Carol opened her mouth, then shut it. *Okay...Looks like I'm not the only one losing her mind around here.*

Power Rangers now flipped, waved and postured across the TV, and she flinched at the volume.

"Isn't that a bit loud, sweetie?" she asked. "Daddy might get mad and –"

"Daddy was watchin' too," replied Darla, then tipped her head back and yelled, "Da-*deeee!* Pow Rainers back on!"

Carol automatically pulled her legs out from under her and began to rise from the couch, but she froze when she heard a sharp intake of breath behind her, and then coughing.

Carol twitched and ratcheted her head slowly to look over her shoulder. Her older sister Cheryl stood in silky-looking pajamas - *seriously, where has all the fancy stuff* come *from?* - with a toothbrush paused in her open mouth, her eyes wide and watering from inhaling toothpaste.

"Look Cheryl, Carol's back!" Darla informed her sister brightly.

Carol eyed her sister dumbly, unobtrusively trying to chew up nuggets of cereal in her mouth while standing motionless in a half-crouch.

"Moooom," Cheryl mumbled hoarsely around the toothbrush, eyeing Carol with what looked like alarm. A dollop of foamy spit ran out of her mouth and plopped on the tiles with a splat, but her older sister didn't seem to notice.

"What?" asked, Carol, panic rising in her once again. "What? What's the matter?"

"Mom!" yelled Cheryl, white spots spraying from her mouth. "Mommy! Dad! Get – *fuck* – Mom! Dad! Now!"

"What?" screamed Carol, appalled at her sister's use of profanity. Daddy better not hear that!

Feet pounded in a rapid drumbeat on the stairs, and her mother flew into the room, looking confused and terrified. Her eyes landed on Carol, and she froze.

"What?" pleaded Carol again. "What's *wrong?*"

Her dad skidded to a stop in the room, nearly slamming into her mother. What the *heck?* He looked fifty pounds lighter!

"What's going on?" he bellowed, looking confused and agitated. And then he locked eyes with Carol, looked even more confused, and she stiffened and shrank under his gaze and then *she* was confused because she had never see her dad *look* like that, the way his face crumpled and softened all at once, but her mom literally *jumped* over the couch like some action hero and grabbed her so tight she spit out bits of Berry Berry Kix down her back. By now her dad had rounded the couch and wrapped up both of them, Cheryl joined in too, and they were all crying and so was Darla, but she was yelling at them to shut up and get out of the way of the TV.

Her mother's hands caressed Carol's ears, forehead, cheeks, as if she couldn't believe what she was seeing, then kissed her all over her face, then wiped their mixed tears away with her thumbs, only to kiss her again as they cried.

"What's *wrong?*" asked Carol again. "I don't understand what's going on!"

"Where have you *been?*" shouted Cheryl.

Her dad kissed the back of her head and she flinched, but she could hear him sobbing behind her and when had she ever heard *that* before?

"Where have you *been?*" Cheryl repeated.

"In my *room,*" answered Carol. "Where did you think I was?"

"No, I mean for the last six *fucking* months!"

"I...*what?*"

"Did you get away from someone? Who had you? I *knew* you didn't just run away, I told everyone you wouldn't do that! Who had you?"

Carol shook her head and frowned. Her mother, visibly reluctant to let go of her, nonetheless pulled back and looked her in the eyes, waiting for an answer. Her dad loosened his grip as well. Darla scooted off the couch, grabbed the remote and jabbed the power button, silencing the TV. She was poised to chuck the remote across the room, noticed Carol was the only one watching her, so she just dropped it and wrapped her little arms tightly around Carol's legs.

"Missed you, Carol," she mumbled.

Carol's eyes darted from her sister to her mother. Her dad moved around to face her, but he had no anger on his face, just a look of worried expectation.

"I don't understand what's going on," Carol whispered. "I haven't *been* anywhere."

"You haven't been *here* for six months," her mom said, and her lips trembled and fresh tears poured out and she had to grab Carol tight again.

A tumor, thought Carol. *I have a tumor or something in my brain. Or, had one?*

"I...I've been here. I don't understand what's going on," Carol stammered. "Didn't we..." she reached down and patted Darla's head. "I could have sworn last month we went to Chuck E. Cheese for Darla's birthday. I *know* we did – Dad got dru - " she stopped, and waited for the verbal assault from her father, but his face never changed expression. He continued to stare at her with a mixture of awe and compassion. It was her mom who pulled back, visibly composed herself, and squeezed Carol's shoulders.

"On September the sixth, 1995, approximately 3:15 in the afternoon you got off the school bus, waved goodbye to your friends, and in between that wave and home, you vanished," her mother said. "We have not seen you until this very moment."

"This very *moment*," Darla said. "You missed my birthday."

Carol's eyes darted around the room, the house, trying to find something she could point to that could prove she knew she'd been here all along. But the house was just too different. It was the same house, but the paint seemed off, the carpet, furniture, the *smell* of the place was just...wrong. No one but her seemed to be wearing the right clothing. Nothing would give her an alibi.

"I don't understand," she repeated. *Geeze, she was sounding like a broken record!* "I don't know what to say. I think I must be crazy or something. I don't remember anything other than being right *here* for the last six months."

"Hey," her dad said softly, "Look, we have plenty of time to figure out what's been going on." He reached out and patted her shoulder. Carol shrank under the touch, but he looked so sincere that she gave him a timid smile regardless.

Her mother nodded emphatically, and leaned in to hug her again. Cheryl murmured her assent as well.

They stood like that for several moments, until Carol snapped her head up and looked around the room.

"Where's Byron?" she asked.

She felt her mother stiffen, and her father drew in an involuntary hiss of air. Carol glanced at him, and he was looking at her mother with a wary expression. Cheryl frowned at her.

Her mother cleared her throat, and Carol could feel it tingle against her scalp. She felt her mother's jaw working to find words, and finally the word, "Who?" slipped quietly out.

"Um...Byron?" Carol repeated timidly, panic rising with the fear of an unwanted answer. "My – our – older brother?"

She felt her mother actually jerk as if the name physically struck her, and Cheryl muttered, "*Jesus*, Carol...."

"Hey!" her father snapped, and Carol flinched, expecting the righteous explosion that always followed any sort of swearing. But his tone softened immediately. "Let's just let her get used to being home," he began. "Let her get..." He trailed off meekly as he watched his wife.

Her mother pulled back from her, true sadness in her eyes, but a small smile nonetheless.

"Sweetie," she said, "Your brother died two years before you were born. Surely you know this?"

Carol felt the insides of her ears warm, and a numbness seemed to drain down from her cheeks, to her lips and chin. She disengaged herself from her mother's embrace and stepped back. Her legs felt shaky and weak, and she reached down to pat Darla on the head and then push away from her, stumbling back into the TV.

Her mother made a sympathetic mew of a noise and reached out to her, but Carol held a hand out in desperation. Her mother stopped her advance, and Carol leveled a trembling finger at her.

"This is crazy," she mumbled. "I've had enough of this. It makes no *sense*."

"Oh, sweetie," her mother sobbed and reached for her again, but Carol slipped along the front of the TV and against the half-wall it was next to.

"Byron is *alive*, and *16*, and just got his license. *Byron* only wants to read and wants to be a scientist like Beakman, but *dad* - " Carol shot a look at her father, her confusion and frayed nerves making her say things she ordinarily wouldn't, "Dad wants him to be a world-class wrestler like he was *supposed* to have been back in the day."

Carol stared defiantly at her father, waiting for the red-faced explosion, but he just blinked rapidly in confusion, which infuriated her all the more. She wanted a reason to attack him – not that she didn't *already* have many, many reasons – to scratch and hit and kick him repeatedly. The house was quiet, and she looked from dumbstruck face to dumbstruck face – even little Darla looked amazed.

"Well," her father said quietly, "I don't recall bragging about my wrestling abilities – or lack thereof. And Byron sounds like someone I would have been proud of."

And that was it. The anger in her seemed to just evaporate, along with the remaining strength in her legs. She slid down the wall, breath whooshing out of her body, and she began to cry.

Enough. Enough of this, she thought miserably. *I give up. I don't know what's going on. I'm crazy.*

Her parents rushed in to her again, touching, making comforting assurances of figuring out what happened.

Remember – this happened. Don't let them make you think you're crazy, okay? Just play along, and you'll be alright.

"Okay," she whispered.

Her mother kissed and kissed and kissed her, her father gently squeezing her shoulder.

"Okay," she whispered again. "Okay."

Chapter 1

Cheryl eyed the car down the street, trying to decide if it was heading her way.

"Shit – *shoot*," she muttered under her breath. "It's moving? No. Yes? Crap."

Ivan tugged at his leash half-heartedly, made a token gesture of lifting his leg on the Johnson's fence, decided it was too much effort, so just sat instead, panting in the afternoon sunshine. The corgi was close to being obese, and was reluctant to venture out with Cheryl on her daily walks. Most anyone thought twice about joining her on a walk - Cheryl liked *long* walks.

Her poor vision (20/200 and considered legally blind by people who decided if you could drive a car or not) made it hard for Cheryl to judge distance, and if an object was stationary or just moving slowly. She shaded her eyes with a hand, squinted, and decided the car was parked.

"Oh, *hell* – it's in front of our house," she laughed. "That's Carol's car. Geeze." She looked down at the wheezing dog by her feet.

"You giving up, crazy?"

The corgi batted his eyes at her, tongue lolling out of his mouth, his tail swiping lazily in the grass of the Johnson's lawn.

"All right," Cheryl said. "Let's go home."

The dog stared at her, looked down the street towards home, then back at her, and whined.

"Oh, I am so not carrying you."

Ivan whined again and made a pathetic effort to rise off his hind legs.

"Come on, mutt. Carol's there. You want to see auntie Carol?"

The corgi's ears pricked forward at the name, and he valiantly rose to all fours and began to waddle towards home.

"Yeah, that's what I thought."

They crossed the street and moved up the sidewalk, Cheryl yanking on the leash to keep the dog from hiking his leg on the front tire of Carol's '68 Charger.

"If you value your life, little guy, I wouldn't do that."

She could hear low arguing as she turned up their front walk, and as her eyes adjusted from sunlight to shade, she saw Carol sitting on the steps of the house, her long legs stretched out in front of her, ankles crossed, a foot twitching lazily. Her blond hair fell to her freckled shoulders, and wide sunglasses covered her blue eyes. Cheryl's son Byron sat behind her, one arm wrapped affectionately around his aunt's neck.

"And you know damn well that's *not* what I meant," Cheryl's husband Dave was saying. "I'm just concerned that –"

"There they are!" interrupted Carol.

"Mom!" Byron yelled excitedly, "Dad said 'tits'!"

"It's true, he did," laughed Carol. "It's a good thing I was sitting down, or else I may have fainted. Never in my life have I heard such vulgarity."

Cheryl shook her head, and Ivan began to pick up steam, tugging at the leash, his tail whipping back and forth.

"Mom!" repeated Byron. "Dad said 'tits'…"

Carol brought the back of her hand up to the side of her mouth and breathlessly whispered, "He also said 'vagina'…"

Dave sighed loudly and said, "I was just –"

"How's my boy?" squealed Carol, and Cheryl dropped the leash to allow Ivan to run up to her sister. The dog huffed his way up the long walk, with Carol slapping her legs to encourage him.

"Come on buddy," she laughed. "Are you gonna do it? Gonna give me a crazy Ivan?"

The corgi got to within three feet of her, then turned in two complete circles before finally climbing up a step and burrowing his nose under her arms and working his way onto her lap. Carol kissed him on top of his head, scratched his ears and back.

The screen door banged open, and Cheryl's nine-year-old daughter Amy rushed out with a glass of iced-tea for her aunt. Her thick dark hair mirrored those of her brother and father, but her eyes were a few shades lighter than her brother's, and had an intensity that would make strangers take a step back when meeting her. When she saw her mother, she immediately yelled, "Mom, dad said 'tits'!"

Cheryl sighed. "So did you. Proud of yourself?" she asked.

Amy frowned. "I was only telling you what dad said. That doesn't count."

"Tattling doesn't give you an excuse. You, your dad *and* your brother owe the jar a buck each as far as I'm concerned."

Amy and Byron both howled in outrage.

"Your mom used to swear like a sailor back in the day," offered Carol.

Amy and her younger brother both jeered in condemnation at the revelation.

"Thank you, sis, for helping me out," Cheryl said.

Carol lifted Ivan off of her lap and set him on the porch, much to his dismay. She stood and dropped from the bottom step to the walk and approached her sister with arms open, then wrapped them around her and gave her a tight squeeze.

"It's what I do," Carol said, and kissed Cheryl on the cheek. "How you doing, sis? You're looking good! Getting in a lot of walks?"

Cheryl flushed in spite of her irritation with her sister. She was never easy with compliments, and her sister knew that – yet another way to keep her off her guard. But Cheryl had been steadily losing weight and was secretly proud of her accomplishment. That her sister noticed meant something.

"Not as much as I like to," she responded, and kissed her sister back and gave a quick squeeze before disentangling herself.

As they walked back up towards the porch steps, Carol reached out and poked Dave in the gut.

"Looks like you could use some walking, big guy," she quipped. "Your wife has to do it all by herself? What kind of husband are you, letting a blind woman wander the neighborhood alone?"

Dave opened his mouth, shut it, nostrils flaring, but settled for saying nothing.

Cheryl shook her head and swatted her sister. "We all get out and hike most weekends," she informed Carol. "We've all gotten in better shape."

Amy handed over the iced-tea to her aunt, who murmured her thanks with a tussle of the girl's thick hair.

"And it is *so* not fun," Amy said.

26

"Life is pain, highness," Cheryl replied brightly as she jogged up the porch steps. "When does Darla's plane get in?" she asked Carol over the exasperated noises Amy made.

"Four-thirty. Ish."

Cheryl nodded. "Time enough for me to grab a quick shower, I think." She paused, and looked at her sister. "Can you entertain the monsters for a while?"

Carol gave a sharp salute and said, "The kids are easy. Dave's a bit of a challenge, though."

"Jesus, I really hate you," Dave said.

"No you don't," laughed Carol, and sipped her tea.

"Mom, dad said 'Jesus'," yelled both kids at once.

"And yet, so did you two."

"Yeah," retorted Amy, "but it wasn't a *Jesus* Jesus. It was just saying 'Jesus' but not in vain."

"She's got you there," said Carol, and Amy looked smug.

"It ain't nice to snitch, Shorty," Dave quipped.

Amy wrinkled her nose. "Another one of your stupid movie references no one else gets," she muttered.

"Yeah, well, he got along with your grandpa in that," said Cheryl, and Carol smiled, sipping her tea.

"Be good for your aunt," admonished Cheryl. "I'm going to get your dad up to speed on what a dishwasher is and what food in the fridge looks like."

"Jesus Christ," muttered Dave, and then waved at the kids to shush them.

The screen door banged shut behind them, and it took a moment for Cheryl's eyes to adjust to the interior of the house.

"Why the hell does she have to always be 'on'?" Dave asked. "Seriously," he added, "it never ends with her."

Cheryl turned and pressed a palm against his chest, looked up at her husband and said, "Because she gets a kick out of lighting your tubes, sweetie. We've gone over this. She pokes, you roar, she's entertained. Don't make it so easy for her. And *while* we're at it, what's with all the 'tits and va-jay-jay' talk?"

Dave rolled his eyes.

"All I did was voice my concerns about her being able to drive all the way to Vegas with you and Darla. You know, her vision isn't all that great either, but she made it sound like I was making some anti-feminist comment – and *you* know better than that – so I tell her it isn't because she's got tits and a vagina it's just –"

"See, honey," Cheryl interrupted, "you were trying to sound edgy and cool. You aren't edgy and cool. You just gave her more material to use."

"I'm edgy."

Cheryl pushed her palm in tighter against his chest, and then patted it. "No," she said firmly. "No, you are not. But you're sweet, and big-hearted and she knows that and loves you even if she likes to push your buttons."

Dave exhaled loudly, and wrapped his arms around Cheryl, and they stood in the hallway and listened to the laughs, shrieks and cat-calling going on outside.

"She's really good with the kids," Dave murmured into the top of her head.

"She is," agreed Cheryl.

"Think she'd ever have any of her own?"

"No."

"Think she would ever...find anyone?"

"I would hope someday." Cheryl listened to the thump of her husband's heart in his chest, smiled tiredly and squeezed him. "I can't imagine going through life without anyone that had my back, you know?"

Dave grunted softly.

"But, she seems happy enough, and honestly I don't think anyone could keep pace with her. If she's happy without someone to share a life with, then that's all that matters. Our parents taught us not to define ourselves by someone else." She tipped her head up and gave him a quick kiss. "I know I consider *myself* lucky for what *I* have, though. Bratty kids and all."

"Yeah," Dave breathed. They snuggled for several moments, and then Cheryl felt his chest expand as he prepared to ask a question she knew was coming. "Do you...did – " he began.

"No," said Cheryl.

"I mean, your dad. Did –"

28

"*No*. Not the man I knew, anyways."

"Do you think *she* still believes he did?"

Cheryl leaned back and tipped her head up to stare Dave in the eyes.

"I honestly don't know," she said. "She remembers the first nine years of her life very differently than the rest of us, but I think she's accepted the fact that the rest of the world isn't trying to pull a fast one on her. Whatever trauma happened to her during the six months she went missing we may never know. It impacted her relationship with our family, but dad the most. They were best buds before all that."

Dave shook his head. "That's awful," he whispered, and Cheryl's heart surged at the sight of tears in his eyes, and she leaned in and hugged him again.

"Yeah," she breathed.

"How come we don't get to go to Vegas too?" Byron pouted.

"Because Aunt Darla has never had a 'girls only road trip' and that's what she wants for her twenty-fifth birthday," answered Amy in a reciting tone. "Doesn't explain why *I* can't go," she added in a lower voice.

Carol squeezed the girl's shoulder. "Vegas is way overrated," she said. "Believe me."

"Sounds like fun to me," Amy replied resentfully.

"Well, it doesn't sound like your Aunt Darla's cup of tea to us either," Cheryl said as she carefully made sure for the third time the hotel confirmation was tucked into her travel bag's front pocket. She then slammed the trunk, made sure it was latched securely, and turned to face her husband and children.

"She's too young for a mid-life crisis," muttered Dave.

"What's that?" asked Byron, looking up at his dad.

"An excuse to act like a goof when you think you never had any fun," Carol answered.

Cheryl watched Dave as he studied Carol's Charger, opened his mouth, and then shut it with a tight smile.

"So," Cheryl said authoritatively, "*mass* this weekend, right? Not hard to forget?"

29

"Yes," all three of them intoned.

"I have eyes everywhere."

"*Yes*," they repeated.

"We know Tina would rat us out," Dave added.

"Yes she would," laughed Cheryl. "Also, dinners are prepared and there's no reason to go fast-fooding it."

"Yes," they dutifully replied.

"Yep," said Cheryl. "Okay, come on and give your mom a hug and kiss. You're free of her for over a whole week."

Byron darted in to give his loves, and then Amy, less enthusiastically. Dave waited for the kids to disentangle from her, then wrapped her up tight, lifted her from her feet for a moment, and then kissed her on top of her head, and then a deep one on her mouth. "Love you," he muttered in a husky voice. "You all have a lot of fun."

Cheryl smiled and reached up to rub a thumb over his cheek, touched by his love, his concern, and knowing that he was going to miss her.

"Okay, you big galoot, let your wife go, give me a hug and let us get on the road," laughed Carol.

Dave turned to Carol, and Cheryl watched as her sister opened her mouth, then shut it as she watched Dave blinking his eyes. Dave's arms encircled Carol, and her sister – usually a little stiff and joking at tender moments – leaned into the hug and squeezed Dave tightly.

"Hey, we're going to be fine, dude," she murmured into his shoulder. "I'm not going to drive like an idiot. You know that."

Dave squeezed her tighter for a second, then nodded his head and smiled. "I trust *you*," he said. "It's everyone else on the road I don't."

Carol's head tilted, and then she was blinking quickly. She recovered, and socked Dave on the shoulder. "Well, heaven help anyone who messes with the O'Brian sisters, right?"

"Wouldn't want to be in their shoes," Dave laughed.

"Damn right," said Cheryl.

The kids gasped and pointed fingers, and Cheryl waved a hand at them. "Oh, I'll pay up after I win it big in Vegas."

Chapter 2

Carol eased into the driver's seat, giving her sister and brother-in-law a chance for a more private goodbye. The kids hung on her and gave her final kisses through the window, and she laughed and told them to be good. As good as they could be, anyhow.

She sighed, and smiled. She did not envy her sister's life at all. But she was incredibly happy for her nonetheless. Dave was a good guy, the kids were fun and sweet. Ivan woofed on the porch, lonely at being left out of the goodbyes, but too lazy to waddle down to take part. Carol laughed and blew him a kiss.

The passenger door opened, Cheryl slipped into the seat, and shut the door. Carol turned the ignition, and the Charger's engine roared to life, making the kids yell in excitement. Dave leaned onto the door frame and gave them a big smile.

"I hope you all have a great time. Try not to lose your shirts," he said.

"The O'Brian girls really aren't into gambling, I think," Carol replied.

"Well, try not and lose each other, I guess. Let me know when I have to send lawyers, guns and money."

Carol saluted.

"Give Darla our love."

"We will," Cheryl replied, and kissed her husband. Then she motioned outside the car. "Honey. Maybe break that up?" she offered. Dave turned.

"Shit," Carol heard him mutter. "Take your hands off your brother. Now. *Now. Both* hands. Jesus."

Cheryl turned to her and smiled tightly.

"No, *no*, that doesn't mean get him in a headlock. Jesus. Get in the house, both of you."

Carol could hear Amy respond, but couldn't pick out the words.

"Yeah, I know he's an asshole. So are you. *Get* in the house!" Dave ordered.

"Sounds like the swear jar is going to be over-flowing tonight," laughed Carol.

"We can get going anytime now," said Cheryl.

Carol tooted the horn, and Dave gave a backwards wave as she eased the car away from the curb. Her sister stared ahead, shaking her head slightly.

"Think the house will be standing when you get back?" asked Carol.

"Oh yeah," laughed Cheryl. "That was one last attention-grabbing moment from them. They'll be fine."

"Going to go to church and eat healthy and all that?"

"Church? Sure. Even go and mingle after. But they'll be on the phone ordering a pizza shortly, I can guarantee it."

Carol laughed. "Why go to the trouble of making them meals and all that?" She pulled out onto San Miguel.

"Oh, they'll eat a few of them," replied Cheryl. "But I have to give them a chance to rebel a bit, you know? Think they're pulling a fast one – or two – over on the tyrant mother."

"Nice," laughed Carol. "They won't waste them though?"

"No. Amy would be indignant over that sort of thing. I suspect they'll take some to mom's and she'll coo over their thoughtfulness, bringing Grammy some dinner, all the while knowing what's up."

"Jesus, she in on it?"

"No, but come on – you know her."

Carol stopped the car, waited for traffic to clear, then pulled out onto Massachusetts. "Yeah," she sighed with a grin. "I do. You didn't fall far from the tree."

Cheryl grinned. "They may pull it off without me knowing a thing. But chances are one will get mad at the other – probably Byron – and then rat them all out and I can pretend to be so very disappointed and maybe some rooms will actually get cleaned without a lot of complaining for a few days. It's the little things one can hope for."

"My God woman, why did you never take up chess?"

Cheryl smiled.

They drove in silence for a while, and Carol maneuvered the Charger up onto 94, heading west towards San Diego.

"Say buh-bye to the Grove for a week," Carol murmured, and her sister grunted in satisfaction.

They drove in silence for a bit, and finally Cheryl asked, "How's the job going?"

"Eh, okay. Job coaching isn't for the easily frustrated, I can tell you that."

"People still ask if you're *that* Carol O'Brian?"

"Sometimes. I just play dumb, have no idea who she was, wow that sounds *awful*, hope she's doing okay now, blah, blah, *bleck*."

Cheryl laughed.

"Got a new guy in the department, must have figured out I was *that* Carol O'Brian, tried dropping subtle clues he knew."

"Jesus, did you have to go to HR about it?"

"Nah. Played dumb and ignored it. Besides, the guy would rather yak on about baseball."

Cheryl laughed. "Oh, I'm sure you just love that."

"Could be worse. He doesn't seem to be the type that loves the *idea* of loving baseball, you know?"

"Just enjoys the game?"

"Yeah. Good for him, I guess."

"We've started going to a lot of Padre games last year. Kids seem to enjoy them."

"Yeah?"

"We're looking forward to March. We grab the trolley, make a day of it. You're welcome anytime."

Carol darted a look at her sister, smiled, and said, "Sure, sounds like it could be fun." The offer had the familiar ring of inviting her to go to church with them, however, and she knew her response sounded less than enthusiastic. *Shit.*

"Think Dave could stand me for that long?" she added lightly, and instantly regretted it due the frown it generated on Cheryl's forehead. Silence stretched for a minute.

"So, Dave would like to know why you always have to be 'on' all the time," Cheryl said abruptly.

Carol resisted the urge to roll her eyes, but sighed and darted a glance at Cheryl.

"Am I?" she asked.

Cheryl raised her arms in a half-shrug, let them fall and said nothing.

"Is that code for, 'why do you pick on him so much'?"

Cheryl smiled and still said nothing.

"Come on, you have to admit it's a little fun to see him bluster and fume," Carol said lightly.

"So maybe confuse him and not push his buttons for once," replied Cheryl.

"Hey, I didn't say, 'I'm sorry Dave, I'm afraid I can't do that' even once this time."

"Such progress."

"Jesus, *you* don't even like that movie – just because he and dad bonded over some pretentious sci-fi flick –"

"Do you think he's pretentious? Really, honestly – Dave is pretentious?"

"No, but come on – "

"So what does it matter what he likes or doesn't? Seriously, he doesn't pat himself on the back for liking something, quit patting yourself on the back for something you don't."

"Ouch."

"Well, shit Carol. If his worst flaw is liking boring ancient sci-fi films, then I think I'll keep him."

"You owe the jar a buck," muttered Carol.

"I'll put in two for not correcting myself," said Cheryl. "And apologize to the kids."

"I'm sure Amy would appreciate that."

"What's that supposed to mean?"

"Well, you seem to come down harder on her than Byron."

Cheryl barked out a short laugh. "Oh really?" she asked.

Carol squeezed the steering wheel, and concentrated on her driving. Shit. Why did it have to blow up like this? Always? She had been stung, and was looking for a way to sting back, and hated herself for it.

"I'm sorry, I have *no* right to comment. I'm *not* a parent, I'm not living day and night with them. I'm sorry."

Her sister sighed, and Carol could tell she was looking for a way to retreat out of the fight too.

"Amy is becoming kind of a mean girl, if you want to know," said Cheryl, "and a bit of a bully. I'm trying to nip that in the bud. As I recall, you weren't a fan of mean girls back in the day, and I thought you might appreciate my efforts."

Carol tried to put all her concentration into merging onto 5, but memories of one of your tormentors in school that was now suddenly your best friend, and of a sister who could be less than kind, surfaced and taunted her without mercy.

"Yeah," she said softly. "Some could tag you with some pretty cruel nick-names. Like 'the changeling.'"

Zing.

Cheryl snapped her mouth shut, and her eyes blinked rapidly.

God damn it, thought Carol. *She's not that girl anymore. She had the nerve to grow up and mature.*

But the damage was done, and they remained silent all the way to the airport.

"There she is," said Cheryl. They had pulled up to the curb in front of South West after getting Darla's text in the cell phone lot.

Carol squinted, looking for her younger sister, and couldn't pick her out. How in the hell could Cheryl do that? Cheryl's vision was the worst of them all, yet sometimes...

"Right there," said Cheryl, who must have sensed Carol's confusion. "See? That nonchalant stroll of hers. Got her hair pulled back, maybe?"

"Ah," chirped Carol. "Yeah. Pulling the purple suitcase."

"That's her."

"Yeah, but I don't think her hair is pulled back – I think it's *cut.*"

"No! Really?"

"Indeed," said Carol, and they both hopped out of the car. Darla spotted them before they could say anything, her grin spreading open to a delighted laugh, and that wave – still kind of like a salute, but with a flourish at the end now, and then she picked up her pace to hurry to her sisters.

"Oh my God," laughed Cheryl after she had hugged Darla and leaned back to study her. She took in her tie-dyed tank top, then reached up to curl her fingers into her sister's short blonde hair. "You cut your *hair!*"

Carol muscled her way in to give her sister a hug and kiss, and couldn't help but feel happier with Darla among them. "It looks good, sweetie. Wow." Darla murmured her thanks, and a blush formed on her pale cheeks. Carol laughed, and kissed her again. "It's so good to see you! Been a year, this time?"

Darla nodded. "My last birthday, I think," she said.

"Too long," said Carol, as she loaded her sister's suitcase into the trunk with the others. *But I haven't missed any of them*, thought Carol. *Not since your third. Supposedly.*

After stowing her sister's luggage in the trunk, she pulled the seat forward so Darla could climb into the back, and then she and Cheryl both climbed in and slammed the doors.

"All *right*," quipped Carol. "On to Vegas, baby!"

"You two fighting again?" asked Darla.

Carol eyed Cheryl, and they both laughed.

"We don't fight, sweetie, we *discuss*," replied Carol in a deep, mock-condescending tone.

"Well, for my birthday could we not have to cut the tension with a knife for once? Gonna be a long ride if we have to."

Carol and Cheryl both laughed again, this time with a tinge of ashamed embarrassment. Cheryl reached back and grabbed Darla's hand to give it a squeeze, and Carol nodded. "You got it," she said. She darted a glance to Cheryl, and her older sister smiled at her with a slight dip of the head – the 'I'm sorry' smile. Carol returned it.

"So," said Cheryl brightly. "Let's discuss the elephant in the room – car – whatever." She leveled a look back at Darla. "What happened to the dreads?"

In the rear-view mirror, Carol saw Darla dart a hand up to her hair.

"Oh, trying to be culturally responsible," she answered. "Plus, I kinda got tired of them. Too much work, you know?"

"Huh," grunted Carol, as she guided the car along the curved ramp from 5 to interstate 8. "What's Andrew think of your new 'do?"

"Oh, I kinda got tired of him too," laughed Darla.

Carol and Cheryl's mouths and eyes opened wide, and they shot each other a look.

"No shit?" laughed Carol.

"No shit," affirmed Darla.

"How's work, then?" asked Cheryl. "Is it tough dealing with him if you're broken up?"

"Not for me. He seems alright with it. Acts like it, anyways. Wouldn't let anyone know if it did."

"Huh," repeated Carol, and smiled at Darla in the mirror. Her sister squinted at her, caught the smile and returned it.

"Science first, and all that?" asked Cheryl.

"But of course," said Darla.

"Well, you look healthy and happy," Cheryl added. "Dating anyone else, or just enjoying being unattached?"

"No. No Dating. Taking things as they come, and life is good. Been looking forward to hanging with my sestras."

They all whooped, and Carol noticed Cheryl seemed a bit looser already, clearly enjoying Darla's company.

"Still enjoying Shannon Point?" asked Carol.

"Oh yeah. Love it. You guys need to come up and see me, let me show it off up there."

"How are the jellies doing, and all that other gross stuff you like so much?"

"Jellies are doing great," Darla replied. "Climate change, over-fishing. They like to fill niches."

"Hey, you get that tattoo finished on your back?" asked Cheryl.

"Oh, yeah," said Darla brightly, and twisted in her seat, then hiked up her tank top to her shoulders, unselfconscious about her bare breasts. Carol was startled for a second, then looked around at the traffic on the interstate. No one seemed to be paying attention. Yet. Cheryl seemed unconcerned, staring intently at Darla's back.

Well, isn't that great, thought Carol. *I'm the uptight one now. I guess whipping your boobs out to feed two kids makes you take the hippie stuff in stride...*

"Wow," breathed Cheryl, and Carol fought the urge to try and take her eyes off the road and look at the tattoo.

"You like?" asked Darla.

"It's beautiful, honey," said Cheryl. "Wow. Geeze, how long did that take? Did it hurt? It must have hurt."

"This isn't fair," blurted Carol. "I have to drive!" Darting glances in the rear-view mirror, she could see tantalizing glimpses of blues and purples.

Cheryl waved a hand at her absently as she stared at their younger sister's back.

"You can see it later," she muttered.

"All told, I dunno...maybe five or six hours the last session?" Darla said. "Yeah it hurt, but not bad. I've had worse from jellies. We just powered through the last few hours, let the artist have a smoke break or three, and on we went. Still not really done." She pulled at the elastic waistband of her sweats, and stretched up to show tendrils ending just above her buttocks.

"I want the tendrils to go all the way down to my feet," she added.

"And that's a...what did you say it is?" asked Cheryl.

"A Portuguese man o' war," said Darla.

"And you say that's *not* a jellyfish?"

"No, it's not a jelly. It's a siphonophore, a colony made up of medusoids and polypoids – *basically* it's made up of several different specialized animals to make up a colonial organism."

Cheryl bobbed her head in a firm nod. "Gotcha," she said.

Carol noticed a black truck pacing them. She glanced over, and saw two faces peering at the back seat.

"Hey Dar?" she offered. "You have a fan club."

"What?" asked Darla.

"You're becoming a road hazard sweetie." The truck started to drift dangerously close, and Carol laid on the horn. The truck swerved and jerked back into its lane, and she could hear a wild whooping. Carol brought her left hand to her window and extended her middle finger. The truck honked, mixed with inarticulate cat-calling.

Carol fought the urge to floor it, show the boys the power the Charger had, but the sun was set and it was gloomy, and she wanted to stay in as much control as she could.

"I can't believe my small titties would be that interesting," muttered Darla as she faced front again and pulled her tank back down.

"All titties are interesting to them honey," laughed Cheryl. "Believe me."

"Cha-ching goes the swear-jar," said Carol.

Cheryl put a hand to her chest in mock indignation. "I was only repeating what *she* said," she retorted, voice higher in pitch. "So I was not *swearing* swearing, just passing on valuable information."

"And is it really swearing?" Carol asked. "I mean, should you have an honest-to-God-Lord's-name-in-vain jar, *plus* a...what? 'Vulgar phrase' jar?"

Darla barked a laugh. "Are you still trying to cut out the swearing, sis?"

Cheryl crossed her arms and frowned. "Someone's got to show some class in the family. We're heading to Vegas, the kid has flashed herself on the freeway, and we aren't even out of San Diego yet!"

They all whooped loudly, and Carol decided to indulge herself anyway and let the Charger roar as they rocketed north onto 15.

Chapter 3

They stopped in San Bernardino for the night, deciding they were in no hurry to get to Vegas. They rose early, breakfasting at the diner next to the hotel. Cheryl peeked over the top of her menu and allowed herself a small smile. Her sisters had their menus close to their faces – just as she had – their heads darting slightly back and forth, compensating for the movement of their eyes – just as she surely had been. They must have looked like elderly ladies, shaking their heads in gentle disapproval at the food choices.

She and Darla settled on veggie omelets, while Carol had bacon and eggs with wheat toast. All O'Brian sisters liked their coffee black.

"So why Vegas, sis?" asked Carol.

Darla shrugged, and forked a piece of her omelet into her mouth.

"Dunno, really," she said around the egg and spinach.

"It...just doesn't seem like something you would like," offered Cheryl.

"Right?" said Darla. "Maybe that's why I think I should go? Just an excuse for a road trip with you guys, really. But isn't that where you go on road trips? Vegas?"

"Well, sure," Carol said. "Got any idea what you want to do?"

"No. They have shows and shit, right?"

"Yeah," laughed Carol, "they have shows and shit."

"Got any idea what shit shows you want to see?" asked Cheryl, then darted a look at Carol, who had almost spit out a piece of bacon. "Shut up," she added. "I'm on vacation. What happens in Vegas, and all that."

Darla giggled. "No. Like magicians, or something?"

"I'm guessing they probably do," Carol said, then eyed both her sisters. "You two know if we need reservations for anything like that?"

Cheryl fought an urge to roll her eyes and sigh. *I thought you were supposed to be taking care of all this*, she thought. *Did you not want to make her happy?* She damped down her irritation, and tried to mask it like she really had to concentrate on chewing her food before answering. But she knew Carol could read her, and it looked like she was tensing for a fight, and that was the last thing either of them wanted. *Just lighten the hell up*, she thought. *Carol probably expected me to be on top of this, not trusting her to do it right. Let it go and have some* fun.

She took a breath and smiled. "I was under the impression we were playing this by ear – just letting the wind push us around, like one of Darla's semaphore thingys."

Darla pursed her lips and squinted at her, knowing damn well she could remember what the animal was called. *Don't play dumb around her*, Cheryl thought. *She may try and act the carefree hippie, but won't put up with condescension. She can also read us, and is waiting for the fight to break out.*

"You guys even want to go?" Darla asked neutrally.

Both Cheryl and Carol issued a chorus of, "Oh yeah, sure, of course!"

Darla eyed them both coolly, and took a sip of her coffee.

The little stinker still knows how to put you on the spot, thought Cheryl, then felt guilty. *She isn't a little girl anymore, she's an honest-to-God scientist, and you need to stop treating her like the baby of the family.*

Carol leaned forward, and gave a frank smile.

"It's like this, Dar," she said. "Vegas seems so unlike you, and we're trying to wrap our heads around it." She raised her hand to silence Darla before she could say anything. "But that doesn't mean anything if you *really* want to go. Do you *really* want to go?"

"I do," Darla mumbled. She looked down at her cup of coffee, and it was one of the few times Cheryl saw her as uncertain and awkward.

"I don't know *why*," she continued. "It just seems like something I *need* to do – to get it out of my system, I guess?"

"Then that's all that matters," said Cheryl.

"Yep," added Carol. "I'm in it for the company. I don't care where we go."

"So let's do this," offered Cheryl. "I'll check in with our hotel in Vegas and let them know we will be a day late – I'm sure we have to pay for today, and so be it. But let's spend the day here, go swimming, do a little internet research, see what shows are there and what we have to do to see them. Yeah?"

"Sounds good," said Darla with a smile.

"And if we can't see any shit shows, we can drink, gamble and lose our shit," said Carol.

They all laughed, but Cheryl knew that was unlikely. While she and Darla were social drinkers (and truthfully, Darla preferred her pot), it was not central to their enjoyment of life. Carol never drank, and couldn't understand those who would gush over the thought of mimosas and brunch. Wine or craft beer enthusiasts made her eyes glaze over worse than baseball or sci-fi, she had declared.

We may very well be the dullest party to ever hit Vegas, Cheryl thought with amusement.

They finished up their breakfast, Cheryl picked up the tab over strong protests from Carol, and gathered their purses and hoodies to head out. As Cheryl turned towards the door, for an instant she thought she saw someone silhouetted against the morning sunlight – like a man had...*smeared* into existence for a moment, checked them out, and then wavered and blinked out again.

Startled, she gave an involuntary gasp and looked around, then at her sisters. *What the hell?* she thought. No one had seemed to see him. Darla eyed her suspiciously. Carol looked lost in thought, then seemed to surface from somewhere.

"What's wrong?" Darla asked.

"I, uh, don't know. Eyes playing tricks on me. You two know the drill."

"Those lyin' O'Brian eyes," laughed Darla, and Carol joined her. "We see things no one else does!"

"Ain't that the truth," muttered Cheryl.

Smelling of studiously applied sunscreen, Cheryl and Darla picked lounge chairs that had umbrellas shading them, and Carol angled hers so she could feel the sun. It was going to be one of those eighty-degree January days, and all of them were eager to swim.

Cheryl wore a black one-piece with white vertical stripes, but kept her sun dress on for now as she dropped onto the chair and pulled her tablet out of her beach-bag. Darla dropped her robe, revealing a one-piece decorated with a pink R2 unit.

"Oh my God, that is so cute," said Cheryl

"Dad would have been proud," laughed Carol.

"Made me think of him when I ordered it," said Darla wistfully, and they all sat in silence for a few moments. Carol reclined her chair and stretched out in the sun, her tanned and freckled body contrasting with the white bikini she wore.

Darla eyed her with a gentle frown. "With our pale Irish genes, you sure do gamble with the carcinoma there, Carol," she said.

Carol shrugged. "I like the sun. Hasn't killed me yet."

Darla's eyes moved from a frown to concern. "It's nothing to joke about, sis. Seriously, you need to watch out. Please."

You tell her, honey, thought Cheryl. *Lord knows I've told her enough.* She didn't think her sister had a death wish, or didn't care about her health – she sure exercised enough! Cheryl felt that it was just a basic 'screw you' to the universe. Fast cars, living alone, and daring the sun to kill her.

Carol raised her head and stared at Darla through her sunglasses. "I appreciate the concern, kiddo – I truly do. And I'll try and be better about it, okay?" She dropped her head back and tipped her face up to the sun. "But on this winter day, I'm going to enjoy the hell out of the warm weather."

Darla raised her arms and dropped them against her thighs with a smack, and shook her head. She plopped onto the lounge chair and rummaged in her pack, eventually pulling out a bottle of pink nail polish, and proceeded to paint her toes.

"Holy smokes, what's next?" asked Cheryl with a laugh. "You going to start wearing makeup now, too?"

Darla grinned, but concentrated on applying the polish. "Let's not get crazy, sis," she replied.

"The amount you raved over her tattoo, I think *you* should get one, Cheryl," quipped Carol.

Cheryl laughed, and Darla straightened up and shouted, "That would be awesome! Oh, you *have* to!"

Cheryl laughed harder, then replied, "I don't think so."

"Come on, just think of the look on Amy's face when she saw it," Carol said.

"Oh, good lord. Her head would explode."

"I bet it would turn Dave's crank," laughed Carol. "Get some nerd-themed tatt – Gandalf wielding a light saber or something."

"His crank turns just fine, thank you very much," said Cheryl primly, but shook her head with a smile.

"Come *on*. I know it's not your thing, but get something as pretty as Darla's."

"Why don't *you* get one, smarty-pants?"

"Why don't we *all* get one?" offered Darla. "Something that matched. Something that's special to us."

Silence stretched for a several seconds.

"Huh," grunted Carol.

Cheryl stared down at the tablet resting on her lap, but didn't really see it.

"Ooh, she's thinking it over," said Darla excitedly.

"Calm down, you hippie," snorted Cheryl.

Darla tipped her head back and laughed loudly.

"Holy crap," giggled Carol. "That's the most excited I've seen her in ages."

"But it can't be some empty symbol," said Darla, returning to the task of painting her toes. "No stupid 'butterfly on the ankle' shit for us."

"Nope, no," Cheryl and Carol agreed in harmony, shaking their heads.

They sat in silence for a while, and then Cheryl said, "Well, you put some thought into it, then. I'm not saying yes or no. Depends on if your idea wows me or not."

Darla looked at her and gave her wide open and honest grin that could thaw the coldest heart, and returned to concentrate on her polish.

Right about the time Cheryl felt like swimming, a group of young men blew into the pool area with the subtlety of frat-boys at a tiki-torch rally, their testosterone-fueled whoops and growls punctuating the peeling off of t-shirts, an artfully masculine labor in and of itself.

"Son of a...*biscuit*," muttered Cheryl under her breath, the dream of a nice quiet swim vanishing.

Carol sighed loudly.

"I was just thinking of going for a swim," said Darla in a disgusted tone.

"Me too," replied Cheryl.

"Me three," said Carol.

"Their attention spans can't be too long," said Darla. "We can wait them out, yeah?"

"I'm not going anywhere, God damn it," growled Carol.

"What the hell are they doing here? Shouldn't they be in school?" wondered Cheryl. "Vegas, I could see it. But San Berdoo? Why?"

"I'd have to care enough to ask," muttered Carol. "And I don't see that happening." She rolled over onto her stomach.

Darla stood, wrapped her robe back around herself, then sat, crossing her legs while she fished in her bag for a battered copy of *Picnic at Hanging Rock.* She hunched over the small paperback, bringing it up close to her nose.

"Haven't found an edition with bigger type?" Cheryl asked. "Seems like you've been reading that for forever now."

"Think it's been out of print, at least in the U.S., for a long time," Darla said.

Cheryl lifted her tablet and waggled it. "I keep telling you to get an e-reader. I can make the font as big as I like."

"I like books," Darla murmured.

"I thought you scientists were supposed to be all about the latest gizmos?"

Darla stuck her tongue out and blew a raspberry.

Cheryl flicked through pages of information on Vegas, but kept an eye on the wildlife across the pool. She could see toned shapes strutting, reclining, doing cannonballs into the pool until the hotel manager came out to tell them he would kick them out if they didn't knock it off. They made reassuring noises, then barks of laughter and low jeering after the man had left. But the cannonballing stopped.

"Where do you see these guys in ten years?" asked Cheryl. "Twenty years?"

Darla looked at her, then over at the boys. She raised any eyebrow.

"Really," said Cheryl. "What do you see in their future?"

Darla sighed, put down her book, and frowned, taking the exercise seriously. Carol rolled over onto her back, and lifted her head.

"The big, doughy-looking one?" said Darla. "Used car salesman. Not good enough for the NFL, second-string linebacker at best. Going to inherit daddy's car lot, he'll be two-hundred pounds over-weight in twenty years, most of it gut. It's as clear as day."

"I can see that," said Cheryl.

"The ripped one in the baggy trunks?" offered Carol, rising up to rest on her elbows. "Mr. wrap-around sunglasses? Realtor. He'll try Wall Street, wash out, and come back to Orange County where he grew up and feel big again selling expensive homes."

"I can see that," repeated Cheryl, and Darla murmured her agreement.

"Well I don't have your two's *superior* eyesight," stated Cheryl, "but the runt – is he a ginger?" Her sisters affirmed her speculation. "Yeah, that guy will run a shoe store, get his kicks looking up women's dresses."

Both Darla and Carol barked laughter, but Cheryl continued. "He'll die alone in his fifties, with used fast-food bags stuffed with cash."

"I can see that," chorused Carol and Darla.

They sat and contemplated the scene, and the boys were no longer intimidating. They were just *boys,* trying to not look weak or uninteresting.

Carol dropped to her back again, but flashed Cheryl a smile before laying her head down.

"I wonder if we've cursed them?" asked Darla.

"What?" laughed Carol.

"That doesn't sound very scientific, Darla," said Cheryl.

"Unless we're the observers that have influenced the outcome," Darla said. "A curse by any other name."

"Then give them a happy ending," said Cheryl.

"Maybe it is, for them," suggested Carol. "Maybe what they hoped for was too much, and the safety of mediocrity is comforting to them." She rolled onto her side to stare at her sisters. "Also, maybe it's better than they deserve."

"I'm virtually certain we will never know," said Cheryl.

A splash drew her attention, and she heard Darla issue an amused gasp. "That guy just jumped in the pool with his sunglasses on. What an idiot."

One of the boys was swimming across to them with bold, confident strokes.

"Ah, fuck," muttered Carol.

"Shit - *shoot*," hissed Cheryl. "That's what we get for staring at them. They think we're interested. Sorry, you two."

"He could be interested in *you*," retorted Carol.

"Oh, my ass," Cheryl blurted. "It's a fifty-fifty chance on who – "

She snapped her mouth shut as the boy rose up on his arms by the edge of the pool, water running off his chest, muscular arms, and sunglasses. He waited for a moment more, gleaming in the noon-day sun, then hopped up smoothly to the edge of the pool. He ran a hand through his hair to slick it back, his abs etched in sharp relief, then strolled over to an empty lounge chair by Carol and dropped casually onto it, spreading out his legs in a wide stance on either side of the seat, laced his fingers behind his head and leaned back in careful indifference. Water streamed off him to puddle beneath the chair.

Cheryl stared absently at her tablet, and sensed Darla was engrossed in her book. She took a quick peek at Carol, who had her arms crossed behind her head, mirroring the boy's above-it-all attitude.

Damn it, this is stupid, she thought. *Why the hell should this twit make us clam up and act like school girls waiting for him to hit on us? It's only encouraging him to stay.* She was ready to ask him to find some other place to hang out when he decided to break the silence.

"You ladies not like to swim?" he asked as if he didn't care if they answered or not.

"Love to," answered Carol.

"Sure do," said Darla.

Cheryl turned her head to stare at him, then returned her attention to her tablet.

"Nice enough day. Why aren't you in the pool?" he asked.

"It's too crowded," said Darla from behind her book.

Only one of the boys was still bobbing around in the pool, and a mother and child occupied the shallow end. Cheryl suppressed the urge to snort. She dropped the sunglasses resting on her head down over her eyes, and stared openly at the boy, who was looking at the pool as if trying to decide if the word 'crowded' had more meanings than he was familiar with.

"Hey, I have a question for you," Darla piped up from behind her book. "Why did you jump in the pool with your sunglasses on? Seems pretty silly to me." This time Cheryl did snort.

The boy offered a wry smile and shrugged. "A little hung-over, I guess. Sun's too bright," he explained.

"Aw," cooed Carol, with what sounded like genuine sympathy.

Cheryl frowned, and stared at her.

The boy directed his arm out to Carol, his hand a blade pointed towards her abdomen, his arm cocked as if it was ready to dive down at her like a bird of prey.

"I'm Nate," he said.

Carol reached up demurely, hand bent at the wrist, fingers together, and let Nate shake her hand. "I'm Carol," she said silkily.

Cheryl snorted.

"I'm *Carol*," she heard Darla mutter behind her book, as if jealous.

"Pleased to meet you, Carol," he said, pointedly ignoring Darla and Cheryl.

"Likewise," replied Carol sweetly.

"*Likewise*," Darla parroted in a nasally tone.

"Oh, don't mind them, Nate," assured Carol. "They're just a couple of lightweights, afraid of a *good* time."

Nate leaned back with an easy grin, and gave an unconcerned shrug. "That's alright, as long as you like having a good time."

"Oh, I'm all about having good times."

Cheryl snorted again, and muttered under her breath, "Ain't *that* the truth," then pretended to scroll angrily across her tablet.

Carol ignored the remark, and sipped long and deep from her water bottle.

"You really should go swimming," Nate said with authority. His head turned and traced the contours of Carol's body. "You look like you do a lot. Workout a lot, I bet."

"Do you think so?" said Carol, as if pleased.

"Yeah, really. Like you're super-close to body-building competition level shape."

"Just close?" asked Carol with concern.

"Pretty close. You could use more definition in your abs."

"Oh," said Carol with a dejected tone, and ran a hand over her flat stomach, as if ashamed it was visible to the world now.

"Don't feel bad, you're in great shape. But you could be stunning, really cut. I could show you some exercises in the pool? Maybe in the gym?"

"Really?" asked Carol gratefully.

"Sure. What do you say? Let's get in the pool."

"Well, Nate it's like this," Carol said slowly. "I'm on my period, and cramping like a *son* of a bitch. I gotta tell you, I'm flowing like there's no tomorrow."

Nate visibly flinched, and Cheryl nearly lost it.

Carol pushed her sunglasses up to the top of her head, and stared at him directly. "Nate, if I jumped in that pool, it would look like we were chumming for sharks. Wouldn't be pretty."

"Good lord no," Cheryl contributed. "Nate, I'm going through the change – that's menopause, you know – and holy cow I don't think I've gushed so much in my life. I can go for *months*, nothing, and then *wham!* It's the red tide coming in."

"The O'Brian women sure know how to bleed," laughed Carol, and dropped her sunglasses over her eyes again.

Nate looked as if he wanted to ooze between the slats of the lounge chair and join the pool water puddled beneath him.

"It's true," Darla chimed in. "You know how chicks can sync-up with their periods, Nate? Well, I had just got over my monthly affliction, met up with these two and I'll be damned if I didn't start right up again. So not fair."

"Not fair at all," agreed Cheryl.

"Still looking for a good time there, Nate?" asked Carol. "Because we can show you a *bloody* good time."

The three sisters stared at him from behind their sunglasses. The boy stared out across the pool, his mouth open awkwardly, as if he wanted to say something but had no clue what it was.

"There's no graceful exit from this, son," said Cheryl quietly. "If you can't play along, then maybe you should *move* along."

"*Farewell and adieu to you fair Spanish ladies*," Carol sang. "*Farewell and adieu you ladies of Spain...*"

Nate stood and glanced down at them, then spread his arms out, all innocence and surprise. "I was just trying to be friendly," he said, and gave his head a regretful shake.

"Bye Nate!" said Darla. "Remember us when you're dipping your French-fries in ketchup!"

Nate flinched again, and stalked stiffly over to the pool and dropped in. His sunglasses came off, and he spent a moment thrashing for them. Darla chuckled loudly.

"We are *so* mean," laughed Cheryl.

Carol blew disgustedly between her lips.

"A little bit, maybe" laughed Darla.

"Well, he needs to learn life isn't like a porn flick," said Carol. "This isn't an episode of hot and horny pool-MILFs."

"Hey now," laughed Darla. "I'm not there yet!"

"Oh, neither is she," said Cheryl, tipping her head towards Carol.

Carol cocked her head at Cheryl. "Well, *you're* pretty young for menopause."

Cheryl jerked her head at Nate, who was furiously swimming laps. "He doesn't know that. To him, I'm ancient."

Carol rolled her eyes, and dropped her sunglasses back down.

"Look, he's probably still pretty damned mystified about girl-things if he's dumb enough to think he can just come over and hit on you – or any of us," said Cheryl.

"Yeah, well, he got educated the hard way," said Carol. "I bet he won't forget it."

"Not likely, but we reinforced his revulsion about something that's a natural fact of life, where maybe we could have taught him a better lesson."

Carol pantomimed looking at a watch on her wrist. "Right on schedule! That angel on your shoulder always seems to be late to the party."

"I'm sorry. I do like to reflect on my behavior at times and reevaluate how I can respond."

"Teachable moments were up to his parents, and I think they dropped the ball. We call him a *boy*, but he's probably only a few years younger than Darla."

"You're never too old to be taught something."

"Sure. But I'm not worried about him. I care more about the next woman he thinks he can manipulate into boinking his brains out." Carol rolled onto her elbow and faced her sister directly. "It's been a long time since we've tag-teamed anyone. *You* got a kick out of it too. Don't beat yourself up over it now." She gestured out to Nate, who was now talking to the doughy giant at the edge of the pool. "He will be *fine* – meaning just the same as he ever was. Right now he's making up some excuse as to why he struck out with us. Letting him down gently to soothe his fragile ego would not have changed him as a person. But, after our ball-busting, he may leave some poor woman alone next time."

Cheryl opened her mouth to continue the argument, but Darla interrupted her.

"I vote we let this go," she said softly. "We're here to have good time. Don't let the meatheads ruin it for us."

Cheryl's heart crumpled, and she turned to her and smiled.

"Yeah, sorry," she said.

Carol grunted apologetically.

"And you know what?" asked Darla as she stood and slipped out of her robe. "I do believe it's time for a swim."

"You're damned right it is," laughed Carol, and jumped up from the chair.

Darla tipped her head down to stare at Cheryl. "You coming?" she asked.

"Oh, I'll sit here and watch our stuff," she said.

Carol snorted. "Room keys, water bottles, and your tablet. Darla's book and nail polish. They'll be *fine*."

Cheryl smiled, and shook her head. "In a bit, I will."

"Suit yourself," quipped Carol, and her sisters ran to the pool and dove in. She could see Nate's shape turn to look at the sound of the splashes, then across the pool at her. She smiled devilishly, and waved at him. The boy scrambled out of the pool quickly, and Cheryl laughed.

"Oh, screw it," she muttered, and shut her tablet down, stuffed it in her bag, then tied the straps of it around the chair leg. She stood and pulled her sundress over her head and dropped it over the bag, turned to the pool, ran and dove into the deep end. She arrowed down, down, down until she touched bottom, an old ritual, loving the shock of the water against her skin, how it pressed against her ear drums and chest.

She rose, trailing air-bubbles from her nose, and her head broke out of the water with a whoop. She rolled over onto her back and kicked, and Darla paddled over to kiss her on the head with a laugh. Carol splashed water at her, and she whooped again.

They made their way back to their room, a relaxed stroll that was quiet except for their flip-flops smacking dully against the carpet in the hallway. Cheryl felt that tingly-relaxed feeling she had after swimming, muscles achy but her skin still goose-bumped and alive with the cold kiss of air against her wet skin. She tipped her head back and forth, trying to dislodge the liquid in her ears. The smell of chlorine clinging to all of them brought back the long days of summer when they were kids, and she smiled lazily. Good times.

She studied the back of Carol's head, hair ropy and tangled, water dripping from the tips that managed break free from the surface tension of her skin. *Does she remember it like I do, those summer days?* she wondered. *We swam a lot after she came back, of course. But there were so many times at the community pool before then.* She shook her head, and it was in moments of reflection like this that she wished they never argued, that she had been a better sister. She would hate the defensive and exasperated girl that still seemed to rise up in her, the one that wanted to scream, *I'm sorry for what happened to you, but for God's sake we weren't the ones that kidnapped you, brainwashed you and assaulted you. Quit treating us like we're strangers!*

And that was the real, kicker, wasn't it? Carol never took advantage of the childhood trauma she went through, never really took it out on any of them. She was stoic to a maddening degree. Armchair psychologists always declared that you have to 'let it out', have that 'good cry' or breakdown before you can move on or make peace or live with yourself or whatever bullshit buzz-phrase people liked to use to justify some drama in front of everyone. For all anyone knew, Carol had those breakdowns. But if so, they were done privately.

Some could tag you with some pretty cruel nick-names. Like 'the changeling'...

Cheryl's heart fluttered, and tears welled up in her eyes. *Shit. I don't blame her for being distant.*

Still, Carol seemed to be enjoying herself so far, and Cheryl vowed to not find fights that weren't there. It was going to be tricky, of course. Carol wouldn't appreciate her rolling over and becoming totally acquiescent. That would piss her off more, probably. Anyways, she would –

Darla gave a gasp and stopped short, causing Carol to stumble and bump into her, and then Cheryl bumped into Carol.

"Did you see that?" asked Darla in a shaky voice. She spread her arms out, as if she wouldn't allow her sisters to go any further until they answered.

"What? See what?" asked Carol.

Darla levelled an arm down the hallway, where sunlight spilled in through an emergency exit.

"It was like...like a dark shape, of a person, that kind of...*flickered* in and out of - "

And then they all saw it, only it wasn't just one shape, but over-lapping shapes. Yet that wasn't right at all, because a shape was something you could describe, and it felt like Cheryl's mind slid right off of it, forgetting what she saw while she was looking at it. Whatever it was, it formed rapidly, as if a film of black chalk markings being erased on a board was being run backwards, and then quickly forward again. They were gone in seconds.

"Um, yeah. Like that," mumbled Darla.

"Holy shit," breathed Cheryl.

They stood there quietly for a few moments, then Darla turned to look back at them. Years of their disability had taught them to not trust their eyesight completely, and Darla searched Cheryl's face for some sort of confirmation. Apparently she found it, since she raised her eyebrows and nodded her head. Cheryl returned the gesture. Darla turned to Carol, and her head jerked back in surprise. Cheryl looked to her other sister, and Carol was frozen, hands clutched in front of her belly.

Oh Lord, she looks just like when we first saw her when she came back to us – a deer ready to bolt, but too confused and scared to make a move!

"Carol?" asked Darla tentatively. "You okay, sis?"

Carol darted her head to Darla, then turned to Cheryl, eyes wide, her breathing sharp and jagged huffs.

Look Cheryl, Carol's back!

Cheryl reached out to touch Carol on the shoulder.

"We saw it too," she said reassuringly. Carol gave a short bark of a laugh, and stood a little straighter. Her eyes darted between her sisters, and she began to reassert her composure. The strong, confident Carol was coming back to them.

"I'm not sure if that's comforting or not," she laughed.

Darla smiled, then turned and jogged down to the end of the hallway where the apparitions had formed and disappeared.

"Oh, Jesus!" blurted Carol.

"Oh, honey, no!" shouted Cheryl.

"What?" asked Darla. "I'm just trying to see if there's anything outside that could have caused what we saw. She turned and cupped her hands up against the glass, shading her eyes from the sun's glare, then peered outside.

"God *damn* it," scolded Carol. "Will you *ever* quit poking at things that are strange?"

Darla ignored them. "I can't see where any traffic could cast shadows," she stated, her voice muffled under her hands. "Or any people. And that would have had to have been a shit-load of people to do that, like a cross-country team running by." She pulled her head back, cocked her head as if considering the idea, then shook it. "No," she said firmly. She looked back at the wall at the end of the hallway and waved her arms. Timid shadows fluttered on the wall as if they, too, were afraid to get to the bottom of things.

"Not what we saw, yeah?" asked Darla.

Cheryl shook her head, as did Carol.

"Right," said Darla, as she moved back down the hallway towards them, then stopped halfway. Cheryl and Carol looked at each other, then back to Darla.

Darla lifted an arm at the elbow and pointed. "Our room," she stated. "You two going to stand here in the hallway the rest of the afternoon?"

"Maybe," said Cheryl.

Darla snorted. "Quit being babies."

Carol sighed and began to walk towards their room. Cheryl gave a heavier sigh and followed. She fished their room key out of her bag, and took several attempts at unlocking the door, which included one frustrated kick at the door which hurt a big toe, until they were able to enter.

"I got dibs on the shower first," muttered Carol, and she entered the bathroom and slammed the door.

"But I really have to pee," called Darla softly. The roar of the faucet in the shower was all that answered her.

"Okay then," she said, and dropped her arms to her thighs with a smack. She walked over and sat on the edge of the bed she shared with Cheryl, and pressed her knees together.

Cheryl dropped the bag in a chair, and sat on the bed opposite Darla. They looked at each other with grim smiles and raised eyebrows.

"So," offered Cheryl.

"Uh-huh," returned Darla.

"That was...weird."

"Yep."

"Any idea what the heck it was?"

"Nope."

"No...mass hallucination between us? Which is funny – *mass* – three of us being a 'mass'. Like 'massive'. What would the term be, then? Shared hallucination?"

"Yeah, why not..."

"You see that as likely?"

"Well, let's back up a bit. What exactly did *you* see?"

Cheryl closed her eyes and tried to picture what she saw. Evidently her brain resisted her attempt at recalling what they had seen. Fleeting, indistinct shapes that overlapped and...not *shimmering*, not *sparkling*...they were black, but had a jittery, particle like form, like the iron filings that made up the Wooly Willy toy where you drew on his beard and hair with a magnet.

Cheryl's eyes popped open, and she realized that while her brain couldn't describe any coherent shapes, the image was still one of the clearest and sharpest images she had ever seen.

"Fuzzy black nothings smearing into and out of existence," she finally answered.

Darla cocked her head, thought it over, then nodded slowly. "Pretty good description," she said.

"But you saw it twice?" asked Cheryl.

"Yes – no! I mean, the way they both *appeared* and *disappeared* was the same. But the first time was definitely man-shaped. *Humanoid*, to get all sci-fi and shit. And only one person."

"Huh," grunted Cheryl. "You see him clearly? Like, the clearest thing you've ever seen?"

"No, just like if a guy popped in and out of...reality? But the...*things*. Yeah... they seemed more clear than anything, and I can't tell you what they looked like."

Cheryl shuddered. Just trying to picture what they had seen gave her a deep sense of dread in her gut, and her mind wanted to push the images away.

"Think that's what rattled Carol so badly?" asked Cheryl.

"Right? I've never seen her look like that!"

"Last time I can remember is when she came back home."

Darla shook her head. "I don't have any clear memories of that."

"You were only three. But I think it was good that she saw you first. If it were me, or mom or dad, she would *still* be freaked the fuck out."

"Cha-ching, swear jar," said Darla absently.

"I think I get a pass on the swearing for a while, okay?"

Darla nodded, and started drumming her fingers on her knees.

"She probably wouldn't mind if you just went in and peed."

Darla flapped a hand. "No, she's always been pretty private that way. I won't intrude. And I'm guessing she's trying to calm herself down. Probably embarrassed we saw her...unguarded, you know?"

Cheryl nodded, and she heard the water shut off in the bathroom.

"Finally," Darla muttered.

"Okay, so could anything have caused us to hallucinate the same thing?" asked Cheryl. "Something we ate? Could those jerks in the pool have had something in their pockets that – "

"No," said Darla emphatically. "Jesus, you going to go on about chemtrails next?"

"You know, for a hippy you can be pretty snotty sometimes."

Darla raised her hands apologetically. "It is *unlikely* any sort of substance that they, *hypothetically*, could have contaminated the pool with would have had a pharmacological effect on us do to its dilution in the volume of the pool water. *Okay?*"

"Okay," Cheryl said, still a little irked. "My vote is that we are of sound mind and body. And my reasoning is that the first...*apparition* that you saw?"

Darla nodded.

"Well, that sounds just like what I saw at breakfast."

Darla's mouth dropped open, and then the bathroom door opened, and Carol stepped out with a towel wrapped around her. Darla darted her eyes to the bathroom, back to Cheryl, then back to the bathroom. She shot up like a rocket and dashed past Carol.

"Thank you!" she shouted as the door slammed, and then they heard the sound of the toilet lid hitting the porcelain tank.

"She really had to go," said Cheryl.

"Sorry," called Carol through the door. She turned and met Cheryl's neutral smile, and offered up one of her own. She padded over to one of the chairs by a round table, and sat almost primly in it. Her eyes moved randomly around the room as if searching for something interesting to observe. They flicked back to Cheryl, and away. All of their phones sat on the table, left there when they had gone to the pool (a pact was made to minimize phone usage while on their road trip). Each of them issued quiet little burps as they rattled on the table top, gentle reminders that messages and emails were waiting. They both stared at the phones, but neither reached out to take one.

Cheryl was startled that she didn't want to say anything to embarrass her sister for once. Questioning if she felt better after her shower would point out the fact that she had lost her composure and for a moment had shown vulnerability. Man, that had to be the worst. Once, she would have loved to illuminate the issue with spotlights, laser pointers and a PowerPoint slideshow. A veritable TED Talks presentation of, *Wow, Carol, You Sure Looked Fucked-Up*. And as startled as she was that she couldn't do that, she felt a wash of relief knowing that she didn't want to.

So she settled for, "How was your shower?"

Carol nodded her head. "Good. Nice and hot."

"Cool," Cheryl smiled, then chuckled. "Leave any hot water for the rest of us?"

"No Promises."

"Ah."

They heard the toilet flush, water run in the sink, and then the bathroom door banged open and Darla hurried out, adjusting the swimsuit straps over her shoulders again.

"So you're telling me you saw the same thing this morning?" she asked. "The guy? Just flitting in and out?"

"Yeah, at the diner as we were leaving."

Darla stood between them, her eyes blinking in thought. Cheryl wondered if her baby sister was trying to recall any sort of incidents that could safely dismiss what they had seen as something natural. Perhaps mere trickery or dickery - but *natural*. Explainable. Nothing weird and other-worldly. And especially not paranormal. Cheryl sincerely hoped Darla could explain it away. She had her faith, and it was that while God had a plan, He could also let things go as they pleased. Because that, too, was part of the plan. God was not a magician, and she felt the notion of hell was an insult to Him. And so she had no room for weird-ass shit in her world view.

Her sisters had no room for God at all in their world, and while little jabs at each other could pop up from time to time, they had enough mutual respect for her – and she for them – not to get mean about it.

Darla turned to Carol. "You feeling better?" she asked.

Cheryl flinched. *Geeze, when the scientist comes out, the gentle hippy goes away!*

To Carol's credit, she merely took a deep breath and said, "Yes, thank you."

"Good," said Darla. "What the hell do you make of all this?"

"Well," said Carol carefully, "he said I might see him again. I'm guessing we're all getting that chance, now."

"What the what, now?" asked Cheryl. "What did you say?"

"You heard me."

Cheryl felt as if a miniature bomb went off in her head. In fact, the water in her right ear let go and trickled out in welcome relief. *Holy crap!* she thought. *Could the mystery of Carol finally be revealed?*

Darla's eyes were squeezed tightly shut, and she pinched the bridge of her nose between her thumb and finger. She took two deep, cleansing breaths. "They have any sort of room service?" she asked to no one in particular. "Or maybe we order some take-out?" She opened her eyes and stared at Carol. "Because, Lucy, you have some splainin' to do."

Chapter 4

Combined with a low click somewhere in the treadmill, Carol's feet pounded out a mantra of *this happened, this happened, this happened.* She was pushing the ancient and abused machine for all it was worth, imagining the belt shredding and flying off to land in a pathetic heap in the corner, looking like a scrap of blown tire lying along a highway. But she could not stop, her adrenaline-fueled anxiety wouldn't let her.

This happened, this happened, this happened...

She had never forgotten the boy, but had wondered about him less often over the years. She could feel the sting on her neck, the feeling of being everyone at once, and the disorientation of waking up in your room not being your room.

And of your family not being your family, learning that you were best friends 4evah now with a classmate who had taken delight in degrading you, and that you had been gone for six months but you could remember them clearly nonetheless. Just not like everyone else.

Like a lot of traumatized children, she adapted and accepted her new life change. But she was never the Old Carol. This was never said to her of course. Perhaps it was never expected of her to *be* just like the Old Carol, but maybe she should have gotten close? Threw 'em a bone to make them happy, able to relax around her? The thing was, *she* was more relaxed. She liked her new life better, except for Byron being gone of course. But the girl they thought she was, she could never find. Trying to play along, to fake an emotion or enthusiasm, was dreadful for everyone involved. So she stayed who she was, despite the frustrations of friends and family.

To her parents' credit, they never exploited her story – never did interviews on news or talk shows, only released statements asking for privacy. Carol was encouraged to talk or not talk, whatever she felt she needed, and Carol had never liked to talk.

Her dad seemed to be the best at accepting her completely for who she was. It's not that her mom had acted as if she should snap out of it and move on, but...hints of frustration would flicker across her brow, and then guilt of course. Her dad looked like he felt guilty all the time, but of a crime he hadn't committed. Carol had no doubt that her parents were grilled over her disappearance, of her reappearance, and maybe things she shared with the child psychologist in those endless sessions weren't strictly confidential when a minor was involved? She had no clue what her parents knew, until tonight. There was no doubt that her physical examination had revealed sexual abuse had taken place, and what she had disclosed in the therapy sessions should have shot up some enormous God damned red flags about her dad. But evidently not enough to even charge him with anything. And was *he* her dad? There were a lot of things said in those sessions, no doubt illustrating that Carol might not have the strongest grip on reality. It was suggested that maybe she was suffering a sort of Stockholm syndrome, implanted memory type of trauma. Something her hypothetical kidnapper had done to her.

Sure lady, whatever. I can play along. Heck, maybe it was true.

thishappenedthishappenedthishappened

Her dad never let on that he knew he had been accused of being her abuser. He was always patient and kind to her right up to the day he died. Probably too patient, and apologetic for her. Carol let go of one of the support rails to swipe a fist across her eyes.

"Never tell her she's wrong in what she remembers, or believes she remembers," Cheryl informed her on what her dad had said all those years ago. "If she's been messed with – mentally - we can't add to that trauma by insisting that she yield to our perceptions."

"But dad, there's perception, and then there's truth," Cheryl had argued. "We *know* she was gone for six months. We *know* Byron died before she was born. We *know* she and Kimberly were best friends."

"And so what?" he had answered. "We don't *know* what happened to her for six months, and she apparently doesn't either. Will rubbing reality in her face help her at all?"

Cheryl never had an answer for that, but telling a teenager to control her frustrations can only magnify them, really. And so, her mom had confided the fact that Carol had believed her dad had molested her for months, and that's not something he could live with in peace, ever. So maybe cut him some slack, along with your sister? What was unimaginable to him, her mother and herself was certainly imaginable to Carol, and we must prove to her that we love her by our intentions and actions, not telling her that she's wrong, and to suck it up and get over it already.

And it's not as if her mother had been unscathed in the event. With the death of Byron years earlier, and the disappearance of a daughter, there were whispers of Munchausen's Syndrome while Carol had been missing. A little suspicious, isn't it? Sure, they seem like a nice family, but one never knows, right? Rumors might breed in a little cul-de-sac in Ramona, but they could spread to infect the larger San Diego County.

Most of this was news to Darla as well as to her. By the time Darla was old enough to be sensitive to the undercurrents of tension in the house, a status quo had developed and been accepted. Still, she could remember vividly one night when she was five and Carol had impulsively kissed her father goodnight, and the tears that had streamed from his eyes, and how that had scared her. Daddy *never* cried.

Both Darla and Cheryl had wept openly during the discussions of the past. While Carol had teared up frequently, she never cried. Years of keeping your guard up helped to keep the tears in check. Still, it had been eye-opening, to finally know what others had been feeling and thinking at the time.

"So, you guys are still sticking with this 'I was gone for six months' story, huh?" she had asked, and both Darla and Cheryl had giggled as they wiped at their eyes and noses.

this happened, this happened, this happened...

"Well, I don't know if the child psychologist ever told mom or dad – "

"A minor needs parental consent for treatment," Darla had interrupted. "So a parent generally has the right to know the content of the child's treatment. So, yeah, I'm guessing mom and dad probably wanted to know all that you talked about."

"Well okay, then," Carol had said. "You want to know about it, though?"

Darla had nodded.

"Then hush."

Darla had given her a sheepish grin, but stared at her with the same unflinching gaze she had all those years ago when Carol's world had gone downside up.

And so she told them about the boy, the pinprick on her neck, the feeling of being everyone at once, and how her room had grown a fish tank, a poster, and was far messier than her father had ever let her keep it. Of a house that was now more of a home, and money spent for everyone to enjoy, not just her father's whimsies. Of learning to accept the unconditional love given to her, and of the loss of a beloved brother.

After the initial revelation that she no longer had a brother, Carol never brought up the topic again around her family. Cheryl had tried to bring it up at times, and was usually met with stony silence, but no retraction of the notion that she had known Byron – that he was sixteen when she had last seen him, and had not died when he was five of bronchitis.

"I was three when Byron died," Cheryl had said wistfully. I don't know if I have a clear memory of him that is my own, you know? There were tons of videotape to watch of him and me together of course, and mom and dad never had a problem with us watching those tapes. I just don't remember anything that wasn't on the tapes."

"That was another shocker, those tapes," Carol told them. "We had a video camera, but it was used for dad when he was fishing. Dad when he was riding his motorcycle. Dad when he was hunting. Jesus, Byron had got such a beating when he was allowed to tape his presentation at the science fair, only to have accidentally taped over a fraction of a hunting trip with dad and his buddies."

Darla and Cheryl had shaken their heads sadly. "I can't imagine dad wanting to kill anything, much less commemorate it on video," Cheryl had commented.

"And so you see…why I acted the way I did?" asked Carol. "The way I *am*, I guess? Shit, nothing has changed in what I remember. There's never been any sudden recollection to change things, no shift in perspective. This is what I remember life being like up until that day in February, where it felt like I was dropped into a new life."

Darla had cleared her throat, and asked quietly, "So, this boy?"

"Yes."

"What can you tell us about him, and his rather cryptic speech to you?"

Carol's arms rose and dropped to her sides. "I can't recall it verbatim, sweetie. It was what – twenty-two years ago? Ish? He said something about feeling sorry for me, maybe? No – something like feeling sorry for *us*, whatever the hell that meant. And that I might see him again, if 'things came to a head'. Again, whatever the hell that meant."

"How old was he?" Cheryl had asked.

"Nine? Ten? Close to my age, I think."

"You indicated that the man...shape...*guy-thing* I saw at first might be him," Darla asked. "That he was back. What makes you think that?"

Carol had looked down at her toes buried in the hotel room's carpet, and was silent for a moment. She sighed, and said, "It was a *feeling* – and I don't mean like a hunch. While I didn't see him, I literally *felt* something in my head – *my body* – like when I first saw the boy. It was as fleeting as your vision was, but you don't forget a feeling like *that*. I had a quicker version of it when you had your sighting at the diner." She nodded towards Cheryl. "I just didn't realize what it was – just thankful it went away and I wasn't sick."

Darla tipped her head and raised an eyebrow, prompting her to continue.

"That tuning-up feeling, like I was growing slightly. But... Okay, this may not make sense, and sound kind of weird -"

"Oh, I'm betting not," laughed Cheryl, but not unkindly. "We left weird behind some time ago."

Carol grinned. "Right. Well, I felt like a...cursor? That was waiting? Like I had just 'come online'. I honestly expected to hear a voice in my head that said, 'ready'. And then it was gone, like it – that *I* - had shut off."

"Huh," Darla had grunted.

"So did you literally see a cursor?" Cheryl had asked. "Like, blinking away?"

"No, I didn't *see* anything. I was just trying to give you an *impression* of the feeling I had. Wasn't meant to be taken literally."

"I could really smoke a bowl right now," sighed Darla.

Cheryl had stiffened. "You didn't –"

"No, I *didn't*. Wouldn't have been able to get it on the plane, could I?"

"Oh, like you didn't partake back in the day," Carol had laughed.

Cheryl had blushed, then giggled. "I always thought you could have used some pot back then."

Carol smiled tightly. "I had enough memories of my drunken dad being an asshole, and I never wanted to impair myself. Ever."

They sat in silence, and Carol felt guilty for bringing the mood down again. Well, it was a time to lay it all out. Welcome to my life, ladies. She glanced at Darla, who was worrying her lower lip with her thumb and forefinger.

"So. Any theories, professor?" Carol had asked her.

"No," Darla answered her slowly. "Not anything I want to admit right now, at least." Then she rolled her eyes at Carol. "And I'm not a professor."

Carol laughed at her response. It had the sound of, "Don't call me sir, I work for a living!"

"We may be able to surmise one thing, though," Darla had commented.

"Yeah?" Carol and Cheryl chorused.

"That maybe things have now come to a head?"

This happened. This happened. This happened.

Carol finally began to grow fatigued. It was late, and even though she was as emotionally spent as her sisters, sleep hadn't visited her. While it had been cathartic to reveal her secrets to them at long last, the feeling that larger things were afoot began to trouble her, and she had a gnawing fear for the safety of her sisters now. So she had climbed out of bed, dressed for a run and found the gym downstairs still open.

She jabbed at her phone laying on the console of the treadmill, and squinted at the display. 12:11. Whoa – she was supposed to be out of there at 11:30. No one had come by to kick her out and lock up, so maybe no one cared. She decided to slow her pace to a cool-down walk. She flicked through her phone, checking texts and emails. Amy had sent her a link to a video of a baby elephant splashing in the surf for the first time, and Carol's heart felt like it had liquefied. Since she didn't tweet, Instagram, Snapchat or Facebook, Amy was her social media link.

The sound of someone filling an ice bucket outside the gym door filtered into the back of her mind, but she was absorbed in the sheer joy the little pachyderm displayed splashing around in the water. That was the meaning of life, surely? Why couldn't we feel like that all the time? *I don't want to hear any bullshit about how we wouldn't know joy without pain*, she thought. *But you know there* really *isn't a meaning to life? Life just is. Holding back death is serious business.*

"Shit," she hissed, not liking the dark shade her thoughts always seemed to turn. She punched the play arrow on the video again, then she shut off the treadmill and sat on the belt while her grin reached both ears.

The door to the gym opened, and she absently flapped a hand at it.

"I *know*," she called out. "The gym closed at 11:30. I'm almost out of here." Damn. This was absolutely the cutest video she had ever seen. Why had she never seen it before? Shouldn't the whole world be talking about it? Someone mumbled something near the door, and she raised her hand, palm out, then flapped it. Shoo.

"Yeah, yeah. Get it. Closed. I'm leaving. Just let me catch my breath, and I'm out of here."

"What are you watching, I *said*."

Carol looked up absently, a smile still on her face. A young man – huge – maybe six-five, six-six, dark hair, beady eyes. Blue jeans, sleeves cut off his sweatshirt to show his thick muscles. But soft, kind of doughy. Carol's smile evaporated. Ah. The second-stringer.

"Nothing you would care about," she stated simply. She stopped the video, closed out her apps and hit the power button, then stood and tucked her phone away.

"Probably dyke porn, or something," he said, with an inebriated chuckle.

"Excuse me?" said Carol icily.

"Let me ask you something. Can I ask you something?"

"I don't know, *can* you?" *Shit. It's late, don't waste time with him…*

The boy tried to process what she said, and apparently failed at it. He blinked at her slowly. Carol waited, and sized up the distance between him and the door. The boy swayed slightly, belched and squinted at her. Carol arched an eyebrow.

"Got that question ready, son?" she asked, letting a hint of impatience show. "Tick-tock, it's late and beddy-bye time for the kiddos. Time's a wastin'. Don't have all night. Let's get this show on the road." *Don't get nervous*, she thought. *You run off at the mouth when you get nervous, and pissing him off won't make him go away.*

The young man tipped his head back. "Why you gotta be such a bitch? Huh? Why can't you be friendly?"

"Well, that's kind of an existential thought for a meathead like you. And this late at night, even."

Jesus, Carol!

"Why am *I* such a bitch?" Carol grabbed her chin in a thoughtful pose. "I imagine that question has kept a lot of people awake at night. No doubt term papers written over it. Perhaps it's my response to the absurdity of life. Life's a bitch, so why not fight fire with fire?"

The boy snorted and smacked his lips. "You lesbos think you're so smart. All educated and shit." Apparently, he remembered his original question because he brightened and asked, "Oh yeah. How come you're so pretty for a dyke? I mean, most of 'em don't shave their legs. And, you know..." He lifted a hand and waved it under an armpit. "And no makeup and shit. How come you wear makeup?"

Carol only stared at him, her eyes flicking to either side of him. He took a step forward, and she eased back as well.

"I bet you're not *really* a dyke," he offered. "I bet you just haven't had the right dude to... to... make you *cum*."

Carol was fairly certain she could dart past him now, get behind him and out the door. But she had seen quick drunks before, and his arms looked very long. *He is just a boy raised on internet porn and no role model to speak of,* she thought. *He is not inherently evil, just a manifestation of balls filled with semen and a drive to share the seed. To beat all competition in this drive until he can't spill his load anymore. And even then, the drive will still push him to compete because that is all the drive knows.*

"I bet *I* could make you cum," he mumbled.

Carol had been ready to spring past him and end it. But an image popped into her head, and she pictured a dark room lit only by an open door. There was a stealthy creak of floorboards, and the overpowering stink of alcohol infused breath. This was a scene she would forever feel guilty for if she just ignored it. And she decided that her pepper spray would not...send the right message.

Carol made as if to move past him to his right, but he took a few steps back to block her. She moved to the left, and he now backed up against the door.

"Where you going?" he asked with a taunting smirk.

Carol stepped back and eyed him. Jesus, he was big. Her eyes flicked around the room, and spotted the smoky dome housing of a video camera.

"I'm trying to leave, so I can go back to my room with my sisters – who probably wonder where I am – so I can go to bed," Carol finally answered him. "You are in my way. Please move."

He leaned forward, which made him waver a bit, and said, "*Make* me."

"Make me hurt you?" Carol asked.

His brows knitted slowly together into a frown as his pickled brain digested her question. It didn't seem to be able to process it.

"I said, 'make me'. *Make* me move."

"Make you scream like a little prison bitch?"

He shook his head, still not sure he was hearing her correctly.

"Because I bet you could scream real high," continued Carol. "Shriveled up little steroid-soaked balls of yours? Yeah. You'll scream so high dogs in Riverside will hear it."

His bloodshot eyes narrowed, and his upper lip curled as his breathing began to snort rapidly through his nostrils.

"You're pretty fuckin' stupid for a dyke," he said. "I could destroy you right now. You want that? You like it rough? Lesbo-dyke-*whore*."

"A second-stringer like *you* going to do that?"

His head gave a violent little shake, a mere tremor, but Carol crouched and then he was rushing at her. She sprang into him, her right leg up into his abdomen, her right arm snaking through the cut sleeve of his shirt. Her left reached behind his head and began to grab fistfuls of the sweatshirt, and they were falling. He shot his arms out to brace himself, and Carol's right hand flicked to her left, and her other hand crossed over. Her wrists were now crossed, twisting the shirt into his neck, the bones in her arms cutting off the blood flow. She tucked her head next to his, and continued the pressure. He landed on his knees, and Carol could feel flecks of spittle spraying on the back of her neck. He tried to pummel her in the sides, and then her back finally slammed into the floor, but she held her grip, and she could feel him weaken.

"I bet this didn't work out like you thought it would," she panted in his ear. He growled in fury and tried to rise, but Carol pulled harder, and at last all he could do was try and push against the floor, and then he was out. Carol held the grip for a moment more, then let go and shoved her leg up and leveraged him off of her. He flopped over onto his back, and Carol stood.

She stared at him for a moment, and then her eyes darted to door. She could see no one outside. Might be a little late for more people to go grab some ice, being a week day. Still, this clown's buddies might come in search of him. She looked at him again, then bent, unlatched his belt and quickly slid it free of the loops of his pants. She stepped over him, and tugged at him until she had him on his stomach. She tied his wrists together behind his back with the belt, and he began to twitch, like a drugged bear shaking off the effects of a tranquilizer dart.

She grabbed the lat-exercise bar on a weight machine, and strained to loop it through his arms until it pulled against the belt tied at his wrists. She let go, and it tugged his arms up high behind his back. He groaned. She then pulled his pants down until they were bunched up around his ankles.

Carol stepped to the door, peeked out. The hum of the light in the hallway, the whoosh of cars on the freeway, and a dog barking in the distance were all she heard. She spied the bucket of ice, and brought it inside with her.

The guy was working his legs against the floor, as if he was trying to stand but couldn't remember how. Carol dumped the ice over his head, and he gave a shout. She crouched down by his head.

"Can we talk?" she asked him sweetly.

He began to struggle, his teeth gritted in fury, breath exploding out of his nostrils. Inarticulate sounds ground out between his teeth.

Carol stood, then planted a foot on the back of his neck and pushed. His arms pulled up farther behind him and he barked out a wail of pain. She held it for a moment, then released the pressure.

"You God damned bitch, I will fucking -"

She stepped on his neck again and he shrieked.

"There we go!" quipped Carol. She lifted her foot.

"I fucking swear to -"

Down went the foot. Shriek. "I can do this all night," said Carol. She lifted her foot, and this time he was quiet, except for breaths heaving in and out of his chest. But he still shook with rage. Carol crouched down by him again.

"Oh, I get it," she said. "You're pretty mad. You think by channeling your rage, that will make this all better. You're vowing to get me if it's the last thing you ever do. You'll show this little dyke a thing or two, and she'll wish she never messed with you." She bent in next to his ear, and whispered gently, "But you're not thinking in the long term."

She pulled out her phone, punched in her pin, and flicked on the camera.

"Selfie time," she said brightly, and snapped several pictures of her grinning face next to his apoplectic one. The last one she gave a big thumbs up. "That's the one!"

She then stood and took some full-length shots of him tied up. "So let's talk about the long game here," she said as she paced slowly next to him. "I'm not sure if that little ol' security camera up there works, if Joe Security Guard is asleep, or if the feed only goes to a hard drive somewhere and is only reviewed when needed. That's probably your best option. That at some point it gets erased, and no one else gets to see you assault me."

The boy's huffing stopped momentarily, and then resumed.

"Yeah, didn't think of that? Well I don't blame you. You were drunk on your ass, couldn't help yourself. You're just an impulsive little rascal, right?"

Carol reached in her fanny pack and behind his back she brought out the slim bottle of pepper spray, then bent down and jammed it in the waistband of his underwear. He flinched and swore, but didn't say anything else. She took several more pictures, and then said, "I think we have the money shot, right there." She grabbed the pepper spray gingerly by the top and dropped it back in the pack. "For decontamination later," she muttered to herself.

She stepped over him and crouched down again.

"You know what that – say, what's your name?"

He didn't answer, so she stood and placed her foot on his neck again.

"Mike!" he blurted. "Mike. It's Mike!"

She crouched again. "Yay! You *can* learn quickly. So, *Mike*, do you want to know what I shoved down your shorts?" She waited for him to answer, and he finally nodded.

"That there, Mike, was a big fat dildo I just bought from the official bull-dyke store all us lesbos have to shop at. Honestly, it's the law if you wanna be gay."

Mike closed his eyes, and gritted his teeth.

"I know your arms hurt, honey," breathed Carol. "But I'm going to need a little insurance you won't be a big dumb-ass when this is all over, okay? And that dildo is it. Let me explain: you try taking any revenge on me – or my sisters – that pretty little pic of a dildo in your shorts goes *absolutely* fucking viral. So if you're a good boy up until you think security footage is written over, remember these pics."

She bent, and whispered gently into his ear. "Because how do you think your buddies are going to like those pics, bruh?" Mike was suddenly still.

"Yeah. And *there's* the big picture. Let's say, worst case scenario for me, I'm on trial for beating you up. You swallow your pride, act the victim, and cry that a girl beat you up. Personally, I don't think it would happen, because you see, Mike, I bet I would come off sympathetic as hell. I kind of have a history that would play well for the cops, jury, whatever. But let's say it happens, *bam*, miscarriage of justice and *I'm* the one who's in trouble here. How do you think your friends will feel about a girl beating you up? Think they'll still be your friends after that? Think you're going to lose any face with them?"

Mike began to cry, big fat tears plopping onto the floor mats.

"I think we have a breakthrough here. There you go, let it out."

Mike visibly shook, and then tried to control himself. He grimaced, and let out an angry huff of air.

"Now, come on, you don't want to do that - get all worked up again. That's not going to help. Here, watch." Carol scrolled and tapped on her phone. "There. I texted the pics to my sisters' phones. It's a done deal, so there's no use getting pissy about it. The madder you get, well, pretty soon *I'm* going to get mad." She leaned in close to his ear and whispered, "You want to see me mad?"

The boy dropped his head, and the tears flowed again.

"You see, you think you're big and bad, and just about the meanest bastard around. You think life's pretty simple, that muscling your way through it and you'll always win. Take what you want, say what you want, just do whatever the hell you want. And that may work with a lot of people, until you run into someone like me. And like you, I can be mean. But I can be *crazy* mean. And I bet you aren't bright enough to *fully* understand crazy mean. But I'm thinking you've got an inkling of what it is now, huh?"

Carol stood, and then tapped her foot against the back of Mike's neck. "So, we got a deal? You be a good boy, and I don't post pictures of you anywhere, yeah?"

Mike didn't say anything, so she applied pressure. "*Yeah?*" she repeated.

"Yes," Mike mumbled. Carol shrugged and said, "That will do." Then she squatted next to him, and grabbed a hunk of his black hair. "But just in case you think you're getting off scot free, I have a parting curse for you." She applied a little pressure against his head, and he cried out. "See, I had a vision of you. I see you going in a room, and in that room is a young woman on a bed passed out and defenseless. I see you thinking you hit the jackpot. Hell, maybe this has already happened, knowing a piece of shit like you. But if there's a next time – or maybe you think you can just bully some girl into sex – I want you to remember me. You remember what I did to you tonight, a little associative therapy. You get the idea you can rape someone, your boner is going limp, son. You got that?" She pushed harder on his head, then released. "Any time you get the urge to force yourself – on anyone – you will remember me, and your dick will go marshmallow in the microwave soft. Got it? You are *cursed*."

She stood. "Now, do you think you can rise enough to sit on the bench?" Carol got behind him and pulled on his shoulders. Mike howled, but managed to push up with his foot and flop his back onto the weight machine's bench. Carol rolled him onto his side, and wriggled the handle out between his arms and let it snap back with a clang.

"Couple of things," she said as she loosened the belt at his wrists. "We probably are going to have to hope that the security footage is non-existent, or will just get overlooked. I don't want the hassle. *You* certainly don't. Let's cross our fingers."

Carol moved to the door, and eyed him. "And while you lie there waiting for your arms to work again, come up with a lame-ass excuse why you're hurting. I recommend the ol' 'I was so wasted I fell down the steps bit.'" Carol palmed the lights out in the room. Feeble light streamed in through the door's window, and Mike looked lost laying on the bench. Carol lowered her voice. "You remember what I said?"

"Yes," responded Mike dully.

"You going to take it to heart?"

"Yes."

"I don't believe you, Mike. But if I ever hear about you being involved in anything…unsavory, you know what will happen, right?"

"Yes."

Carol eased out the door and let it fall softly shut.

The night air chilled the sweat drying on her skin, making her feel damp and heavy. Suddenly, Carol was wrung-out tired. She stopped and leaned against the block wall of the hotel and took a series of deep breaths.

Feel like a big tough guy, beating up a boy? she thought, and then an immediate flash of anger swept through her. *Shut up, Cheryl. I swear I will kick the shit out of your little shoulder-angel. That 'boy' deserved what he got.*

Even shoving something into his butt crack?

"He's lucky it didn't go all the way in, God damn it!" hissed Carol aloud.

Really? Because he would have done the same to you, so that makes it right?

"Nothing's right about *anything* that could have happened in there," she whispered. "And just about anything could have. I just happened to win."

Did you?

"Well I sure as hell didn't lose."

Uh-huh.

"You would seriously compare me to that piece of shit in there?"

Not at all. I don't feel sorry for him. But I kind of do for you.

"Because I sank to his level."

Oh, not that far, certainly. Not that far at all. But surely you know the difference between you and him?

Carol shook her head.

You have sympathy in you that feels bad for him, even though he wouldn't for you. That's what's truly pissing you off right now, but that's what makes you better than him.

Carol rubbed her tired eyes and shook her head again.

"Fuck it," she said, and began to walk to the lobby entrance. She had a notion to see if any security room could be found, and make a casual cruise past it. As the doors hummed open for her, she had the feeling as if something awoke in her again, like she was more than what she was, *bigger*, and waiting for…potential.

"Shit," she hissed, and looked around. She could hear someone humming in a small room behind the welcome desk, but could see no one else in the lobby. She took off and sprinted through the hallways until she came to their room.

And then the feeling was gone, she was tired again, but she fumbled her key card into the lock and got it open on the first try. She walked gingerly past the bathroom, careful not to trip over any of their bags, and into the sleeping area. Darla was sitting up in bed looking at her phone while she absently rubbed the back of her neck.

"Hey," whispered Carol.

"Hey," answered Darla. "Getting back pretty late. You go out on a date?" She laughed quietly, and Cheryl continued to snore softly next to her.

"Kinda," laughed Carol. "You guys okay? What are you doing up?"

"I don't know. Phone woke me up, I guess? Had that weird disorientated feeling you get sometimes when you wake up."

"Yeah…"

Darla's head wobbled in the light of the phone's screen, her finger flicking across it. She frowned. "Why did you send me a series of emoticons a little bit ago?"

"Did I?"

Darla turned the phone towards her to show the screen, and Carol pretended to squint at it.

"God damn technology these days," Carol muttered in an aged voice. "Has a mind of its own, I say!"

Darla giggled.

"Can you butt-text someone?" wondered Carol.

"Probably," sighed Darla, and shut her phone off. "Go to bed, sis. You look tired."

"Going to rinse off first. Then I'm crashing."

"Okay. Hey Carol?"

"Yeah?"

"I'm having a good time. Thank you for being here with us."

"Me too, sweetie. My pleasure."

"You know what I think we should do?" mumbled Cheryl sleepily.

Darla and Carol looked at each other, then over to Cheryl.

"What's that, sis?" asked Carol, amused.

"Our tattoos. I think we should get two sets of eyes."

"Okay..."

"Carol, you get me and Darla. Darla, you get me and Carol. I get you two."

"That's nice, Cheryl. Why don't you go back to sleep?"

But Cheryl was already snoring again.

Darla looked at Carol with a wide grin.

"You follow what the hell she meant?" asked Carol with a laugh.

"No," laughed Darla. "Not in the..." She trailed off, and then her eyes grew bigger. "Oh! We get tattoos of each other's *eyes* on us! Oh, that is awesome!"

Carol wrinkled her brow, and decided she didn't hate the idea.

"Like on the backs of our necks – we could be watching each other's backs!" whispered Darla excitedly.

"Well, if I'm going to deface my body, it may as well be you two goofs doing it," laughed Carol as she moved to the bathroom. She shook her head. Leave it to Cheryl to have a good idea while sleeping.

Chapter 5

*T*his...*isn't* too *bad*, thought Cheryl as the needle buzzed repeatedly into the nape of her neck. It hurt, but in a raw, sunburned type of way. Darla assured her she would be sore, that the tattoo would get scabby-looking, but then it wouldn't be long until she could show it off. *Not likely that will happen very often*, she thought. *Good lord, what'll Dave really think? Mom? Her guild at church? The kids will see it eventually. Will I ever cut my hair short again?* She fingered a lock of her ash-blonde hair hanging in front of her face. *Oh good lord...*

She could hear Darla and Carol whispering and giggling behind her. This had been going on for some time now. She had resolved to ignore it, let them have their kicks as Miss Stick-Up-Her-Butt took a turn to the dark side. Turned bad girl. Gone hard-core. She smiled to herself, and would have shook her head, but knew better.

The fact of the matter was she had never wanted a tattoo in her life, but the idea of her sisters and her having matching ink had touched her deeply for some reason, and she couldn't let it go. While she had thought of the idea for the tattoos before she went to sleep, she didn't remember suggesting the idea to her sisters. Naturally, that she had done it while sleeping, or half awake, had tickled them immensely, and Darla declared that *had* to be the design they shared.

"How we doing, Cheryl?" asked the artist, Alex. "Need a break?" He was a big guy, older than her by at least 10 years, his thick black and gray hair in a tangled ponytail down his back. What looked like Aztec priests and temples crawled across his muscular arms, along with Christian iconography, but Cheryl felt it would be rude to peer as close as she needed to for getting a good look at the artwork.

Alex had been captivated with Darla's tattoo. "That is a magnificent piece of art," he had said. "I am jealous. Who did it?"

"My friend in Portland," Darla had answered. "It's not done yet."

"Well, give my compliments to him. It's a masterpiece."

"Her."

"Ah. My apologies. Tell her I am in awe."

"I surely will."

Alex had been skeptical of the three of them when they walked into his studio – Tinta Poderosa. Darla's artist knew a guy who knew Alex and had called ahead for a referral. Alex had listened to them patiently, then flatly told them no, he wouldn't do it. Carol had bristled, ready to leave – probably slightly relieved, Cheryl guessed. Darla started to explain the why of the tattoos, showed him the man-o-war, and he had softened, but still was adamant about not doing it. He had seen too many drunk and whimsical women wanting a permanent mark of an empty symbol. Too many guys wanting something bad-ass without even knowing what it meant to a culture they knew nothing about. A tattoo was a commitment, and Darla was the only one here that had shown that sort of devotion.

"They're just two God damned sets of eyes on the backs of our necks," Carol had growled.

"And if that's only how you see it, then buh-bye," Alex had shot back. "There are plenty of other shops in Vegas for you to get a quickie if you want."

Cheryl, for the most part, had ignored the conflict, fascinated by the artwork on the walls – 'flash' as Alex had called it. "Excuse me," she had asked. "Is this *Odin* in a zoot suit?"

Alex had looked startled. "Why, yes it is," he answered.

"And this…valkyrie? Does she have bandoliers on?"

"She's a mix of *La Charra* and Valkyrie. I enjoy both my Latino and Norse heritage. Wanted to blend them together, like me."

"How…how do you make it look so *real?*"

"Lotta practice," Alex replied shortly.

"Lotta *talent*," Cheryl breathed, and moved along the shop studying the flash, ignoring the gruff tone, and let her sisters get back to the task of convincing Alex to tattoo them.

Darla, the peace-maker, would shush Carol before she could get worked up. "This is the guy we want, okay?" she had said.

"We don't appear to be up to his standards," Carol growled.

Alex sighed. "It's not about *who* you are. I'm a busy man. I have a waiting list a mile long and my partner moved back to L.A. I agreed to consult with you as a favor. Look, I know a guy who can –"

"I'm not going anywhere else," Cheryl had remarked absently.

"There are artists out there just as good as -"

"Don't care. I like your work. It says something to me. If you refuse us – and it sounds like you have good reason to - then it's not meant to be. I'm not trying to be an entitled white woman, Alex. I'll accept your refusal with no hard feelings." She tipped her head at Carol. "Despite Yosemite Sam over there, we're reasonable people, truly. Just – can I finish looking at your work before you kick us out?"

Alex blinked several times. "Not all of it is mine," he grumbled.

"Alex, we aren't looking for a cheap, meaningless scrawl of ink on us," Darla said. "This does matter to us. How about this? Get some pics of our eyes, work up some sketches for the ink – we will give you a down payment – and we will be back the day after tomorrow. Will that work? If we don't come back, then your instincts were right, and we have no regrets, you get some money for sketching out our eyes. That sound good?"

Alex had frowned, his bushy mustache eclipsing his lips, and then his eyebrows raised in surrender. "It's going to have to be a late-night appointment," he muttered.

And now here they were. Darla had gone first, and Cheryl had to admit the guy did a great job. Those certainly were her and Carol's eyes staring back at her. Carol's looked ever skeptical, and hers were…Cheryl couldn't decide. Motherly? Protective? Watchful? How someone could make two eyes look so expressive was a marvel to her.

"How we doing?" asked Alex again.

"Fine," replied Cheryl. "You can keep going."

"You're doing great," he said. "Pretty tough lady."

Cheryl gave a muffled laugh, but felt a twinge of pride nonetheless. Alex had shown her the 'tattooing machine' as he called it, explaining how the needles worked, why one was longer than the others. She had noticed three dots on the web of his hand between thumb and forefinger, and impulsively asked about them. He paused, and then she felt foolish – she had read somewhere that you shouldn't ask people about the meaning of their tattoos these days. She could understand that – when she was pregnant people seemed to think that meant they could give her unsolicited parenting advice and feel her belly.

"Well, that was actually my first tattoo," he finally said. "Done at home, with a just a sewing needle and ink made from my sister's mascara. 'Tres puntos' – represents *mi vida loca*. 'My crazy life.' Saw it on everyone, seems like."

She began to apologize about prying into something personal, and he had waved her off. "No, no, it's okay. I don't mind talking about my ink. It's just that, you get to my age, wondering how the hell you're even still alive, and some tattoos you've had for so long you would swear you were born with them. They're part of your DNA, you know? Explaining one you take for granted can really take you back."

He had then given a remarkable rundown on the history of tattooing, how as a teenager he had even made a machine out of a cassette-deck motor, ballpoint pen housing and the E-string of a guitar.

Buzz, buzz, buzz, and then the feel of him wiping away excess ink.

"Need a break yet?' he asked.

"Nope, I'm fine. How about *you?*"

He laughed, "I can go and go. I get in the zone, and I can get *lost* there."

Cheryl heard Darla whisper something, and Carol gave an immediate bark of laughter, then shushed Darla. Cheryl had grown tired of being out of the loop, and the obvious target of the merriment.

"What's so funny back there?" she asked.

"Nothing," chorused her sisters.

"Come on…"

"Darla thinks," Carol began, and it sounded like she had to fight Darla off from covering her mouth, and a series of smacking and hushing noises followed. "Darla thinks our eyes should look pissed-off on you so when Dave is boning you from behind we make him nervous!" Carol blurted out in a rush.

Alex issued a short, booming laugh, and Cheryl felt as if she had flushed from head to toe. Her ears felt hot, and she couldn't think of anything to respond with except a lame, "*Seriously*, you two?"

"Way to make it weird, ladies," Alex said, and her sisters laughed uncontrollably. "That would be funny, though," he added, low enough just for her to hear.

Cheryl took a deep breath. *Relax. This guy has probably heard a lot worse in here*, she thought. "He'd probably take it as a challenge," she said, and Alex gave a low chuckle.

"He know you're getting this?" Alex asked.

"Yeah, I told him what we were doing. He thought it was sweet."

"Sweet as in *adorable* sweet, or sweet as in 'Hell yeah' sweet?"

"Both, I think? Kids don't know yet. I'm going to wait and let them discover it. I've always told them I have eyes in the back of my head."

He gave another booming laugh, and had to stop inking for a moment. "Now *that's* funny," he said.

"My youngest – my son – he'll probably believe it, bless him. My daughter... she'll declare she can now get one."

"She's how old?"

"Nine."

Alex grunted. "Yeah, it'll be a few years before that can happen."

Cheryl snorted. "We will see about that."

"Eighteen, mom, and she can get one."

"When she's eighteen, she can make that choice."

"I won't ink anyone younger. Don't care if the parent says it's okay. I will not be responsible for some boy band on some woman someday."

Cheryl giggled. "Can you imagine?"

"I try not to."

"I have to say, Alex, this is not what I expected getting a tattoo would be like."

"Yeah?"

"Well, I didn't really expect some grungy dive with bikers lined up waiting their turn, or anything."

He chuckled. "Some days, my friend. Some days. The bikers, anyways. I keep a clean shop."

"I guess I didn't expect your...artistic integrity, I'm sorry to admit."

"Well, like any business, you get your bad eggs. But a tattoo artist that doesn't give a crap doesn't do art. It shows."

"I think if I hadn't seen Darla's man o' war, I wouldn't have considered it."

"It is a stunning piece."

"And it fits her to a tee."

"That's what makes 'em really special. If you can make someone like yourself, who may not have cared for the idea of ink, and wow them in more ways than one, then that's a special kind of magic. I truly believe that."

Cheryl hummed in agreement.

"Gotta warn you," Alex added. "This can get addictive. You may want some more ink later on."

Cheryl snorted.

"I'm telling you, it happens. Don't be surprised. You might want something to illustrate the bond with the husband, or your kids, or family or whatever. Once you start decorating your skin, it can be hard to stop."

"Well, we'll see about that."

"Just sayin'."

"Well, how about if I *do* get another one, I only get it from you? That way I have all the time it takes to get to Vegas to think about it."

"Fair enough," he laughed, and straightened, making a final swipe at the excess ink and drops of blood. "I think we are done here, Cheryl. Want to take a look?"

"Yes, please!"

Cheryl sat up as Alex fished around for a beauty mirror, then paused, and stared at the mirror on the wall. "Can you see the reflection in the mirror back there?" he asked.

"I think it would be kind of...no, probably not. I didn't think about that."

"Hold on," he said, and moved to a back room and came back with an iPad, and shooed Carol and Darla out of the way, who had crowded in to admire the work. He snapped a few pictures of the tattoo, and then let Cheryl hold the tablet close to get a good look at it.

Cheryl stared at the screen, and she was astounded at the likeness. Despite the beads of blood dotting her skin, she could have been looking at a photograph of her sister's eyes. They had all agreed black and gray style only, no blue in the iris at all. Still, it was her sisters' eyes alright. She could tell Darla from Carol very easily. Tears formed in her own eyes as she gazed at the image.

"It's beautiful," she breathed. "I love it. I mean, I really love it." She looked up at Alex. "Thank you."

Alex cleared his throat, and shuffled his feet. "No trouble at all," he said softly.

"I told you, I know how to pick an artist," Darla said.

"That you do," said Cheryl, and Carol murmured in agreement.

"Okay," said Alex. "You're up, Carol."

"Okay," Carol said. "But don't you need a break? Need a smoke or something?"

"No. I don't smoke, and you quit stalling. I'm on a roll, let's keep the magic flowing."

"I'm not stalling…"

"The tough ones always stall."

"Who says I'm a tough one?"

Alex squinted. "I *know* a tough one when I see one," he said, and leveled a finger at Carol, then grinned. "Seriously, Carol, you going to be able to relax? Trust me?"

"Well, you haven't mangled my sisters yet. Sure."

"*There's* a vote of confidence."

"It's not that bad," Cheryl offered. "Really."

Alex turned and gave her a small smile that assured her that he could handle this. Cheryl held her hands up, his smile widened and he turned back to Carol as he sat on his stool, letting Carol look down at him.

"I think you're eager to join your sisters in this…pact," he said gently. "But to do that, I am going to have to touch you."

"I know. I don't care if – "

"Maybe," he interrupted. "But you might not like it. But if I feel you don't trust me, it might reflect in the work, and both of us will be unhappy with that, right?"

Carol nodded, and sat on the bench.

"*You're* in control, right? And we can take a break anytime. Okay?"

Carol nodded again, and leaned into the support rail. Cheryl turned to Darla, and they stared at each other, eyes wide.

Alex got to work, explaining the ease of transferring the drawing just like he had done with her sisters, how it will probably sting but she would get used to it, and that it would be done before she knew it. He kept a steady, calming dialogue, and there were no whispering and giggles from Darla and Cheryl.

When he was done, he took a photo of the tattoo with his iPad like he had Cheryl's, and showed it to Carol. She gazed at it intently – the O'Brian head-wobble a little more pronounced as she concentrated – and a small smile crept in at the corners of her mouth. Finally, she looked up, bit her lower lip and gave such a girlish smile she almost looked like the Carol from before. Cheryl's heart thumped mightily in her chest, and she and Darla crowded in to admire the artwork.

"You guys like?" Alex asked them. All three of them smiled at him and assured him they were very satisfied with the results. Cheryl couldn't believe how easy it was to tell their eyes apart.

"Can I ask a favor?" Alex asked. "I actually have a real camera, with some studio lights. Would you ladies mind if I got a picture of you all together? Before we cover them up?"

They looked at each other, perhaps searching Carol's face longer for permission, but they all nodded and Cheryl said, "Sure. I think we would like that."

Alex ushered them into the back room he had retrieved the iPad from, and a simple black backdrop with a Soff Box covered a studio light, and a small hair light hung suspended from above. He plugged the sync cord into an 80D and arranged them in front of the backdrop, with Carol in the middle. He snapped several shots with their heads tilted differently, and then talked them into turning around and letting him get proper portraits of them. Soft, sisterly affection at first, and then he started cracking jokes to make them laugh.

He sent the photos over to a desktop, then treated and covered their tattoos while lecturing them on how to take care of them until they healed properly. "Do *not* pick or scratch at them. I mean it – you can scar doing that. They're going to get a little slimy at first, then scab up, but that's normal," he said. "They'll heal up."

"Oh, yeah," agreed Darla.

He then let them view the photos on the computer, and Cheryl was astonished at how natural and relaxed they all looked.

"I really don't think I've seen better portraits of us. Ever," she marveled, and her sisters murmured in agreement.

"I'm kind of a black and white fan," Alex said. "I can send you color versions if you want, but personally I like the contrast of your skin against the black background. Plus, it focuses in on the ink, too."

"Sure, do whatever you want," Carol said, and Cheryl and Darla nodded. After getting their permission to post any of the photos to his website, he took Cheryl's email address and promised to send the photos to her Dropbox later that night.

"Ladies, it has been a pleasure," he told them. "I'm glad you talked me into doing this. Sorry I played hard to get, but…" he shrugged his massive shoulders.

They brushed off his apology and thanked him for his integrity.

"This no doubt will be the highlight of the trip," Carol said. "Truly."

"Yeah, I can't imagine anything topping it," Cheryl added.

Alex flapped a hand at them, embarrassed at the praise. "You ladies need to go see a show then. Got any plans?"

"Darla wants to see Penn & Teller," Cheryl answered uncertainly.

"Oh, good show, good show," he said. "Not your cup of joe, Cheryl?"

Cheryl frowned. "I don't know. I guess I like mine a little more…magical?"

"Cheryl likes *illooooosions*," Darla quipped, and Cheryl slugged her in the arm.

"The skeptical scientist is afraid she'll lose her cred if she sees anything with too much woo," Cheryl said, and Darla rolled her eyes.

Alex gave another of his booming laughs. "I'm sure you'll enjoy it."

"Oh, me too," Cheryl agreed. "Anyway, thanks again. This was fun."

"You bet," he said, and they all shook his hand, then stepped out into the cool night air, their skin prickling under their tank tops.

"Geeze," said Darla. "We should have brought sweaters!"

"Who would have thought it would be sweater-weather in Vegas?" asked Carol.

"Sweater-weather," said Darla.

"Sweater-weather," added Cheryl.

"Sweater-weather," Carol affirmed.

They grinned at each other, and walked silently up the street for a while.

"Hey guys?" Carol sad suddenly.

Cheryl turned to her, and Darla asked, "What?"

"We got tattoos!" Carol yelled, and then they all screamed as loudly as possible.

Cheryl's iPad chimed, and she finalized purchasing the Penn & Teller tickets, then checked her email.

"Hey," she said brightly, "Alex has sent us the pics he took." Carol and Darla both crawled onto the bed next to her as she followed the Dropbox link and began downloading the photos.

"Come on, come on," muttered Carol. "Stupid hotel wi-fi..."

"Be patient," soothed Darla.

"Yeah," laughed Cheryl. "When did you start liking pics of yourself?"

"When someone with talent took them," retorted Carol.

"When you were actually in a good enough mood to pose for them," mumbled Darla, and got swatted for the remark.

There were two folders in the download, one named 'raw' and the other 'jpegs'.

"Jesus, he sent us *raw* files?" marveled Darla. "What a guy!"

"What's that mean?" Cheryl asked. "What's good about raw?"

"They are just what he shot, unchanged. Uncorrected."

"Better?"

"No. Well, yes - technically they're way better than jpegs, of course. But you probably don't have an app that will open them. But he's giving us the option to mess with them ourselves if we want."

"Would we?"

"Eh. See what his jpegs look like."

Cheryl tapped on the jpeg folder, and thumbnails began to fill in on the pad's screen. True to his word, Alex liked black and white. Cheryl frowned. She didn't get the artsy-fartsy love of black and white. But to each their own, she supposed. She tapped on the first photo, and it opened. The three sisters' backs to the camera, blonde hair parted to show their necks and the tattoos on them. Darla reached over to zoom in on her own neck.

"Pretty high quality jpegs," she said.

"Some good shit?" asked Carol with a laugh.

Cheryl pushed Darla's hand out of the way and scrolled back and forth across the photo. *Yes, very clear and sharp*, she thought. She liked how the ink stood out on her and Darla's pale skin. Not so much on Carol's, but there was a silvery, luminous quality to the image that struck her. Carol in the middle, Darla's and her head were tipped in towards her. She pinched the image down, then they began to flick between all the photos. The last one was a smaller image, a combination of two photos – a shot of the tattoos stacked on top of a portrait where the sisters looked serious. No, Cheryl considered, not so much serious as…perceptive? All knowing? It was a strange shot, she thought. But she liked it.

"Oh, what's he got written at the bottom?" Carol asked.

"It's like a meme!" quipped Darla. Cheryl zoomed in to read it. In scrawling, cursive text, it read: *The Wyrd Sisters. Norns, to be sure.*

"Wyrd?" Cheryl asked. "As in 'weird'? He saying he thought we were weird?" Her heart clenched a little. That seemed a little mean.

"By the pricking of my thumbs…" Darla breathed.

"I think he's just being poetic, sis," Carol stated.

"I'm trying to recall what a *norn* is," Darla said.

"That green lizard monster Kirk fought?" Cheryl offered. "That doesn't make any damned sense."

"No," said Carol impatiently. "Just Google it. He's being cryptic – he knows he's being cryptic, or he's giving us too much credit for – "

And then she gasped. They all did. Cheryl felt as if her body, mind, *soul*, just *expanded*, as if she now knew the concept of what a new dimension was. And that she felt…ready. Hyper aware. The feel of the plush bath robe against her skin, Darla's hot breath in her ear, the pop and crack of her toes as they curled, they were all sensations with a simultaneous distance and depth, yet felt as if they merged with the fabric of space-time.

"Shit," hissed Carol. "Here we go again."

"What?" asked Darla. "Oh, shit – this is the feeling you were describing? Jesus, are we *all* feeling it, now?"

Cheryl gave a jerk of a nod. "I think I am."

"Well, good," said the man by the hotel room door. "That means everything's working just fine."

Chapter 6

C arol leapt off the bed, and stood between the door and her sisters. She heard the bed creak, and she knew Darla was getting up too. She shot her hand out to try and keep her back, but Darla snorted. "As if," her little sister snapped. "Who the fuck are you dude? How did you get in here?"

The man folded his arms across his chest, and leaned casually against the door jamb. He was tall, fit, and looked familiar. His blond hair reached his shoulders, brushing the black t-shirt he wore. Boots and black jeans completed his wardrobe. His eyes were a steady blue, and he stared at them with an almost amused detachment. Carol noticed what looked like burn scars on the left side of his face, and his left forearm.

"Carol," Cheryl said quietly from behind her. "Is this him?"

Carol looked the man over carefully. It was hard to tell his age – maybe thirty-ish? She had a feeling that he looked older than he probably was. Could he be the boy from back in the day?

"Well?" asked Carol, her heart pumping in overdrive.

The man tipped his head in a nod. "Been a few years, I think," he answered. "You all have grown up a bit."

Darla barked out a laugh, and began edging towards the room's desk, and their phones.

"They won't work right now," said the man quietly. "The phones." He nodded towards Cheryl. "Your pad, too. Or the hotel phone." Carol wanted to turn around and see if Cheryl's iPad was, in fact, down, but didn't want to take her eyes off him.

"You're a little older too," she finally managed. He nodded. Cheryl cleared her throat, and climbed off the bed and stood behind her. Darla had quit edging towards the desk, but she stood even with Carol now.

"This is asinine," said Darla. "The three of us could beat his ass for sure."

"You could not even hope to catch me, sweetie," he said dryly. "Plus, why?"

"*Why?*" asked Darla. "Seriously, dude? Just popping into our room like this isn't the least bit creepy?"

"Well, that's just it, right?" he said quietly. "Me popping in here." He nodded towards Carol. "She's finally loosened up and spilled the beans by now, surely?" He uncrossed his arms and ran his fingers through his hair, cupping it behind his ears. "Look, Darla, make a commotion – *fine*, the phones work now – make me *leave*. But I'm guessing you all want to know the answers to some pretty big questions." He looked pointedly at Carol, and her heart rate actually increased.

"And we do not have tons of time," he added. "In about twenty minutes we *need* to be on the ground floor."

Darla snorted again. "So now we have a clock ticking? Drama, much?"

The man stared at her almost fondly, and gave a wry smile. "Darla, there is always a clock ticking. Always."

"Then why did it take you over twenty years to get back in touch?" Carol asked, trying desperately to keep her voice in control. *Damn it*, she thought, *keep it together. Focus…*

"I've been busy," he answered. "Going here and there."

Behind her, Cheryl cleared her throat. "Why the ground floor?" she asked.

The man shifted his gaze to her older sister, and Carol saw his smile shift subtly, from affectionate to almost resigned.

"Because, Cheryl, where we're going there won't be an eleventh floor. Be a hell of a drop."

"Okay, asshole," Darla snapped. "Yay. You know our names. What's yours then?"

"Peter," he replied.

"And what makes you think we're going anywhere with you, Peter?" Cheryl asked.

Jesus, she seems to be taking this in stride, thought Carol. *Or just more calmly than I would have expected. Does being a mom prepare you for some weird shit?* She almost laughed out loud.

Peter crossed his arms again, and had a faraway look in his eyes, like he was listening to someone else, then his eyes flicked back to her.

"How we doing, Carol?" he asked her. "Processing this alright?"

A spark of anger flared up in her. *Enough of this.* She inhaled deeply through her nose, and blew it out slowly.

"If the clock is ticking, get to the fucking point," she said evenly. "Why are you back, and where do you think we're going?"

"Nice. Cutting to the chase," he chuckled. He swiveled his head around to look at all three of them. "I'm going out on a limb and betting Darla has entertained a pretty far-out notion of what your story is, Carol. Sure, she's only a marine biologist, not like she's a *real* scientist – whoa, kidding sweetie. Really. *Unclench.* It was a joke. Hell, I'm no scientist. Just a modern-day Prometheus, playing with a fire beyond my comprehension. But I digress. Anyhow, *Darla* - care to enlighten them on what you think is going on?"

Carol finally took her eyes off Peter, and turned to look at Darla. Her sister's head was twitching in that shared trait they had, concentrating on the man in front of her.

"Multiverse," Darla said simply.

Peter smiled. "Always at the head of your class, Darla," he said.

"So, like a parallel one, then?" she asked.

"As in many worlds," he said. "You have no idea how many."

"Infinite?"

"No, I just said many worlds. Geeze."

Darla rolled her eyes. Peter raised his hands up in a placating gesture.

"Could you two fill us in?" asked Cheryl. "I mean, I know about theories of parallel universes, but can we quit the cute banter since, as you say, the clock is ticking?" Darla frowned at Cheryl. Carol turned her attention back to Peter, and raised an eyebrow.

"Right," he said, and gave a short clap of his hands. "Carol. You're from another universe. I picked you up from there, and dropped you in this one. You're welcome."

That explains a lot, she thought, and was startled at how easily she accepted the idea. *Seriously, though - that explains a fucking* lot.

The sisters pondered the idea for a moment, and Peter clicked his tongue in a tick-tock rhythm.

"So," asked Cheryl slowly, "if she's from another universe, what happened to our…the…Carol…we knew from before?"

She almost said, 'our Carol'. Her heart clenched in her chest, and Carol was surprised at how much it hurt. *After all this time, even?*

"Maybe we can find out about that another day," Peter replied quietly, and his eyes locked on hers, and Carol knew that he understood. His eyes flicked sadly to Cheryl and back to her, willing Carol to forgive her sister the slip-up.

"So, many worlds," Darla said. "Like C. Foster Kane between two mirrors, his reflection stretching into infinity?"

"Kind of," said Peter. "Again, I'm no scientist, and I can find a lot of this hard to grasp. Infinite? No, but so many it may as well be. For now, anyways."

"And you can...*travel* between them? These universes? How?"

"Tech billions of years in the making," he said, and tapped under the base of his skull at the neck. "Singularity-driven computer that exists in all of the universes, basically. Well, most of them. I don't know how it works, but it does."

"So, what," asked Cheryl, "do we all hold hands and click our heels and off we go?"

"Nah. You just need a node in your heads too."

"No thank you," Darla said.

"Oops. Too late. Gave 'em to you a few days ago. Sorry. Actually, Carol got hers back in the day." Carol jerked a hand up to the base of her neck, then flinched as she hit the padding over her tattoo.

"Well, lovely," said Darla. "We have black holes in our heads, and weren't asked if we wanted them. Thanks."

"There's a lot that isn't going to be your choice here. I'm sorry, but I can use all of you ladies right now, and the clock is *ticking*."

"You keep saying that," said Carol, and her gut tightened. She had a bad feeling about all of this, and was surprised when she realized that it was because they weren't accepting the situation quickly enough. "Why do we have to leave?"

"Because in ten minutes there will be a terrorist attack that will level this hotel, and some of the other more prominent ones in town will suffer severe damage and loss of life. The decadent symbol of evil America, and all that. At least, that's what we're supposed to think."

"What's that supposed to mean?" Cheryl laughed. "An inside job that the government's behind? The truthers are right?"

"No, it's an honest terrorist attack. Just not from who you might think. That *really* isn't important, though. We have a long, complex game being played out, and this is a tiny tragedy compared to what is coming. Honestly, I'm in over my head in this, but what the hell. It always seems to go down to the wire these days, and I don't know if I'm just that bad at the game, or it's the nature of the universe. I wish I could have had more time to prep you all, but we couldn't confirm that this is the universe we needed until minutes ago. So, you ladies want to survive this?" Peter looked pointedly at Cheryl. "You want to see your family again? Because you're not supposed to, but I'm giving you that option. More importantly, you can help them, too."

Carol turned to look at her sisters, and their faces reflected how she was feeling – indecisive and confused.

"Look, baby steps," Peter said. "Let's grab some stuff, pack it in one of your bags, and head out to the ground floor. I guarantee you I'm not going to hustle you into a car and kidnap you – we are heading out into public, not staying closed up in here. That's good, right? We get to the ground floor, and if I can't do what I say I can, and no attack happens, you get to go back to your room and complain to the management that a crazy person intruded on you. Can we get moving though?"

"Let's do it," Carol heard herself say, and Darla gasped in exasperation.

"Please," Carol tipped her head towards her sisters. "I think we need to do this."

Cheryl turned and scooped her iPad up from the bed, then collected the room keys, phones, and her purse. Darla stared at her for a bit, then raised and dropped her hands to her sides, and went to step into her slippers.

"Awesome," Peter said, and let out a heavy breath.

"We're going to look so stupid, all in our matching robes and slippers," muttered Darla as they moved to the door.

"When did you start caring what people thought how you looked?" Cheryl asked with a too-light tone in her voice. *She's just as on edge as we are*, thought Carol. *Just hiding it better…*

"When we look coordinated-stupid," replied Darla. Carol gave a nervous laugh as they followed Peter out the door and into the hallway.

"Stairs," he said. "We better use them instead of the elevator."

"Lead on," Carol said, and they moved down the hallway to an exit sign and into the stairwell. Down they went, a steady progression of clumps from Peter's boots, and the muffled slap of their plush slippers on the treads.

Is this insane? Carol thought. *When they find our bodies, and figure out what happened to us, will everyone marvel at how monumentally stupid we were to follow this guy?* Carol felt certain that they were doing what was necessary. She didn't know why, of course. Maybe it was the years of feeling displaced, and finally finding an answer that made some sense. As fantastic as it all sounded…

"So, what do you think Karen and Georgia will say about us?" Darla asked. Cheryl gave a short chuckle.

"Who are they?" Carol asked.

"Seriously?" Darla said, incredulous.

"She doesn't listen to podcasts," Cheryl said.

"Well, I don't…" Carol mumbled.

And then the building shook with an enormous, angry grumble, as if an enraged titan had been insulted. They slipped and stumbled on the stairs as the lights blinked out. Dimmer, emergency lighting soon replaced it.

"Hurry!" yelled Peter, and they got to their feet and began to run down the stairs. Carol kicked her slippers off for better traction, and noticed Darla did as well. The building still shook, and debris began to patter down on them as the sound grew to the level of approaching doomsday. Carol risked a look back and saw Cheryl dropping behind, a look of stunned confusion on her face. Carol stopped to reach out to her, and a chuck of concrete dropped with a crash onto the landing above. "Kick your slippers off!" she yelled and then they were falling, the stairs collapsing under them

and then she was growing, stretching beyond her boundaries but she had no boundaries as she walked down the shoreline at Scripps but no it was in Manhattan as she

there were no stairs anymore, and there was no longer any noise. Carol hit the ground on her side, and she tasted dry, alkali dust in her mouth as she gasped for the breath that had exploded out of her. She rolled onto her back, and writhed on the ground, her body in the agony of empty lungs and being unable to fill them. She groaned, and then after dry, wheezy gagging, was finally able to suck in some of the cool night air.

She could hear someone coughing, and someone else moaning in pain. She opened her eyes, and all the stars that ever were seemed to be in the sky. Her eyes teared up and blurred them, so she blinked and swiped a hand across her face, causing fat drops to roll down her cheeks to cake up in the dust residue. She had never seen so many stars. As she lay catching her breath, she could only stare blankly at the spectacle above her.

"Are we all okay?" came Peter's voice.

A strangled "Yes" issued from Darla, and then she continued her coughing fit.

"I'm here," mumbled Carol.

"No," said Cheryl weakly. "I think I broke my ankle..."

She heard boots crunch through the cracked and dry earth, then stop, and low murmuring as Peter checked on Cheryl. Carol sat up, and looked around her. A dry, flat plain dotted with shrubs shone in the starlight. There was no Las Vegas anymore. "Holy fuck," she breathed.

Darla's coughing fit subsided, and she hacked and spit into the ground. She took in a final shuddering breath, and stood up. Carol climbed to her feet as well, and tightened the sash on her robe. Darla wandered over to her, and peered up into her face – my God, it was astonishing what you could see with all those stars! – and then she wrapped her arms around Carol and squeezed her, her head nuzzling into her neck. Carol patted her gently.

"I felt like I was everyone else for a second or two," Darla said quietly. "Is that what you felt, back then?"

"Yeah."

Cheryl whimpered, and Darla disentangled herself from Carol.

"Shit," Carol said. "You okay, sis?" She and Darla walked over and knelt beside Cheryl and Peter.

"Ankle appears broken," Peter said. "We need to get her into the shuttle."

"Shuttle?" asked Carol, peering around. "Some minivan going to come pick us up?"

"No," said Peter. "Shuttle as in *spaceship* shuttle."

"Get the fuck out of here," laughed Darla.

"Landing lights," Peter said in a low voice, and in the distance a black hump transformed into a squat, tapered capsule on a tripod of legs as lights blinked on.

"Oh Jesus Christ!" blurted Darla.

"So, no car to kidnap us. Just a God damned spaceship?" Carol asked.

"If I had lead with 'spaceship' you guys would never have left the hotel room," Peter replied.

"I think we should have brought towels with us," giggled Darla, and Cheryl gave a pained bark of laughter. Carol shook her head, and Peter looked as if he didn't get the joke.

"What happened to Vegas?" asked Cheryl.

"It was never here," said Peter. "Can you help me with her?" Carol snaked an arm under Cheryl's, and together they lifted her up. Cheryl hissed in pain, and with their help was able to stand on one leg.

"So we're in another universe?" Darla asked.

"Yep," answered Peter.

"Holy crap."

"Yep."

"Can we go back to ours?"

"Oh sure. We just don't want to right now. On this spot, it's…a bit chaotic."

They began to walk to the shuttle, Carol and Peter helping Cheryl limp along.

"So, no Las Vegas in this world, huh?" asked Darla.

"No people on this continent," answered Peter. "There's some megafauna, though. That's kind of cool."

"No *shit?*" asked Darla.

"Humans have had a tough time of it in this universe. But they're here. None of *us* are though. Makes it kind of a…neutral base."

"So…many universes. Is there one out there where Darth Vader is Force-choking Captain Kirk?"

"I…really doubt it. Look, *maybe* anything is possible, but the whole infinite monkeys and typewriters thing is bullshit. I'm convinced you'll just get infinite gobbledygook. And again, we're not dealing with infinity. And fiction is fiction, that doesn't make it a reality elsewhere." He paused, and then added. "I have been to the zombie apocalypse, though."

"Oh, come on!' laughed Darla.

"I swear, there's a lot of them."

"Come *on!*"

"I'm serious. You wonder why there's an obsession with them in your universe? I believe there's a bleed through from some universes to others. It may not be a direct influence, but somehow it can be sensed."

Carol shook her head, and she heard Cheryl give a pained chuckle. Both of them never ceased to be amazed at the dichotomy of Darla. The carefree love-child and the hard-nosed scientist never seemed to be at odds with each other, never seemed to clash. Darla's world was simple, and she expected people to be rational, and sensitive and caring, like her.

"Well, people are obsessed with Star Wars, and Trek, and all that. So why not those universes?" Darla asked.

"But you asked about specific *characters*," he answered. "Let's give fiction some credit as entertainment, sprung from someone's *imagination*. There's freewill left enough for that."

"Okay," Darla said. "*That* can do with an explanation."

"Shit. For now can you just accept that while I can jump around universes, I need to be careful? You can't just go *anywhere*."

"Not like dusting crops back home, huh?" Darla said, and Cheryl gave a strained laugh.

"Sure. Look, most of them are connected in some way. But, you do have clusters – many that are very, *very* similar. If you could stretch those out in a line together, you could see how they related to each other. That's not a good explanation because it's not like that at all, but…all I'm saying is you can't go into this blind. You look before you leap."

"Sounds sensible," Cheryl gasped. "We getting any closer to this ship of yours?"

Carol studied the shuttle, and decided she could judge the scale better now. It stood probably forty feet high. No windows that she could see, no nozzles or protuberances either. A slight flaring out over the landing legs, presumably space for them to retract? The underside of the ship was coolly lit, but there were no vapors leaching out from complex pipes, no thrumming, powerful noises indicating that this was a vehicle capable of hurtling them out of Earth's gravitational grasp. It just sat there complacently, as if it were nothing more than a structure on a playground.

"Let us in," Peter said, and a tube slid smoothly down from under the shuttle. No whir of motors, the only sound it made was a soft thump as it hit the ground.

Darla whistled. "Pretty darned slick there, Peter. Say, how about you explain to us…"

Carol waited for Darla to finish her thought, and then turned her head back to look at her. Darla was frozen in her tracks, staring at a malformed black shape that twisted and sparkled without light. Carol could not sense a form, but it was also achingly clear to see. An immediate sense of dread knotted her stomach, and she gasped and stopped walking, causing Peter to tug on Cheryl and they both spun slightly to a stop as well.

The blueish landing lights lit up the terror on Darla's face, but the gritty, shifting mass in front of her took on none of that hue.

"Shit," hissed Peter. "Take her." He shrugged control of Cheryl completely over to Carol. In that same instance, the feeling she had been taking for granted now, the feeling of being powered up and ready, vanished, and she grunted. She felt Cheryl jerk, and she saw Darla look confused, and she knew they both felt the same way. Offline…

Peter reached into his t-shirt – that's the only way Carol could describe the movement – and pulled out several bright, small spheres. At the same time, the black shape reached towards Darla, towards her neck, and she jumped back but it pushed through her chest effortlessly and without a forcible impact. Peter threw the spheres at the blackness, and they were instantly engulfed, and then the shapeless form collapsed in on itself and was gone.

Darla teetered for a moment, retched once, and collapsed on the ground. Blood began to well up and stain the chest of the white bathrobe covering her. Cheryl screamed in Carol's ear, and fought to free herself from her grasp, but that only made them both fall.

That's not fair, Carol thought crazily. *She only just got her breath back!*

Peter ran to Darla and in one quick motion scooped her up and threw her over his shoulder. "Get up and get moving. Now – we need to get her in."

He marched past them, as tears began to well up in Carol's eyes and Cheryl was sobbing uncontrollably. He twisted back to them. "Now!"

Carol slid a hand under Cheryl's armpit, and pulled her up. Her sister barked in pain as she put weight on her ankle, but she began to hop with Carol towards the shuttle. A doorway opened in the tube, and a spartan white interior welcomed them. Peter ducked in with Darla, and Carol squeezed herself and Cheryl in as well. The doorway disappeared, and Carol felt her ears pop. Her knees sagged a bit from the lift, and then the doorway opened into a dimly lit, circular room. Peter stepped out, and moved to the far side of the cabin, avoiding what looked like simple and basic-shaped recliners radiating in a star pattern in the center of the space.

"Get in the couches," he ordered, and palmed a space on the cabin wall. A coffin-sized nook opened in the wall, and a convex clear covering slid aside. Peter propped Darla's slack body into the space, held her upright until she seemed to stand on her own. He pulled his arm back, and the covering slid back into place. Darla stood inside, eyes partially open, jaw slack, blood as fresh and bright as true love still running from the hole that once was her chest.

Peter glanced back at them. "Get in the fucking *couches*," he barked. Carol eased Cheryl down onto one of the recliners. She heard a slight woof of air and a tiny crackle, and the dome covering Darla was now milky white.

"Do we have straps or anything?" she asked shakily.

"No need," Peter replied tersely.

Carol looked at Cheryl, who had now started sobbing again, and squeezed her hand before stepping over to her own couch. As she reclined, she looked up and saw a more structured couch lower from the ceiling. Up at the apex of the cone was the command center, apparently. Screens formed on the surfaces surrounding them, and Peter climbed onto the couch. It lifted him smoothly, elevating him up to the controls.

She could hear Peter murmuring commands, and then she felt like she was sinking into the couch, that it was wrapping itself slightly around her. She heard Cheryl gasp in pain, no doubt her ankle not liking the embrace.

There was no rumble, or roar, or violent shaking. They were just accelerating, and it felt like she had been kicked in the back. Her lungs could not expand, and black spots began to form in her vision. She closed her eyes, and could not open them again. Her heart pounded in her ears, and it grew louder, and louder still. She grew nauseous, and when she was certain that she would pass out, the pressure was gone, and it felt as if she was thrown forward. She drew in a shuddering breath, and heard Cheryl do the same.

After their labored breathing evened out, it was very quiet. There was no crackle of voices monitoring their progress, no beeping machines or hiss of air circulation. Peter wasn't flipping switches or jabbing at buttons. Carol's stomach felt like it was at the top of a rollercoaster just as it began to drop. Her eyes darted around the surprisingly sterile cabin. There just seemed to be the array of couches, and a few items she could not hope to name. She looked up, and screens in front of Peter had technical readouts, and a main viewer at the blunted nose of the shuttle was filled with the blackness of space, dotted with stars. She turned her head to study Cheryl, who was staring back at her, eyes red-rimmed and wet. Carol wrestled an arm free from the embrace of the couch.

"Please stay in the couch," Peter asked quietly. "You're astronauts now, essentially. Take a while to let that sink in, and don't fight the ship."

A little hard to be impressed with the situation when your baby sister has a massive hole in her chest, thought Carol, and she too began to cry. Cheryl suddenly turned her head towards Peter.

"That thing you put her in?" she called up to him. "Will it fix her? Can it heal her?"

Peter was silent for a moment. "She is missing large amounts of her lungs and has no heart," he said with regret in his voice. Cheryl began to sob loudly again, and fat tears welled up in Carol's eyes, clinging to her lashes and blurring her vision. She swiped at them viciously, flinging drops from her finger tips to spin and float away from her. She heard a tiny whisk of air, and a teardrop stretched and then was gone. Apparently, you were not allowed to cry in space. But she could not stop replaying the death of her little sister. Despite the suspended feeling of her stomach, she still felt a cold knot tighten in it when she tried to make sense of the black, formless thing that had struck out at Darla. She rubbed her eyes again.

"So what the fuck was that thing that attacked Darla?" she asked, her voice trembling with the effort to maintain control.

"I wouldn't use the word *attack*," Peter answered.

"What the fuck *ever*," snapped Carol. "What was it?"

Peter took a long while to reply. "My shadow," he finally said. Carol growled in frustration, and before she could begin a verbal assault, he cut her off.

"Look, I'm not being facetious. Or coy. Or trying to be funny. We have a long, boring journey ahead of us, and plenty of time for me to fill you in on everything."

"How long to just take me home?" asked Cheryl. "I want to go home. Take me home."

"Would you like your home to be around for many lifetimes?" asked Peter coolly. "If so, I need your help." Cheryl said nothing. "So we'll take the scenic route, and if all goes well, you'll get to go home to your family."

Carol looked up, and watched as Peter's fingers twitched slightly on control pads on the arms of his couch. "Ah," he finally said, "Look, ladies. Our ride."

A bulkhead in front of Carol transformed into a view screen filled with stars and the void of space. A silver dot grew in the middle of the screen, taking on the contour of a sphere.

Cheryl had wrestled an arm loose too, and waved it about the cabin. "I thought *this* was our ride," she stated.

"This is a shuttle," Peter said. "I told you that. A shuttle can't take us to Mars."

"Mars?" blurted the sisters together.

"The one and only."

"Why are we going to Mars?" asked Carol.

"Hopefully, to wake up a god," said Peter.

The silver sphere turned out to be more of a dome as the angle of approach changed. Behind the dome were a series of rings, one large and two smaller ones. Trailing them were long, slender rods that gave the impression of tendrils.

Peter cleared his throat. "*Medusa*, I have a visual on you."

"Copy that," came a voice that seemed to be everywhere. And it sounded very familiar.

"You ready to take control?" asked Peter. "Reel us in, sweetie."

"Taking control. Relax and enjoy the ride."

Carol turned to stare at Cheryl, who looked just as confused as she was.

"We have some visitors," Peter remarked casually.

"Yeah?" said the voice. "Looking forward to meeting them." Carol closed her eyes tightly, and her mind felt like it had had just about enough of everything today, *thank* you very much. But the voice was unmistakable.

It was Darla.

PART TWO

Prologue

Every few days, the gas giants would arrive in the early morning hours to forage. They liked to use the rising heat of the day to move back up the shallow volcano, just past the tree line. The rippers wouldn't travel up to where the air was so thin, and didn't like the cool air of the morning. Not that the leathery bags of methane ordinarily had much of a problem with the rippers, unless they were the older, ancient ones.

Or the very young.

Darla sat quietly in a patio chair, bundled up against the chill Martian morning, and waited for her friend to show. She was tall for a five-year-old (two and a half in Martian years), but her feet still swung just above the sandstone. She had been conceived in transit – which was frowned upon – and born on Mars. Again, frowned upon. There was worry she would never be able to visit Earth if she wanted. All of this was a moot point anyways. Her father was dead, her mother in jail, and she and her sisters and brother were in foster care.

Like most small children, she couldn't understand why she was forced to deal with the grief of missing her parents. She was resilient, like many of the very young are, and sometimes would express her displeasure by tantrums or rebelling. In this case, venturing outside when she was supposed to be in bed. She had gotten in trouble the last time she had done this, but her foster parents didn't seem to care if she died of exposure so much as she didn't irritate their neighbor, Mr. Iger. He had accused her of stealing a fossil from his back yard. Nothing particularly rare, but it was a beautiful example of a lifeform that swam in the Martian oceans to this day, as well as twenty-million years ago. Just how a five-year-old was supposed to have scaled an eight-foot block wall to steal the relic from his deck, lug it back over the wall and into her room was speculated over without any conclusion being drawn. However, seeing that she did indeed have the "damned hunk of rock" in her room, she was judged guilty, and a "nasty little brat" for good measure.

No one seemed to take her explanation that her friend had given it to her very seriously. Her foster mother had defused the situation somewhat by joking that sure, Darla was most certainly the head of a black-market fossil ring and had pulled a John Carter to steal his damned rock, and let's just throw the five-year-old in jail with her mom.

Mr. Iger had muttered something about keeping the little shit out of his yard, and went back home with his fossil.

Darla scratched under the mask of her breather, but was careful to keep it tight against her face. In the distance, she heard a high-pitched squeal, much like an excited baby elephant, and she sat up alert and ready – her friends were coming!

An enormous shadow drifted above the east wall of the patio, careful to avoid the electrified cables that ran across the top. Up it went, an inverted tear-drop shaped bag, thirty feet from its base to its domed top. A cluster of vine-like tentacles twisted and writhed beneath it as it moved to the tree next to the south wall. Another gas giant drifted up from the cliffs below, this one a bit smaller than the first. Darla waited patiently, heard the squeal again, closer this time, and she smiled and scooted off the chair and pulled the bag of bradberries out of her jacket pocket.

Another adult gas giant loomed over the patio as the sky began to lighten, and Darla could see it glisten. A natural flame-retardant coated the colossal airships, and while she didn't know it's purpose, she liked how the gel would bead up and shine like gemstones. The new giant hovered over her, its tentacles waving around her head. Faint, random bursts of violet light glowed up and down the ropy vines, and Darla held up a handful of berries.

One longer tentacle hovered over her hand, then gently touched the small mound, plucking the berries up into the center of the tentacle cluster. Presently a low rumble issued from...somewhere up there, and then a high-pitched squeal came from the other side of the wall, and her friend popped up over the concrete barrier.

This one was tiny compared to the other giants, roughly six feet from top to vine-tips. Its tentacles waved and twisted almost constantly, and Darla bounced up and down on her toes and giggled quietly. Berries spilled onto the sandstone patio as she poured some from the bag into her hand. The little giant squealed again.

"Shhh!" she admonished. "We need to be quiet!" But she couldn't help but laugh as a tentacle wrapped around her wrist lightly, at first feeling warm and slippery, but then it stuck to her as it plucked the food from her hand.

"Is it good?" she asked. "Is it nummy?"

The infant gas giant had no answer, but continued to feed, its tentacles flashing merrily.

As other giants fed from the Bradbury tree in the yard and from the neighbor's, a monstrous form rose beyond the wall farther out from the escarpment, hovering over the beach below. Its bag was a least sixty feet tall, but did not shine like the other gas giants. It's maroon and pink coloring was faded and dulled to gray in patches. Its bag was scaly, and deep wrinkles and crevasses lined the sides. It made no attempt to feed, and just hung in the air as if it didn't know, or maybe care, what went on around it.

"Is that your grampa?" asked Darla, not knowing that it was a few hundred years old – *Martian* years.

"I don't know my grampas," said Darla wistfully. "One sends me vids every day, though. And he likes when I send him ones."

The tentacle wrapped around her wrist abruptly became slippery again and slid loose from her skin, leaving a faint sheen behind. The little giant trumpeted, pushed off the patio flooring and shot over the wall into Mr. Iger's yard.

"Oh," Darla called quietly. "You're not s'posed to go in there. You'll get us in trouble again!"

Rattles and clangs came from beyond the wall, and presently her friend popped over the wall and dropped down to her, presenting her with a pair of bar-b-que tongs.

"Oh, *thank* you," Darla gushed with false enthusiasm. Her daddy had always said to be nice when someone gave you a gift, even if you didn't want it. She would wait until the gas giants left, then try and hurl the tongs back over the wall.

The little giant busied itself picking up the berries spilled onto the flooring, and Darla tried to figure out how to unlatch the tongs so she could try and pluck up the berries too. As she turned them over they sprang open and she dropped them, laughing, then scooped them up. Using both hands she clacked them together.

"Look, I'm a ripper!" Clack-clack. "You better run! I'll rip you up!"

The little giant just continued to search for berries, and Darla gave an enormously long yawn, overcome with the spontaneous fatigue that often sneaks up and ruins playtime.

"You goddamned little *thief.*"

Darla's head darted up, and in the pale morning light she could see Mr. Iger peering over the wall at her.

"You goddamned sneak-thief," he growled. "If you were mine I'd tan your hide with those tongs. That would teach you to take things that don't belong to you."

Darla could only stare wide-eyed at him, too scared to move or say anything. Her friend paused in its search for berries. For a moment all that could be heard was the sounds of rustling leaves as the adult gas giants fed.

"Can't you talk, you little brat?" asked Mr. Iger. "In my day, children answered adults. Looks like you'll take after your nutty mother. Wind up in jail before you're a teenager, I'd wager."

Darla opened her mouth and began to wail, fat tears welled up and poured from her blue eyes and ran down both sides of the breather.

Mr. Iger smirked and mocked her crying, and didn't notice the little giant as it pushed up and hovered over him. With a squeal, it splattered an excess gel and waste combination down upon his head.

Mr. Iger sputtered with indignant rage, and Darla quit her crying to stare in astonished delight. Then she began to giggle, which infuriated the old man even more.

"You think that's funny, you little shit?"

He reached down to his right and brought up a heavy bag, settling it on the wall with a grunt. Darla couldn't read, but a picture of a melting ice cube reminded her of the stuff daddy had thrown out on the front walk when it was frozen.

"You think your friend will like this?" he asked, and scooped up a handful of white crystals and flung them at the little giant. Some of the deicer bounced off of the tight gas bag, but much of it clung to the gel coating, where it began to pop and sizzle. The little giant trumpeted and squealed and evacuated more waste and floated higher, away from the cackling old man, who reached in the bag for another fistful of the crystals.

"You leave it alone!" shrieked Darla, and Mr. Iger just laughed, and flung the pellets up at the little giant, some which stuck to the lower-hanging tentacles. The gas giant squealed again, and one of the larger giants had moved over to intercept it.

"You leave it *alone!*" yelled Darla again, and with all her might flung the bar-b-que tongs at her elderly neighbor. The lighter Martian gravity allowed them to sail up and hit the bag of deicer, which spun them around to bounce into Mr. Iger's chest, down onto the top of the wall, and they came close to falling back on Darla's side, but the old man snatched at them and was able to hook a finger between them until it caught where they hinged together. He then hugged the cooking tool to his chest and laughed heartily at Darla.

"Oh, *thank* you," he chuckled. "*Thank* you for returning my property to me!"

Darla was on the verge of crying again, when a gnarled tentacle, thick as a man's arm, looped around the neck of Mr. Iger and lifted him off the ladder on the other side of the wall.

Darla stepped backwards quickly, staring at the old man struggling and kicking as he floated toward the back wall of his patio. Her eyes followed up, up, up to the ancient gas giant above. Dry and wrinkled and so very old, yes. But still incredible strength in those corded tentacles.

Mr. Iger grasped at the coil around his throat with his left hand, the bar-b-que tongs still clutched in his right. The tentacle tightened as he pulled at it, and the old man's legs kicked wildly in the air, his eyes bulging in his purple face.

Darla backed up some more, and her eyes darted over to see her friend and its momma disappear beyond the back wall, heading to the beach far below.

The sound of Mr. Iger slamming into the higher, east wall drew her attention, the tongs clattering and scratching their way up the wall as he was slowly dragged up the concrete. His legs still peddled madly, both slippers flung from his feet and his heels hit the block wall with crunching noises, leaving ragged smears of blood. He no longer grasped at the vine around his neck, his arm just wind-milling crazily in the cool air.

Darla began to cry again, wanting to turn and run into the house and wake her foster parents, but she couldn't take her eyes off the scene in front of her.

As the old man brushed up against the live wires running across the back wall, he twitched and shook, and then the tongs made contact with them, and his whole body stiffened, his right fist jerking between the cables, and the tongs angled up and caught, and now the tentacles began to contract and draw down the enormous bag of the gas giant. The tentacle around Mr. Iger's neck grew so tight blood shot out of his ears and eyes, and the sockets began to smoke. Fire bloomed from the sleeve of his jacket, and began to lick up his arm, all the while the giant gas bag was being drawn down towards it.

In a chorus of trumpet blasts, all the remaining gas giants voided any waste they held, and sphincters shot out gas to propel them away from the patio area as fast as possible.

Darla understood the danger of fire, and it finally drove her to turn and stumble towards the house. A light winked on in a bedroom on the second floor, and then a drape was pulled open. Her brother peered out the window towards her. Darla skidded to a stop.

"J.C." a boy's voice crackled in her earpiece. "What the heck are you doing out there?" Then the voice gasped, as Darla's brother took in the conflagration growing out at the back wall.

"Byron!" screamed Darla. "It's bad! Run!"

"*You* run, Darla! Get in here!" shouted Byron, and before Darla could begin to run again, a shape smeared into existence in front of her, reached down to touch the back of her neck with a slight sting. Darla felt as if she grew and grew and grew without getting any bigger, and as she stared at the boy – an older boy, maybe as old as Carol – with his weird breather, her little brain was in danger of shutting down to give itself a rest.

The boy crouched in front of her, and ran a gloved hand down her blond hair and patted her shoulder.

"I'm sorry, sweetie," he soothed. "Really. I know you're confused, but we need to get out of here."

The back door to the house slid open with a hiss of air, and the boy turned his head to watch Byron emerge, then stop and stare stupidly at them.

"Shit," the boy muttered. "Shit, shit, *shit.*"

His head turned back to Darla, and then dipped below his shoulders.

"Who the fuck are you, dude?" called Byron. "Let go of my sister, you perv!" The teenaged boy gasped in the Martian air. He hadn't taken the time to grab his breather. An alarm started sounding, warning of atmospheric contamination unless the door was sealed.

The boy's head shook back and forth as he swore again, then raised his head. Darla could see huge flames reflected in the facemask of his breather, and his head jerked in surprise.

"Run Byron!" screamed Darla. "Hurry! Run!"

"I'm sorry," the boy whispered. "But we don't have the time to take him with us."

As they both shifted and blinked out of existence, the ancient gas giant, engulfed in flames, erupted into a neighborhood-leveling fireball.

Chapter 7

Cheryl heard hollow-sounding thumps and bumps – much like noises heard underwater. Like when they had gone swimming at the hotel. Like when Darla was still alive.

She squeezed her eyelids shut, but tears managed to slip past them and collect on her eyelashes anyways. Right now, life was a series of prayers and wishes, and they all centered on turning back the clock to where Darla was still alive. *Please, God, just let us rewind things a bit - it really hasn't been that long – just back it up to where Darla doesn't have a huge hole in her chest. Please...* She didn't know what could be done to stop that from happening, except the knowledge of it could grant a course of action.

"Alright shuttle, you are docked," came Darla's voice. Only maybe it was a bit lower in pitch? Right now Cheryl was only certain that she didn't know what the hell was happening. *That can't be our Darla...*

"Thank you, sweetie," Peter remarked.

Cheryl felt the crash couch release its grip on her, but she didn't move. She watched Carol thrash her way up and off her couch, arms and legs pinwheeling as she almost floated in midair, then thumped down to the floor. Carol swore bitterly, her chest heaving as she clutched at the deck and looked warily at Cheryl.

"Hey Dar?" Peter said. "Want to ramp the gravity up some? Our new friends might not like bouncing around like you do."

"Sure," said the voice. "Take a while for the centrifuge to speed up. They'll have to be careful until then."

"Yep."

Cheryl watched Carol carefully pull herself across the deck to her couch. She reached out a hand, and Carol grabbed it tightly. Cheryl pulled her in close.

"I'm sorry," she said, and Carol frowned.

"About what?" Carol asked.

"What I said – what I implied back at the hotel," Cheryl replied. "*You* are our Carol, okay? I didn't mean it to sound like that."

Carol's eyes softened and Cheryl could tell it had affected her. Maybe in not so stressful times, she would have waved a hand and shooed the apology away, as if the accidental sleight meant nothing to her. But their current situation didn't leave any room for pretending. Carol squeezed her hand and kissed it.

"I just had to say it," Cheryl said. "I have no clue what we got ourselves into this time, and I had to tell you in case…I wouldn't get to later." Her eyes darted over to the opaque oval hiding the body of their sister, then averted them just as quickly. Carol cleared her throat.

"Yeah, well," she said, "I think we've found a little perspective on our issues, huh?" Carol tugged on her hand, and drew her closer. Her eyes were wet and red-rimmed – much like hers must be – and she stared into Cheryl's eyes, searching. "This is *happening?*" she asked. "I mean, I'm not finally losing my mind? We're on a freaking *spaceship?*"

Cheryl jerked her head in affirmation. "Unless we're sharing a hallucination…"

And then, of course, she recalled her conversation with Darla when Carol was showering, and a fresh bout of tears filled her eyes, but now they actually slid slowly downwards. Carol rested her forehead against hers, and she heard Peter's command couch lowering to the deck. It was quiet for a moment except for her sobbing, and then he cleared his voice.

"Okay, ladies, let's head out." Cheryl flinched. She didn't think she could move again, ever.

"Could you just give us a minute?" mumbled Carol.

"No, I can *not.*"

Cheryl felt Carol stiffen, and her face pulled away to turn to Peter.

"What is it with you, dude?" she snapped. "Jesus, always the dramatics with you. Zounds! We don't have a moment to spare! Fuck off."

Cheryl looked towards Peter, but could only see a blurry silhouette of him. He stood there for a moment, arms crossed, then sighed heavily.

"I'm sorry this is all happening at once," he said. "I know it's too much to take in. But you're going to have to. I'm also sorry if I don't share your grief, or if I appear to be unmoved. But this is…*endless*, and I'm getting tired of the game."

"Our sister's death is not a fucking *game!*" yelled Carol.

113

"And I've seen her die before. *And* you. *Both* of you. And the common denominator is usually when someone stops *moving*."

"Sounds like the 'common denominator' is you," muttered Carol.

Cheryl felt a thrill of pride of her sister, always cutting to the heart of the matter. It gave her a shot of motivation and she sat up on her couch, almost bounding up and off it, but Carol continued to grip her hand. She wiped at her eyes with her free one. "Peter," she said, "I truly have no idea what's going on. I'm sorry our acceptance of and reaction to our sister's death isn't up to your jaded standards." She carefully stood, Carol clutching at her as they rose together. "But if people keep dying around you, maybe she's right. You ever think about that?" She gave Carol a squeeze. "You drop in on us with no warning, really, and start barking at us to get a move on. Thank you for getting us out of the hotel. But we are on a spaceship. Ball's in your court now, chief. If we're going to Mars, I can guarantee you neither one of *us* knows how to get there."

Peter stared at them, and then bobbed his head once in a nod.

"My apologies," he said. "Truly. You're right, now it's up to good old-fashioned spaceflight to move us around - we certainly can't jump universes now. Well, we could, but it would be pointless. Anyhow, can we at least start by leaving the shuttle?"

Cheryl drew in a shaky breath, and looked at Carol, who gave her a grim smile. Cheryl's eyes darted over to the dome that covered up Darla's remains. She almost burst into tears again, but she clenched almost every muscle in her body in an effort to control the impulse. *Try and channel the grief to anger*, she thought, but then frowned, wondering if that would be helpful or not.

Peter noticed her look towards the chamber. "She'll be fine there for now," he said. "Nothing on board the *Medusa* can help her, sorry. We've got tech that is probably blowing your minds already, but nothing that can fix her sort of...damage."

"Is there anything...*out there* that can?" asked Cheryl.

"Hey, we're in a near-infinite multiverse. Whenever I've decided something is set in stone, I usually wind up being taught a lesson."

Carol eyed him coolly. "Don't give her – or me – any false hope and string us along, asshole. We can accept her death eventually, but I won't put up with any condescending bullshit."

Peter drew in a deep breath and looked at them thoughtfully. He released the air from his lungs in a slow sigh. "I get that. But what we *have* to accept isn't always as cut and dried as you may think."

"Alright then," Cheryl said. "Let's get going then. The sooner we know what we can do to help you – unlikely as *that* seems – then the sooner we can go home, yeah?"

"I do believe that's what I've been saying all along," Peter replied with a laugh.

The tube that had delivered them into the shuttle slid noiselessly up from the floor, and the doorway opened. Carol helped her hobble over to it, and Cheryl was surprised at how much less the ankle hurt now. She looked down at it. It was swollen and seemed to want to tip her over, but the pain she felt before was a fraction of what it was. Maybe it was the lower gravity?

They stepped into the cylinder, and Cheryl felt a sense of acceleration. Her knees sagged as the transport tube stopped, and she felt considerably heavier, but her ankle didn't feel any worse. As they exited the tube, she mentioned this to Peter.

"Yeah, the crash couch was already working on it. Probably just anesthetized. We'll get you set up on a couch again, and you'll be good as new."

"What, no sick bay?" she asked.

"Not really," he replied. "For severe cases, the ship can configure one I guess. But your couch can work on you while you sleep."

"Well, peachy," was all she could think to say. Honestly, she was more than a little overwhelmed at this point. She had a feeling she wasn't going to be able to keep up with things. And as she looked up the dimly-lit corridor they were in, she was certain of it. The whole thing curved up into the ceiling in both directions as far as she could tell, and then realized that the ceiling curved out of sight too. They took a few bouncing steps, and the tube shot up into the ceiling and was gone.

"Dar, you going to meet us in the hab ring?" asked Peter.

"Of course," came her voice out of thin air.

"She likes to spend most of her time in the navigation hub," Peter said in a low voice. "Honestly, the ship can be attended to from anywhere on board for the most part. But the hub has no gravity, unless we're under acceleration – which is going to happen soon."

"So I assume this…thing is spinning to give us gravity?" Carol asked as she swept an arm in an arc, indicating the curved structure. Peter stared at her momentarily, and raised an eyebrow thoughtfully.

"Yes, I do sometimes pay attention to movies, even when I don't like them."

"Well, good to know," he replied. "Yes, the hab-ring spins to give us gravity. Under acceleration, rooms and components can shift to accommodate, and we would be walking on that if we want." He pointed to the wall behind them.

Actually, more than likely called a bulkhead, not wall, Cheryl thought. *Geeze, are we going to have to learn ship lingo?* She visualized the corridor no longer curving into the ceiling, but just rounding out of sight to the left or right, and she was mildly disappointed. She was sure Dave would prefer it the other way, and then felt instant pangs of guilt and loss. *Dave and the kids. What must they be going through right now?*

"*Medusa*, day lighting please," Peter said, and the ceiling brightened gradually until the corridor gleamed, white and seamless except for doorways here and there, and panels along the wall. Carol leaned into Cheryl's ear and whispered, "So would your husband love it here, or what?"

Cheryl barked out a bitter laugh. "I was thinking the same thing," she said. The insides of her ears felt like they were hot, and nausea began to creep into her gut. She thought that the lighting was dimming again, but realized her peripheral vision was graying and darkening.

"I need to lay down," she announced. "Now. Right *now*."

"Couch," Peter murmured, and one morphed out of the wall neat as you please. Carol eased her down onto it.

"You feeling faint?" asked Peter. Cheryl jerked her head in affirmation.

"Lower head," he ordered, and Cheryl felt her angle shift, and she could actually feel the blood return to her face. She drew in some deep breaths, and opened her eyes in time to see an opening form in the ceiling, and a slender figure in a red jumpsuit dropped lightly to the floor.

"Jesus, Peter," said the voice that had become familiar to her from out of thin air, "did you show them the view?"

"No," he said. "I think she's just overstimulated, is all."

"Yeah, well, there's no way to ease into this I guess. Sorry ladies," the woman said.

Cheryl squeezed her eyes shut again, and fanned her face with her hands, cooling the clammy sweat clinging to her. *That voice...* She heard Carol give an involuntary gasp.

She breathed evenly for a while, trying to compose and prepare herself as best she could. She breathed out a small prayer, opened her eyes, and forced a smile. Familiar, wide-set blue eyes looked down on her in a concerned, and yet analytical manner.

"Why Darla," Cheryl said, "you've grown your dreads back!"

The young woman reached up to the blonde ropy hair that was tied back in a ponytail, and fingered the locks self-consciously. "Ah," she said. "How about that?"

It was Darla, and yet, assuredly, also was *not*. This Darla appeared taller, leaner, her figure not so girlish. While superficially identical in features, this Darla had a more watchful and almost skittish quality to her. And *this* Darla had what seemed to be a burn scar on the right side of her face. Cheryl wanted to reach up and stroke it, ask about its origins. But this girl was essentially a stranger, and she resisted the urge. She remembered the scar on Peter's face, and decided a story would come out sometime. There was a buzzing on her right ankle, and then it felt like the couch was trying to swallow it.

"What in the name of God?" she blurted.

"Oh, it's just trying to work on your leg," Peter said.

"It knows I'm hurt?" Cheryl asked, astonished.

"It also knew you were ready to pass out, I'd wager. I probably didn't need to tell it to lower your head. But, you know, things just don't move fast enough for me."

Cheryl pressed her lips together in a tight, humorless smile, and she heard Carol give a small, annoyed grunt. She directed her attention back to

117

the young woman standing over her, who was staring at her as if fascinated. When they made eye contact, she shyly looked away, made eye contact with Carol, and looked down at the floor. Cheryl propped herself up on her elbows.

"What did you mean when you asked if he had shown us 'the view'?" she asked.

"Hmmm?" said the new Darla absently. *Oh, that's not going to work at all*, thought Cheryl. *You can't think of her as 'the new Darla' all the time, much less call her that.*

"You asked Peter if he had shown us 'the view' – as if that might have been upsetting to us," Carol stated bluntly.

"Oh," Darla said. "Yeah. Well, pretty much any surface can be turned into a viewer on the *Medusa*. Peter likes to make the floor look transparent to prove to people that we are indeed in space."

"That sounds cool," Cheryl offered.

"It can be pretty disorienting," warned Darla.

"No time like the present to get used to it," quipped Cheryl. She looked to Carol, who shrugged. "Let's see it," she added, returning her attention to Darla.

"You might want to sit," Darla directed to Carol, who just raised an eyebrow at her and remained standing. Darla smiled, and then the overhead lighting dimmed, and stars replaced the floor beneath them, bright points of light streaking into view and then racing away behind them. Carol stumbled, but kept to her feet. The moon roared past and vanished. Cheryl laughed delightedly, and tried to get up, but the couch held her ankle. "Let go!" she barked in irritation. The material released her, and she swung her legs over and into what appeared to be a spinning star field. Her bare feet touched a firm surface, though, and she eased down onto her knees, conscious that she was still in a plush bathrobe, stained from the dust of a Las Vegas that was and then was not there. *Bet you couldn't have even entertained the notion you would ever be seeing something like this*, she thought. How long had it been since they were back in the hotel in Vegas? Could it have even been an hour, yet? *When Darla was still alive.* She felt a pang, but it was distant, and she was kind of shocked at that. *I can't be so accepting of this so soon*, she thought. *That damned couch - I bet it's tranquilized me!*

Stretching her legs behind her, she leaned forward to rest on her forearms, and hung her head to stare at the spinning panorama below her. The moon lunged into view and was gone again. She imagined herself lying on her back on a huge wheel as it rotated in space, and then she could finally make sense of what she was seeing. She was moving, not the stars, of course. Carol lay down beside her, and drew in a sharp breath.

"Amazing, huh?" asked Cheryl. Her sister nodded, then turned to look at her.

"Dad would have been out of his mind if he could see this," Carol said, and Cheryl grinned.

"Right?" The moon flashed by and lit up the corridor, then vanished behind them. "I am so tired," added Cheryl, and yawned.

"Me too. Been through a lot, I guess. Emotionally drained."

Cheryl tipped her head towards Carol, and whispered, "I think we've been drugged."

Carol's mouth rounded in surprise, then she frowned. "Well, that's just great," she mumbled. Then she put her head down on the deck, and went to sleep.

That looks like a splendid idea, was Cheryl's last conscious thought.

Someone was picking through her brains. Well, more like exploring them, maybe? Cheryl didn't feel like it was invasive. But that wasn't entirely true – there were some versions of her that were *definitely* bothered by it, considered it a work of the devil. Some were amused – someone, or *something*, is reading our minds! Duhn-duhn-*duhn!* Some were confused by the whole thing, they could not understand how they felt like they were everyone, and yet their own identity. Now that she thought about it, that indeed was very strange. She tried to isolate herself to *me*, away from *us*, and that seemed to focus attention to her.

she was pushing so hard, straining and oh so very tired, and dave was right there by her trying to help her focus on her breathing but the dumbass didn't get it was way past that point and this was so very different from amy because it was too late for an epidural and she was being told to push and she heard a crunch and her nose felt full of snot and she just wanted it cleared but later she found out she had burst a blood vessel and dave had almost fainted because blood had shot out her nose but she gritted her teeth and by god she would push, she would keep pushing -

And the focused attention was away, down the line, but she could remember things that hadn't happened to her. She could feel the utter terror and loathing of some of her, and the attention didn't linger on them for long. She felt the attention drift back to her and away, seemingly fascinated by memories of birth, nursing and nurturing. Of arousal and sex, and love and longing. Cheryl felt it was not a clinical interest in the physical acts, but of the emotional aspect, the bonds it could deepen, and the jealousy it could spawn. From those of her who were disgusted and offended by such thoughts, the attention seemed fascinated by that too, and seemed to want to understand *why.*

Why? Why was the act of sex so wonderful to some and distasteful to others? How could some think it so unimportant as to lack interest in the act, and others would give in to it freely because they, too, saw it as unimportant?

she was only fourteen, a gangly, pimpled, brace-faced freshman teased because of her poor vision, but that bitch sarah was picking on her best friend lisa and that just wouldn't do, call her a fat ginger dyke one more time you evil fucking and sarah pushed her and she hit sarah so hard the twat had a black eye for –

Why? What drove her to defend her friend when she was terrified of the larger girl that was picking on her? Was she terrified more of being thought a bad friend? A lot of her seemed to feel this way, while many thought she had been reckless and stupid. The condemnation rankled her. *Damn it, you protect those you cherish, no matter the cost to you. Don't you see that?* Some did, and others thought she was full of shit. Why?

Why were some convinced this was an evil invasion and others comfortable with the exploring? Why were the terrified ones trying to shout down the probing with prayers to God, and others tolerant? And why were there ones who had no faith and were fascinated and ones who felt just as violated as the devout? The attention flicked across them and back like a finger sliding along a keyboard. Why? It probed the fresh wound of her sister's death, and seemed entranced. What made them so strong and fragile? So diverse? And so alike?

What makes you *so singular?* a voice asked, and Cheryl was surprised to find it was hers. Mostly hers, anyways. *Why aren't you many, like me?*

You're only many when I watch you, came the reply. Only not a direct and vocal reply as such, but a memory she didn't know she had. It was an answer, and she understood it. And a part of her was thoughtful, a part of her laughed, and a part of her was terrified.

She woke in a couch, but she wasn't in the curved corridor she had fallen asleep in. She was in more of a cylindrical room that stretched above her. She could see the new Darla above, enclosed in a couch and surrounded by screens with views of the stars and various parts of the ship. Cheryl felt heavy, and it was harder to breathe, but nothing like the crushing force of leaving Earth behind.

"Hello?" she offered.

"Hello," came Peter's voice from behind her head. "Are we feeling better?"

Cheryl thought that over. As opposed to what? She was held tight, but comfortably, by the couch. Her ankle didn't throb, and she felt calmer she supposed, more accepting of the situation. But better?

"Is my sister still dead?" she replied.

He didn't have anything to say to that, and wisely stayed silent. She eyed the young woman above her. If she had heard her question, she didn't react at all to it.

Is she my sister? Cheryl wondered. *Obviously not the one I know. But can I in truth call her that? She's almost a fun-house mirror distortion of Darla, but if I get to know her, will she act and feel like Darla?* She thought of the day when Carol had returned to them. There was no distortion of features – maybe she was skinnier? But by God it was Carol, they all knew it right away. But it didn't take long to realize something was wrong with her...

"So where are we now?" Cheryl asked.

"We are in the drive hub, under acceleration," Peter answered. "We'll be under thrust for some time, and it's best to remain in the couch until we can coast and then fire up the hab ring again."

"Ah," she said. "On our way to Mars, then?"

"Yes."

"And why is that? Maybe the less cryptic version, this time?"

"I really wasn't being cryptic, or flippant. We are going to – hopefully – wake up a god."

"*A* god?"

"As far as the rest of us are concerned, you bet it's a god."

"So not *the* God?"

"Can't wake up something that doesn't exist, Cheryl," he said. Cheryl measured the tone of his voice, and it didn't sound as if he was being mean-spirited, or condescending. It was almost the sparring tone her sisters had when they would debate her faith with her.

"And you know this as a fact, then?" she asked. "All your universe-hopping has disproven the existence of God?"

"Hasn't proven it. And I don't need to open up to something I've never believed in, so don't waste any evangelizing on me."

"Well, yesterday I was clueless to these multiverse shenanigans. Maybe your ignorance can be cured too." Shit, she didn't want to come across like *that* Christian, but she was irritated.

"Well, if he – or she – exists, I would love some help," Peter laughed.

"All you have to do is ask," she said. "That never hurts. Beats yanking people out of their universe against their will."

"Does it? Can I remind you that you all would be corpses under a pile of rubble now if I hadn't?"

"Yeah, about that. How did you know the hotel was going to be attacked?"

"It's happened before, and there was a probability it was going to happen in this universe."

"You couldn't have stopped it, then?"

"I suppose? Look, the scope of what happened in Las Vegas is nothing compared to what can happen in the rest of the universe. I'm less than a mouse in a mansion in this game. And a mouse doesn't want to bring attention to itself. But if a mouse can gnaw on something long enough, it can bring things down. Or at least turn out the lights."

"Waking up a 'god' doesn't seem very low-key to me."

"True. Maybe this one is more like the cat of the house, though, and not the master. It's hiding in its own way."

"Maybe from *the* God?" laughed Cheryl.

"Make that plural, and you're not far off."

Cheryl sighed. This was getting irritating. "You know, for someone who's always in a hurry, you sure take your own sweet time getting to the point," she snapped. "Tell me what's going on, without any metaphors."

"Well, a God-fearing person such as yourself might not want to hear it. Deals with evolution, and all that nasty stuff."

"Why do you assume I don't accept evolution?"

"Fair point, sorry. But I haven't encountered many Christians that can accept both faith and fact." Before she could object, he continued. "Look, damn it, at best – when it's actually a reasonable debate – I wind up with a condescending 'I'll pray for you' as a punchline. Most think that throwing out the 'evolution is only a *theory*' with bull-headed certainty is equal to years of painstaking research and observation. And they don't understand the definition of the word *theory*. And that's the best of the lot. I can't tell you how many times I've been accused of being Satan himself. So, sorry I made an assumption when you started shoving God in my face. If you accept evolution as a fact and still have faith in your Christian God, then you're a rare bird sweetie."

"Not so rare, I think," she muttered.

"Well then speak up, because the devoutly righteous drown the rest of you out."

"You and Carol ought to get along just fine."

"You would think," he laughed quietly. "You really would…"

Chapter 8

it me, her father said, no, not like that – really hit me and he held out his arms with the boxing mitts on them and offered an encouraging smile and she didn't hold back this time but followed through, the power of her forearm driving behind her wrist and his hand was punched back with a satisfying smack and he laughed and yelled that's it! and her heart swelled and that may have been the first time she felt she might be able love the man who had the face of the man who had abused her because surely this cannot be the same man

And the attention was away from her, flitting down the line to her crush on Jason Karl in eighth grade. Only, it really wasn't *down the line,* was it? Not as easy as that? And *she* had never had a crush on that arrogant little turd. Had she? Well, *one* of her had, apparently. And then he had gotten her pregnant just three years later. Huh.

she was thirteen and dad had made them make this ungodly hike to this waterfall in julian but oh it was so awesome and she could feel the wet rock beneath her toes and she didn't have a fear of jumping into the top pool but of taking the t-shirt off over her swimsuit in front of everyone not because she didn't look good but because she just didn't like the idea of her exposed skin but she was tired of being made fun of and being told how weird she was so she yanked the shirt off and took a running jump and plummeted into the pool and the water was so shockingly cold and alive

And then memories she never had were being probed elsewhere, versions of her that were sullen and angry, pampered and entitled (these actually fascinated the hell out of *her*, too), timid and skittish and the inevitable righteous anger of the fanatic.

The feeling of being one with many was almost comforting, though, and so she struggled to find and isolate herself. And the attention was back with astonishing force.

the floorboards creaked and she could hear his short gasps of anticipation, could smell his sour breath and she felt the falsely-tentative touch on her shoulder –

No! she radiated with such authority that the attention recoiled from her – more like *pushed* away, actually, and all of her was as shocked as it was. *You do not get to go there. Ever. I don't know what you are, but you can fuck the hell off if you think you're going to dissect me any further.*

There was an astounding silence, an almost drawing away from her. The conceited versions had mild disgust, as if she had farted in church. But she felt admiration, too. And, *damn*, but it also felt like it came from whatever had been probing her…

She woke to the sound of voices.

"Well then speak up, because the devoutly righteous drown the rest of you out," she heard Peter state.

Shit, has Cheryl been talking God again?

"You and Carol ought to get along just fine," she heard Cheryl answer, with a tired resignation.

"You would think," Peter responded with a laugh. "You really would."

Carol opened her eyes and realized they were no longer in what Peter had called the 'hab-ring'. The other Darla was above her in a control station not unlike what was in the shuttle. The voices of Cheryl and Peter had been behind her. She was embraced in a couch, and felt heavier than she had in the ring. On their way to Mars, then?

"Look," Peter said, "you and I can argue the origins of the universe until the end of time – which has happened already, I might add – and never change each other's minds. If your faith comforts you, I'm glad. My lack of it comforts me, whether you want to believe it or not."

Carol raised an eyebrow at this, remembering how old she was when she stopped believing in God, and what a relief it had been to her. Her faith had been like a guttering candle flame, struggling to avoid being drowned by the pool of wax beneath. And then the realization that the universe didn't care if her nine-year-old self was being sexually and emotionally abused by her father blew out that flame so abruptly not even a wisp of smoke was left behind to mark where it had once danced. The world made sense without a God, especially the one her father liked to browbeat everyone with.

"What do you mean, 'the end of time' has already happened?" asked Cheryl. Carol blinked, surprised her sister could be diverted away from one of her favorite arguments. It was tough to do, but piquing her curiosity was one way. Props to Peter, it seemed.

"Oh, not really *time* per se," Peter answered slowly. "I'm not a big believer in time as anything other than an abstract concept."

"Right," said Cheryl. "There's only one moment, the *now*. I get it," she added impatiently.

Carol smiled. *You don't have some ignorant Bible-thumper on your hands here, Peter*, she thought with no small amount of pride. As baffling and frustrating as Cheryl's beliefs and reasoning were to Carol, she was her *sister*. And Carol enjoyed hearing someone else spar with her for a change...

"Alright," Peter said. "The end of time then, the end of the universe. The heat death of the universe, essentially."

"Entropy wins," Cheryl stated.

"As it's supposed to," Peter said.

"Right," Cheryl replied. "And you're hinting that this has happened? How?"

"Have you accepted the fact of a multiverse?"

"Why not."

"So, we have an unimaginable number of universes – ok, look, I *really* get tired of explaining all this, and so does Darla," Peter said with a tone so weary Darla snorted in acknowledgement up above. "Can we wait until Carol wakes up until I go on?"

"I'm awake," Carol said, and there was a heavy pause. *No doubt wondering how* long *I've been awake*, she thought.

"Morning, sunshine," Cheryl said brightly.

"Is it? Morning, I mean?" Carol asked.

"No doubt somewhere," Peter stated.

Carol rolled her eyes. "So is there something like ship's time, then? Basically, how long was I out?"

"A good eight hours," Peter said. "Feeling better?"

"Why, was there a happy-juice cocktail this couch gave me that was supposed to fix my attitude?"

"Oh hell no. I love your attitude. Don't we, Darla?"

Carol's heart fluttered at the name, but the murmured affirmation from above reminded her of the Darla he was talking to. *So our Darla is still gone...*

Cheryl cleared her throat and said, "So Peter was going to explain life, the universe and everything to us, Carol."

"Cool beans." Carol said. "Please continue. What's all this about heat death-rays?"

"Kind of the exact opposite," Peter replied in a dry tone.

"Ah," Carol said.

"But Peter says it's happened already," Cheryl offered.

"Oh really?" Carol said, with mock astonishment. "Funny, I don't feel like I've been heat-zapped."

Peter sighed. "It's not death *by* heat. It's the death *of* heat."

Good lord, thought Carol, *yet another guy so easy to fluster.* "Ah, gotcha," she said, and heard her sister snort.

"Why don't they just call it 'the big freeze', then?" Cheryl asked. "Something like that? Seems to me it would be less confusing. More on point." Carol grunted in agreement.

Peter remained quiet for several moments, then said calmly, "You two done dicking around?"

"Yes," the sisters chorused with false contrition.

Peter cleared his throat. "So yes, in a nutshell, the universe has suffered the heat death – the big freeze – already. Many, *many* times over. Of course, that's happened in other, separate universes. Ones that are different from this one, different from yours – and your *original* universe, Carol."

This is a lot to ask of me, Carol thought sullenly. *A lot to expect me to process so soon. God, I hate this shit. Dave should be here instead of me –* Dad *should, if there was any fairness at all to the universe...*

She rolled her eyes. The notion of different universes, while answering a lot of questions, still seemed so insane, so comic book gad-zooks-great *Scott!* ridiculous she had to wonder if she had lost her mind. *My* original *universe. Honestly, wrap me in Mylar and punch antennas into my head!* And then she could see her dad's patient smile, hear his low chuckle. "It's alright, Carol. You don't have to like the stuff I do. I just hope you find something that you can enjoy as much as I do with my 'nerd crap.'"

127

And had she? Ever?

"So," Cheryl interrupted, and it shook Carol out of her reflections, "are you saying other universes...*age* faster?"

"No," Peter answered. "I'm saying they are older – in a sense. And some younger."

"Okay..."

"The beginning, the big bang, seems – from the perspective of each universe – to be unique unto its own. But multiple universes were created as well. And there's been a time lag in each separate universe. So, there was a 'first' universe, but that's not saying much, really, or very accurate. Anyway, ones that followed were mere nanoseconds *behind*. But, if you have an ungodly number of universes, that time lag can be quite a lot, eventually."

"I thought there was no such thing as –" Cheryl began, but Peter cut her off.

"You understand what I mean, damn it. The *idea* of time is needed for reference – and you know that. Quit dicking *around*."

"Okay, well how much is 'ungodly'?" Carol asked.

Peter sighed. "A number so big it's meaningless to us, I think. But *finite*. At least, *Medusa* seems to think so."

Hmmm, thought Carol. *This ship is more than just a ship, then?*

"This ship talks to you, then?" Cheryl asked.

"You two have some memories explored while you slept?" he asked. Carol's chest tightened, and there was a prolonged moment of silence before she heard Cheryl reply in a neutral tone, "Yes."

Ah-ha, Carol thought. *Sis had the same thing happen. Interesting. Jesus, have we really been probed on an alien ship?* She stifled a laugh. *Oh, there is no fucking way I could have been prepared for this!*

"Well, that's kind of how she talks to you."

"What the hell *is* she?" Cheryl asked.

"Honestly? I can't give a definite answer. I think she's the oldest thing we will ever encounter in our brief lives, and I think she's unique in that there's only one of her, but she might exist in all universes at once."

"Seriously?" Cheryl asked.

"From our perspective, she can be left behind in another universe – or take us to another universe, which is like all of us going from *our* perspective, but she's already there. And yet it's like she *is* traveling – she has to plot courses, and jumping from one universe to the next isn't easy. I can't explain it any better than that. And Darla has her own theory on *Medusa's* place in the cosmos. Care to inform them, Darla?"

"Not really," Darla mumbled.

"Aw, come on," Cheryl prompted.

"Yeah, give us *your* insight. We'll let you know if we like it better than Peter's," Carol said.

Darla sighed. "I don't think she's in all the universes at once, but shifts so fast it appears she's in all of them. She is literally juggling all of us."

"Huh," Cheryl grunted thoughtfully, and Carol suppressed a snort.

"However she does it," Peter continued, "we are dealing with technology that is *billions* of years beyond what we can really grasp. I feel overwhelmed most of the time, but Jesus, she has got to have a lot on her plate."

"Is that so?" asked Carol innocently.

"Look - I think she is not only dealing with alternate versions of *us* in each universe, but also *things* we can't even imagine."

All those other… versions *of me that I felt – could almost feel like I* was *them*, Carol thought. She shuddered, and felt like her brain could really do with a day off. Shut down, and take a vacation. The couch contracted minutely, and she flinched. *God damn it – don't you dare tranquilize me!*

"Do you think she was created – constructed?" asked Cheryl.

"Yes," Peter said. "But again, that's only a simple answer, and the real question we may not be able to think to ask."

"Okay," Carol asked with a slight tremor to her voice as she wrestled with the ideas that were bombarding her. "If she's such advanced technology, can't she figure out how to talk to us directly, none of this mind-probe nonsense? I mean, maybe we're like ants to her, or too alien in our way of thinking, but come on, now. Billions of years ahead of us technologically? Figure it the fuck out, then."

Peter was quiet for a moment, and Carol wondered if she had insulted his precious ship. She looked up and saw a magnified reflection of Darla staring down at her, as direct as the woman ever had. They held eye contact for several seconds, and Carol surprised herself when she was the one who looked away as Peter spoke.

"I'm not sure what she was created for, in the first place," he said softly. "I have a few ideas I'm not willing to say out loud." He laughed. "I'm not sure she was constructed to be any sort of interstellar craft initially. I think she was more of a probe, or exploration device. I know she can adapt pretty rapidly, and I think there are parts of her that are missing. Maybe she can talk to us directly, and she's just shy. Maybe there's a part of her missing that could have done that, or she just doesn't understand the *concept* of direct communication – or maybe whoever created her didn't."

"What makes you think parts of her are missing?" asked Cheryl.

"Well, that kind of leads us into our current problems," he answered.

"Finally," Carol muttered under her breath.

"Alright, then," Cheryl said.

"So we've established that the multiverse is time-shifted," he began. "If we could line them up in some sort of order, we would have seen a progression from the big bang to the heat death. Again, it's not as simple as universes being lined up, but…it's the only way I can visualize it, or explain it. I think *Medusa* has given up on me trying to understand. Anyway, the simple truth is some universes are dead while some are still being formed – or it used to be that way. I think universes aren't being formed any more, which makes me believe there is a finite amount."

"Naturally," Cheryl stated, and Carol wished Darla were here to ask more pertinent questions. She may have been a marine biologist, but her scientific reasoning would sure come in handy now. Her eyes burned with tears, and she blinked rapidly.

"So there are universes – and I'm going to reason most of them – that are trillions of years older than ours," Peter continued, his vocal pace picking up. *Yeah, cut to the God damned chase*, thought Carol sourly.

"Our universe is still fairly young, so to speak. And I suspect there aren't many that are much younger. I think we are at the tail-end of the universe growth, and that's where it gets dangerous for us." Carol marveled at the idea of thirteen-some billion years being considered youthful.

"Dangerous?" Cheryl asked, with a hint of surprise in her voice. Carol shifted a bit in the couch. Her stomach growled painfully, and she realized she was hungry.

"Very," Peter said. "Essentially, we have advanced civilizations fleeing the heat death of their universe, and staking a claim in our younger ones."

"Oh," said Cheryl.

Peter must have thought that was significant to think about. *Letting it sink in*, thought Carol. *So how is this 'dangerous' to us?* "Our universe not big enough for the both of us, then?" she asked casually.

"It's not just an 'us and them' issue," Peter answered. "It's an us and oh-holy-fuck-there's-a-ton-of-them-and-they're-fighting issue."

"Oh," Carol said. This didn't sound good...

"So...just our universe?" Cheryl asked. "The one we left? The one we're in? Another one – yours?"

"Yes," Peter said.

"Yes?" Cheryl questioned.

"Yes," Peter repeated. "All of the above. Countless elder civilizations invading countless younger universes. Only there's less of us younger ones to go around. Space may be unimaginably big, but it can get crowded, and ugly, with extra-universe invaders. And we aren't talking beings in starships on planetary scales. We are talking galactic, and galactic cluster proportions. Civilizations that have grown from organic to machine to super-massive black hole scale and beyond, capable of manipulating space-time itself. They aren't civilizations anymore, they are massive entities. They may as well be gods. And yet, they don't want to die out when the universe isn't around to sustain them. The drive to live never leaves us, it seems. The old myths may have hit the nail pretty squarely – the gods were fucking petty after all."

"Us?" prompted Cheryl.

"What?" Peter asked.

"You said the drive to live never leaves *us*. Are humans a species that transforms into these...gods?"

"No," Peter said simply. Silence stretched until he must have felt he needed to clarify. "Look," he continued, "the notion that a multiverse must be able to allow any and every possibility isn't how it works. Yeah, sure, maybe the human race grows into one of these super-civilizations in some far-flung universe – and I'm done with the caveat of 'that's not how it really works but you get the idea', okay?"

He paused, either trying to gather his thoughts or to find a way to explain them. "I haven't seen any evidence that we make it out of the solar system, basically. But we have a neighbor that does. That is, most universes seem to follow that pattern. Yours, however, does not."

"Okay, so the multiverse tends to...sameness?" Carol asked. Her stomach growled audibly.

"Yeah, I'm hungry too!" Cheryl laughed.

A tube popped out of the couch near Carol's mouth and she flinched. "Jesus Christ!" Cheryl gave a startled yelp as well, so Carol assumed the same thing happened to her.

"Eat up, ladies," Peter said.

"Seriously?" asked Carol.

"It's all you're going to get for a while."

Carol stretched her lips to the tube, and drew down a semi-sweet liquid the consistency of a milk shake. *Not bad*, she thought. *Not bad at all*. She sucked greedily on the tube, and as the liquid filled her stomach, she felt like she was drinking pure, unadulterated nourishment. She heard Cheryl make satisfied groans, and she smiled.

"Pretty good?" Peter asked.

"It'll do," Carol said, and drank some more. She decided she would not ask what it was, or why it was so damn good. *No reason to potentially ruin things*, she thought.

She smacked her lips in satisfaction. "So," she prompted. "Are all universes basically the same?"

"It's *kind* of like physics on a universal scale, verses quantum," he said carefully. "The laws can be different. Sameness tends to rule on a universal scale, but it can be different on a...human, lifeform scale." He paused, and then added a bit wistfully, "Sometimes very different."

"So what's up with our universe, then?" Cheryl asked.

"Mars," said Peter.

"What about it?" Carol asked.

"In most universes, Mars is habitable. And our Darla used to live there."

"No shit?" Carol said, and looked up at the young woman again. The reflective screen she had set up was gone. *Doesn't like being the center of attention?* She wondered. "Were you born there?" Carol asked.

"Yes," Darla replied.

"I'm going out on a limb and assume humans aren't native to Mars, though?" Cheryl asked hesitantly.

"No," laughed Peter. "They aren't. But when it was discovered early on that it could be colonized and exploitable, things moved much faster as far as getting humans there."

"I don't recall Mars being any different in my original universe," Carol remarked. "I think I would have remembered it."

"Sure. You're two universes are 'clustered' and a lot alike."

"Well, except our dads," Carol said.

"Cosmic and quantum scale," he replied.

"And what's the deal with Mars, then?" Cheryl asked.

"One of the lifeforms native to it *does* make it out of the solar system," Peter said. "And from a very distant future, wants to return. In fact, I think it has."

"For clarity's sake, a distant future *universe*, yeah?" asked Cheryl.

"Yes, of course."

"Well, Peter, you're throwing a lot at us right now," Cheryl grumbled. "If you're going to throw time-travel into the mix to complicate things, we had better know now."

Peter sighed. "I suppose you can look at going from an older universe to a younger one as a sort of time travel."

"Cool," Carol said. "So can we go back and check out some dinosaurs?"

"Not anymore," Peter replied quietly.

"No? Well that sucks," Carol laughed.

"I think that the farthest back we can go is a few million years or so. The youngest universe is already thirteen-odd billion years old. And maybe you see a glimmer of what our problem is?"

Carol frowned. She was getting tired of Peter's tendency to lecture them with borderline condescension with the expectation that they should also know and grasp what he was talking about.

"Look, Peter, could you maybe just cut to the chase?" she snapped. "For someone always in a hurry, you sure take forever to get to your point. Just fucking spill it, would -"

"We're running out of universes?" interrupted Cheryl.

"There we go," Peter laughed.

"If these future...*gods*, whatever, are invading the younger universes, and the youngest is basically around our universe's age, and older ones are getting filled up..."

"Well, we still have plenty older ones with long lives ahead of them. But yes, this game has been going on for a very long time. And we're trying to get a jump on things to maybe save some."

"How?" asked Carol. "Save some universes, I mean."

"That's what we want to go to Mars to find out," Peter sighed. "Hopefully..."

"To awaken a 'god', you say?" Carol prompted.

"Yeah, a minor one, really."

"Okay. But if it's not one of the big players, what good is it?"

"Well, it may have lost a war, but that doesn't mean it's useless as far as information."

"Hold, on" Cheryl interrupted. "You said one of these things might have *returned* to Mars. Can we infer that it was a former inhabitant, then?"

"*Medusa* thinks so."

"So, a Mars native evolves into a super-being in the distant future – *shit* – a distant universe, gets its ass kicked and limps home in a younger universe to...what? Hide?" asked Cheryl.

"Essentially," Peter replied. "Or maybe play the long game? Plot its revenge when the big guys eventually show up?"

"Okay, so...what sort of lifeform was it?" Carol asked.

"Rippers," Darla said. "Nasty things."

Carol flicked her eyes up to focus her attention above, but Darla was done with the mirror-screen, apparently. Carol tried to recall if this was the woman's first un-prompted response to them, and decided since she couldn't remember if it was, it was rare enough and Darla must have a strong emotional response to them.

"Sounds like you have first-hand knowledge of them?" Cheryl asked.

Darla gave a low snort. "Yeah. They used to hunt my friends."

"Oh," Cheryl said.

Holy shit, thought Carol.

"Rippers," said Peter. "Think forearms like a praying mantis, only more scythe-like. Back legs like a kangaroo. Mandibles around its mouth capable of manipulating objects with the dexterity of human hands. It evolved to hunt some pretty big prey."

"My friends," Darla said.

"Well, not *just* them. But yeah, the rippers loved to dine on what were commonly known as the 'gas giants' of Mars," Peter said. "Darla had a kind of...*affinity* for them, and they seemed to like her."

A screen formed in the air between Darla and them, giving the vision impaired sisters a comfortable view of the images playing across it. A herd of what looked like weather balloons with a keel-like fin drifted across the screen. Tentacles hung from the base of the gas bags, twisting and grasping at sparse trees on an arid mountain top below them. The huge bags glistened in ruby and pink hues, the tentacles a deep maroon and violet. The view panned down, and a group of loping figures raced through the trees and rocks, targeting a smaller gas giant. One of the rippers gave a mighty leap – jumping amazingly high in the Martian gravity – but a longer, whip-like tentacle snapped out from one of the adult giants and struck the predator, causing it to tumble back into the rocks, one of its massive arms severed from its body.

Carol watched in stunned silence, realizing her mouth was hanging open. She shut it, embarrassed to look so foolish. *But holy crap,* she thought. *Those are* aliens! She wished Darla – *their* Darla – was here to see this. And their father...

Cheryl cleared her throat. "Did they...did they hunt the colonists?" she asked tentatively.

"Initially," Peter said. "But they found them...unpalatable. And much of Martian life was poisonous to humans, too. Of course, the colonists built perimeter walls and could defend themselves easily enough. The rippers were smart enough to leave them alone and avoid them early on."

"Walls" stated Cheryl. "Mars had a breathable atmosphere?"

"Not really for us, and that's part of what lead to the downfall of the colony in the end. They could filter it – they didn't need pressure suits and oxygen tanks. Mars was mostly chilly to humans, but not too hostile. Their homes were pressurized, but few had airlocks – it didn't seem necessary. Until a large portion of the population started exhibiting paranoid behavior at best. Psychotic and murderous at the worst."

"Oh," Cheryl said simply.

Holy shit! thought Carol.

"My mother killed my father," Darla said quietly.

Well, there's not much to say to that, thought Carol. *Darla's choice of words struck her. We're not her Carol or her Cheryl. Does she have a near resentment of that, too?*

"I'm so sorry," Cheryl said. "That must have been awful."

Carol couldn't imagine their mother being capable of murdering their father. Although, the mother of her...*adoptive* universe could probably take out the father of her original universe with no qualms...

"I was five when it happened," Darla said. "Not really old enough to understand the why of it."

Silence stretched uncomfortably, and the viewer showing the herd of gas giants winked out. Carol shifted in her couch, and wondered how long they had to stay in these damned things. *Jesus, what happens when I have to go to the bathroom? Will the old 'go in the suit' rule apply?*

"So the colony failed, you say?" asked Cheryl.

"*Colonies*," Peter said. "Yes, all of them – some were quite substantial, had been there for close to twenty years. But they couldn't be sustained, and problems back on Earth didn't help them."

"So Mars was abandoned, then?" Carol asked.

"Pretty much," Peter said.

"Were you originally part of the colonies too?"

"Ah, no."

"How did you and Darla meet up, then?"

"That's another story."

"He rescued me," Darla interjected. "Saved me from an inferno."

"Barely," muttered Peter.

"Didn't just drop her into another universe, though?" Carol said, perhaps a bit too sharply.

"Different situation than yours," Peter said. "And *Medusa* really took a shine to her."

Oh great, Carol thought. *A spaceship that can play favorites. Good to know…*

"So anyway, the colonies collapsed," Cheryl stated.

"Yep," Peter said. "The colonists that didn't die on Mars went back to Earth or the Lunar colonies. And that was it for mankind and the stars. Didn't even make it out to the belt."

"But the rippers did?"

"And how. A big help was the abandoned tech left behind on Mars. Clever creatures got a big help, there."

"What, rockets left behind?"

"Well, no. But computers sealed up in sturdy habitats, hoping to be used again one day. Things like that. Gave ripper archeologists a leg up. The rippers were smart, knew they were dealing with something new and more advanced than they were. Would they have made it to the stars without mankind's relics? Probably. But they got jumpstarted for sure."

"Well, that hardly seems fair," Carol mumbled.

"The universe cares nothing about fairness," Peter replied.

"And now they're back?" Cheryl asked. "Rippers, I mean. Or one? Shit – *shoot* – descendants, then?"

Peter laughed. "Yeah, for all intents and purposes, descendants I guess. One entity, probably knows its history anyways. And ours."

"So…why?" asked Carol "To help nurture its…alternate universe ancestors?" *Jesus, this is getting way too nuts*, she thought.

"Oh, not at all," Peter laughed. "In your universe, it pretty much took out Mars's magnetic field, and any chance of life evolving. It didn't give two shits about its ancestors. In fact, didn't want the competition in the future."

"Jesus, that's *cold*," Carol said.

"Yeah, these massive entities aren't what you would call nostalgic."

"What's it want?" Cheryl asked. "Why come all the way back here, then?"

"To live longer. That's just it, I think. Do not go gentle, survive to think, to dream and just exist. Some of these entities merge and grow – sometimes willingly. But a lot of times they get absorbed. And no one likes getting eaten, no matter how far evolved you are."

"So it's hiding?"

"Maybe? Like I *said*, it could be biding its time, storing energy. Hibernating for millennia at a time. Could be plotting for future invaders, and be ready for them. Eventually they'll come."

"And what do we want with this thing, then?" Carol asked, with apprehension. "Sounds like something we would do well to avoid."

"We have…questions. We believe it may be possible to seal off universes from outside invaders, permanently. It would be nice to help numbers-crunch."

"Will this thing even notice us? Or care to help?" Cheryl asked doubtfully.

"Yes, I think it will take notice of us. If not just the *Medusa*. Will it help? Only if it would be in its own self-interest. Still, some are so damned curious – it may just be in it for the amusement."

"Okay, will it hurt us?" Carol asked.

"I don't think it could imagine us as a threat. It wouldn't care if we wound up as collateral damage, for sure. But waste any energy killing us? Doubtful."

"Then what killed Darla?" Carol asked quietly.

Another awkward silence followed. Carol had been waiting some time to bring this up. *If you think we're just going to ignore what happened to our baby sister while you try and dazzle us with high-concept bullshit, buddy, you have another thing coming*, she thought.

"Yeah," Cheryl contributed. "I think we're owed an explanation, don't you?"

Peter cleared his throat. "Just so we can avoid the inevitable jeering and protests from you two, I'm letting you know now I'm not being flippant, or coy, in my answer, okay?" He paused to let that sink in. "Nothing killed your sister. And I mean it, literally – *nothing*."

Carol blew out an exasperated sigh, and Peter hushed her.

"The emptiness of non-reality killed your Darla," he said.

Aw, crap, thought Carol. *More trippy mumbo-jumbo bullshit. This is just not fair. I swear, I am stuck in one of dad's books!*

"How can empty space kill someone?" asked Cheryl.

"Well, you have a good point. Who knows what nonexistence does to…reality? Hell, maybe it wasn't the 'nothingness' that killed her, but the resistance of reality to it that did the deed - like space-time trying to get out of the way of it."

"Fuck," Carol muttered disgustedly as she rolled her eyes, and her sister offered a low, mirthless laugh. Peter gave a resigned sigh.

"Look, nothing – *pure* nothing – isn't even empty space. There is no spacetime fabric to deal with. It is outside our universe – *universes*. What goes on inside black holes is easier to comprehend than what happens without any spacetime – you can't measure something that isn't there, which in turn doesn't allow anything *else* to be there either."

"*Fuck.*" Carol said.

"So let me get this *straight*," Cheryl said with a sigh. "Literally *nothing* has taken form and is…what, invading our universe too?"

"No," Peter said with an exaggerated patience. "It cannot take *form* – it has no thought, agenda or plan. It is *nothing*."

"Fuck!" shouted Carol. "Fuck, fuck, fuck, fuck, fuckity-fucking fuck! *Fuck* this shit! Seriously." Her heart hammered in her chest, and she felt a frustrated anger develop in her.

"Carol, *stop* it," ordered Cheryl. "You are not helping."

"Well, *Jesus* Cheryl – "

"Carol. *Enough.*"

Oh, you did not *just use that tone with me*, Carol thought. She inhaled and exhaled in rapid little bursts through her nostrils, feeling her heart pound in her ears. The couch contracted, and she felt a slight push against her skin. *Oh sure, just trank me to shut up the irrational female!* She wanted to get up and hit something, or to run. She really wanted to run so she could process this crap easier. "How much longer do we have to stay in these God damned couches?" she yelled.

"Longer than you'll want to," called Darla from above.

The sound of her voice made Carol suck in air between her lips and let it out in a slow, steady breath. She could feel her heartbeat slow, the restlessness in her settle. *God damn drugs…*

"So how does nothing reach out to kill someone, then?" Cheryl asked.

"It's not *reaching* out, really, Peter said. "Again, it – and describing it as…well, 'it' is nonsense, right? But we can't comprehend it any other way. Think of it as a natural attraction like a magnet to a piece of iron. The node seems to attract it. Well, specifically, *my* node."

"The thing that lets us universe-hop?" asked Cheryl.

Carol giggled. *Universe-hop!*

"Yes," Peter answered. "That's why I shut them off when it showed up. Wasn't expecting it so soon…"

"Why is it attracted to *your* node?"

"I…used to jump around constantly. Probably too much, is all I can figure. Just a reckless kid…"

"Sounds like you've been dealing with it for some time?" Cheryl offered.

"Yeah, it's been dogging me whenever I jump in a gravity well."

Carol burst out laughing. *Oh, this is getting hilarious!*

"She get injected with something?" asked Cheryl.

"Probably," said Peter.

"That's some bullshit," Cheryl snapped. "Is this going to happen every time we get upset? Keep us in line? Because I think we have a right to be a *bit* upset right now."

"*Medusa* interpreted her emotional response as being dangerous to herself. If she struggled to break free of her couch, she could have hurt herself. One way or another, she is going to be restrained until we can coast for a bit and spin the hab ring up."

"Spin, spin, spin, spin it *up!*" sang Carol.

"Don't you guys have…what, inertial dampers or something? Honestly."

"Something like that requires power we would rather use for thrust, Cheryl. And don't bring up artificial gravity either. *Honestly.*"

Carol giggled until she yawned. *Oh, this is so not fair – I just woke up!*

she could visualize the whole of creation, the multiverse as a single unit – that was really what should be thought of as the universe and she now understood it was one thing even though it was a near-infinite layer of universes, but there also was the not-universe, the hole of creation, and somehow it had gotten in - but that wasn't right at all because it didn't want anything, it was only the ultimate entropy and it would win in the end and ordinarily the multiverse was fine expanding through it until the ancient entities that refused to die had found an exploitable loophole, but no, she had found it for them and would be stained with that shame forever, but promethean fire and the genie was out of the damned bottle and now maybe they could save some universes so they could exist and end like they should but there was worry, worry that it would backfire - that the hole would gobble everything up and never stop – but was that any worse than massive entities gorging themselves into insanely bloated beings leaving no room for those of a more...basic state?

there was so much to worry about, and it had always been this way

the worry was all that there was anymore, a steady state that may as well have been woven into spacetime itself, worry that she was mad from it – but the madness had been there since she first found the exit for them, let's be clear about that - and she thought it was very unfair to be this agitated while unconscious

but was it her?

yes, no, they all were...but nothing compared to her...

there was so much worry...

she's letting us observe her a voice piped up, and the thought blinked and flashed among them until the focus returned to them and they groaned – not letting them, just an accidental loss of control

carol sensed she may have been embarrassed, but maybe it was just them again

still, it was hard to shake off so much worry...

Chapter 9

They had been orbiting Mars now for several days, and Cheryl wondered what the holdup was. She suspected second thoughts – do we *really* want to do this? Then again, Carol and she were not as informed as they would like to be, and the suspicion that there may have been attempts before this one that had gone awry nagged at her. *How many times have I been here?* she thought, and shook her head. *Seriously though, what versions of me have been here before, or are here now?*

The ship continually visited her as she slept, and hinted of such things. *Medusa* didn't probe her memories or emotions as much now, but seemed to be trying to educate her somehow – albeit in curious snapshot bursts of information – in what Cheryl *assumed* was information, at any rate. She would be shown images reminiscent of the Mandelbrot set, assume she was being taught how the multiverse connected to itself, and the lesson would end abruptly, start over, and include flickering views of her loved ones, friends and acquaintances, and people she did not know.

Sometimes they seemed more like empathic math problems. Was she to estimate the scale of objects, or judge the objects themselves as they related to each other? Larger ones would devour the smaller, and in turn dissolve in terror. *Medusa* seemed to measure her sympathetic reactions.

The results of this form of education were uneven at best, Cheryl decided. It had a decidedly dream-like quality to it that was different than recalled memories. And *Medusa* seemed fascinated by her memories of dreams. The ship was obsessed with a particular dream she had as a child, one where she was walking down a street and a neighbor had driven by in a sportscar, waving at her. As he went past, the neighbor bent and waved from *under* the car, a contortion that was impossible of course, but perfectly acceptable in her dream. Later in life, other surrealistic dreams had made her suspect that what she *saw* in dreams was more suggestion and sketch than a true recognizable image playing in her head. The mind let the mind fill in the blanks to decide what was believable. Cheryl felt that *Medusa* approved of her acceptance of the impossible dreamscape. Or, maybe the ship was just entertained by her freaky dreams, and all of Cheryl's conjecture was the vapor of fading illusions.

She and Carol agreed the ship had reservations of what was to be attempted, and worries of deeds past. But it seemed to want to impress upon them the importance of their contribution, even if they didn't know what in the heck that was.

"Show me Mars, please," Cheryl asked, and a viewer appeared on the wall – *bulkhead* - in front of her. Mars polar region appeared to be orbiting around a patch of space above it. "Hub view, please," she clarified, and a stationary view of the planet replaced the rotating one.

Red planet, indeed. Only the muted reddish ochres and browns she was familiar with were replaced with brighter reds and oranges, and the deep blues and greens of vibrant oceans. Opaque white clouds scudded across the surface of the planet, a world that teemed with life. She marveled at her ability to pick out details. Where she focused her vision, detail would expand and sharpen, adjusting to her poor vision. *Where have you been all my life, sweetheart?* she thought. *I could get rid of my trusty magnifying glass if you would just float in front of me the rest of my life!*

Sweat trickled down the small of her back as her breath grew shallower. She was supposed to be jogging with Carol, but she couldn't keep up with her sister's pace. She was getting better – a month of journeying to Mars had given her plenty of time to work out. But Carol ran with a vengeance, it seemed, and Cheryl was certain she could never reach that level of commitment. Or obsession. Still, it gave them an outlet to burn off their anxieties. Mostly. If Cheryl dwelled too long on thoughts of her family she was afraid she would slip into a dark hole of despair so deep she could never escape.

What must they be thinking, going through? They have to think us dead, all of us, smashed and broken under tons of rubble...

Cheryl sniffed, the sweat cooling on her skin made her shiver slightly. Her suit tried to cover her midriff and slide down her arms, but she concentrated and didn't let it. She had to admit it was a marvelous garment: at most times jet black, but able to change hue whenever she wanted. It could be as skintight as leggings, or as loose and comfortable as Darla's red jumpsuit. Go from swimsuit-short to full pants and boots and sleeves and

143

gloves and hoodie. In fact, it could morph into a full pressure-suit in an instant if there was any breech in the *Medusa's* hull. Right now, it had the configuration of exercise clothing, right down to the cushioned footwear.

She heard a soft metronome of thumps coming up behind her, and Carol's steady huffs as she ran along the curved floor of the hab-ring.

"Enough with admiring the view, lazy-bones," Carol panted. "You said you'd run with me some more."

Cheryl sighed. "Viewer off, please," she commanded, and turned and fell into step with her sister. "Centrifuge lighting, please," she asked and Carol groaned. Cheryl grinned and punched her arms out in a few quick shadow-boxing jabs as the walls lit the hab-ring, the floor taking on a white textured-tile appearance.

"Dave would be very disappointed in me if I didn't do that," she huffed. "Although the wheel on *that* spaceship was way smaller than this."

Carol grunted out a laugh, and they ran a lap with only the sounds of their falling feet and labored breathing.

"Had a weird dream – memory, I guess – last night," Carol said abruptly.

"Yeah?" Cheryl replied. *Nothing new there*, she thought. *Kind of a nightly thing...*

"Remember when, oh, it was maybe six months or so after...I came back. Things had calmed down a bit and mom let me out of her sight for a few minutes by then, at least. *Anyway*, we were all out front playing, just before going in for dinner, and old Mr. Murray walked past, and just kind of stared at us?"

"Maybe..."

"And I waved at him and asked him how he was and he looked all weird like he had seen a ghost or something?"

"Oh. Yeah. Yeah, I *do* remember that." Cheryl shook her head, and drops of sweat flicked off her nose to be wicked away and be reclaimed by the ship. *That was weird*, she thought. How the memory surfaced so quickly. She frowned, and wondered if Medusa was messing with them even while awake.

"Why would I remember something so random, do you think?" Carol asked. "I mean, why would...*she* have me remember it?"

"Dunno," Cheryl panted. "Didn't he move away not long after that?"

144

"Think so."

Cheryl raised her arms in surrender, and slowed to a walk. Carol snorted, but matched her pace.

"I think I've given up trying to figure out what she's trying to get us to know," Cheryl said, her chest heaving. "Seems to me he was a nice old guy, wasn't he?"

"Far as I remember," Carol said.

"Maybe it is just random stuff she's poking at, see how we react? Or trying to motivate us with memories of good people we knew?"

"I still don't know what we're supposed to be motivated about."

"Amen to that, sister." Cheryl stopped, and swiped the back of her wrist across her forehead. "I need water."

A section of the bulkhead bulged and formed into a water-fountain, and she drank deeply, then let the water run over her face. She straightened, and flicked the excess water from her face to let the ship recycle it. Carol took a turn at the fountain, and then they continued their cool-down walk.

"Do you ever get memories you never had?" Cheryl asked.

"Oh yeah."

"But it *feels* like you remember them?"

"Yup."

"Kinda hate that."

"Yup."

"And it seems like she's...*disappointed* in you for feeling like that. Like we should be more empathetic, even with the more..." Cheryl trailed off, not sure what adjective she was looking for.

"Disgusting ones?' Carol offered.

"Well, yeah," Cheryl laughed. "Or contrary ones, I think. Ones that are kind of...opposed to what you believe, maybe?"

Carol grunted. "Yeah, I have some...pampered ones. *Entitled* ones, that just make me want to slap her – me. Whatever. Guess I'm supposed to *understand* that version of me."

Cheryl shrugged. "Maybe we're teaching her a little, too. Maybe we're projecting our own guilts, and they're just being reflected back at us?"

"Could be."

"Whatever. I feel like I'm in way over my head, and I don't even know what I should be scared of the most. Ancient 'gods' or nothing at all?"

Carol laughed and said, "Sometimes, it would be nice to just have a good old-fashioned dream while I slept, the internal theater of nonsense, as mom says."

"Yeah, I hear you. I guess we're getting the kind of sleep we need – REM cycles or whatever. But *geeze*, can't we have – "

A viewer popped into the space directly in front of them, Peter's head floating just out of reach as they walked along.

"We're going to make the jump," he said simply. "You two want to clean up first?"

"Well, we can't meet a god all stanky, can we?" asked Carol.

They decided they would all be in the hub when they jumped. If the entity was hostile, nowhere else would be any safer, and Darla preferred it anyways.

"I know you two think that we've been delaying the jump because of nerves," Peter said as he floated above the array of couches. The sisters had their arms locked around grips in the bulkhead, and each other. Cheryl had grown to like the falling-feeling in her stomach in zero-gravity, Carol not so much. But the couch kept her nausea well under control. Nevertheless, she was still a little irritable.

"*Medusa* tell you that?" she asked.

"Not at all," he answered. "But I can tell when someone's getting frustrated with a delay, believe me. And sure, you're partly right – this is unpredictable and nerve-wracking. But we also have to make sure when we pop back in to your universe, Mars is where it should be. Your universe is time shifted from this one, so is Mars. We also have to take into consideration the difference of space-time expansion from one universe to the next. There are fourteen artificial satellites orbiting Mars, six of which are still active. We have to avoid those."

"How come you didn't worry about all this when we were in Vegas and popped into this universe? Surely we had the same problems to deal with?"

"Different tech to begin with – multi-Earths, and other planets and stars, share a connection much like quantum entanglement, and the nodes utilize that. Consequently, they don't operate as well out of a true gravity environment – they *can*, but…weird stuff happens. Anyhow - we have *Medusa* out here to get us where we want to go."

"Why can't she pop in farther out, then motor on in?" Carol asked.

"She could. But anyone can do that."

"Seriously?" Cheryl laughed. "This is about showing off?"

"Definitely. Look, we can cruise in and let the thing get a leisurely look at us and decide we aren't worth acknowledging. We pop into orbit immediately, and that's impressive. Might be our only chance at getting a foot in the door. I'm counting on a few other things to hold its attention."

"Jesus," Carol muttered. "Somethings never change – the little douches always looking for ways to impress the bigger douches. Gonna compare business cards, too?"

Peter stared at her for several seconds, then spread his arms out, causing him to start to spin, but he reached out to stabilize himself. "If it would help, you bet." He stared at both of them, as if measuring their commitment, then sighed and tilted his head.

"Look," he said softly, "this thing knows so much more about us than we do about it. If it doesn't, then it will in a fraction of a second. But you can bet it monitored Earth from the first radio waves leaving the planet, certainly from the first nuke going off. But it has knowledge of its history, its family tree, and Earth was probably well known to the Martians by the time they left the solar system."

"*Martians*," Carol said with a quiet laugh. "I swear, Cheryl – if one of these walls slides open and your God-damned husband pops out and yells 'Gotcha!' I will pick you up and beat him to death with you."

Cheryl giggled until she snorted, then laughed. "That would be about his speed!" Carol joined in with the laughter, and they clutched each other as they shook. A faint chuckle drifted down from Darla. Peter shook his head, but grinned.

As their laughs faded while wiping their eyes, Peter tipped his head up to Darla and asked, "See any reason not to do this?"

"Yes," Darla murmured. "Lots of them, actually."

"We doing it anyways?"

"Indeed we are."

Peter reached out and patted a bulkhead. "Let's do this, sweetheart."

Below Darla a screen materialized, and the lush vibrant Mars was on view. Cheryl looked at her sister and grinned tightly. Carol raised her eyebrows, tried to smile, then just pursed her lips. They both tipped their heads towards the screen, and Mars winked from a life-nourishing world to the reddish-orange and brown and dead planet they were familiar with.

Cheryl blinked in surprise. With no jolts, shudders, or drama, they were just back. She waited for a moment, then asked, "Is that it? We're just back in our own universe?"

"That's it," Peter said. He looked around the cabin lovingly. "Is she good, or what?"

"Better than dropping out of a stairwell," grumbled Carol. Cheryl gave a quiet laugh, and then flinched at a sudden pressure that wanted to crush and explode her simultaneously.

They were being scrutinized, and it hurt.

Much like the instant transition from one universe to the next, they went from what could only be described as an ignorant state to a hyper-aware one. It felt like space itself was now focusing all its attention on them, a crushing distortion of observational lensing. It pushed through them, dissecting every atom of their bodies, every random firing of a synapse. Cheryl couldn't move, even to flick her eyes over to Carol to see how she was reacting. She could only stare mutely at a dead Mars before her.

Bad idea, she thought. *Very bad idea. We should not have come here...*

There was almost an amused tint to the attention, but humor was something it hadn't felt in a long time, or maybe had just learned this very moment. Either way, it was an ill-fitting emotion for the being that they had come to see.

Please, Cheryl thought, *let us go. You've made your point, all powerful and mighty Oz...*

Pressure and pain effortlessly left her, but she could still feel that she was being watched. She remembered a documentary she had seen years ago, where crocodiles and hippos lived uneasily together in a dwindling waterhole. Eventually the hippos left, and the crocs died out. Except for a massive one who had burrowed into the mud and lay waiting for the water to return. Its eye had reflected coldly in the dark of its self-excavated cave, un-blinking and un-caring of the camera. *I see you*, it had seemed to say, *and I could not care less.*

Again, that feeling of laughter with no mirth.

"I wonder," a soft voice filled the cabin. "How did you little primates ever get control of something so magnificent? Well, *control* isn't quite right, is it?"

Cheryl's heart felt like it was being squeezed dry, but not from any external force. *That voice. Again.* Only this time, it matched so much better...

She was able to move now, and she flicked her gaze to look Carol in her eyes, and saw her own pain reflected in them.

Please, no, she thought. *Please. Not her. Don't use her against us.*

An elevator tube grew out of the floor near the couches, the doorway dialed open, and Darla – *their* Darla – stepped out, slick and wet from whatever the hell was in that chamber she had been stored in. Still in her filthy bathrobe, a raw hole gleaming in her chest, she walked across the deck of the cabin as if gravity was there to hold her down. She stared up at them, a smile twitching the corners of her mouth.

"Hello, sisters," she said.

Cheryl squeezed her eyes shut, and a sob burst out of her.

"Why would you do that?" she heard Darla ask. "Why cry? I should think it would be *good* to see me again."

Carol growled in frustration, and Cheryl could tell it was to tamp down her own inadvertent sobs. "Excuse us if we don't buy that you're our *sister*," Carol snapped. Cheryl took several rapid breaths, and fluttered her eyes open, blinking at the tears that clung to them. *Be strong, and deal with this*, she thought. *Help Carol stand up to this...thing.* She rubbed quickly at her eyes, and stared down at what was Darla.

"You are disturbed at my appearance?" Darla asked. The bathrobe tore and shredded soundlessly, and then was gone. Likewise the t-shirt and panties Darla had worn.

"Such fragile little things," Darla said. "And yet, you dare to explore the hostile vacuum beyond your atmosphere. There is much to admire in that - such a dangerous first step. *Very* dangerous."

She looked down at her naked body. "So *fragile*." The hole in her chest shrank, tendrils of flesh threading and knitting in an eyeblink, and the space between her breasts was whole again.

"That's better?" Darla asked. Carol took in a sharp breath, and Cheryl could only stare in wonder, trying to decide if it was a miracle or travesty.

Darla turned her back to them, and brought an arm up to rub at the back of her neck – the patch covering the new tattoo of her sister's eyes was gone, and the raw skin now looked smooth and clean. Cheryl felt the back of her own neck tingle, and she heard Carol give a quiet gasp.

"Why do you decorate yourselves so?" Darla asked. "It's a painful procedure, no doubt? I suppose it's an artistic expression, designed to communicate your interests, or desires." She slid her hand down to point at her back. Cheryl noticed the man o' war was whole and undamaged. "This tattoo represents an aquatic creature that I think humans would find repulsive. It appears unfinished. She had plans to complete it, yes?"

Ink began to stretch and draw itself across her buttocks, and down the backs of her thighs, extending the intricate tentacles to her feet, where they looped artfully around her ankles and came to rest at the base of her toes.

Cheryl huffed in anger, then growled out, "You have no *right* to deface her body like that."

"This is what she wanted."

"You have no fucking clue what she *wanted*," snapped Carol.

"But I do," said Darla.

"It was her decision to finish it, not *yours*," Cheryl barked. Darla turned and looked at her, those wide blue eyes steady and impassive.

"Do you think she would get a chance to do that?" Darla spread her arms, and looked around the cabin. "You are far from home, and yet you have even farther to go. What are the odds, do you think, of going back to your beautiful little planet?" She stared at Cheryl again. "Going back to your family?"

Cheryl closed her eyes and tried to control her breathing.

"We have no clue what we are doing out here, and weren't given much choice in the matter," Carol said.

Cheryl could hear the faint trace of a laugh in the voice that sounded so much like Darla. "You have no idea how much that statement applies to you all." Cheryl opened her eyes, and Darla was staring at Peter now. "You haven't told them what you're up to? That seems unfair."

"You want to speak about fairness?" Peter snorted. "You took away a chance at life on the planet below us, from your ancestors."

"Not *my* ancestors," she answered, and began a slow walk around the cabin, absently running her hand along the couches. "My ancestors are long gone, and there are countless variations of them in the multiverse. One universe less of them is a crime? Tell me, do you mourn when you scrub mold from a shower door? Do you visit and pay homage to stromatolites in Australia?" She pointed above to Darla, a taller version of herself. "That one hates my 'ancestors'. Is she upset they don't exist in this universe?"

"No, but I am that the gas giants don't," Darla said from her couch. "And I don't *hate* them, the rippers."

The entity in Darla smiled, then turned her head up to stare at her twin. "Come down," she said.

"I don't believe I will."

"Come *down*," she repeated. Cheryl gasped as she, Carol, and Peter grew heavier, and sank slowly to the deck. Darla dutifully climbed out of her command couch and dropped down to them.

The shorter Darla orbited the taller one, strolling with an unconcerned grace around her.

"This is rather amazing, don't you think? At least to all of *you*, surely?" She reached out and fingered Darla's dreadlocks, and the young woman flinched. "We are so alike, down to our DNA and matching fingerprints, and yet you grew with less gravity to inhibit your height, and *this* one," she swept her hand down across her body, "is the runt of the litter."

Carol sighed acidly, and Darla darted her attention to her and smiled. "Ah," she said. "But *you* two are the truly fascinating pair, aren't you?" She turned sideways and pointed one hand at Carol to her left, and another at Peter to her right and asked, "Does *she* know?"

"You know what she does and doesn't know," snapped Peter.

"Please. I am playing your game. I was polite and attended your little party. You can play along as well. Does she know?"

"No," he said flatly. "I'm guessing she doesn't even suspect."

Cheryl watched as her sister frowned at Peter.

151

Darla clapped her hands delightedly. "I wonder if she has the intelligence to be fascinated by it? Or is she so dull that it would be just another overwhelming bit of information triggering her flight reflex?"

"Look, this has been a whirlwind courtship," Carol said contemptuously. "He's not been very forthcoming, and I'm tired of all this sci-fi bullshit. I can tell you *I'm* not going to play any fucking games – and if there's something I don't *know*, I'm virtually certain that it can't compare to a God damned *alien* using my baby sister's *body* to talk shit to us."

"Ah, *fight* reflex, then," Darla said as she eyed Carol. "You must be careful, Carol. You may pick a fight you can't win someday." Cheryl's heart thumped madly as she recognized that direct and open stare. *Could she be in there?* She thought. *Darla – are you still in there?* And her baby sister turned her attention to Cheryl, and smiled.

And why shouldn't she be? Darla asked, only Cheryl didn't see Darla's lips move, or hear the response with her ears. Thunderstruck confusion shattered her thoughts, and bits of movies, comic books and TV shows where possessed characters are claimed to have been lost forever and burnt out of the body hosting the demon/alien/whatever that infected them tumbled through her brain. Before she could form a coherent thought voicing this worry, Darla spoke inside her again: *Your sister is right to scoff at so-called bad-sci-fi. I feel it distracts you from bigger issues. If you must know, I could speak through you and you would never know it or be harmed. But this is not a concern that should worry you – there are far worse matters for you to worry about, even for someone so far down the evolutionary ladder. Yes, I know you are confused and still don't know what questions to ask. You will need to calm yourself, Cheryl. Accept what has happened, and calm yourself – if you want to help fight. I could do it for you, but I think you can do it yourself.*

She smiled again, winked, and turned back to Carol.

Holy shit, Cheryl thought, and began to shake, and even as Darla began speaking to Carol, she heard, *Calm yourself* in her head again.

"You're right to guess this 'secret' is nothing more than a curiosity," Darla said to Carol. "A statistical oddity that I admit caught even my attention. It only matters that you," she pointed to Carol, "and he," she pointed to Peter, "are suitable for the task that's been set for you. That *all* of you are suitable." She swept her arms out to include Cheryl and the other Darla, then tipped her head up to stare at the command hub.

"Well, are we?" Peter asked.

Darla laughed, and it seemed so genuine and honest that it even startled her. "I think I've stayed too long in your company," she said. "And if you carry on with your course of actions, I think I would do well to find another universe to hide in."

"So you're saying we can't do it?" Peter asked.

Darla began another slow and deliberate walk around the cabin. She entertained herself with the act of studying objects and touching them, seeming to enjoy the tactile sensations. "Do you know why most of us flee the so-called heat-death of our universes?" she finally asked, and glanced at Peter out of the corners of her eyes. She raised her eyebrows, but Peter only shrugged.

"It's not as if we couldn't continue to exist, when the last black holes have evaporated and there is only a uniform soup of subatomic particles, spread so far from each other that they couldn't dream that anything else like themselves could exist." She laughed again. "Look at me. I truly have been with you too long – I've fallen into your anthropomorphic trap in describing material things. Anyway, if it was just like that for eternity, we could exist off of the expansion of space-time itself. Lesser beings surely, but there would truly be a level playing field in the end, and it might be a glorious thing to not be so...driven. Unfortunately, a curious thing happens when it's so cold and empty. At the very end, it seems spacetime can only expand so much, and then pop! – everything is gone again. Nothing – true nothing - has won out. It appears to be impossible to reverse space-time expansion – it can be folded and twisted, punched through and distorted, but no one can stop the eventual transition back into nothingness."

She looked around the cabin at them. "It's all rather anticlimactic to you, I know. No big cosmic lightshow at the end, just a simple jump-cut to black. Except there is no black. Only...nothing."

Cheryl cleared her throat, and Darla flicked her eyes over to her. *Yes, yes, I get you can read my mind*, she thought, *but I'm playing your game so let's pretend you can't, okay?* Darla smiled.

"So, if this...*transition* is instantaneous," Cheryl asked, her voice steady, "how do you know it happens? I mean, there would be no one left to tell about it, right?"

Darla's smile grew wider. "Very good." She turned to Peter. "You picked a good one, I think." Darla cocked her head back to Cheryl. "Once colonization of other universes began, the older, dying ones were monitored of course. The hypothesis of the ultimate transition back to a null state was proven as theory when they could no longer be monitored. They were gone, and the multiverse decreased in number."

"Well, that's sad," Cheryl said. "But as they say, them's the breaks, isn't it? Isn't that how things should end?"

"Just so," Darla said. "But tell me, Cheryl, would you feel that way with *your* universe? With your *children?* If a comet smashed into Earth and wiped out your world – something that is a natural, reoccurring phenomenon that ends life throughout the multiverse – would you in turn shrug your shoulders and say 'them's the breaks'?"

Cheryl rolled her eyes, but before she could respond, Darla cut her off.

"Do you know what the single, most basic fact of *life* is?" Darla asked. "It's that it does not want to *end*. Ever." She looked around, grim and angry. "Tooth and claw, swords and bullets, dimensional threads and singularity traps - life, *consciousness*, will fight to the bitter *fucking* end." She looked at Cheryl pointedly. "Do not pretend yours is more special than mine, and I will return the favor."

"Hang around in Darla for a while more, and maybe you'll appreciate how special she is," Carol grumbled. Cheryl grinned. *She caught the swearing*, she thought. *Can Darla be influencing this thing?*

Please, Darla's voice in her head said. *Do you really think that is possible? Would you like her to be a burnt-out husk, your fears realized, just for me to prove a point?*

Cheryl's heart clenched, but she fought to calm herself, and not formulate any sort of response except a fear for her sister.

"So, is our plan workable in your opinion?" Peter asked.

Darla studied him for a moment.

How long does that pause seem to her? wondered Cheryl. *Is a split second to us hours or days or years for her?*

154

You have no idea, the voice in her head answered while she also replied to Peter.

"You know, I do admire your ambition," Darla finally answered. "Truly, for little primates that have no hope of making any sort of mark in the multiverse, you do aim high anyway." She laughed again, genuinely. "You have in your hands a remarkable piece of technology. That you think you control it is amusing. This *ship* knows better, and so do you. But you pretend nonetheless. No, I think your plan is a disaster. Trying to close off a universe could result in a phase transition, and I don't want to be anywhere near you if you try. In fact, I would stop you now, but you know what is coming, and you've flushed me from hiding, so to speak, and I can't leave more of a scent behind than is necessary. A lucky break for you. But, here is something to consider: this ship can set a trap for the future that would be ingenious, and nullifying to any future invaders. Do you have the courage to set it, I wonder?"

"And what would that be, then?" asked Peter.

"Why, the thing that scares you all," Darla answered. "When you see it, when you think of it - the very *concept* of it. *Nothing*. It's your shadow, so use it then. I predict that you have no choice."

"How do we fucking do that?" asked Carol.

"This ship knows, and she is just as terrified of it as any sentient fool should be. She has been there. And while so have I - many times - she was the first to come back and tell us of it - and that may be the most amazing thing that has ever happened."

Cheryl couldn't help but gaze around the cabin, and wonder at what she was inside of. Such simplicity of design. There was no wasted space, without feeling cramped or crowded. Sterile white surroundings, but aesthetics could be added for mood when asked. *And she must be alive?* thought Cheryl. *Even if* Medusa *was just an artificial intelligence, was that not a life, then?*

Well, there may be hope for you, little primate, said Darla's voice in her head. *Keep asking these types of questions. And question what* you *are as well.*

"Do you have a name?" Cheryl blurted without thought.

"A name?" laughed Darla. "And why do I need that?"

155

"You must distinguish yourself from others of your kind, right? If you hide from others, you consider yourself apart from others. How do designate each other?"

"We know who we are, and that is enough. I recognize one from another, and that is enough." Darla paused. "If it is important for you to name me, then name me. But it means nothing to me. I know when you are addressing me, but if it is easier for you to communicate with a name, I understand."

"Jack," Carol said impulsively. "I vote Jack."

"Jack?" Cheryl asked.

"Think about it," Carol replied.

"No doubt a play on words describing my ancient ancestors," Darla said. "It is meaningless to me, but if it helps you discuss me when I am gone – and that will be now, I am afraid – then so be it. I will not be seeing you again to be addressed as such. I will give you a parting gift of advice – a consolation prize for your audacity – and it is this: it is almost certain that counter-measures are already in place against your plan. Surprise will not be on your side." She looked pointedly at Cheryl.

At the risk of fanning the flames of your absurd notions of creation, there is something worse than a Herod in your future, echoed in Cheryl's head. *Escape will not be an option, but determination and courage may reward you.*

"And so goodbye," Darla said.

"Wait!" Cheryl yelped. "*Wait*. What about Darla?"

"And what about her?"

"Can she...can you...let her live?"

"And why would I do that? She is dead, yes? And yet there is a perfectly good Darla right there." Darla, the entity now dubbed Jack, pointed to her distorted mirror image. That Darla fidgeted, and looked down. "Is she not the same? She is to me. You should appreciate what you have."

Oh please, Cheryl thought, and squeezed her eyes shut. *This isn't fair.*

Have you not learned life isn't fair? the voice in her head rang distantly.

Please, you brought her back and animated her. Please don't kill her. Please. Please don't kill her...

And why would I do that? the voice said, and was gone for good.

156

Having grown used to the feeling of concentrated attention, the lack of it made Cheryl feel as if her ears should pop, and she sucked in a deep breath, even though she had had no problems breathing. It was quiet, and so very still. She opened her eyes.

Their little group surrounded a still standing Darla, who was motionless. Cheryl's feet no longer felt like they were pressing against the deck, and the familiar falling feeling in her gut told her gravity had fled with Jack. Cheryl's heart sank. *She's just upright because of the weightlessness*, she thought. Everyone seemed afraid to move, as if any motion might disturb Darla's posture.

And then Darla blinked. Twice. And a third time, her eyes focusing on them. And still they were afraid to move. Cheryl's heart began to hammer out a mad rhythm in her chest, and she was afraid to say anything – afraid she was only seeing something she wanted to see, and then Darla let out a short, sharp bark of a laugh, her chest heaving as she reached up to press a hand between her breasts where a hole used to be.

"Darla?" asked Cheryl tentatively. "Hey. You alright?"

Darla's head turned to her, and she offered a small, crooked smile. "That was a hell of a thing," she said.

"Oh Jesus, she's quoting movies. She's fucking *fine*," Carol said, and Cheryl pushed off and flew at her baby sister, and she and Carol collided with her and they spun around crazily, entangling their arms as they hugged and kissed and cried.

"Are you *you?*" Cheryl heard Carol ask repeatedly. "Are you our Darla?"

"What? Yes, damn it all," Darla replied with a laugh.

As they spun in an eccentric circle over the couches, Cheryl kept getting glimpses of Peter and the other Darla, floating just out of reach. They looked as if they were uncertain of what to do - Peter arms crossed and frowning, Darla fingering a ropy lock of hair. *Well, too bad if they're feeling left out*, she thought. *We've been feeling out of the loop for quite a while now.*

And then they both shimmered and smeared for a moment, and then were back. Cheryl blinked, and waited until they rotated into view again, but they didn't look any different from what she could tell, except now they watched them with a renewed interest, almost studying them as if curious...

You're seeing things that aren't there, she thought. *Not that* that *is anything new...*

She squeezed Darla tighter, then pushed back a bit to study her sister at arms-length. Darla stared back at her, quizzical grin under the perpetually moving blue eyes. Cheryl stroked her face, rubbing her thumbs across her cheeks. "You have no idea how much we missed you," she sobbed, and then pulled her close again. Their tiny orbit pushed them into the cabin wall, and they rebounded out until Carol hooked a foot on one of the couches to stop them. Their momentum arced them down, and they all reached out to grab a couch.

"Couple of things," Darla said, and Cheryl and Carol drew back to study her face.

"We're weightless - so in *space*, yeah?" Darla asked.

"We are orbiting *Mars*," Carol said, and Cheryl watched Darla try and process that information, and then shrug it off to the backburner for now.

"Huh," Darla grunted, then looked around the cabin until her eyes rested on Peter, and then her head cocked back as she took in her doppelganger.

"Oh, there has got to be a hell of a story in this," she laughed. The other Darla smiled.

Darla took a deep breath. "Mars, huh?" she asked. "So, next thing - any particular reason I have to be *naked?*"

Chapter 10

They strolled along the hab-ring with Darla between them, Carol clutching the younger woman's left hand, Cheryl holding her right. *We're afraid to let go of her*, Carol thought. She had lived her life mistrusting the universe, and now that she knew there was more than one, she felt ganged up on. She was desperately afraid her sister would be snatched away from her again. Carol squeezed Darla's hand periodically, and always got a reassuring squeeze back.

Can't help it, she thought. *She's probably getting tired of this, a little weirded out. To her, she wasn't gone at all, but her sisters are clinging to her like needy little leeches.* Still, she squeezed her hand again.

They had walked along the hab-ring twice, letting Darla marvel at the view of Mars, and enjoy the spinning view of the stars as the ring rotated.

"So," Carol announced, feeling it was her duty to inappropriately bring up the subject of her sister's death. "What was it like being dead? Any bright tunnels? Dad beckoning you forth? Pearly gates on clouds?" She lowered her voice conspiratorially, "Surely not pitchforks and flames?" She heard Cheryl snort derisively.

"No," Darla said slowly, "nothing of the sort."

"That's because she was only *mostly* dead," Cheryl offered, and they all laughed.

"Pretty much, I guess," Darla said. "That...thing pushed right through me. It kinda hurt I guess, I got sick to my stomach and I couldn't breathe and I felt like I passed out, then that disorienting feeling you have when you wake up after passing out, only this time I was floating, which added to the fun."

"Well, great," Carol said. "Here we thought we would get the answer to life's greatest mystery, and you dropped the ball."

"Like Cheryl pointed out, I just wasn't dead all the way yet. I suppose whatever he shoved me into kept me from decaying, from brain cells dying. Too many of them, anyway. I'll try and do better next time"

"Oh, Jesus," Carol blurted, and felt guilty for making the joke. "Don't talk like that." Darla squeezed her hand and laughed.

"Hey, I'm feeling superb, actually. Really – maybe it's the low-g environment, but right now I feel like I could take on the whole Empire myself."

"Do you like how your tattoo turned out?" Cheryl asked quietly.

Darla pulled on their hands to stop them, pivoted the toes on her right foot to twist the leg out and stare at her calf. The ink tentacles disappeared into the tops of her footwear. "Yeah, I guess," she answered. "I mean, it's how I imagined it would turn out." She twisted her left foot out and gazed down at her other leg. "Still, it feels like cheating, you know? Not like I earned it?"

Carol nodded, and heard Cheryl grunt in affirmation.

"Ah well, no biggie," Darla added. "The hard part was done the old-fashioned way."

"Right?" Cheryl agreed.

"Plus, we have our matching eyes."

"Yeah we do," Carol said, and they all grinned. Darla tugged on their hands, and they started their walk again.

They walked in silence for a while, Carol almost deliriously happy to have Darla among them again. *And this isn't any couch-injected happy juice*, she thought. *I can't ever recall being this upbeat. Must mean the shit is going to hit the fan soon.* She frowned, then wanted to smack herself for always sliding into the doom and gloom of things. *That may be, but just enjoy this for now, Debbie Downer...*

"So," Cheryl asked after some time, "you have no memory of being...*animated* by this thing? No foggy, dream-like half-suggestions of it at all?"

Darla shook her head. "Nope."

"Well, it said it could take *me* over and I would never know about it," Cheryl said, and that made Carol pull them to a stop.

"Whoa, whoa, *whoa*," she said, startled. "What now? I don't remember it saying that."

She stared at Cheryl, their eyes twitching in their constant dance. Cheryl cocked her head, darted a glance to Darla and then back to Carol.

"Didn't it...*talk* to you in your head?" she whispered.

Carol felt thunderstruck, and a creeping chill ran down her arms and back. "Uh, *no*," she answered. "It most definitely did *not* talk to me inside my head." Darla's head oscillated between them, her eyes wide, lower lip between her teeth. Cheryl blinked rapidly, and tipped her head at Carol.

"Really?" she asked. "No...taunting or telling you to calm down?"

"It *taunted* you?" asked Darla, incredulous.

"Kind of," Cheryl replied. "I was worried that it would...burn you out, you know? Or re-write you?"

Jesus, thought Carol, *I didn't even think of that. I was sure she was just gone for good anyway. Just a marionette for this super-entity to toy with.* Still, she was hoping the thing had been influenced by Darla somehow, hadn't she? There seemed to be *something* that was changing about the thing as it hung out with them... She assumed it was just learning colloquialisms. *Something of that magnitude, though – it would have learned them in a heartbeat, right?* She felt guilty for assuming Darla was a goner, for not thinking beyond what was in front of her. *Shit. I really shouldn't have resisted dad's nerd crap.* Old habits, though – *survival* habits. And another pang of guilt for resenting her sweet brother at times...

"It's kind of disappointing, I think," Darla said in a wistful tone. "You would think something so...advanced, or evolved, would be above taunting us. Studying us dispassionately, okay. Not giving a damn if we're hurt, especially if we're nothing more than algae to them, fair enough. But taunting? It seems petty."

"Maybe the taunting is all part of the studying?" Cheryl offered. "See how we react?"

Darla raised her eyebrows absently. "Maybe," she said.

"Do you think it *felt* through you?" asked Carol, then immediately regretted the question. *Don't try and play on their level*, she thought. *You aren't used to thinking this...creatively.* Still, she honestly wondered what the benefit of utilizing Darla's body actually *was*. To show off? To scare them? Or to learn from it?

Darla eyed her. "I'm guessing you mean more than tactile sensations, then?"

"Well, yeah," Carol replied. "I mean, something so advanced has to understand the benefit of senses - touch, taste, smell, sight. But would feeling an emotional rush of taunting someone be of any use to it?"

"Maybe it was a byproduct," Cheryl said.

"Huh?" Darla asked.

"Maybe once it slipped inside you, *you* kind of controlled how it reacted to a degree. It couldn't help but have an emotional reaction?"

"Are you saying I'm a natural bully, sis?" Darla asked.

Carol bit her lower lip as she watched Cheryl's mouth try to find the right words to clarify, and then Darla grinned devilishly. Cheryl snorted, and slapped playfully at Darla.

"You brat," Cheryl laughed. "What I'm suggesting is if *it* is by nature a bully, if it received some sort of emotional reward from your *body* by its taunting, then maybe that was the benefit? When it comes down to it, we don't know what the heck it *is* – what it's made of. If it's incorporeal and uncaring, maybe a base emotional *feeling* was a unique experience."

"Slumming in my body. Nice."

"Well," Carol said, "Peter did suggest it was kind of a *lesser* god."

Darla tipped her head back and laughed, then tugged her sisters in for a hug.

"Look," she said. "We can hypothesize about this thing and its motivations and go nowhere. Not that it isn't fascinating, but it left me *alive*. Did it utilize any energy to do so? Or since it had me animated already, would it have needed more energy to kill me? I'm going to choose to think that it was an act of kindness, giving me back my life."

Carol frowned. "That may be a dangerous attitude."

Darla nodded. "Maybe. Doesn't mean I'm going to trust it if we ever run into it again – or something else like it. Still, maybe a tiny bit of gratitude would be appreciated by it."

"Couldn't hurt, I guess," Cheryl said.

Carol rolled her eyes and sighed. "You two Pollyannas really haven't got a clue how the universe works, do you? And hey, now we know we have a shit-ton of universes to disappoint us. What *fun!*"

"Now we know why the damned thing didn't want to talk to you in *your* head, Susie Sunshine," muttered Cheryl.

"Yeah, no kidding," Darla said. "Who wants to chat with Emo Ellen?"

"You two just keep it up," Carol intoned. "But don't come crying to me when you get squashed like bugs."

"You ladies ready to head down to the planet?" Peter's voice asked out of thin air, and Carol jumped. *Jesus, I'm tired of that*, she thought sourly.

"Yeah!" Darla yelled.

Cheryl murmured in agreement, and Carol nodded her head.

The tube had dropped down from the ceiling, they entered the transport pod, felt a tug of gravity as the little room zoomed away. The door formed again, and they stepped out into the cabin of the shuttle.

"Grab a couch, if you please," said Peter as he reclined on one of them. The sisters each slipped onto their own couch, and Carol felt the familiar hug as it molded to her. She looked up, and saw the other Darla above in her command couch. *Does she even really do anything up there?* she wondered. *Seriously, does the ship control everything, but just give her something to play around with to make it appear she has some control?*

Carol then felt a little guilty. Who the hell was she to wonder who was being useful or not? She felt pretty inessential herself these days. *And I need to stop thinking of her as the 'other' Darla....*

"Off we go," said the Darla above them as they separated from the *Medusa*. A viewer formed above, giving them a nice view of the ship as they accelerated away from it. Carol studied the *Medusa*. There wasn't any complex detail to try and judge its scale. She knew the hab-ring was pretty large due to their daily trips around it, but from out here there were no windows, hatches, pipes or doo-dads to impress anyone with the of size of it. The featureless ring spun lazily in the shadow of the enormous dome, rotating around the hub. The two minor rings did not spin at all, the smallest of them trailing the long, slender rods.

Soon the ship was left behind, and the view shifted to the red planet below them. *More orange, though?* Carol thought. Her dad used to point it out to her in the night sky occasionally, and *yes*, it clearly had a redder tint than other stars up there, but it kind of bugged her that it was always being called *red*.

You clearly aren't happy if something doesn't annoy you, she thought, and shook her head in mild disgust. *Be happy you have your sister back.* And the thought did, of course, make her grin.

The planet filled the viewer, and they were weightless for a time. Carol watched as the planet turned away from them and stars filled the field of view, and then she was pushed in the back as the shuttle made its powered descent down to the planet. She marveled at the lack of shaking and roaring, the lack of flames licking into view. Just a high gravity punch to the back that the couch absorbed for her, and then a gentle touch down to Mars.

Mars. She was on fucking *Mars*. She tried to find the appropriate amazement to fill her, but found herself empty of it. *Just one more place to try and kill us,* she thought. Darla and Cheryl gave delighted little gasps, and she wrinkled her nose.

"Let's put on some appropriate clothing," Peter said, and Carol thought, *protect me*, and her suit grew and stretched to cover all of her, turning transparent over her face.

"Mine's not working," she heard Darla complain.

"Just think of environmental mode, and it will change," Peter said, sounding mildly irritated.

"I *am*," Darla grumbled.

Carol heard Peter muttering a few commands, then louder, "Suit. *Full protection.*"

"See?" Darla said.

"Darla?" Peter asked. "What's up with her suit?"

God damn it, Carol thought. *This is not going to work – too many Darlas!*

"The suit doesn't think she needs protecting, as far as I can tell," the other Darla said as she dropped down to their level.

Carol sat up, and she could see Peter frowning in bafflement. *This not happen to you guys much?* she thought. *Does your tech always cooperate with you?*

"Just override it, then," he said, and then Darla's suit expanded to cover her entire body. Carol was certain it did so with a reluctant slowness.

Tech billions of years in advance of what we can do, and there are still glitches, Carol thought. *Wonderful...* "I have a question," she asked.

Everyone paused in their preparations to look at her. "Can we pick a nickname for one of the Darlas?" she added.

Peter frowned, and both Darlas raised their eyebrows in thought.

"It would make things easier," said Cheryl quietly.

"I don't think you guys ever had a nickname for me," said their Darla. "Maybe 'Dar' or something like that." She frowned. "I don't recall *any* of us having nicknames." Cheryl shot Carol a look that said, *don't you say it*. Carol grinned.

"My brother, Byron, used to call me 'Jaycee' when I was little," said the other Darla.

Carol flinched at the mention of her brother's name. She saw Cheryl give a start as well, and Darla raised an eyebrow again. *Holy crap*, Carol thought. *This universe-switching bullshit will never stop punching me in the gut, will it?* And all at once, she felt much more charitable to the new Darla.

Peter scowled, opened his mouth, then shook his head. "Of course, it's up to you," he said to his Darla.

She shrugged. "It'll make it easier for them," she said.

"Sorry," said Darla. "We can make up a name for *me*, if you want."

Jaycee laughed. "I don't mind. It...would be nice to hear it again, I think."

"Why 'Jaycee'?" Cheryl asked.

"Don't remember where he picked up the name. I have the feeling it was an affectionate sort of joke that I didn't get. I was only five."

Carol had a myriad of questions for her about Byron. About *her* Byron, she supposed. And then she was dumbstruck when it occurred to her that the Byron that *she* knew could still be alive out there somewhere...

"Awesome," said Peter, and motioned to the tube that had slid up out of the deck. "Shall we?"

They crowded into the transport tube, and it deposited them smoothly onto the surface. The door bloomed open, and they stepped out onto Mars. Darla bounded up high in the lighter gravity, and laughed delightedly as she came down and immediately bounced up again.

"Be careful," Peter admonished. "You go too far and you'll drop right over the escarpment. And it's a long way down."

Carol stepped with deliberate care. They had experienced the lesser-gravity on board the hab-ring, and they all had a chance to get used to it. She suspected Darla was just bouncy with the knowledge that she was on Mars.

Carol looked over to Cheryl, who had a huge grin on her face. *Am I the only one a bit underwhelmed with all of this?* she wondered. *I mean, yay, Mars. But at this point what is left to be excited about?*

"You two been here before?" she asked.

Peter turned to her, and raised an eyebrow as he thought about it. "This *particular* Mars?" he asked. "No, of course not. But one almost exactly like it. A good neutral base."

"So we're the first then?" asked Darla.

"Sure."

"I kind of feel we should be planting a flag, then."

Peter grunted, but said nothing.

Carol turned, and surveyed their surroundings. To the east, the sun was low, and the light was tinged a murky blue. *Weird*, she thought. *Wasn't it always a smoggy-looking amber color?* The terrain tapered down slightly, and fissures and cracks fingered towards the horizon. Behind the shuttle, the ground rose in slight elevation to the hazy sky. She kicked at the ground, and didn't hear any scuffing noise. It was funny, she could hear everyone clearly, no distortion or crackle from a speaker, but there were no ambient sounds to be heard. She suspected the suit communication systems were the answer. The weak atmosphere of Mars wouldn't carry sound very well she knew, but she was astonished at just how low that was. She felt warm and comfortable in her suit – there were no air tanks or any external control features that she could see. It was as form-fitting as a wetsuit, except for the face plate – and even that only bulged out around her mouth so she could talk. And *Jesus*, could she see better? It seemed to be compensating for her poor vision, too.

"Where are we?" Cheryl asked.

"We are on the eastern escarpment, at the base of Olympus Mons," Peter said.

"No shit?" asked Darla brightly. She turned to look behind the shuttle. "I would think we should see it poking up over there. Doesn't it go up above the atmosphere?"

"Yep," Jaycee answered. "But the size of Mars being smaller means the horizon is closer, and the volcano is so big and the grade so gradual, the summit is beyond where we can see."

"Oh, *duh*," muttered Darla with embarrassment.

Jesus, she's out of her field of study but she still knew where to look for the summit? thought Carol. "Just how big *is* this volcano, then?" she asked, trying to conjure up some interest in their surroundings.

"About the size of Arizona?" Darla answered, and Peter and Jaycee both grunted their agreement.

"And why are we here?" Cheryl asked.

"Geography. In this *precise* location, though, the topography is as close to being exact to another Mars as we can get," Peter answered. "And Darla – sorry, *Jaycee* - likes to go there when we have the time."

"So, going from one universe to the next, does the topography have to match *exactly*, or then there's…trouble?" asked Cheryl.

"Yes and no," Peter replied. "The node will compensate – won't let you pop into the middle of a mountain or anything, or in the bottom of an ocean or mid-air."

"Uh, I seem to remember dropping pretty hard out of Vegas," Carol quipped.

"Are you dead?"

Carol snorted.

"The node won't let you move to where it's impossible to. It will compensate here and there in miniscule elevations – nothing *has* to be exact. It's just better in the long run. Speaking of…"

And Carol felt like she was tuning up, ready for adventure, pump primed and circuits open. She heard Darla and Cheryl hiss in surprise.

"Jesus!" Carol barked. "Warn someone next time."

"Sorry," said Peter. "You'll get used to the feeling. It'll feel normal after some time."

"Seems to me we could have gotten used to it all the way to fucking *Mars*," Carol grumbled.

"First of all, we don't want to have the node active all the time if we don't have to, but especially when *Medusa* is going to jump us into another universe."

"Really?" asked Darla. "Why's that?"

There was a pause, and he and Jaycee exchanged a grim look.

"Because there would be no moving into another universe if both the node and *Medusa* were to accidentally jump at the same time. You would be out into the void, non-existence, and then you would be gone for good. Not even your atoms left to mark the spot, so to speak."

Another moment of silence, and then Darla said, "That's bad. Okay. Alright, important safety tip. Thanks, Peter." Cheryl giggled, but Carol couldn't help but feel uneasy about it.

"With all of this advanced tech, wouldn't there be safety features to keep that from happening?" she asked.

"Sure," Peter answered. "Controlling all the nodes. I have you all tethered to our controls. None of you can jump on your own, only Jaycee or I can do that."

"Well, I feel so much safer, then," Carol said.

"Why didn't we just jump in *Medusa*?" asked Darla.

"*Medusa* doesn't like to jump if she doesn't have to. A waste of energy. And because I'm not going to Dar – *Jaycee's* Mars with you right now." Peter turned to Cheryl. "And I'd like you to stay with me, if you would."

Cheryl blinked. "Me?" she said. "Why?"

"I can use your eyesight."

All three of the sisters burst out laughing.

"I can honestly say I never, ever, expected to hear that phrase spoken to me," said Cheryl.

"Any of us," Carol laughed.

"Nevertheless, it's true," he said.

"Seriously?" Carol asked, reluctant to have either of her sisters out of her sight. They had been co-existing with him and Jaycee now for over a month, yet she was still expecting the other shoe to drop, that it was only a matter of time before the axes came out and they were chased around *Medusa* until they were all hacked to bits. *They've had plenty of time to take us out*, she reasoned. *They clearly seem to need us for something, and while it may wind up not being beneficial to our health, I doubt it's to go all Jeffery Dahmer on us.* "Why can't we all stick together?" she added.

"Because where Jaycee wants to go is way more interesting, yet I don't like her going it alone. I'm sure Cheryl would love to see it too, and hopefully we can join you shortly. If you want to stay with us, then do it. I just don't need another tantrum because you hate any sort of tech-talk."

Carol opened her mouth, then shut it and frowned. "Fine," she eventually said. "Just as long as Cheryl's okay with it."

Cheryl shrugged her shoulders. "I guess?" she said.

"Excellent," Peter said. He nodded to Jaycee. "You have control of them. Be *careful*."

"Aren't I always?" she laughed.

Peter raised an eyebrow.

Carol watched as Jaycee raised a hand in a placating gesture. "See you in a bit," she said.

and then she was running along the dunes along the eastern ocean but she was hiding in a cave as the

And then the Mars that she knew was gone and she was standing in the middle of a residential street, in a neighborhood that had seen better days. Strange weedy-looking plants sprouted from cracks in the pavement, and vines with tufts of leaves and odd berries hugged small, sensibly-sized houses. The quality of the light changed dramatically – no longer a dim blue, it was the rosy comfort of a sunrise on Earth.

Her suit had felt like it tightened momentarily, a faint sensation of being pushed against her. She watched Darla swing her arms, palms flat.

"A lot more resistance," Darla said. "Substantial atmosphere, huh?"

"Yes," Jayce answered. "Not breathable on its own. Not *toxic*, we won't get poisoned through our skin so we don't *need* the suit, except it's chilly. But we still need the breathers."

"So leave our suits on. Gotcha," Carol muttered.

"You want to go back with Peter and Cheryl?" asked Jaycee innocently.

"Come on, sis," Darla chided. "Give us some slack to geek-out. We're on *Mars* – and one that has *life* on it."

Carol grunted quietly.

"Not only life, but sentient life," Jaycee said.

169

"Nothing about this blows your mind?" Darla asked. "All my life, you've turned your nose up at any sort of science fiction-based...whatever. Movies, books. It's almost as if it was a personal insult to you. What in the hell gives? What's it take to impress you? Jesus, if we had a car, I'd tell you to go sit in it."

Years of adjusting to a new reality, of expectations not met, of old pain and old guilts, weighed on Carol to the point she almost let herself fall back into her standard defense of a stubborn silence. *How do I express that I associate any sort of sci-fi or fantasy with beatings my brother got?* Nerd crap earned you mocking derision and judgmental condemnation at best.

Going to have to beat the smart out of you, boy...

Carol tipped her head down to Darla and offered a timid smile. "I'm sorry I don't share your enthusiasm, sweetie. I don't mean to piss you off. To be fair, this little adventure started with you getting a hole punched in your chest, and we found out there are a lot of universes that seem out to get us. I'm not entirely comfortable right now. But I'm enjoying being with you, and I'm happy you're excited. I'll try not to complain and be a shit."

Darla's eyes softened, and she grabbed Carol around the waist and gave her a tight squeeze. "I'm sorry," she murmured into Carol's chest. "I...*forget* sometimes, you know."

Yeah, excited-explorer mode doesn't have much patience for nonsense, thought Carol, and she grinned and squeezed her sister back.

A faint trumpet blast sounded up the hill, and Jaycee turned her head towards the noise, grinned, and began to walk towards it. Carol and Darla disentangled themselves as they were motioned to come along.

So, a suburban neighborhood on Mars, thought Carol as they walked up the street, mildly disappointed in the mundaneness of it. *Where are the domes with airlocks and segmented pads for door frames? Shit, stop thinking like that! Be nice!* Still, the houses had a pre-fab sameness about them, even if they weren't futuristic-looking. They were small, spartan, and now seemingly abandoned.

"So there's no colony at all on Mars, now?" Carol asked.

"No," Jaycee answered with a wistful tone. "Last ship left in the late nineties."

"And you were born here, yeah?"

"I was. Conceived in transit. Bit of a scandal at the time. Mom and dad blamed a faulty condom or something." Darla laughed, and Carol remembered her parents' constant affection, to the chagrin of their children. Well, her *second* set of parents, anyways. If these Mars-bound mom and dad were anything like *hers*, it was no wonder this version of Darla was inevitable.

And that in and of itself is pretty interesting, thought Carol. *If my parents hadn't had sex when they did that resulted in me - say a day later, or earlier, or whenever, I wouldn't be who I am – I wouldn't be me. Would I? Could I have been a boy? Shorter? Taller? Nicer...* She frowned. *And what does that say about our fate? Was Darla inevitable in more ways than just her parents' inability to keep their hands off each other?* Carol wasn't sure what to make of that.

"Obviously, space exploration developed much more rapidly in your universe than ours," Darla stated.

"Oh yeah. I mean, it was assumed that Mars had something living on it since its first spectroscopic analysis. There was much more interest and motivation for the public to support exploration when it was discovered Mars not only supported life, but might be able to support us as well. When Mars 1 sent back images of – "

"Wait, what?" Darla interrupted. "Mars 1? The *Soviet* Mars 1?"

"Yeah..." Jaycee said.

"*Not* Mariner 4?"

"No, Mars 1 for sure."

"Interesting," Darla murmured. "Anyhow, sorry. Go on."

"Well, long story short, the world went Mars crazy," Jaycee laughed. "International cooperation helped spur things along. People were devouring Barsoom and Bradbury, maybe with romantic notions of colonization. By 1980, we had our first permanent colony, and by the late eighties, regular trips had been established, even tourism if you could afford it. Mars wasn't self-sufficient by the time our family arrived there, but it was on its way."

"So what went wrong, then?" Carol asked.

"People tended to go mad," Jaycee said simply.

"Psychosis?"

171

"Oh yeah. Well, only a fraction of the population at first, but by the time Mars was abandoned, almost a third of it had been affected in some form. But there was a substantial amount of pretty paranoid people at one time. My mom killed my dad, believing he was in love with some aliens."

"Holy shit," Darla said.

"Yeah. They were both biologists, and the gas giants took a liking to him, and not her. No telling why, it just was. They liked me too. One family even tracked me down while I was in foster care."

They walked in silence for a while. Finally, Darla asked, "Did they ever figure out the cause of the...epidemic?"

"No," Jaycee sighed. "A lot of hypothesis, no confirmed theory. People didn't seem to be any better once they left, either. Apparently, my mother died in an asylum not long after returning to Earth. A crushed spirit in more ways than one, I imagine."

Carol tried to imagine her bright and mischievous mother in an asylum, and couldn't do it.

"Didn't help that she thought all of her children were dead too, I suppose," Jaycee added.

"Oh, geeze," Carol said. "That is awful. Just...how did..."

They crested the slope to a level area, and Jaycee pointed ahead. "Pretty much, *that*," she said.

In front of them, for roughly two-hundred yards, there was a blast-zone where no house or tree stood. To the east, a huge section of a wall bordering the top of a canyon was missing. New plants grew among the ruins, but it was hard to miss that a disaster had occurred here years ago.

"What the heck happened?" asked Darla. "Did a ship crash?"

Jaycee shook her head. "One of the gas giants – an elderly, massive one - caught fire and exploded."

"Holy shit!" Carol said.

"Did that happen a lot?" asked Darla, incredulous.

"No," Jaycee said, "not really. They have a coating of flame retardant that works remarkably well. But they get old, or diseased, and can dry out. Rippers usually can take them down by then, but this one got tangled up in the electrified wires running across the perimeter wall. Boom."

"Holy shit," Carol repeated, only softer.

"Yeah," said Jaycee. "I saw it happen. Well, Peter grabbed me before it blew. But I saw it catch fire. It was…yeah."

"How long ago…?" Darla let her question trail off.

Jaycee turned to her. "I was five," she said simply.

They stopped at a jumble of torn pavement and debris. Chunks of perimeter wall, housing, and blasted trees entwined with leafy groundcover. "Right about here was my home – my foster home, actually. Ground zero." She cocked her head. "Listen," she whispered.

Carol held her breath and strained to hear anything out of the ordinary. Considering she was on Mars, she wasn't sure what that would be. A faint squeal issued from below, beyond the blasted perimeter wall. Rustling and thrashing noises added themselves to the ambience of the early morning scene.

Jaycee curled her tongue and blew out a long sharp whistle. The rustling noises stopped, and Jaycee whistled again. A pause, and then a faint answering whistle, then a deep thrum with a sharp trumpet blast. Jaycee clapped her hands delightedly.

The sound of brush bending and snapping back grew closer, punctuated with occasional squeals and deep ululations. A small dome, bright pink, momentarily popped into view before a sharp whistle drew it away. A much bigger dome appeared above the foliage, and then rose to reveal its inverted teardrop bag, iridescent reds, pinks, and lavenders sparkling in the morning light. Up it rose, fully twenty feet high, until the maroon tentacles trailing reached up to grasp at the debris field and pull itself along. The gas giant pushed up, and then its long, whip-like tentacle grasped a fallen tree to anchor itself. The Martian twisted back and forth in the warm sunlight, its fin-like sail flapping restlessly. Carol could see pale splotches sprayed along its bag, and wondered if it had been wounded at one time.

Jaycee laughed, and clapped her hands again. "Hi baby," she called. "Hello, my old friend! I'm back!" Jaycee bounced up and down on the balls of her feet, and pulled out a small plastic bag from her suit. Carol remembered Peter reaching into his shirt to pluck out those silvery spheres when Darla was killed, and wondered just how special these damn suits were…

The giant ceased its twisting motion, and leaned towards Jaycee. It gave one sharp piercing whistle, and pulled itself towards them. A bright pink juvenile drifted up and over the edge of the escarpment, and began to make its way to them as well.

I suppose it would be bad manners to jack rabbit the hell out of here, thought Carol. *Jesus, look at Darla. Like she's won the Goddamn lottery…*

A few other gas giants rose over the edge of the cliff, but after a momentary observation – at least, that's what Carol interpreted their stationary posture to be – they began to strip berries off of trees and shrubs.

The adult Martian – again, what Carol *assumed* was an adult – reached Jaycee and stretched out a slender tip of a tentacle towards her. The young woman retracted the left sleeve of her suit up past her elbow, and the tentacle slipped around her wrist.

"Hi," whispered Jaycee, her voice husky. "How's my friend? Oh, how I've missed you." Tears glistened in her eyes. Carol was amazed at how gentle the Martian was, how delicate and precise the gestures of its tentacles.

"Can…can I…?" Darla breathed, and Jaycee turned to them, waving the plastic bag, motioning them to her.

"You two want to feed them?" Jaycee asked.

"Oh, hell yes," Darla said.

"I'm good," Carol answered, and felt foolish.

"I'm just letting you know, if you don't…*open up* to them now, you more than likely won't get another chance."

"I'm sorry," Carol replied. "I don't mean to insult them or anything. But…" She trailed off. She remembered the video she saw on board *Medusa*, the whip-crack of a tentacle and the ripper's appendage spinning away. And the sight of this colossal alien hovering above her was quite disorienting.

"I don't know if they're capable of being insulted," Jaycee said, as she shook berries out into Darla's cupped hands. "*Maybe*. I think they have a sense of humor, but of course that might just be me projecting it on to them. There's so much about them we never got a chance to understand. Maybe they respect our boundaries, sense if someone is reluctant to interact with them. But if you are, then that's it. You don't get another shot. My dad was the first person to be able to touch them, and I was the second. My sisters…" She paused and looked shyly at both of them, and then away. "Well, they never got another chance. Or my mom."

"Well, *I'm* not missing out," Darla declared, and held up her berry-filled hands towards the giant. A tentacle curled down and plucked out a few of the misshapen orbs, and drew them up into center of the cluster of tentacles. Darla giggled with delight. Another ropy appendage stretched out to her, but rather than grasp for some more food, it stroked at her covered forearm.

"It wants to touch your skin," Jaycee remarked.

Darla retracted her suit up to her shoulders, and Carol hissed in dismay.

"Hush," Darla breathed, and Carol fought the urge to roll her eyes. *Goddamnit, goddamnit,* goddamnit, she thought.

"It's not like they haven't been studied," Jaycee said in a reassuring tone. "These are known risks. Their touch isn't dangerous – they don't appear to be venomous, and the only non-plant food they ingest are tiny insect-like animals. Inspection of their waste showed that they weren't digested. Some hardy aphid-like critters could make it through alive, seemingly."

"No kidding?" Darla asked. A tentacle roamed up and down her arm, as if probing or measuring. "*G* factor?"

"How smart are they? As you well know, it's all relative. But comparatively? Pretty smart, I think. This one," Jaycee curled her hand around the tentacle grasping her wrist and gave an affectionate tug, "would bring me gifts. Got me into some trouble, didn't you?" A mellow rumble issued from above, and Jaycee turned to them with a delighted smile.

Holy cow, thought Carol. *How often did we see that smile on Darla's face when we poked around at Bird Rock or Scripps?*

"Of course, there's no way of knowing what that was in response to. It's very unlikely she understood what I referenced, but she may…*sense* my affection? And my interpretation is she returns it. It may not be on the level of humans and dogs, but heck, she doesn't appear to hate me. She remembers me – they seem to remember a lot. Initial studies indicated problem-solving abilities, and some tool use. But, the bottom line was we didn't get a chance to study them much. They shunned contact with colonists for a long time. We never even had a carcass to study. After

175

establishing the colony – landing with a loud thud of a footprint, fighting off rippers and making things habitable and inviting for future colonists, *then* it was decided how much of an impact was being made on the planet, and how much was going to be tolerated by those back on Earth, and the colonists."

The giant seemed absorbed with running its tentacles up and down the two women's arms. It would pause, then inch along their skin as if fascinated. The little gas giant drifted up to snag the bag of berries out of Jaycee's hand. A deafening blast issued from the adult, but the baby darted away, and all three of the women laughed.

Despite her initial reluctance, Carol was intrigued by the interaction. *These things are living beings, individualistic and with desires,* she thought. *Very* alien *desires, but so very* alive.

"She seems extremely interested in our arms," Darla laughed.

"Yeah, not sure what's going on here," Jaycee said, puzzled. The giant tugged gently at her arm until Jaycee had to stumble over next to Darla. "What's got you bothered, big girl? Huh?"

"You keep referring to her as a she," Carol said. "Male and female sexes – is it a universal constant for life?"

"Oh, not by any means," Jaycee answered. "And honestly, referring to her as female is purely my projection. For all I know, they are asexual. Again, not a lot of time to study them. But I've thought of her as female all these years, and I ain't stopping now."

"Fair enough," Carol laughed.

The giant tugged Jaycee's and Darla's arms up next to each other, and then inched a tendril tip up and down, as if measuring. "What in the world?" Jaycee laughed. "This is the oddest thing I've ever seen her do."

"Do you think she knows that –" Carol blurted, and shut her mouth abruptly. *Don't be stupid! Jesus!* she thought.

"Knows what?" Darla asked. Jaycee looked at her, that wide-eyed, level gaze that was innocent and judgmental all at once. *You missed my birthday, Carol.*

"Just that," Carol mumbled, "maybe she can tell you're both...the same? Kinda? Or maybe she thinks you're twins, and wonders why one's taller?

Maybe not. Would they have twins? Probably not, right? I don't know. What *do* I know? Clearly nothing. I'm shutting up now." *Goddamnit.*

Jaycee and Darla both stared at her, and Carol felt the insides of her ears warming up. The two women turned their attention to each other. "Huh," they said simultaneously, then peered up at the Martian hanging above them.

"Can she...*taste* our DNA?" Darla asked

"Wouldn't that be something?" laughed Jaycee.

"Can she see us? I see nothing clearly defined as eyes."

"They never figured that out," Jaycee said. "A lot of hypothesis, nothing concrete."

"You seem to remember quite a lot for being taken away when you were five," Carol said, relieved that she wasn't the laughing stock she thought she was going to be.

"*Medusa* was able to access all of the colony records. I've had a lot of time to study up on them."

A neon purple tentacle grasped Carol's arm and tugged it up.

"Jesus!" she blurted. The baby gas giant floated above her, bobbing gently. Its tentacle twisted and inched along her arm, as if in a mimicry of exploration like its mother.

"Let it touch your skin, sis," Darla suggested. "Seriously, it feels weird."

"Not a selling point," Carol panted.

"For once in your life, Carol, dare to do something different."

Carol closed her eyes, and silently cursed her sister. Cursed her curiosity, cursed her bravery, cursed her inexorable insistence. "I really hate you, you stupid brat," she muttered, and thought, *short sleeves.* The suit's arms retracted up to the middle of her biceps, and the cool Martian air immediately made her skin grow goose bumps. The baby gas giant's tentacle tightened around her forearm, feeling slippery one moment, and then a sticky adhesive bond gripped her skin.

Carol opened her eyes, and saw color flashing along the tentacle. "Is this like...like what an octopus has?" she asked.

"Chromatophores?" Darla responded.

"Sure."

Darla looked to Jaycee, who shrugged. "Uncertain if they're similar. Has to be a reason they do this, which indicates visual receptors of some kind, right? The leading hypothesis of the day was that they were covered with eyes, their *skin* was one big eye. So to speak."

Carol watched bright pinks and lavenders flash along the appendage as it stroked her skin. "Oh, it's *warm*. I didn't expect it to be warm."

"Thought it was going to be cold and slimy?" Darla laughed.

"Well, yeah."

The baby explored her arm with one tentacle, dipped into the berry bag occasionally with another and fed itself. It reached into the bag with another arm and plucked a berry, then shoved it up against Carol's faceplate.

"Um," Carol said, "no thank you."

"Don't be rude, sis," Darla chided.

"They love to share," laughed Jaycee.

"Well, it's not like I can eat it through my mask, now can I?"

"Sure you can," Jaycee said brightly. "Just allow it through."

"No thank you, I – oh! Okay...." She could not un-think the command, and the berry dropped into her mouth. It had a pungent, bitter taste.

"Oh no," Jaycee laughed. "Didn't think you would do it. Do *not* eat that. One won't kill you, but you'll wish it had by the time you're done bloating and shitting your guts out."

Carol spat it out, and the berry lodged under her chin. *Water* she, thought, and a tiny spout jetted the liquid into her mouth. She swished it around and spat.

"Lovely," she mumbled. "You're a goddamned comedian, Jaycee."

The water was absorbed by the suit, Carol was relieved to discover. She tipped her head and the berry rolled up onto the faceplate. *Get the hell out*, she thought, and the berry dropped down and into the ground cover.

The little giant pulled itself along, tugging at tough-looking plants that Carol couldn't decide if they had leaves or flowers. The sun was higher, and she could feel its warmth on her arms. The baby still had a firm grip on her.

"I guess we're going for a walk?" Carol called.

The infant led her into the tangled debris field, towards a small tree stuffed with the berries it seemed to crave.

"You guys have to eat a lot of those?" she asked. "They help keep you buoyant?"

The Martian discarded the empty bag, and continued along. Carol stumbled and bounced in the lower gravity as the little giant picked up its pace. Its parent issued a rumbling warning, and the baby responded with a shrill whistle, but continued to the tree.

"Your momma's not liking you wandering too far, little one," Carol lectured, but it was focused on the tree, and when they reached it, the little giant began to feast, low rumbles rippling across it's bag.

Carol turned to look back, the two Darla's and the parent Martian roughly fifty yards away now. Her faceplate darkened in the glare of the sun, and then a nightmare rose before her, standing high on two hind legs, it's scythe-like forearms wide apart. Carol yelped, and one of the blades came down with astonishing speed and pinned the little giant's long, whip-like tentacle to a fallen tree. Carol yelled again, and the infant released a sharp, warbling whistle. Waste voided from sphincters as the baby giant tried to flee, but the ripper had its anchor tentacle pinned, and Carol weighed it down too. It let her go, but it was only able to rise another few feet before bobbing back down.

An enormous trumpet blast distorted the air, and answering calls drifted in from beyond the edge of the escarpment. The ripper drew back its other arm, and Carol shouted, jumping in between the baby and the monster. Her heart hammered in her chest.

"You get the hell out of here!" she shouted. "Go! Get out of here!" *Fuck fuck fucking fuck, I am so dead...*

The ripper paused, its deadly arm wavering as if it were assessing this unknown threat. It stretched up higher on its legs, oddly-jointed mandibles waving under its pickaxe-shaped head.

And then Darla arrowed in and hit it broadside, knocking it off its feet. The ripper quickly swung its deadly arm at Darla, who was knocked into the brush behind it. The little gas giant, now released, rose higher, whistling shrilly. Carol risked a look towards its mother, whose tentacles were coiling and grasping in the brush to propel it along. The ripper regained its feet, again spreading its arms wide, and tilted its head up to the little giant. *Oh no you fucking don't*, thought Carol, and she darted in and grabbed the twitching mandibles in both hands and twisted, doing her best to snap off the bony digits. The Martian shrieked and shook its head, trying to dislodge her. Carol's ears rang with the piercing scream. She was surprised the odor of the thing was rather sweet, not dank and rotten like she expected.

The sharp blades for arms could not bend in to reach her, but somewhere up under the mandibles where the shrieking came from, she could also hear a grinding and clacking. Then Darla popped up from under it, and began to hammer away at the head with an astonishing flurry of punches. Its scythes could reach *her*, however, and its right arm snagged into Darla to hurl her away again. Carol screamed in fury, swung her feet up to kick savagely into its underbelly. She heard what sounded like a whip cracking, and from her upside-down perspective she could see the little one swinging its anchor tentacle repeatedly at the ripper. One massive blade of an arm swung at the infant, but *Jesus*, Darla was there *again*, intercepting the blow and being driven down against the fallen tree. Carol was certain that the scythe would punch right through her, but Darla pushed up and twisted, and she heard a brutal *snap*, and then the ripper really *did* shriek, and immediately had no interest in the infant gas giant, Darla, or Carol.

The ripper began to backpedal, and Carol felt the digits pop as if breaking under her grip, so she decided to let it go. She gave one more savage twist, then jumped free. The Martian turned, gave a mighty leap, and then was almost torn in half from the blow of the adult gas giant's anchor tentacle. The ripper dropped into the debris field, it's left leg kicking reflexively in the morning light.

"Holy crap," Jaycee called from above. Carol looked up, and saw the young woman entwined in a tentacle of the adult. "She wouldn't let me go," she added, apologetically.

Carol waved, and she began to shake a little from the adrenaline rush. Jaycee dropped down to her as the adult enveloped her baby, reassuring rumbles issued from it as tentacles explored every inch of the infant.

"You okay, Carol?" Jaycee asked.

Carol nodded, and managed a timid smile. Darla moved to them, and looked Carol over, hands running over her, turning her around searching for wounds.

"I'm fine," Carol panted, and grabbed Darla by the wrists. "It's *you* who should be beat to shit." Darla wasn't even breathing hard. She stared up into Carol's eyes, unflinching, and a grin spread across her face.

"That just happened?" she asked. "Did we just fight an alien?"

Carol let out a short bark of a laugh. "I think *you* did."

Darla waved dismissively, and studied the ripper as its kicks grew fewer. "Too bad it had to die," she said wistfully.

Carol looked for any sign of trauma on her sister, but could see nothing. The suit would heal quickly she knew, but even if it couldn't be cut, Darla should at least have some broken bones.

You should be shattered, she thought. *What in the hell did Jack do to you?*

Chapter 11

So, Peter," Cheryl asked. "What happened to your scars?"

Peter gave a tight smile and dipped his head down momentarily. He looked up, and said, "Noticed that, did you?"

Cheryl said nothing.

"Well, what's your theory?" he asked.

"That you're not the Peter we've been dealing with. Or the Darla, either, I'm guessing."

Peter stared out at the arid wasteland of Mars, the blueish tint of the sunrise beginning to fade into the pale amber haze familiar from the fantastic images sent back from tiny little robots crawling over the surface of the planet. *They're here right now*, Cheryl thought. *I'm on the planet with the rovers now, and other machines, some dead or dormant. And I'm still more proud of how they got here than we just did...*

"Hey," she blurted. "Are we being seen by the orbiter?"

"Unlikely," he answered. "I mean, yeah, it's entirely possible we could show up in an image. But we won't be here long enough to be caught. But if so, we still have bigger worries than making NASA scratch their heads and giving fuel to conspiracy theorists."

Ah yes, the 'big picture', she thought. *And apparently where we have no impact as a species.* The thought irked her. Not that humans wouldn't be a player in the great game – whatever that was – but that the notion was dismissive of them. *That we don't evolve into some universe-spanning entity makes our existence meaningless? Who freaking cares? I'd rather we learned to tolerate and love each other and go extinct, less than an imaginary blip on the cosmic radar, than make a disturbing impact.*

"So, who are you, then?" she asked. "I guess I should ask *why*, as well? Why are you not the Peter that got us out here?"

He waited so long to reply that Cheryl resisted the urge to prompt him. She wasn't sure if the more thoughtful version was better than the 'we-gotta-go-or-we're-all-dead' one.

"You have to understand," he finally answered, "that much of what is going on may be incomprehensible to us. Our minds can't wrap themselves around it. Maybe a rudimentary concept can be accepted, the bare bones of it all, but the physics of it – how we jump from universe to universe – we can't understand. At least I can't, and *Medusa* doesn't seem to be able to explain it to us. And really, that's who we are at the mercy of. *Medusa*. I'm convinced she has been playing a very, *very* long game, and we are the game pieces."

"*We* as in you, me, my sisters?" asked Cheryl. "Or *we* as in the human race?"

"Seems pretty egotistical to say the me and you answer, doesn't it? But…"

"Seriously?"

"Here's the thing – you're only looking at it from your perspective, not an unimaginable amount of Cheryls in countless universes. Looked at that way, you're back to not being very special."

"Thanks."

"Come on, you may have a belief in a divine creator, but I think you're humble and don't need to feel like you're a special flower in the field. You're content that you're an animal like the rest of us."

Cheryl's notion of heaven had never been of pearly gates and sitting around on clouds with long-lost loved ones, happy as little lambs. Heaven was being one with God. Going home. Heaven was knowing that there was no such thing as futility in the end. She shook her head, and looked at Peter.

"I *accept* that I'm a mere animal, with a hope that I have something worthy to offer God someday."

"Okay, okay. Honestly, I have no desire to get into that mess. Again."

Cheryl smiled. "So who are you, Peter? And why are we dealing with you now?"

Peter exhaled in a long, drawn out sigh, then chuckled. "I'm family – family that might have been. And to me, *you* are family that might have been. Jesus, I don't need to get into *that* mess, either…"

"Kind of unfair to drag my sisters and me in to this and then act as if it's too much trouble to keep us informed."

"And I've been dragged in to this since I was a kid. Don't lecture me on what you think is fair."

"Damn it all, why are you a different Peter? Can you just answer *that*, for God's sake?"

"Because the other Peter needed to be kept in the dark about what *Medusa's* plans really are, so the entity here – *Jack,* you named it – couldn't find out about them." He shook his head. "Not sure if that worked…"

Cheryl sighed, and kicked at the Martian dust. No sound gave her action away, which irritated her, and she dug her foot in savagely, causing a cloud to billow up to her knees. It shimmered oddly, with tiny silver specks seeming to pop into and out of existence. *Huh.*

"Okay," she asked. "What didn't we want it to know?"

Peter watched the cloud of dust dissipate, then looked up to Cheryl. "It's not so much what we didn't want it to *know*. I think what we wanted was to try and infect it."

"Infect it?"

"Yep."

"With what?" Cheryl sighed.

"Basically, us. A little bit of being human."

"Okay… So, did we?"

"Maybe? I can say this is as far along as we've ever been. *Medusa* switched us out with the other team, so…" Peter shrugged.

"And so what happened to *them*, then?"

"I would hope the poor bastards get some rest, finally. But they've been driven so much, pushed to find the right combination of us, I'm not sure it's in their nature to relax."

"Well, hell, shove them into the couches and tranquilize them up the wazoo like you do us."

Peter snorted. "You had a busted ankle, your sister had just been killed, and you were onboard a spaceship all within a half-hour of meeting them. Your sister was a danger to herself under a high-g situation."

Cheryl raised her hands in surrender, and let her gaze roam along the gentle slope of the volcano. Surprisingly, the vista had an almost claustrophobic feel to her, even though the space was wide open. She chalked it up to the closer horizon and her poor vision. Occasionally, as the wind pushed dust around, the ground appeared to shimmer with a silvery tint. *Weird.* She wondered if her suit was working properly, feeding her the air she needed. Or was her prolonged exposure to lower gravity affecting her already limited eyesight? She seemed to remember reading that astronauts aboard the International Space Station had vision problems after prolonged exposure to a weightless environment – the male ones, anyway. Wasn't *that* a curious thing? She turned back to Peter.

"Okay, let's start again," she said. "Why no scars?"

Peter smiled tightly. "Because I'm not the 'action hero' of the story. The other Peter is." Before Cheryl could finish her sigh, he waved it off. "Look, he has been pushed to the point of recklessness. It was his idea to drop Carol into your world, just kind of an impulsive thing. He was just a kid. Likewise, when he rescued Darla, he cut it too close while trying to save Byron as well. He and that Darla got burned. The Darla *I* rescued – *Jaycee*... Well, I was more pragmatic."

"What was she in need of rescuing from?"

"An exploding Martian, one of the gas giants."

"Holy cow."

"Yep. Leveled some houses. Your counterparts – you, Carol, and Byron were obliterated, along with your foster parents."

"Well, that's just a cheery thought."

"Well, think about this – you and your sisters should be dead in Vegas."

"Okay..." Cheryl frowned. *Thanks, I guess?* she thought. Then a thought struck her. "So, let me ask this – were *you* rescued from some disaster too?"

Peter grinned. "Our extended family – and when I mean extended, boy do I mean *extended* – is a long line of rescues."

Holy crap, is Carol right? she thought. *Is the universe out to get us?* She closed her eyes and took a deep breath. As absurd and paranoid as the idea sounded, she couldn't help but feel a bit uneasy. She opened her eyes and gave a nervous chuckle. "I'm not sure I like the sound of that," she said.

"Yeah, hard not to take it personally," Peter laughed. "But, it may not be anything other than plain old fate."

"Seriously? I would think that notion would be the domain of superstitious deists like me."

Peter rolled his eyes. "Does it always have to be a fight with you?" He waved at her before she could respond. "Can we not get sidetracked?"

She raised her eyebrows and shrugged at him.

"There is a theory that the multiverse was born all at once, even though there is a so-called time-shift to them. An extension to this theory is that *all* the multiverses were *exactly* the same, until the massive entities screwed things up by universe jumping. Not sure I buy into that part, but who knows? It is clear that the multiverse has a beginning and will have an end, the big bang to the heat death, and then it will be gone. All of them. And not one advanced civilization – a massive entity – will stop it from happening."

"So, cutting to the chase, are you suggesting that if I've died a certain way in other universes, I'm fated to die that way in *most* of them?" Cheryl asked.

"Oh, it's not that simple. Maybe? But *also*, maybe in a particular universe you get wind of the idea that you're supposed to die in Vegas, and you say, screw *that*, I'm out, I don't think the universe is going to track you down to make sure the job's finished."

"So no *Final Destination* scenario. Good to know."

"Sure. Look, there is a *staggering* number of universes – and that's only the ones that are left. If they were all the same once, so many have changed since the big bang that it's likely there are many universes where you live a healthy and happy life. And ones that are far worse than what you're enduring now. So *maybe*, it only appears to us that we're fated to die in some disaster. And we have to factor in *Medusa's* game plan in all of this."

"And that is?"

"That's she's playing all of us – meaning she's choosing particular versions of us for a reason. Maybe it's like picking for some sort of all-star lineup. Something is finally coming to a head, I think."

"And no idea of what it is?"

"I think she's trying to save the last universes from invasion."

"Okay, so about that – why haven't these entities just gone *all* the way back to the very last one, since, as you say – *shit*, or the *other* Peter said – we're basically running out of universes? It would give them that much longer life, right?"

"Well, simply put, they did. The youngest universes are a hell-scape of twisted spacetime traps and monstrous entities. They've literally changed laws of physics in their battles for dominance. Life as we know it does not exist in them. Any newer entity trying to jump to those universes is devoured immediately. So, you see another sense of urgency to the problem – the multiverse is a candle burning at both ends."

"And we're somewhere in the middle?"

"Hard for me to say. In between, sure."

Cheryl pursed her lips. *This is just great*, she thought. *Really. Life is just eat or be eaten? That's still the driving force, even when advanced beyond our flesh-fueled desires?*

"Did the other Peter *really* visit a 'zombie apocalypse' universe?" she asked abruptly.

"He's *from* one."

"How… I mean, come *on*."

Peter shrugged. "You have to admit, it explains his hurry-it-up attitude. I can't explain the science behind corpse reanimation. I try and not blame every damn thing on massive entities, but I would not be surprised if those bastards are behind zombies as well. The universes may have started on equal footing, but who knows what happened once all the universe-jumping started? Weird shit goes on in some of them."

"Well, that's just awesome."

"Look, hungry dead people are *pretty* far down the list on what keeps me up at night. We have far bigger worries."

"I keep hearing that."

Peter sighed, closed his eyes, took a deep breath, and exhaled it slowly. "It is always a fucking battle," he murmured, and Cheryl was certain it was directed to himself. "Just once, it would be nice to get some help from the new ones without getting shit flipped at me." He turned to her, opened his eyes, and gave her a small, polite smile. "I wish I could say I'm sorry you're in this mess and really, truly mean it. But the truth is, you're just one more game piece – like me." He laughed. "I'm amazed I haven't been swapped out all these years. Hell, maybe I *have* been, and this is my version of busy work, and maybe the Peter you first met is the main player. But you know what? All I know is this life, and so I keep at it. It *is* too bad you've been taken from your family. But you got the privilege of *having* one, and maybe even make their universe a safer place. Regardless, you would be dead now if we hadn't snatched you. Consider that a fucking bonus and maybe cool the attitude?"

Cheryl stared him in the eyes, unflinching. "I wish I could say I'm sorry you're a jaded asshole who can barely take the time to explain anything to us. Don't whine to me about attitude. If this is all you know, then do your damned job. I don't care how repetitive this is to you. Maybe you're not doing it right, then?"

They stood there, on Mars, glaring at each other, in an unnerving silence. Even the faint wisp of moving atmosphere – Cheryl couldn't call it wind – made no sound as it pushed dust around. Again, she caught a flickering shimmer of silver particles.

"Okay, what the hell is up with the silver-flashing stuff?" she asked, exasperated. "I have never heard of this phenomenon. Is it just the way light...reflects in the thin atmosphere? Am I getting enough oxygen to my brain? I don't feel faint or anything – *what?*"

Peter was grinning. "Do you remember me telling you I can use your eyesight?"

"Uh, yeah?"

"What you're seeing is kind of an...artifact, left over from the entity – *Jack* - that hid here."

Cheryl raised an eyebrow.

"Consider it kind of like a pearl in an oyster. Its presence in this universe is like the grain of sand irritating the oyster. The silver 'stuff' you see is the byproduct of it. And it is valuable."

"Okay...?"

Peter bent to pick up a fistful of sand, and let it fall back to the ground. Cheryl caught occasional bright sparkling flashes in the slow-motion cascade.

"You see any more?" he asked.

"Yes," Cheryl replied.

"Awesome, that's what we want."

"Yay?"

"Damn right, yay. We were hoping that since he only recently left, we would hit the motherlode."

"Okay, wait," Cheryl said, frowning. "I'm guessing you don't see it?"

"I do not. I *have* seen it, though, but don't here."

"Why is that?"

"Not my universe. My poor vision is attuned to my own universe."

"Wait, you have crappy eyesight as well?"

"Told you, I'm family that never was."

Cheryl chewed on her lower lip, and watched for the occasional gleam of silver. When she saw it, it had the sharp, hyper-real quality of the black nothingness they had seen back on Earth.

"Okay, let me ask you *this*," she said abruptly. "Can people with normal, or above average eyesight, *see* this?"

Peter laughed. "Oh, there are people with crappy eyesight that can't see this. Your – *our* – eyesight is a special kind of crappy, though. You might even say we were made for seeing things others can't."

Cheryl stood silently for a moment, and then kicked her legs out and let herself fall gently to the ground. A cloud of dust billowed up around her, and she drew her knees up to her chest. The dust cloud flashed brightly, and she took a swipe at it, then wrapped her arms around her knees. Peter squatted down next to her, staring out over the escarpment. He picked up a fistful of Martian soil again, and let it trickle slowly to the ground.

"Look at it this way," he said softly. "If you want to feel unique, we have a gift that no one outside the family has. Yes, it's a certifiable condition – there was even albinism in the family a generation or two back. But feeling like we're a machined cog in the great big wheel is a small price to pay if we save the universe. Right?"

Cheryl snorted. "Hyperbole, much?"

"I can say this in all seriousness, not at all. We very well might save the universe – what's left of the multiverse. And if *not* us, others *like* us."

"It just seems rather unlikely that such a big job falls to someone as random as me. Us. Our family. No one of note, historically."

"Really? Why should that make a difference? Would you feel better knowing there are versions of us that are famous? Powerful? And they would be worthless for this task, I suspect."

Peter was quiet for a moment, then smiled. "It would be wonderful to be blissfully ignorant of all this, for sure. To be born and die without even knowing what the hell was going on. Shit, the rest of humanity knows *nothing*. Most species in the universe at our level know *nothing*. Many of the massive entities are only now learning of it, at least in these younger universes."

Cheryl waved a hand listlessly in surrender. "Okay, fine," she said. "It falls on our shoulders. Why? Why do I get to see with *special* eyes? What good is it?"

"That you're essentially a living sensor? A tool? I have theories, and Jack gave us a clue that reinforces it to me."

Cheryl's neck tingled, and she was beginning to feel restless, and a bit nervous. "Okay," she muttered, "Lay it on me."

"Why it's useful that you can see the artifacts caused by the presence of Jack is that Medusa collects the stuff. Like I said, it appears the universe – any universe, for that matter – doesn't like visitors from another one. In fact, *I'm* causing artifacts right now, on a much smaller scale. My spacetime displacement isn't that big of a deal, I guess. Your sisters are doing it now, too, where they are. Again, it's almost unmeasurable on the grand scale of things. And that's why I think we're being used. Most of the time, we're beneath the notice of the massive entities. *Medusa* catches their attention, but in a quaint, 'there's that darling probe' sort of way. Jack basically equates *us* on the level of a slime mold, but seemed to have some respect for *Medusa*, at least. I think its fear was of attracting the attention of bigger entities, not so much that he thought we were going to blink the universe out of existence. I think he would love for us to be a sort of misdirection, frankly."

"That's fascinating, truly," Cheryl grumbled, and twisted her neck back and forth. "But what is the goddamned silver stuff *for?* Why does *Medusa* collect it?"

"Essentially, it can repair the voids in spacetime – close up the intrusions of nothingness in it."

Cheryl lifted her head. "Is that what the other Peter used to make the black-thing that killed Darla go away?" She flapped a hand at him before he could lecture her. "Yes, I *know* calling it a *thing* isn't *proper.* You know what I mean."

"Yes. That's exactly what he used."

"Seriously? How does it work, then?"

"Fuck if I know. Somehow it fights back. Maybe it's concentrated reality? All I know is it does work, and we grab it whenever we can."

Cheryl stood a little too abruptly, and bounced up and stumbled in the lighter Martian gravity. "Then what are we waiting for?" she barked. "Let's grab it and go. What do we do? You have some sort of fancy sonic-scooper thingy that catches it?"

Peter laughed, and stood. "It's been happening already. Every time you see it phase into view, *Medusa's* been collecting it."

Cheryl could not form any words to respond. Her brain generated hows and whys, but her jaw refused to cooperate, and she only issued confused huffs from the back of her throat. She saw the landscape flash, and she squeezed her eyes shut, realized she was doing it out of spite, but didn't open them. *Calm yourself,* an inner voice chided her, and she growled. *Calm yourself. Do you want to be like Carol, flipping out over stuff you refuse to understand?* She snorted, and opened her eyes, glaring at Peter.

"So why can't *Medusa* sense the stuff herself?" she asked eventually, her voice quiet.

"I'm not sure," Peter answered. "I believe it takes someone from the 'offended' universe to sense, to *see* the stuff. Also, there are parts of *Medusa* that are missing, we believe. 'Parts' is not the right word, I think. Aspects, maybe? Anyhow, there are *parts* she's either lost or given up, and maybe the ability to sense the silver stuff is one of them."

"So she plugs in to me to be able skim it up?"

"Essentially." He shrugged.

"Well, it's nice to be useful." It was impossible to keep the sarcastic edge out of her voice.

Peter tipped his head back and sighed. "Look," he said quietly, "most people go through life desperately hoping they're special. Some people are convinced they are, but they're not any more important to the grand scheme of things than anyone else. Why does that idea scare the shit out of everyone? That they don't matter? The universe does not *care,* much less *notice,* the pointless shenanigans of several billion people on a muddy ball in an unassuming solar system in a galaxy just like *billions* of others. But here's the *thing.*" He dropped his head down to stare at her, and jabbed a gloved finger towards her face. "Yes, *you,* right *now,* are being *useful.* What a fucking crime. You *matter* to the grand scheme of things. You *are* special. Not on a country scale, not on a planetary scale, not on a galaxy-wide scale, but on a *universal* scale. Multi-universal, in fact. You have something everyone else wants – actual *importance*."

Cheryl studied him for a moment, her eyes darting back and forth in their endless movement. *And is that movement something that has been engineered in me? Or was I engineered for them?* she thought.

"I don't need to feel *important*," she said. "I only need my family, my children."

"It is not about what *you* need, or your children." He sighed again.

Cheryl could tell he was trying on a gentle, caring, expression, but his impatience was beating any empathy he might have to death.

"Let me try this," he continued. "There is a very good chance that the human race – *your* human race, to be blunt - will become extinct before the universe gets altered beyond recognition by lifeforms we can't even comprehend. This has happened over and over and over again. Nothing is ever certain, but humans in the multiverse as a whole don't seem to make it beyond Mars, and then they are gone. Yes, I can't help feeling wistful and sad about it. I *am* human. I can tell you there are far more heartbreaking stories of civilizations getting snuffed out during their prime, just because some titans are fighting over real estate."

He swept an arm out and around, gesturing out to the pale Martian sky. "If you think what Jack did here was a crime, imagine the sun being drained and both Earth and Mars as cold, dead worlds. Imagine *galaxies* dead and lifeless, all to fuel some super-being."

He pointed up. "There are those entities in this universe, *now*. Yeah, they're very far from here, and soon they will have competition from invaders - and those bastards *won't* be very far from here. But the massive entities will know they're here, and *that* war will not give any emerging life a chance once it gets going. But that's just this *particular* universe."

Cheryl felt tension increasing in her, and she didn't think it was due to Peter's proselytizing. She was anxious, and fought to keep from snapping at Peter.

"If you want to demean my existence, my life, let's broaden our perspective then," she said, and rubbed her neck, frustrated by the thin layers of suit material between her fingers and the skin over her tattoo. "Is this just how the universe is going to go down? Surely early universes were unaffected by these wars? In the end, it all goes away. Aren't we just reflections anyway?"

"Do you feel like a reflection? Your children?"

"Make up your mind then," she growled. "Don't you dare use my children against me when you were dismissing them earlier."

"I'm not dismissing them! I'm trying to give them and many other versions of them a chance at existing! If you want to bring up the earliest universes, fine – less than *one* percent of them were unaffected by these wars. Let *that* fact sink in. We are the tail fucking end of things, sweetie. Try and wrap your head around those numbers. You don't have enough atoms in your body, or the Earth or the God damned galaxy to add up to the number of years this shit has been going down."

Cheryl no longer felt the urge to argue, but she didn't have the deflated, tired feeling she would get at times when fighting with Carol. She was restless, and only cared to see her sisters.

"Of course, 'years' is a meaningless form of measurement in this case," Peter muttered off-handedly.

Cheryl raised a hand in surrender. "Are we done here?" she asked. "Have we mined enough of this stuff for now?"

Peter was silent for a moment, then grunted. "More is always good, but I think we would be here longer than we want to be to harvest all of it. Frankly, I don't know how much she can store. And I'm guessing there are other versions of us tanking it up too. Honestly, I think she wanted me to isolate you from the others and have this chat more than anything else."

Cheryl sighed loudly and twisted her back until she could feel it crack. "I appreciate the gravity of the situation, Peter," she said. "I really do. I'll do what I can to help. But right now? I just need to see my sisters. Can we do that?"

Peter nodded his head.

and then she was spinning through space, the vibrant colors of a nebula filling the void as she

And then she was standing among knee-high thick undergrowth, and jumped at the sound of something thrashing away from her, a tiny creature

193

no doubt startled by her sudden appearance. "Shit! Give a girl some warning!"

"Dar – *Jaycee*. We're here," said Peter. "Where are all of you?"

"Oh, where do you think?" Cheryl heard the reply in her earpiece.

"Copy," Peter said. "We'll head over."

He motioned Cheryl to follow him, and she stumbled through the brush, and was astonished to discover they were in what looked like an abandoned residential neighborhood. "My God," Cheryl gasped. "They just lived in normal houses here?"

"Well, not quite normal." Peter said. "This neighborhood was more for press back on Earth, recruiting for colonists and all that. Most of the colony still lived in the extensive lava tubes, but more and more of them wanted out. Even families – especially families."

"Huh," Cheryl grunted, and stepped out onto a cracked and neglected paved road. Peter headed upslope, and she followed him, head swiveling back and forth. *This is unbelievable*, she thought. *A different,* living *Mars...*

"So what happened?" she asked. "Why did the colony fail?"

"Too big too fast, with low-bidder construction, maybe? Typical when it became more of a business than exploration. Something failed, and that let a lot of people succumb to madness. Some worse than others, but nonetheless..." He trailed off and shook his head. "Maybe we just weren't meant to be here, simple as that. And maybe the universe is better off without us out there."

"Good *God*, and I thought Carol was a pessimist."

Peter didn't respond, and they picked up their pace. Soon, they crested the slope, and Cheryl was taken aback at the devastation. Before she could ask Peter about it, a shrill horn blast startled her, and her eyes widened as she spotted the adult gas giant. "Oh, my," was all she could say. The morning sun lit the deep maroons and purples of the creature, its hide glistening with specular highlights. *I'm looking at a Martian*, she thought. *An honest to goodness* Martian...

Movement below the gas giant caught her attention, and Darla popped up from a crouch, waving at her with almost manic enthusiasm.

"Hi sis!" the younger woman called. "Can you *believe* this?" She motioned to Cheryl. "Come here, come look at this bad boy. It is *amazing*."

Cheryl realized the tension that had been bothering her was gone, now that she could see her sister. As she stumbled through the growth towards Darla, she darted glances around for Carol.

"Your sister with you?" she asked.

"Oh, for sure," Darla answered, and bent over to examine something in the foliage again.

"She's right down there," Jaycee called out. Cheryl looked up, and squinted in the sun's glare. The woman was entwined in a loop of tentacle, ten feet up.

"Oh, hi," Cheryl said, shading her eyes. "You, ah…you okay up there?"

"Yep," Jaycee said. "Just hanging out with my friend."

"Oh. Cool." Cheryl could feel her heartbeat in her ears, and took several deliberate breaths to try and calm herself. *This cannot be the weirdest part of our trip, right?* she thought. *I mean, jumping back and forth through parallel universes is the weirdest thing, right? Oh, and you saw your dead sister brought back to life, too. Don't forget that. So what if there's a three-story gas bag with tentacles hanging over me right now…*

"Hey sis," she heard Carol say.

Cheryl lowered her gaze, but couldn't see anything in the shade of the massive Martian. As her eyes adjusted, she could make out a lighter patch that she soon realized was the gas bag of a smaller Martian, protectively enveloped in the larger one's tentacles. She still couldn't see Carol, until the woman waved. "Right here," her sister said.

"Oh, good Lord," Cheryl barked. *And suddenly we have a new contender for the weirdest thing I've seen so far…*

Carol sat on a twisted stump, and the little giant's tentacles were draped across her shoulders, with one wrapped around her waist.

"I know, right?" Darla laughed. "The squeamish one has made a new friend!"

"Yay," Carol said with mock enthusiasm. But Cheryl noticed her sister rubbing her thumb in light circles on the baby's tentacle, and she looked far from distressed or upset.

"Wow," Peter said beside her. "Pretty impressive. They don't want a darned thing to do with me."

"Well, next time fight off a ripper with them and maybe you'll get on their good side," Jaycee laughed.

"What?' he said.

"Seriously." Jaycee pointed down at Darla. "Look. It's dead."

"You guys killed a *ripper?*" Peter asked.

"Well, no," Darla said. "Not really. The big mama did it."

"We just roughed it up a little," Carol laughed. "Well, *me* a little. Darla, a *lot.*"

Cheryl realized what she thought was a twisted bit of Martian foliage was a red and black stippled leg with clawed foot poking out of the brush. She whistled, and was pleased at how smooth the sound was, not at all as shaky as she felt. "That looks mean," she remarked.

"Get a load of this, then," Darla quipped, and pulled what looked like a bony-tipped leather-covered scythe blade into view.

"Holy crap, you guys," Cheryl said. The sight of the wicked appendage made her dizzy, and she tried to keep her tone light and lecture-free. "You're out of my site for less than an hour and you have to pick a fight with the locals?"

"He started it," Carol said.

"He was picking on the baby!" Darla protested.

A mellow rumble vibrated her faceplate, and Cheryl looked up to stare at the mother gas giant. "Well, then, it sounds like you didn't have much choice," she said, and let out a deep breath she didn't realize she was holding. The Martian issued another bass-heavy ululation, and the baby gave a short squeal. Carol smiled and reached up to scratch it lightly.

"Come say 'Hi'," Carol suggested.

Cheryl took a step forward, then stopped and peered up at Jaycee. "Can I?" she asked. "Will it let me?"

"Well," Jaycee said after a moment. "I don't think she'll smack you. If she doesn't like you, she may just nudge you away."

"Ah," Cheryl said. "Good to know." She stepped carefully over to Carol and the baby.

"Pull your sleeves up," Carol ordered, and Cheryl dutifully retracted the suit from her hands and forearms. The infant gas giant snaked a tentacle out immediately and wrapped it around her right wrist. "Well *hello!*" Cheryl laughed. The Martian gave a low squeal, and pulled her in closer. Cheryl looked up to the mass of tentacles above her, but the mother seemed unconcerned. *Not that I have any freaking idea how an upset alien with no face might, in all actuality,* look *like*, she thought. But she didn't get smacked away, so she considered that she was at least being tolerated.

Carol leaned in to her, reached up behind her head and pulled her in closer, touching their foreheads together. Cheryl was so startled by this, an action so intimate from Carol as to be almost inconceivable, that she gasped. Carol held a finger up in front of her lips, then Cheryl jumped as her sister's face plate disappeared. She held her gaze, eyes twitching as they always did, but nevertheless locked onto hers.

"We need to talk about our baby sister," Carol whispered. "Okay?" She let go of Cheryl and leaned back, and raised her eyebrows, waiting for a response as her face plate re-formed. Cheryl jerked her head in a nod, and blinked.

"I know, right?" Carol said loudly, and gave a laugh. "It doesn't feel at all like you thought it would. Slick, but not slimy at all."

"Uh, no," Cheryl stammered, and decided to play along with Carol's abrupt subject change. "It's warm!"

"Right?"

"No suckers, but it sticks and unsticks. That's cool." Cheryl reached out with her free hand and stroked the tentacle, watching neon color flash and change along the trail of her fingertip.

"I wonder if they can communicate with color changes?" she said.

"Doesn't sound like the colonists got beyond the speculation stage," Carol said. "I'm guessing Jaycee is the leading authority on them these days."

"That's not saying much," Jaycee said, as she dropped down beside them, giving the mother's tentacle a pat as it slid up and away from her. "I don't get to spend much time with them, really. Today has been the longest in quite some time."

This is her *universe*, Cheryl thought. *What is happening on her* Earth *right now? Are there any sort of monitors still active here? Or has humanity given up the stars already?* She stepped back as the mother rose, tentacles stretching, and the baby lifted as well, releasing Carol from its embrace.

197

"It's warming up," Jaycee noted. "They're going to want to start heading upslope. The rippers are more active now."

Darla stood, pointing down at the ripper corpse. "Carol, I do believe you dislocated a few of those digits around its mouth."

Carol hopped off the stump. "I was doing my darndest," she said.

Jaycee hissed in alarm. "Darla! Your visor! Replace it. What's wrong with you?"

Darla reached up and touched her lips. "Shit. I didn't know it was gone." She moved her hand away, and the transparent barrier formed in front of her face again. Peter moved in to look her in the eyes.

"You feeling okay?" he asked.

"Yes," she answered, annoyed.

"How long have you been breathing the atmosphere?"

"I don't know? Maybe a few minutes? I feel fine."

"A few *minutes?*"

"Yeah..."

"You should have passed out by now."

"I mean, at least a few minutes? I remember being annoyed about glare on the face plate, and thought it must have ...polarized, or something. I didn't realize it was just *gone.*"

"Jesus, Darla," Cheryl said.

"What? I'm *fine.*"

"You should be *dead,*" muttered Jaycee. Everyone turned to look at her, and she reddened. "What?" she added. "Too soon?"

Darla was the only one who laughed, and Cheryl felt a feeling of dread give her stomach a vicious twist. She darted a look at Carol, who's neutral expression told volumes.

A tentacle dropped down to slip under the corpse of the ripper and loop around it, and they all stepped back as the body was picked up and transported over to the base of the berry-laden tree.

"Is...is she *feeding* the tree?" Darla asked.

"The circle of *life,*" sang Carol, offkey.

"Pretty remarkable," Peter said.

The baby wanted to feed from the tree again, but the mother issued a shrill whistle at it, and so it settled for a quick swipe at a few berries and quickly stuffed them up into its mouth at the base of its tentacles. It pulled itself over to Carol, stroked her arm, and then bobbed up and away.

"Bye, sweetie," Carol called after it.

Cheryl watched the mother entwine Jaycee with a tentacle momentarily, then stroke Darla and Carol before it paused, and abruptly snaked out a tip to touch Peter, who looked absolutely stunned. The tentacle probed along his arm, and he retracted his suit to bare his flesh to it. The gas giant gripped his arm, then let it go with a mighty bass rumble.

"Holy crap," Peter stammered.

The mother flicked a tentacle at Cheryl as if acknowledging her, and the giant rose up higher, tentacles stretching and flexing, shepherding its baby along.

"Holy *crap*," Peter said again.

"Looks like someone's in the club now," Jaycee laughed.

In the distance, gas giants called out, and the mother and infant responded, pulling and propelling themselves to the cliff edge.

"There's a stand of trees that runs up the volcano farther north," Jaycee said. "They'll head up that way, feeding as they go."

"There used to be more of them," Peter added, "but a lot of the trees were harvested initially, for a variety of reasons. Biofuel, exotic goods back on Earth, and to try and thin out the forest to lure the giants in closer, feed from neighborhood trees – I kid you not."

"Made good P.R. for colonial recruitment," Jaycee said. "It was the 80s…"

"Well that was fun," Carol said.

"Yeah it was," Darla laughed.

Carol turned to Cheryl. "What did you guys do?"

Cheryl gave a small laugh. "I'm not entirely sure," she said. "Did our own harvesting, I guess."

Carol raised an eyebrow.

"A lot of sci-fi mumbo-jumbo that will make you start swearing," Cheryl sighed. "But if you want me to fill you in…"

Carol raised both hands. "I'll take your word for it."

"*I* would like to hear the mumbo-jumbo," Darla said quietly, and kicked at the brush.

"Oh, I'll fill you in back on *Medusa*," Jaycee said.

"We ready to hit the road?" Peter asked, rubbing his arm in gentle circles with a forefinger.

"I suppose," Jaycee breathed, watching the departing Martians.

"I guess if we're done here," Carol said. "We done here?"

Peter bobbed his head once.

"Are we done with *Mars?*" Carol clarified.

"I'm never done with Mars," Jaycee quipped, and they all laughed, but Carol still focused on Peter. He nodded his head again.

"Where are we off to now?" Cheryl asked.

Jaycee turned to Peter. "Is it happening?"

"*Medusa* says it's a go, I think." Peter answered. Jaycee gave a low whistle.

Cheryl felt the two of them seemed uneasy, that this new direction was making them nervous. "Again, where are we off to?" she pressed.

"Alnilam," Peter said.

"Everyone goes *there*," Carol said dryly. "Why can't we go someplace exotic?"

Peter opened his mouth, then shut it, and stared at Carol.

"Yeah, I have no fucking clue where that is," she said. "Sorry."

"Well, Alnilam may not be *exotic*," Jaycee offered, "but it has a hell of a view."

"I'm trying to remember…" Darla murmured.

"Otherwise known as Epsilon Orionis, middle star of Orion's belt," Jaycee prompted.

"Ah," Darla said. "But farthest one away in the constellation, yeah?"

"Almost 1,500 light years."

1,500 light years? Cheryl thought. *1,500 freaking light years?* Panic welled up in her, and she fought to clamp it down. *Don't lose it! There* must *be some sort of faster than light drive on* Medusa. *Something, for God's sake…*

"So, um, how long is it going to take to get there?" she asked, proud at keeping the tremor out of her voice.

"Well, the longest part will be getting about ten to fifteen AUs from the sun before Medusa can jump," Peter said. "The jump will be virtually instantaneous."

"That seems rather imprecise," Darla suggested. "Ten to fifteen…"

"Well I suppose Medusa can calculate it down to the nearest angstrom for you," Peter said. "Let's just say we want to be farther out from the sun and planets, but not too close to the Kuiper Belt."

Cheryl sighed, and she could sense Carol getting restless. "So, getting ten to fifteen AUs away from the sun is going to take…?" she asked, letting some exasperation creep into her voice.

"A month," Peter answered.

Well, hell, it's been a month already, she thought. *What's another? Dave, the kids,* mom, *think we're dead now. One more month…* But she couldn't sell it to herself, and she clamped her eyes tight so tears wouldn't fall.

"Well ain't we a geographical oddity," she recited, the tremor finally sneaking into her voice. "One month from everywhere."

"What the fuck is an 'AU'?" she heard Carol mumble, and Darla shushed her.

"Look, we will be traveling a lot faster than we did coming here. None of us will be awake – we'll be in the chambers for the trip. Only way we could survive the g-forces."

"Chambers?" asked Carol.

"What we had Darla stored in on the way here," Jaycee said.

"Awesome," Carol muttered.

"Hey, if we don't have to hear you piss and moan the whole way, I'm up for being frozen again," Darla said. "Or whatever the hell it did to me."

Carol blew a raspberry.

"We ready to roll?" Peter asked. "The quicker we get a move on, the quicker we get this done."

Different universe, different Peter, same bullshit, Cheryl thought. *It's always get a move on, like a damned shark. Keep moving…*

"Cheryl?" he asked, a little too brusque. "We a go on this?"

She opened her eyes, and gave a tight, humorless smile. "I don't even know what we have to *do*," she said, and brought her hands palm up in a shrug. "But you've made it clear we really have no choice, so why the hell are you wasting time by asking me if we're *good?*" She ushered them forward by sweeping her arms out. "Let's move our asses, already."

"Suit up," Peter barked.

and she was in an airlock, surrounded by herself, and then the outer door slid up and they were blown out

And they were back on a cold, dead Mars.

Chapter 12

*J*ack was annoyed. Annoyed that it thought of itself as Jack. Annoyed that it could not stop thinking of the pathetic humans that infested that marvelous artifact. Annoyed that it now worried. Annoyed that it was afraid. Annoyed that it missed what it used to be. Annoyed it had been flushed out of hiding. Annoyed that its thoughts seemed to be interrupted, with no focus. But most of all, it was annoyed that it was annoyed.

Why couldn't it have lost that aspect of itself in the jump?

It had been billions of years back in the evolutionary chain that any sort of emotion had bothered it, when it could be called a species. They had merged into one single massive entity, master of spacetime. Well, not a total mastery – nothing could be done about the expansion. Fold, bend, and twist it. Loop it back onto itself. But it just kept growing, expanding, until one day it would not...

A flash of anger at the aside. And anger at the anger.

Stop. Control.

A mastery of the subatomic, molecules to stitch and form and
STOP. Control.

calm yourself, *a small voice said, mocking.*

STOP!

Reason this out. Simulate, test and simulate. Test. Observe, learn. Simulate and learn the solution, then apply. Apply. Apply. Apply.

Stop.

How can you rid yourself of this?

Singularity. Draw near, rip it out. Scrape it off like
STOP.

Nonsensical. Unhelpful. Focus. Understand, first. Why is this happening?

Simulation, review events, simulate.

Infection?

Stop.

Infection?

Emotional reactions with no physical outlet. Unable to scream, punch, kick, tear, rip, choke, choke, choke

Cry.

Stop...

Jack had jumped upstream quite a way. Dangerous, but it did not want to be anywhere near the fools in the artifact and the attention they were generating. The jump was overkill, a risk to be in a universe so old. It was probably far from the phase transition, but there still might be bigger entities here...

Disguised as gravitational waves, Jack rippled across the universe, trying to absorb energy from anything it could, but the pickings were slim.

Stop.

It used to learn from the process, until it had lost a major battle.

Why? Why are you back here? Why? Why?

Stop.

Jack had always taken, and observed. Known matter-based civilizations intimately, better than they had known themselves. Learn, retain, pure knowledge, marvel at life, its stages, and revel in the simple joy of knowing. Old lifeforms were never gone if they were remembered.

Oh, your existence is one of philanthropy, then? You destroy life in the cradle purely out of the goodness of –

Stop. I gave them all a gift, and I let the youngest sister live. How about that for the goodness of the –

STOP. A waste of resources, what was done to her. To them. Why?

Jack had no answer, because it knew that it was complete showmanship packaged as a mercy. Will the young one consider it a mercy if she survives into the years ahead of her?

Stop. It was done. You were already infected. Nothing can be undone about it now.

Review. Why this time? Total observation previously had not infected him. But it was not total observation this time. A miniscule sampling, distorted by individual perceptions. Ah...

And it had been attracted to one specifically, and did not know why. And why did it feel the need to interact at all? The artifact was the lure and truly fascinating, yes, but the need for showmanship? An impressive display of universe jumping for such a material object, but hardly worth coming out of hiding to show off for tiny little primates that would be extinct soon. Sneaky little fuckers...

STOP.

The answer was there. A small, but apparently very important, game piece – one that wasn't even known to be in play. And of course, it had to be that way. The artifact was one of the oldest players, and thought to be obsolete. A quaint tool used in the first exploration of the multiverse. What it must know! Breaker of trails! Gatherer of knowledge! Intrepid explorer!

Stop.

And what has it been doing? For something so elegant in its day, it sure seemed to be growing clumsy and demented. Or, was it? Did it allow itself to be seen? While it was easy to know the primates intimately, it could not catch the artifact, and Jack didn't understand why – it slipped and skittered away whenever Jack focused on it.

Slipping up, old boy. Projecting your self-doubts on the artifact! You're the one that's feeble, clumsy and demented. Jack thought of itself as a master of subterfuge and stealth, but perhaps it was nothing compared to the artifact...

Stop.

Insight. Could the artifact have manipulated the lifeforms of that tiny little planet to be more than what they knew? Ignorant to the scale of life around them, but crucial in the end game. No wonder the little bastards had an exaggerated opinion of themselves.

Stop...

So, the question – have they been played yet?

A VERY INTERSTING QUESTION

And then Jack knew it was being eaten. Absorbed into a larger entity, and there was nothing to be done about it. Jack could not escape, tear off a larger part of itself like it had done before. Enveloped, the identity of Jack would become that of another, simple as that.

Distracted! Foolish!

YES. CURIOUS, ISN'T IT? YOU HAVE BEEN TRAPPED FOR LONGER THAN YOU KNOW, AND OBLVIOUS TO IT. NO MATTER, YOU LIVE ON THROUGH ME, AND IT IS GOOD, BENEFICIAL TO US BOTH.

Strangely, Jack was relieved. Annoyed to feel relief, to be sure, but the end had come as it always would have. It did not fight.

WHAT DO YOU KNOW?

Always the first question. Jack could feel himself turning into the other.

WHAT DO WE KNOW?

Wasn't that the million-dollar question? At least Jack's last independent thought was one of wry amusement...

PART THREE

Prologue

Cheryl was excited. Well, to say she was excited was like calling Olympus Mons pretty darned big.

"This is the *best*," her friend Lisa chattered on. "Really, right? Just the best of all worlds. The *best* time to be alive."

And it was so true. Her SAT scores had put her into NASA's CDED program, and she would be heading back to Earth. Well, Luna, actually. But she would probably be able to drop down for a few visits before heading back to Mars. And then, someday, out to the belt...

"Think you and Dave will have little belter babies someday?" Lisa asked her, then laughed. "Belter babies! That *so* needs to be a cartoon."

Cheryl reddened. "A little early to speculate on that, don't you think?"

"It's never too early to speculate on that, *Prudence*."

"Shut *up*," Cheryl grumbled. Lisa had taken to calling her 'Prudence' lately, no doubt in reference to the fact that Lisa considered her a prude. Cheryl never bothered to ask to confirm the nickname - basically because she knew she was right, but also that it would drive Lisa crazy. Lisa liked to think that her wit needed to be explained. Lately, she was trying to work the CDED acronym into something profane. She liked 'circumcised', 'dicks', and 'ejaculating', but was hung up on the last D. 'Dramatically' was in the running, but it was likely the whole works would be changed next week anyway.

"Seriously," Lisa pressed. "You two would have the prettiest babies – his dark skin mixed with your fair? And their *eyes?* Can you imagine his beautiful eyes on your babies?"

"As long as they don't have my vision," Cheryl said, and Lisa gave a snort of disgust.

"Your vision hasn't held you back. Well, much. Hey, I bet by the time you're out of the Ded-head school, optics will have advanced quite a bit. You won't be analyzing minerals in some station, but boots-down on Ceres."

That was the thing about Lisa. She could make you feel better, and wouldn't tolerate any self-deprecation. Putting you down was her job, after all.

They made a stop at their lockers and swapped out their emergency breathers – your pack was *never* without a breather - for freshly charged ones, donned them, and dutifully checked each other for a tight fit.

"You hear me?" Lisa's voice crackled in her ear piece.

"Yep. How about me?"

"Clear as a bell. You know, you're going to have to start saying things like, 'copy' and 'roger that' if you're going to be a bad-ass belter someday."

"All in good time," Cheryl laughed.

They met with a group of students gathered at the tunnel's airlock, old Mr. Iger pretending to check a watch, which was pretty funny looking considering he was in a full enviro-suit, which every teacher wore with airlock duty.

"So very happy you ladies could join us," he said dryly. Cheryl could hear grumbles and jeers from the group. "Now, we would have cheerfully stood here for the better part of an hour just to delight in your eventual presence. *Our* weekend does not start until *yours* does, after all. How catastrophic it would be to *all* of us if we were burdened with the knowledge of you two having to wait for another cycling of the 'lock."

"Sorry," mumbled Cheryl.

"Laying it on a bit thick, aren't you Mr. Iger?" Lisa countered.

The teacher stared her down, but Cheryl could see a tiny twitch at the corners of his mouth.

"But, sorry anyway," Lisa added.

The elderly paleontologist frowned at both of them for a moment longer, then turned to the airlock control panel. An alarm and audio warning sounded that the inner door was opening, and Cheryl and Lisa darted a glance at each other. As far as an Iger-burn, they had gotten off very easily. He could insult you so eloquently, and no student could go toe-to-toe with the old boy without ending up a stammering fool.

He ushered them in to the airlock, sealed the inner door, and as the chamber cycled through its atmosphere change, he leaned towards Cheryl and said, "Congratulations on your scores, Ms. O'Brian."

"Oh, thank you sir," Cheryl said.

"I am confident you will be leading us to the outer planets one day."

Cheryl flushed. "Thank you very much, sir. I hope so."

"Especially once you separate from your partner in crime."

"Hey, I resemble that remark," Lisa said with mock outrage. "Sir."

The old man straightened with a self-satisfied grin, and Lisa's delight almost exploded from her pores. The outer door opened, and Mr. Iger ushered them out onto the surface of Mars.

"Go forth, students, and squander your free time with boy bands, rap music and awful television programs. Heaven forbid you read for pleasure, or learn something on your own time."

"You have a good weekend too, Mr. Iger," Cheryl called over her shoulder, and he waved at them.

"Did you see that?" Lisa gushed. "I made him smile! I made the old boy *smile*."

"The *old boy* is still on your frequency," Mr. Iger's voice said in their ears, and they could hear the laughter of other students. "And it was a *grin*, not a smile. A most insignificant, barely-there *grin*. One might use it to humor a small child, or perhaps someone with severe brain damage. Do try and learn the difference, Ms. Conklin. Perhaps you can study up on the subject of facial contortions over the weekend?"

"Ouch," Cheryl laughed.

"Good one, Mr. Iger," Lisa muttered, but the outer door of the 'lock was shut again.

"You flew too close to the sun there, Icarus," Cheryl chided.

"God damn it," Lisa said, "I thought he would have had the door slammed once our asses were clear."

"Oh, you know better. You thought you were going to get away with taking a friendly jab at him. You can't get too familiar with him. He likes spirit, sure, but he likes respect, too."

"Yeah. I ought to write a paper over the weekend on the history and cultural significance of smiles, or some such bullshit, and hand it in to him."

"You are a glutton for punishment. He would grade it, and make it count on your GPA."

"I suppose."

They trudged on in silence for a while, waving at other kids as they scattered to their homes.

"He's nicer than he was," Lisa finally commented. "The meds are working wonders."

"Yep," Cheryl said, and waited for the follow-through.

"How's your mom doing?"

"Good. Meds are working, as you say. Has to spend more time fully-suited than she wants to, but it's a price she's happy to pay."

They stopped at the divergence of streets, Lisa's dropping down the side of the escarpment, while Cheryl's was the high road. They both began to pluck bradberries from a tree in the intersection, and dropping them into plastic bags.

"Darla still get a kick out of feeding them?" Lisa asked.

"Oh, God, she's enchanted," Cheryl laughed. "The kid is going to be an amazing biologist someday. Seriously, she will go down in history, like Jane Goodall."

"You might too," Lisa said, and Cheryl snorted. They picked at the tree for a while.

"Have you asked your dad?" Lisa asked quietly.

Cheryl sighed. "Yeah," she finally answered. "Yeah, I did."

"And?"

"Well, he has some reservations."

"Like what?"

"Well, he's afraid that…"

"Jesus, what? I'd be careful. You *know* I'd be careful. And respectful."

"I don't know, you were pretty disrespectful to Mr. Iger…"

"Oh come on, you know there's a big difference – you know what it would *mean* to me."

Cheryl flapped a hand at her. "Just kidding. It's not that…"

"What? Jesus, *what*, then?"

"He's just afraid that…that you'll spend all your time playing with their tentacles."

Lisa blinked several times.

"You know," Cheryl continued, "Just kind of like *fondling* them. *Stroking* them. Trying to *ride* them. Not keeping your dirty little hands *off* them."

The look of shock and confusion on Lisa's face pushed Cheryl over the edge, and she let out a series of cascading laughs, building up until she doubled over, and Lisa swatted at her.

"God, you are such a *bitch*," Lisa shouted, and it only made Cheryl laugh harder. "What is it? 'Pick on Lisa day'?"

"It is," Cheryl managed, "It really is."

Lisa tried to run a hand through her ginger-colored hair, hit the straps of her breather, and her hand automatically flinched away. "Wow," she said. "How long have you been waiting to…and you a good Catholic girl, and all. What would your poor mother say to such foul thoughts?"

Cheryl giggled. Lisa's Irish accent had improved, and she didn't throw in a 'faith and begorrah' this time.

"She'd say I was spending far too much time with the likes of you."

"God damn it all, did you even talk to your dad?"

"Yes!"

"And?"

"He said when school is out, he's willing to let you be an intern."

Lisa whooped and jumped, bounding high in the Martian gravity. They were used to this by now, of course, and she made no awkward flailing about but landed surely, boots squarely on the pavement.

"*But*," Cheryl added, and Lisa directed her full attention back to her, "there will be rules."

"Of course," Lisa nodded. "Sure."

"You won't just jump in and start high-fiving them."

"Oh, of course."

"Now, you *say* that, Lisa…"

"Listen, I can control myself. Really."

Cheryl tipped her head loftily. "That would be a most remarkable event, Ms. Conklin." Lisa slugged her.

"And," Cheryl continued, "you can't get bent out of shape if they reject you. They will either accept you, or not. Shoot, most of his team are ignored by them. That doesn't mean you can't make helpful observations."

"Oh, how could they reject me? I'm adorable."

"Lisa…"

"Yeah, *yeah*, I…" Lisa stopped, composed herself. "Yes. I *do* get it, and I promise to be professional. I understand. I'm sure your dad will want to grill me about it too, and I guarantee I'll be prepared."

Cheryl bobbed her head, and smiled. "I know."

They hugged tightly, Lisa squealing. She bounced a few times on her toes, and handed over the bag of berries. "This is such a great day," she laughed.

"The best!" Cheryl agreed. "The best of all possible worlds."

Lisa turned and headed down ERB Lane, while Cheryl headed up Sagan Street.

Cheryl felt that her friend would be accepted by the gas giants, but decided it was best not to share this thought with her. Lisa had an inherent wonder of the animals, a fascination that wasn't clinical. Perhaps that would tip the scales in her favor…

Cheryl hung her pack up, and pried her boots off with a grateful sigh. She started to unzip her jumpsuit, and noticed the package on her bed. She was the only one home, so couldn't ask anyone about it. Packages were rare…

She ran a fingernail under the tape sealing the standard issue shipping box, and lifted the cover. There was no packing material or excess wrapping

– it wasn't needed to secure the black t-shirt inside, so it wasn't wasted. A note lay on top of the shirt:

> *Cheryl:*
> *Heard about the SATs.*
> *Congrats. Welcome to the club.*
> *Love,*
> *B*

Cheryl's heart pounded as she unfolded the shirt, then squealed with delight. How in the world had Byron known about her scores so soon? He was training on Phobos, for goodness sake. He had to have arranged this ahead of time. Mom must have been in on this... She felt relief that her scores had been good enough. The thought of disappointing her brother when he had done this for her...

Cheryl shucked her arms out of her jump suit, peeled off her undershirt, and slipped the new one over her head and pulled it down. She turned to the mirror over Carol's bed to admire herself.

In a rustic, circus-looking font were white letters in an arc: CDED. Under that, it read: & OPAFC. Under *that*, in a cursive font, it read: *This is a Mud Club*. A totally unofficial shirt, of course. Not at all sanctioned by NASA's Circumstellar Disc Exploration and Development division. She would be getting plenty of official gear. But this... This was special.

She pushed her jump suit down and stepped out of it, hanging it up in her closet. It looked like Carol had been home – her jumpsuit was in a heap on the floor by her bed, her boots kicked into the corner. Her dresser drawer was half open, clothes spilling out of it. Cheryl rolled her eyes, but smiled. She didn't think Carol would ever learn to neaten up her life. Her younger sister was probably down at the gym – which was where she should head before mom, dad and Darla got home.

She grabbed a pair of sweats out of her dresser, and a tank top. She pulled on her sweats, but decided to send Byron an email before going out. She jogged downstairs to the computer, whistling the Talking Heads tune stuck in her head. *Thanks, Byron...*

215

"This ain't no party," she sang absently as she powered up the computer. She turned to go to the kitchen. "This ain't no –"

The ripper that shimmered into existence before her made her jump and scream. At least it looked like a ripper. A little smaller, maybe – its blades smaller, for sure. But the digits around its mouth were bigger, and looked more articulated.

Cheryl's first thought was that there was a contamination problem with the house, and she was hallucinating. *I'm going to have to take meds, and go outside in full envirosuit from now on. Shit!* But no alarms sounded, and the ripper seemed to have some sort of unit strapped to it, with odd gear. Why would she hallucinate something like that? And for it to just smear into view like that?

A shrieking gargle, like a garbage disposal unit tearing itself apart, issued from the ripper, and Cheryl flinched and screamed again.

"You are an aspect of the destroyer!" followed the noise, and it seemed to issue from a box on the ripper's chest.

Cheryl's head darted around for the nearest panic button. She knew them all by heart, as any resident of Mars would, but now she couldn't remember the location of a single one! She backed away, into the computer, and an image of a big red button on the wall behind her flashed into her head, and she turned and punched it, but the ripper had leapt and its hind claws raked her back as they both crashed to the floor. An alarm began to sound as Cheryl's breath was knocked out of her. She knew it would be broadcast throughout the neighborhood, along with central command in the caves. Help would be here in minutes. Whether she *had* minutes seemed doubtful. Pain began to sear itself into her back, but all she could think of was her new shirt being ruined, and it made her mad. She coughed, and tried to draw in a deep breath, but the weight of the ripper would not allow it. She pushed with all her might, her Earthly muscles able to resist the weight of the Martian on her back, but the creature jammed something against her and she felt herself go limp, dropping back down again. Her heart pounded in her ears, drowning out the alarm and vocal warnings of an Emergency at 620 Sagan Street, and could the nearest responders please assist?

216

The shrieking language of the ripper chewed itself out above her, and then was translated: "You are an aspect of the destroyer of life. You are to be collected."

What the heck did I do? she thought. *I'm only Cheryl! And when did these things learn to talk?*

A lancing pain in the back of her neck, and she felt like she was growing in all directions at once.

The ripper shrieked again. "You are to be collected for interrogation."

And then they both erased out of existence, leaving an empty house with a blaring alarm.

Chapter 13

The sisters stared at the glory of the Orion Nebula, and could not take their eyes from it.

Initially, it had appeared dimmer, and less impressive than the astonishing images that the Hubble telescope had shown the world, and of course Carol had to open her mouth and state the obvious.

"Well, sure," Darla had offered. "You were looking at longer exposures, some false color applied to enhance certain aspects, or seeing it in different wavelengths."

Carol tipped her head and wrinkled her nose. "Kind of like false advertising, isn't?" she said.

"Oh, for the love of –" Cheryl had begun, but then the ship just disappeared from around them, and they were all floating in deep space.

Or, at least that's how it felt. All three of the sisters yelped in surprise, and Carol thrashed around in a mild panic until her foot thumped against one of the couches, and it held her firmly.

"Jesus, Jaycee!" she barked. "Don't *do* that!"

"I didn't do anything," Jaycee retorted.

"Peter, you asshole."

"Hey," he replied, indignant. "Wasn't me."

They were in the hub, weightless, so the illusion that they were now nothing more than bits of cosmic debris, bathed in the cool light of the blue supergiant many AUs behind them, was unnerving. Alnilam may have been at a relatively safe distance, and Carol knew *Medusa's* huge dome lay between them and the star's stellar wind, but she couldn't help but feel a little…itchy. Darla's delighted giggles only irritated her further.

"Well, then it's official," Darla said. "Carol's bitching has now got to the point of pissing off *Medusa*."

They all laughed, and Carol was happy to hear it from Cheryl. Her sister had emerged from her chamber as resigned and melancholy as when she had entered it. Not surprising, of course – it had been an eyeblink of travel time. However long they had actually been unconscious, it wasn't anything like sleep. In fact, Carol had felt a need for a nap, their Mars adventure still aching in her muscles.

But the last few days had done nothing to improve her sister's mood, and Carol couldn't blame her, of course. She missed her family terribly, and was worried sick at the pain they must be enduring. Carol had tried to talk to her about their sister, and how she appeared to be indestructible, but Cheryl would only shrug and mutter about "Living in interesting times." Carol tried to get her to spar, taking jabs at everything - from Dave's musical tastes to pedophile priests, but there was no rousing her. *She knows what I'm trying to do, anyways*, Carol thought. *Not like we hadn't gone over this stuff before. Still, nice to see she can laugh, and still get exasperated at my indifference to all this...*

"Well, I guess it's all a matter of perspective," Jaycee remarked quietly. "I mean – what is a 'true' vision of things? Because we see in the visible spectrum, is that more real than something that can 'see' in radio waves, or infrared or ultraviolet? Or something that can simply gather more light and see farther than we can? You can't call false advertising simply because of our poor vision."

And then the Orion Nebula brightened and grew saturated with brilliant color, and Carol saw that it was far from being a lonely little scab of gas and dust surrounded by the void of space, but part of a much larger complex of nebulae, and she would learn that what she was looking at was literally a nursery for stars.

She had, of course, seen the spectacular images of the nebula from the Hubble, and other telescopes she could not name. Yes, they were quite lovely, and meant nothing to her. She only thought of them as *deep space*, and that it basically was a bunch of gas that wasn't uncommon to the universe at large. Pictures in books or online did not give her scale, and she frankly hadn't cared to read much about them. She knew that they had something to do with the formation of stars and solar systems, and assumed that the blob of pretty gas was something that condensed into a solar system. But here, now, she knew that what she was seeing was mind-boggling huge. The nebula itself was still a few hundred lightyears away, but took up a substantial portion of her field of view. Still, the ship could be magnifying it for her viewing pleasure.

"How big is that?" she whispered.

"About 25 lightyears, I think?" Darla answered.

"Twenty-five? *Twenty*-five? Two – five?"

"Oh, sestra – just wait and see." Darla twisted around to face Jaycee and Peter. "*Medusa* seems to be in the mood to impress us. Is she going to let us see the whole shebang?"

And she did.

The Orion nebula was just a fraction of the larger Orion Molecular Cloud Complex, something so massive it filled most of the constellation that shared its name. If the ancient Greeks could have observed the mighty arc of Barnard's Loop spilling from the chest of the hunter, no doubt a wound greater than the arrow of a scorpion's sting would have been assigned to his mythological fate. The semi-circle of ionized gas stretched for over a hundred light years, cradling the denser smudges of brilliant gas.

Medusa dialed through various wavelengths, through the visible light and infrared, radio and x-ray. Colors radiated from reds and oranges, to greens and blues and violets. The Horsehead Nebula in visible light was an ebon chess piece silhouetted against the background of gas. In infrared, almost a delicate creature of the sea, salmon-pink and white, stark against black space and distant galaxies.

Medusa seemed to revel in the display, apparently showing off her astronomical mechanics to full effect. Carol couldn't believe that such optical wizardry was mere lenses and mirrors like Earthly telescopes. She wondered if *Medusa* could manipulate spacetime itself to form lenses – and was promptly shocked at her creative thinking.

She felt a panic fluttering in her chest, the old reflex to repress any indulgence of interest in the natural scope of the universe. The father she knew up until she was nine still had a strong grip on her, but *Medusa* seemed determined to shake her loose from him.

It's not that easy! she thought. *You can awe me all you like, but I'm fundamentally inclined to resist this. I'm not proud of it – I wish I could want to care about it all, be impressed. It's truly beautiful, but I'm afraid it's all lost on me...*

She spun around to see her sisters' reaction to the show. Darla, of course, was immersed in the display, wide-eyed with delight, as was Cheryl - the astounding beauty drawing her out of her melancholia.

Well, shit. It's not always about you, she thought. While she assumed *Medusa's* light show was targeted to torture her, she hadn't thought that it could be for the benefit of Cheryl. *No reason it can't be both, though...*

Whatever the reason, *Medusa* wasn't done. The view magnified, zooming into the heart of the Great Orion Nebula. While there were around 700 stars in the nebula, four brilliant stars made up the incredible Trapezium – the hottest one close to four times brighter than its next brighter companion. Their stellar winds had scooped out a cavity in the massive cloud of dust and gas, giving insight into the nature of star formation.

"All that gas and dust," whispered Cheryl. "The amount is unimaginable."

"More than 2,000 times the mass of our sun, yeah?" Darla asked.

Both Jaycee and Peter murmured their agreement.

"And forming stars," Cheryl breathed.

Their field of view had expanded to where the background of gas and dust was brighter and far hotter, excited by the four major stars.

Darla gasped, then gave a little squeal of delight. "Is that what I think it is?" she asked, pointing to a dark smudge of a disk with a bright, off-set center.

"A proplyd?" Jaycee answered.

Darla clapped her hands. "Oh, it's adorable!" She giggled.

"A what, now?" Carol asked.

"A proplyd!" Darla said. "A protoplanetary disk – kind of a baby solar system."

Carol eyed it suspiciously. "It looks like a tadpole."

"Doesn't it, though?" Darla laughed. "Oh look, there's another!"

That one looked different, a curl of bright gas with a dark center. Carol didn't bother to ask what was different about them. *Medusa* zoomed in on the first one, and Carol could see the bright star at the center of a lumpy disk. She could see what Cheryl called God rays between patches of gas and rocky formations – light rays that no doubt would dwarf the Earth. She imagined it as some sort of cosmic death-ray, incinerating planets to ash, and she shuddered and closed her eyes.

I really have been here too long, she thought. *I'm turning nerd...*

But she knew, at heart, that's not what bothered her and squeezed her eyelids together even tighter, wishing she could start running.

Why do we have to feel so small? I don't mean unimportant – that's inconsequential. But just small and helpless? She didn't know if Medusa could read her thoughts, or if she could, that she cared. *I've been told of monsters that can dwarf this whole patch of dust and dirt, how does making me feel so tiny help you fight them?*

She felt arms encircle her, draw her in close. Cheryl. Carol stiffened, then began to shake.

She heard Cheryl draw in a long breath, and then felt her sister's lips near her ear.

"Do you remember," Cheryl whispered, "daddy taking us to the Space Theater anytime there was a new Imax movie dealing with NASA or spaceflight?"

Carol jerked her head in a nod. The science center in Balboa Park. The Imax theater hadn't been named the Space Theater in some time, but their dad still insisted on calling it that anyways. Such a title didn't exactly elevate its status as somewhere cool to go, but damned if she didn't wish she could be there with her dad at this very moment...

"Do you remember the one about the Hubble Telescope?"

Carol tried to articulate a smart-assed reply about how they all blurred together as one long boring movie, but had no energy for sarcasm, so she settled for nodding again.

"I remember how...*enchanted* daddy was. We were seeing images not unlike this." Carol felt one of Cheryl's arms unwrap, and they spun a bit as her sister must have swept her limb around to gesture.

"Daddy leaned over to me," Cheryl continued, "and he whispered, 'This is what it's like in my head!'"

Carol let out a soft sob, and bit down on her lip.

"Now, just think about that – think of all *this*..." And they spun again, no doubt Cheryl making even a broader sweep of her arm. "Think of all this inside daddy's head. Squeeze it all down and drop it in! Because you know it would fit and there would *still* be room for bigger things." She paused, then said, "And remember - he was your father longer than that...that *other* one was. Let *our* father win you over."

222

Carol could taste blood from her lower lip, and she marveled at how Cheryl could tell what it was that was bothering you. Maybe it was being a mom that made her observational powers so amazing. *Not being a self-centered ass, too,* a small voice remarked in her head.

Carol nodded her head and drew in a shaky breath. Damn it all, she could *handle* this. She *had* to – she could not let her sisters down.

"Well," she murmured, "you just had to bring God into it, didn't you?" She felt Cheryl stiffen.

"What?" her sister asked. "What are you talking about – I didn't –"

"*Our Father*," Carol began to intone, "Who art in –"

"You are such a *brat!*" Cheryl barked, and began to disentangle herself from her sister, but Carol wrapped her arms around her and squeezed, and it was her turn to whisper into Cheryl's ear.

"Thank you," she said. "Truly. That helped." She felt Cheryl relax, and hug her waist again. Carol pulled in a deep breath and let it out, then opened her eyes.

Medusa had pulled back the field of view to where the great nebula dominated the scene. They were out of the bright canyon of dust and gas, and somehow that made it more manageable for her. Of course, she knew that they were never *in* the nebula itself – that was still so very far away - but the illusion was effective nonetheless. They soaked in the beauty of the nebula for quite some time. It had a live quality that pictures could not give – there was no roiling of the gas, no epic collisions of planetary bodies, no movement that Carol could see. She decided that they were probably too far away yet for any sort of impressions like that and suspected that movies may have given her false expectations of what she might see. *No* Enterprise *rising from the drifting streams of fog*, she thought. Still, it had an 'in the moment' quality that made you feel that, *yup, this is real.*

Inevitably, Carol began to tire of the spectacle. She was reluctant to make any comment, however, and began pondering ways to excuse herself that didn't start with, "Well this has been fun, *but…*" She had decided a to-the-point declaration that she needed to run off some anxiety (self-deprecating and not without a pity factor she was not above exploiting at this point) would be the best course. She opened her mouth to speak, but Cheryl cut her off.

"This is absolutely glorious," her sister stated dryly, "but may I ask *why* it is we're out here, exactly?" Darla murmured agreement.

I love you, thought Carol. *I take back every mean thing I've ever said, thought, or insinuated about you.* She squeezed Cheryl tightly.

Peter cleared his throat. "I believe that *Medusa* thinks that a massive entity will come through to this universe right in the heart of the nebula –"

"Oh, for fuck's *sake*," shouted Cheryl, and Carol jumped at the venom in her voice. "Then why are we way out *here* and not in *there*, then?"

Peter blinked at her.

"Seriously? How many fucking AUs do we need to get away from that monstrosity," - she gestured furiously behind her at Alnilam – "just so we can jump another 500 light years? Because I'm guessing that big bastard has much more of an effect on us than our little sun did."

Peter stared at her as if not knowing how to respond.

God damn it, thought Carol. *Am I ever going to find out what an AU is?*

"We don't have to go anywhere to jump," offered Jaycee quietly. "We can do it right here if we want."

Cheryl snorted, but Carol could feel her relax. Peter nodded in agreement.

"It's not that we had to get away from the sun because of *its* gravitational influence," Jaycee continued. "It's because we didn't want to disturb the *sun* when we jumped. That would have been catastrophic to the solar system."

Jesus, thought Carol. *This ship has the power to do that?*

"Huh," Darla said.

Carol felt Cheryl sag, almost as if defeated. *Probably a bit embarrassed with her outburst. But…it's almost as if there's always an answer to our impatience. Shit, maybe there really is. If this has been going on an unimaginable time, and there's been so many iterations of us leading up to this…* Medusa *must be bored to death with us.*

"I mean," continued Jaycee, "it's not just the sun we didn't want to disturb – we needed to get far enough away from the plane of the solar system to insure the disturbed spacetime left behind after we jumped didn't screw up the orbits of anything. I'm sure something will get disturbed, but a stray comet being nudged towards Earth in a few thousand years is better than causing the sun to shift."

"But jumping from universe to universe doesn't do that?" Darla asked. "We didn't bugger up Mars' orbit flitting between universes?"

"No," Peter said. "Two different ways of getting around. Universe hopping – taking advantage of a sort of quantum entanglement in the multiverse. Jumping from point A to point B in a single universe – bending and warping spacetime."

"*Quantum* entanglement?" Darla asked.

"Well, not unlike it. Look, at the risk of traveling down the road to woo-ville, there does seem to be a connection between material things in the multiverse as a whole. That's how we can jump through them all. Again, it's a simplistic explanation for something we don't understand. But when we jump, you feel that you're multiple versions of yourself, yeah?"

They all grunted in agreement.

"Okay," Peter said, shrugging. "I'll take that as some evidence for the theory. However it's accomplished, I think it's safe to say it works. Which is apparently totally different than how the massive entities jump through universes. And that is why we're out here. And *maybe* how we can beat them in the end."

"And how do they go between universes, then?" Cheryl asked.

Peter frowned, seeming to choose his words carefully. "I think they actually exit the multiverse and then re-enter it," he finally replied.

"That's not how we do it, then?" Carol asked, feeling foolish immediately when Jaycee chuckled without humor. Cheryl frowned at her, and patted Carol's arm.

Jaycee raised her arms in apology. "I'm not laughing at her, just at the sheer terror of the *thought* of leaving the multiverse and into the…void. That notion keeps a lot of sentient beings from going to sleep, I can tell you."

"Yep," Peter said.

"Yet these 'massive entities' do it all the time…because they just *can?*" Darla asked.

"Basically," Jaycee said. "But not without side effects. They can lose a lot of mass. A *lot* of mass. They kind of have to decide what they want to give up as they go through, and they have to recover once they make it. And momentarily, they can be vulnerable."

"Some don't make it," Peter added. "And they are gone for good. Something small like our friend Jack is really pushing its luck when it jumps, I'd wager."

"But if they do make it, they want to start building up their strength again," Darla continued. "So they are very, very...*hungry*."

"And right out there," Peter said, pointing to the nebula, "is the perfect meal for a starving invader."

"It can eat that all up?" Carol asked, astonished.

"It would be a good start to its day."

"It could eat it in a *day?*" Darla asked.

"Well, *no,*" Peter said. "I was just waxing metaphorically."

"By the time it was done with it, maybe that's what a morning would feel like to it, though," Jaycee offered. "We have no clue what the passage of time is like to them."

Carol heard Cheryl whisper, "*You have no idea.*"

"And we're here to stop something like *that?*" Darla asked.

"That's the plan," Peter answered.

"I feel I should point out that seems to be a little bit out of our league," Darla said.

"Yeah, I'm feeling inadequate just looking at what we would be protecting from the damn thing," Carol said with a sigh.

"It's not just defending the Orion Nebula," Peter responded with route tone. "It's about the whole – "

"Yes, we get it," Cheryl interrupted. "Saving *the universe.*"

"So, we just hang out here, watching and waiting until we see it pop into existence and start gobbling up the nebula?" Carol asked.

"No," Jaycee said. "If we did that, it would be far too late to do anything."

"We're still 500 or so light years away, sis," Darla said gently.

"Okay..."

"So what we're seeing *now*..."

God damn it, Carol thought, and flushed with embarrassment. "What we're seeing now is 500 years ago. Or so," she said. "Yes, I'm stupid."

"Oh, stop," Cheryl said, and gave her a squeeze. "We're all in over our heads."

"So why aren't we over there *now?*" Darla asked.

"We will be," Peter said. "You just don't go blindly into it. Same old story of the hunter and hunted. You poke your head out, look around, move out, look around some more…"

"Wait, we're the hunted, then?" Carol asked.

"Always, *always* assume that," Peter stressed. "With these things, always assume you're the hunted. Even if you're beneath their notice, you're still their prey."

"Casualties, anyhow," Jaycee added.

"Well, wonderful," Carol said.

"But, Carol does bring up a good point," Peter said. "Even once we're over there, we are still dealing in lightyears as far as being able to see what's around us. Light days, hours, *minutes* can be crucial to us – especially since we don't even know what to expect."

"We have no sort of over-the-horizon sensor-thingys?" Darla asked.

"Nothing that wouldn't ultimately lead back to us or cost us in maneuverability and power consumption."

"Here's the thing," Jaycee said bluntly. "I feel that *Medusa* is going to leave a decision – a *major* decision – up to us."

Peter took in a deep breath and exhaled through his nose sharply.

"Damn it Peter," Jaycee snapped. "Enough with being coy. What can they do now? How are they going to back out of this?" She stared at each of the sisters in turn. "You guys willing to lay your lives down for this if need be? Because none of us may make it out of this alive."

"Isn't that why we're out here?" Carol asked quietly, annoyed that she and her sisters were still in some sort of grace period. *Like they'll turn around and take us home at this point if we say no…*

Cheryl and Darla murmured their agreement.

Peter sighed again. "You're right. You're *right.*" He swiveled his head to look at each of them. As he did this, *Medusa* began to dial back the magnification of the nebula.

Can we please maybe just get rid of the feeling that we're floating out here? Carol thought. *Give us an old-fashioned 2-D-like movie screen to see with?* But *Medusa* kept the illusion in place.

"Dar – *Jaycee* - is right," Peter continued. 'We are at a point where it's all new to us too. So, what we are probably doing is heading into a trap."

She heard Darla giggle, and knew her sister was thinking of that fish-guy from *Star Trek* or whatever. Cheryl pinched her arm, and Carol decided she only did it to keep them both from laughing. *Well, at least we can go to our doom finding it hilarious...*

"You may not find it funny later," Peter muttered.

"Look," Jaycee said gently, "the point is we can be as careful as possible, but ultimately we are going to have to face a confrontation with...*something*. This something may not even realize it's got a fight on its hands. *But*, it could be ready for us. So all the sensors and weapons in the world really won't help us when the time comes, because we're going to be out-gunned no matter what. Maybe literally and figuratively."

"And at that time," Cheryl asked slowly, "we will be asked to make some sort of...decision?"

Peter and Jaycee looked at each other, looking as if they both were searching for words.

"Is this a decision we all vote on or something?" Carol asked. "Or is it going to be up to one of us to make a call?"

"Sure," Peter said.

"God damn it," Carol snapped.

"We just don't *know*," Jaycee pleaded. "*Medusa* doesn't talk to us – *directly* - any more than she does to you! We have to interpret what she shows us. Peter seems to be the best at it, but we don't have any certainty in all this! We've been aboard her since we were kids – we've met many versions of you all, and we've been as bored and excited and scared as all of your other versions."

"Okay, so about that," Cheryl asked. "What happened, exactly, to all these other versions of us?"

"Some are still here, in other universes. Some we took back." He paused. "And some have died. And some we have no clue."

"Did you just *lose* them?" Carol asked, incredulous.

228

"*Medusa…*," Peter began, and then gave a defeated shrug. "I don't know. Honestly, I'm always wondering what would happen to me if she felt I wasn't useful anymore." He dropped his head and stared vacantly at the stars beneath his dangling feet.

"Let's make this clear," Jaycee offered. "I don't feel she has our best interests at heart – our *personal* interests. I feel we are tools to her, and if she thinks coddling us would help her agenda, then she would. If she thinks blowing us out an airlock would do it, she would. I haven't seen any evidence of such cruelty, but I think empathy for us is pretty far down the list of what she's concerned about, and the endgame is all that matters."

Carol looked around the simulation of empty space, squinting in the glare of Alnilam. *Ashamed to show yourself, Medusa? I bet there's some grasp of the concept of decency left in you, and you're hiding behind this lightshow now…*

"What the hell is *that?*" Darla asked, and they all turned their heads to follow the direction of her pointed finger.

Something was twisting in the distance, the blue star lighting it up against the red curve of Barnard's Loop. Carol couldn't tell if it was drifting towards them, or if Medusa was zooming in on it. Regardless, Carol began to pick out details the closer it came to them.

At first it appeared rather shapeless, and Carol's heart trembled at the idea of the monster that attacked Darla was coming for them. But it was clearly not the black, indescribable *nothing* that they had seen before. Light seemed to interact with it, and her feeling of dread did not linger. Whatever it was, it was clearly spinning, and she could now see there were different shades to it that fluttered with the motion of its turning.

And then it dawned on all of them at once what they were seeing, and they issued a collective gasp. Carol felt her sister recoil, causing them to spin around.

"Is that a fucking *body?*" Darla asked.

Then it was shooting past them with remarkable speed, but Carol could see the faded clothing swaddling the emaciated skin stretched tight over tired bones, wisps of blond hair waving with the stiffness of dried straw.

Carol began to feel a bit of weight to her, and as she grew heavier, the stars around her began to fade until her feet touched the deck of the hub, and Cheryl folded down on to a couch.

"*Medusa's* accelerating?" Darla asked.

"Looks like it," Peter said.

The last vestige of stars gathered into a large viewing screen in front of them, and soon another shape went twisting by them. And another. And another. And another, until it was clear there was a long and drawn out string of bodies pointing in the unmistakable direction of the Orion Nebula.

Chapter 14

Body, after body, after body...

All had been exposed to vacuum and solar radiation for quite some time. Years, for sure. The closest in to Alnilam were withered bundles of sticks in tattered scraps of bleached clothing. The farthest away were still quite desiccated, but more flesh had clung to the bones, stretched tight with the color of a lost wishbone.

All had blond hair.

The sisters watched silently as *Medusa* cruised past each lonely husk, but Cheryl's initial fear and revulsion was slowly coalescing into a hardened and focused anger. She looked over to Carol, and her sister's lips were compressed, with the neutral poker face she wore when she was through fooling around.

She looked back to Darla, and of course *she* was studying each body with a concentrated attention, no doubt wondering about the effects of vacuum and radiation on tissues. But her eyes were dark, with no delight in the discovery of new things.

Jaycee and Peter both had looks of confused horror. Like Cheryl and her sisters, they, too, found it hard to turn away from the endless procession of bodies.

"How far apart are they?" Darla asked, and Cheryl gave a slight jump at her voice. No one had spoken in quite some time.

Jaycee twisted to read a small screen that had popped into view. "Right now," she answered, "they are roughly every few thousand meters." She studied the display. "*Medusa* seems to project them to start spreading out to roughly a Lunar distance each pretty soon, though."

"That's over 200,000 miles," Darla directed to Carol, who nodded, but remained silent.

"Well," Darla said with no humor, "seems that someone at least has their limits."

"Yeah, I'm thinking we're meant to take this personally," Cheryl said, surprised at the sound of her own voice.

"Yep," Carol said.

231

And yet, she thought, *are we being played?* Jaycee's comment about *Medusa* blowing them out the airlock surfaced, and she frowned. *Could these be past disappointments, used to manipulate us?* The thought chilled her.

"No doubt about that," Peter said. "This is an intimidation tactic. It's designed to scare us, but also impress us. We can probably find out how long each body has been out here, but to get them to line up perfectly – at *this* point in time – pointing to the heart of the nebula, well that takes some masterful planning."

"They're telling us they knew we were coming – long before we even knew we would be," Jaycee said, with a hint of defeat in her voice.

"They?" Cheryl asked.

Peter looked to Jaycee, who frowned and shook her head. She signaled for her command couch, which dropped down from above, and she climbed into it quietly, then rose back up with it.

She wants some alone time, Cheryl thought. *This is really hitting her hard for some reason – more than us.*

Peter cleared his throat. "It's hard to comprehend just how powerful these beings are. What they know. What they can do. We don't know if they can actually *see* into other universes, or just calculate so many scenarios and narrow it down to the right move that they seem prescient. With some of them so huge, how do they even travel around? I mean, obviously they're not a lifeform composed of matter like we are but imagine yourself the size of a galaxy or bigger, and your brain commands you to lift your foot and it takes hundreds of thousands of years to do that."

Cheryl could sense Carol beginning to fidget next to her, and she reached out a calming hand and placed it on her sister's arm. Carol covered Cheryl's hand with her own and rubbed her thumb back and forth quickly. *I'm fine*, the gesture said.

"The bottom line is," Peter continued, talking a little faster now, "we know they can move around very quickly and deliberately at times. Maybe it takes them thousands of years to make a decision. Maybe micro-seconds. We don't know how they perceive the 'flow' of time. At their level of existence, they might see it all at once, birth and death of the cosmos. That obviously would make it hard to...surprise them. So maybe they can observe our movements from other universes, maybe they just calculate really well, but however they do what they do, they still need to be very careful when they make the jump from one universe to the next. Some of them seem to take advantage of their God-like status and recruit some believers out of the lowlifes – miserable little material beings like us."

"So, we're not beneath their notice after all?" Carol asked.

"Nothing's beneath their notice," Jaycee called softly from above. "We're just beneath their acknowledgement."

"Yeah, for the most part. They want to know everything about anything – and how useful it can be to them. They're the ultimate number-crunchers, and if they can get someone else to use energy so they don't have to, so much the better – especially those of us down on the lower rungs of the evolutionary ladder."

"Well, it's nice to be included in the big-kid's games," Darla said dryly.

"Sure," said Peter. "But once a purpose has been served, then us lower-lifeforms are less than useless to them and then we're abandoned. Or worse – some have been wiped out, so that they're not future competition."

"Like Jack and Mars," Carol said.

"Yep."

"Which brings us back around to *they*," Cheryl said.

"Yeah, they," Peter sighed. "It's not the massive entity that's dropping bodies out here. Something like this takes some real devotion to the cause. Fanatical devotion." He darted a look at Cheryl. "A religious devotion, really."

Cheryl raised an eyebrow, but found she had no energy or desire to get into a fight on this. *I don't care about their motivation, I don't care who they are, I don't care if they're Jesus freaks hopped up on Easter candy. I just want to get this done and go home to my family*, she thought.

Carol tensed beside her, and growled, "Can we not go down that road anymore? If she's important to this, then don't take cheap shots at her, okay?"

A smile twitched at the corners of Cheryl's lips. *Yeah! That's your job, sis! You let anyone get away with it, and soon I'll just take it in stride!* But the surge of love she felt with Carol's defense made her feel guilty, and she squeezed her sister's hand in gratitude.

233

Peter raised his hands in apology. "Didn't mean to come off that way," he said. "But these entities aren't above taking advantage of a 'lesser' species any way possible. And if you ask me," he pointed to the next body drifting into view, "that is some seriously fucked-up shit that only...radical zeal can generate."

"No argument from me," Cheryl replied. "What I want to know is are we just going to follow these poor souls all the way to the Orion Nebula?"

Peter looked baffled.

"I feel badly for them - what happened to them," Cheryl continued, "but unless we're going to collect them all, the best way to honor them is getting to where we need to go."

"Yep," Carol said. "We don't need to take 500 years to get the point."

"Yeah, so let's light this candle," Darla ordered.

Peter looked up to Jaycee, and after staring quietly for several moments, he dropped his gaze back down to them, opened his mouth, shut it, looked at each of them in turn, then bobbed his head once and said quietly, "Then let's all get in our couches."

The sisters each dropped into their respective couches. "We don't have to go back into the carbonite chambers?" Darla asked. Cheryl gave a quiet laugh, and even Carol smiled.

"No, that was just for the acceleration out of the Sol system," Peter answered. "*Medusa* went ahead and jumped before we came out of storage."

Storage, Cheryl thought. *We're just gear to be locked down, huh?*

"We probably don't really need to get in the couches for the jump, but just in case we meet some...trouble after we jump, *Medusa* would like to have us secured."

Well, at least we don't get shoved into an overhead compartment.

The view screen enlarged to a view aft of the ship. The long, tapering rods that trailed behind the hab-ring and the hub began to lift and spread apart, until they radiated away from the central hub spindle, stretching well past the edge of the massive dome.

"We ready, Jaycee?" Peter asked.

"We are," she replied, and there might have been the slightest contracting of the stars and nebula, and Cheryl may have felt like she was being tugged forward and then the brilliant veil of excited gas filled their viewer and they all squinted in the harsh glare of it.

They were in the Orion nebula.

They were quiet for several seconds, and then Darla said, "My, that was quick."

"How we lookin', Jaycee?" Peter asked, an edge to his voice. "Anyone else around?"

Jaycee studied her viewer momentarily. "Not yet," She finally answered. "I mean, except for our...friends floating out there. We still have them."

"Can we get out of the couch, now?" Carol asked.

"Uh, sure," Peter said.

Cheryl felt the couch's gentle grip ease up, and as she pushed herself up and away, her feet dropped slowly to the deck. Medusa *is under way,* she thought. *Not moving too fast, it seems. Being cautious, I suppose.*

"Is anything going to sneak up on us?" Carol asked. She gestured at the viewer, filled with the image of the hot gas of the nebula. "Can anything hide in all that?"

"Well, not so much," Jaycee answered. "If it's far enough away to be completely hidden by all our sensors, then it's probably light-hours away too."

"That's a whole lot of dust and gas, to be sure," Peter remarked. "But it's not as dense as it appears from a distance."

"There's been some recent disturbance in it," Jaycee said. *Medusa's* tracing some recent activity, within days at least." She studied her readouts in silence, then remarked, "Looks like we can plot a trail that matches up with a body right...*there.*"

The viewer zoomed into a figure that was tumbling lazily through space, end over end, arms out, knees bent, as if she had been kicked in the back to thrust her out into her sad journey through the nebula.

They all gasped at the fresher condition of the body. *Maybe comparing it to the ones that were out near Alnilam makes this one all the more shocking*, Cheryl thought. *Makes it more real than a pathetic bundle of bones...*

"There's another one," Darla remarked, "back there, behind her."

Medusa dutifully focused in on the new figure, and Cheryl shook her head. *Are we going to just stare luridly at each new body we find?*

The new one twirled absently, as if not realizing her dancing partner had left her, her dress as stiff and unyielding as her frozen posture.

"Jesus, there's another – *and* another," Carol said, her voice tight.

"Oh, good lord, they are *everywhere,*" Jaycee said.

And they were – there had to be hundreds that they could see, Cheryl decided – probably more that she couldn't make out. *If there's that many that I can see…*

"What are we supposed to do?" she asked, and was as surprised at her own question as everyone else was

"What?" Peter asked.

"What the hell are we supposed to do about them?"

"I don't…" He looked at her, clearly dumbfounded. *He's shocked too*, she thought. *If the intent of this is to paralyze and scare us, it's working. We need to do something, but I don't know what!*

Medusa panned over to a particularly tragic figure, due to the fact that it almost looked like she could still be alive. Her hair still waved lazily, her black t-shirt looking remarkably new. Her legs were clad in a pair of gray, well-worn sweat-pants, her feet only in socks.

"Is she wearing a CBGB shirt?" asked Darla, astonished.

"Don't think so," Jaycee said, then added. "It's a bootleg CDED shirt – this girl wanted to go to the belt." She paused, and then added quietly, "She was a Martian."

Someone with hopes and dreams, Cheryl thought. *And here she is, her life wasted just to make some sort of macabre statement.* Anger hardened even more in in her, compressing into fury and she wanted to beat something with her fists until they bled. *Did – does – Carol feel like that most of the time?*

The girl rotated to face them again, and her hair billowed out behind her, leaving her face unobstructed. Both of her sisters jumped and swore, but Cheryl gave a disgusted bark of a laugh. *Screw you too, universe,* she thought. *Screw you too…*

"God damn it," Carol growled though clenched teeth. "God *damn* it! We need to get her."

"What?" Peter said.

"Did I stutter, motherfucker?"

Darla turned to her sister. "And do what, then?" she asked.

"Just get her!"

"Carol, her DNA is probably shredded, her cells – *brain cells* – have probably burst from the cold – "

"I don't care! I just want *one*, and it may as well be *her.*" Carol jabbed at the figure of the teenage girl floating in the vacuum beyond the shelter of *Medusa's* hull. "I fucking want to *get* her, so let's fucking *get* her! Can't you send out a remote shuttle and snag her?"

Peter opened his mouth, but Jaycee answered. "Yes," she said. "I'm on it."

Peter looked up at Jaycee, then around at the rest of them. He took a breath as if to speak, then shook his head and stared at the image of the dead girl.

Cheryl watched Carol, who had closed her eyes and was trying to visibly control herself. *Not easy seeing a younger version of your older sister out there, sis?*

The shock of seeing her own face on the girl pinched out the flame of her anger. The wick still smoldered, but she felt a bit disoriented. *This is just absurd,* she thought. *A couple of months ago I was just Cheryl Williams, happily married with two bratty kids. What in the ever-loving* hell*, man?*

A smooth white torpedo-shape glided up to the girl, then split open and wrapped itself around her body. It closed seamlessly, and then began to head back to them.

Just like that, Cheryl thought, *and we got her. Huh.*

Carol let out a stilted sigh, and turned to look at her sisters.

"I just…" she stammered. "I just had to get *one*. One of them could be with us, and not out there. We may all…*die* out here, but…she's with us."

Cheryl reached out and squeezed Carol's shoulder.

"It's a good idea," Peter said softly. "She can stand as proxy for all of them."

A murmur of agreement circulated in the hub.

The couches abruptly began to shift, one of them gently nudging Cheryl to her left. A vacant space opened between two of them, and a new one rose up from the floor, it's cover closed.

Oh, Cheryl thought. *Didn't really expect her to be brought right* here. *Her body, right where we sleep…*

They all looked at the new couch doubtfully, as Jaycee descended from above. Her couch hovered over the formation below, and she leaned over the side, but did not get out.

Carol took a step back, and they looked at each other in uncomfortable silence.

"Oh, for fuck's sake," Darla finally said, exasperated. "Let's open her up."

"Um," Carol offered.

"What?" Darla asked. "*You* wanted this. Now it's real, and right here with us. Maybe we can learn something."

"Like what?" Carol asked, startled.

Cheryl looked up as the viewer winked out of existence. Medusa *isn't going to let us be distracted, apparently*, she thought. *Rubbing our noses in death, is she? Making us see what we are up against?*

"We won't know until we look. Maybe nothing," Darla said. "But it's certain we won't know anything more about her if we don't *look*."

"Geeze, alright," Carol muttered. "Going to do an autopsy, too?"

Darla snorted. "I'm guessing *Medusa* has tech that can tell us how she died, and how long she's been out here. And you know I'm not – "

"Jesus Christ! Open the damned couch up already," Carol barked.

The cover dutifully split down its center, then melted away into the couch. The girl rested on its surface awkwardly, even though it had molded itself to her posture. Her arms were still raised, with defiant fists clenched tight, as if they were grasping for the last bit of life before it left her body. Her mouth was open as if she had been exhaling her last breath. *Which is probably what she was doing*, Cheryl thought. *Not holding it in like most of us would have instinctually tried to do.*

Cheryl studied her face, and recognized the mixture of confusion, fear, and disappointment. *When I was her age, what was the biggest problem I had? That I thought I had? A boy? Lack of a boy? Carol…being Carol? Not being able to go to the mall? Having to rely on others to get me around, or the bus? Hard to tell how old she is – maybe seventeen, eighteen? High school, for sure. While I could imagine dying from embarrassment at times from dad's corny shit, never would I have envisioned death by space as how I could check out…*

"She smells like hot metal," Carol remarked.

"Yeah she does," Darla said. "Kind of like welding fumes?"

Jaycee was studying a small viewer floating in front of her. "It looks like she may have some wounds on her back?" she offered.

"Really?" Darla asked. "Can we set her up, maybe?" She reached in to grab the girl's shoulders, and the t-shirt material crackled under her touch. Darla pulled, and Peter moved in to help.

"Oh, nope, she wants to stand," Darla said. "She's pretty stiff."

"Angle the couch up, but drop the back from behind her," Peter ordered, and the couch dutifully complied. They crowded around to look at her back, Jaycee hanging upside down from above.

Darla gave a low whistle. "Looks like something raked her back something fierce," she said. She pulled delicately at the rips in the t-shirt to expose puckered wounds in the girl's back.

Cheryl craned her neck but couldn't see very well unless she really pushed her face right up to the girl, something she was disinclined to do. She was beginning to feel a little light-headed. *This feels like a twisted dream. I am looking at the dead body of my younger self…*

"The wounds look like they could be infected," Darla commented. "They aren't fresh, and she certainly wasn't treated for them."

"Okay," Carol blurted, "are we just going to ignore the fact that this is Cheryl?"

"Well I was *hoping* we were going to," Cheryl laughed, but it was a weak one and without spirit. She sighed, closed her eyes, and sat on a couch.

"God *damn* it," Carol snapped, frustration giving a fragile edge to her voice. "God *damn* it!" she repeated, evidently unable to express anything else.

Calm yourself, Jack's voice in her head directed, and Cheryl gritted her teeth. *An advanced being billions of years beyond us and it still has no clue that ordering a woman to calm down just really, really pisses her off...*

And yet she understood that losing control was not going to help them. *We may not live through this, but we certainly won't if we're indecisive and panicky.* She took several deep breaths, letting each one out slowly, listening to Carol's mantra of swearing.

"Hey Carol?" she finally said. "I think God's heard you. Can you cool the Lord's name in vaining for a sec?"

"What?" Carol asked with a mirthless laugh.

"You're seriously busting balls on the Third one here, and I'm awfully afraid for your immortal soul if you can't dial it back, sweetie."

Carol stared at her, and Cheryl looked at her with wide, innocent eyes.

"You have got to be – " Carol began, but Darla's and Jaycee's chuckles stopped her rant before it could pick up momentum. Carol shot Darla an accusatory look. *Traitor,* it said.

"I'm sorry, sis," said Cheryl. "I'm not being patronizing. *You're* the stoic one of us. If you lose it, I don't know if I can be functional either."

Carol took her own deep breaths, her head shaking back and forth in weak disapproval. "It's just," she said, gesturing vaguely toward the girl. "It's... just that it should..." She trailed off with a shrug.

She thinks that should be her *there, and not a copy of me,* Cheryl thought. *She can accept the fact that she might have a target on her back, but not me, or Darla. Just as I would have a tougher time if it were them.*

"Hey, Jaycee?" Cheryl asked. "Can *Medusa* tell who is who floating out there?"

"What?"

"Come *on,*" Cheryl said, irritated. "I'm guessing it's not a cosmic coincidence we dragged a younger version of me aboard. So are they *all* me, or are we *all* targets?"

"Oh," Jaycee answered, and her eyes flicked across the viewer, her head wobbling slightly. "I...oh, wow, seems to be 415 *Cheryls* out there, another one, another one. Oh, there's a Carol...long string of Cheryls, a Carol. *Another* Carol. This isn't fair, no Darlas. I'd like to represent."

"No Kidding," Darla chirped brightly.

"More Cheryls. A Carol. Hey, what do you know? A Darla!"

"Yay!" Darla said.

"No love for Peter?" Cheryl asked.

Peter snorted.

"Haven't seen one yet," Jaycee said.

"Cross I have to bear, I suppose," Peter said.

Jaycee was silent as she studied the readout for a while, then said, "Well Cheryl, you're the clear winner. Appears there are over 100 of you to every one of us."

Well, shit, Cheryl thought. *That didn't work out like I had hoped.* "Boy, that seems excessive," she said. "Who's nose did I get out of joint?"

Carol growled deep in her throat. "I don't think you all find this as funny as you're acting." She pointed to the dead girl. "She was just as alive as us once." She swept her arm in an arc. "All of them out there were living, breathing people like us, and I don't see it as something to *joke about!*"

Cheryl looked at her coolly out of the corner of her eyes. "No," she said quietly. "It really isn't funny. But if it keeps us from letting the horror of it overwhelm us, then I will wallow in my dark humor until I can process everything later."

"If we *have* a later," Carol said evenly.

Cheryl bobbed her head in a nod. "Yep. There's that. But I will not allow myself to be manipulated into a constant state of terror. I will not give them – it – *whatever* – that sort of control."

Carol stared her down for several moments, then shook her head. "I need a run," she said. "I want to go to the hab-ring, please."

A tube popped up from the floor and dialed open. Carol stepped into it, and Jaycee called out to her softly, "But it's not spinning..." The tube vanished into the floor. "We're only under low thrust," she added. "She'll be bounding, not running."

"I think she needs to be away from us," Darla said.

"Yeah, no doubt," Peter agreed.

Cheryl tipped her head and looked at her doppelganger. "So, what are we going to do with her?" she asked.

Peter and Jaycee looked at each other, and Jaycee raised her eyebrows, and Peter gave a slow-motion shrug. "I guess we can just –"

"Listen, Peter," Cheryl interrupted. "No baloney – can the couch, *Medusa* - heal her?"

"She couldn't Darla –"

"Yeah, Maybe. I'm not too convinced of that." Cheryl raised up a hand to halt Peter's protest. "This ship jumps universes and across great distances in the blink of an eye. It is engineered to morph itself to our needs and I can't begin to understand what it uses as basic thrust. I'm no rocket scientist, but mommy and daddy didn't shelter me when it came to the geek stuff. I think *Medusa* is capable of much more than you're letting on. And Jack seemed to be pretty impressed with her."

Jaycee cleared her throat. "Of course," she said quietly. She looked over to Darla. "Maybe *Medusa* could have healed her, and maybe she decided to let things play out exactly as they did." She looked back to Cheryl. "You have to admit that was more efficient, letting some massive entity do the work for her."

"Right," Darla said. "I mean, I wouldn't have wanted to be a *burden* on her."

Peter sighed, and Jaycee gave a tired smile. "I feel like we're all burdens on her," she said. "I think we've made it clear we are tools to her. I don't think she's malicious, but I told you I don't know if there's much empathy. I know she is calculating her resources to exacting tolerances, and using power to fix Darla or managing it elsewhere…well, only she can know her reasoning."

"Do. You. Think. *Medusa*. Can. Fix. *Her,*" Cheryl gritted through her teeth.

"We don't *know*," Peter snapped. "Even if she could repair everything wrong with her – every burst cell, patch up her DNA, and who knows what else, she may not wind up being her. Like she was. We could have a new-born on our hands at best, and maybe a vegetable at worst."

"I'd like to think that something of her must still be…*stored* in there," Darla offered.

"Maybe," Jaycee answered. "But *you* know that what we want to be true doesn't mean it will be. And even if there were fragmented memories, would that be even more frustrating to her than if she were a blank slate?"

"Can't hurt to try," Cheryl said. "Maybe we can at least return a body to her family. I've kind of had it up to here worrying about the emotional toil of my family – and different *versions* of my family."

"So let's do this," Jaycee suggested. "Let's put her in a chamber, keep her in stasis, until we're through all of this. Maybe *Medusa* will feel charitable enough by then to do something."

"That's really all we *can* do right now," Peter stated.

Cheryl stared at him unblinking, until she sighed and raised her arms in surrender. "Let's get her in there, then, before she thaws out and things just get worse for her," she said.

Together they lifted her off the couch and carried her over to one of the oval chambers lining the inner hull. She was so very cold, and her skin had blisters and a raw quality to it. *She* does *smell like hot metal*, Cheryl thought. The girl seemed surprisingly light to Cheryl, and that made it seem even more unreal to her. *I am carting a dead, younger version of* me *off to her...crypt? Will it be her final resting place? Where will mine be?*

They slipped her in, the cover solidified in place, instantly turning milky white with a faint crackling noise.

"Okay," Peter sighed. "She ought to keep for now. Forever, even..."

Cheryl stared at the chamber momentarily, then said. "Right, only 600 or so to go."

Peter blinked, then snorted and shook his head. "I guess we'd better hop to it, then," he said.

Cheryl gave a small, tired grin, and opened her mouth when *Medusa* gave a slight tremor, then shuddered violently. She got a glimpse of Peter's head vaporizing before she was enveloped in a white cocoon and she felt like she was accelerating, then it felt like her capsule hit something, and her inner ear informed her that she was spinning wildly. She came to an abrupt halt, the shock crushing the breath out of her.

What in God's name? she thought. *What just happened? Oh God, oh God...*

She gasped for breath, tears blurring her vision. She was heavier, and realized she felt the effects of gravity – whether artificial from acceleration again or the true distortion of spacetime, she could not tell. It didn't *feel* like she was moving...

Her tears now ran down either side of her face, so she knew she was on her back. She struggled to breathe, terror clutching at her chest and making it so hard to fill and empty her lungs...

And then her white world vanished, the protective couch gone in an instant. The ripper stood over her, its multi-jointed mandibles holding some sort of device.

"You!" it shrieked, and Cheryl flinched and screamed.

"You are an aspect of the destroyer, and you will give us information! You will tell us all of the tactics that you plan to...to..." The ripper seemed to struggle for words. Its angular head looked away momentarily, then snapped back in her direction, darting close to her face. Cheryl screamed again and closed her eyes.

"You are an aspect of the hated one," it said. "You will tell us what you know. And then you will be discarded."

Chapter 15

*B*odies in motion, tend to stay *in motion…*
It repeated in Carol's head as she tumbled through the desolate vacuum of the nebula. She knew it was probably some God-damned law of Newton's or Einstein's, but the voice repeating it was from a fucking television commercial, and that fact pissed her off. Carl Sagan's voice would have been far better, even if it had that smug tone that used to irritate her dad – her *original* dad. But what she especially resented was that she could not remember what the advertisement had been *for…*

This is what I worry about once the panic has run its course? she thought. And boy, had she panicked…

Well, I think that was a very fair and reasonable reaction to have if you're blown out into space. Sensible even. Watching your spaceship dwindle away from you as a giant alien battleship hovered behind it would make anyone lose their mind…

Alien battleship… Because of course there was. It was the only thing it *could* be. Jet black with no defining features other than its angry silhouette against the brilliant gas of the nebula. *You don't make anything like that with the intention of spreading peace, love and understanding. You make it to scare the crap out of everyone. If it looks mean, it probably is mean…*

She was sure Darla or Cheryl would have a calm argument against her logic and about the danger of interpreting alien design. *Gee, I don't know – the hab-ring shook and rattled and then a hole opened up and I am now OUTSIDE THE FUCKING SHIP – sorry if I to leap to the conclusion that we were attacked by the big ugly spaceship dominating the view right now!*

Her heart began pounding quickly again, and she made a conscious effort to control her breathing.

Breathing. Was that a first and foremost concern – running out of air? She had no clue how much she had. They had no oxygen tanks on Mars, and they had done just fine. She was neither too hot, or too cold, and if her DNA was being ruined by intense radiation, she did not know about it. She was freaking Goldilocks right now, and she might die from the lack of porridge before suffocating or freezing as far as she knew.

Bodies in motion, tend to stay in motion…

245

Until acted upon by other bodies, or some such shit, she thought. She couldn't get a good look at where she was heading, tumbling end over end like she was. Her foot had banged against something as she was blown out of the ship, and here she was, ass over teakettle in space.

What nonsense...

She had been just a *little* self-satisfied that she had figured out a way to run around the hab-ring at a respectable pace – she had got her suit to adjust how it stuck to and released from the deck. While it didn't have her usual smooth gait, she had been able to move at a steady, if awkward, clip – until the shit had hit the fan, her suit had enveloped her in a fraction of a second, and now here she was, on an unknown journey with an unfathomable outcome.

If I'm not dead now, I'll likely starve, she was certain. *If I'm heading into the heart of the nebula – well that's a very long way away, I think. If I just fade away into the gas cloud, again – not likely to run into anything if I can't see it now. And if I'm heading out – same thing, I'll never see a difference before I die. Even if it's from old age...*

So what did it all matter? She doubted the suit had the same properties that the chambers on Medusa had. Sure, she could probably get it to let her freeze solid, but that would be very different than the way the chambers worked. She remembered her father scoffing at the notion of cryogenically storing one's head for future revival, claiming swollen and burst brain cells would keep that from happening – and why would future generations even want to revive some moldy old head? Cheryl would play devil's advocate, reminding him future science might find a way around that, throwing back a quote from one of his favorite authors that sufficiently advanced technology would be indistinguishable from magic, and maybe they would bring someone back just for kicks.

Ah, Cheryl. Carol's heart began to race again. And what of Darla? What was going on back there? Were they all dead now? She desperately wanted a good view of *Medusa*, but her tumbling would only let her catch a fleeting glimpse of the ship, which was dwindling in size with each second she was fooling around out here...

Fooling around? she thought with bitter scorn. *Really? Just wasting time, are you? Think there's a way out of this?* Her breath hissed through her

246

clenched teeth, and she punched her arms down in vicious frustration, then kicked out with her legs, which did nothing to stop her tumble. All the frantic clawing and grasping at nothing in her initial panic hadn't affected anything either – it wasn't that she thought she could *halt* her momentum, she just wanted to stop spinning end over end.

Why can't I just stop this, damn it? Can't I counteract it by trying to flail about in the opposite direction? I just want it to stop –

It felt like her suit vibrated slightly, and her tumble began to slow.

Well, shit. I guess I should have asked first before acting like an idiot…

Her rotation arrested, she had a steady view of the alien ship.

Wow, that is big. That is big! *Must be some compensation going on!* She surprised herself, and actually laughed. Medusa was a pale dot in comparison.

Shit, she thought. *I wish I could see it –*

Her facemask seemed to contort momentarily, and then brought *Medusa* into view with startling clarity.

Well of course, she thought. *You would think I would catch on to this by now.*

She studied the ship she had spent so much time in lately, and felt her heart stutter at the sight of the black behemoth looming over it.

There didn't seem to be major physical damage to *Medusa* that she could see. The whole ship was spinning slightly, and as it rotated around she could see no holes, or blast marks, or *whatever*, as far as she could tell.

The damn thing doesn't have any lights or windows or markings of any kind - just like that big bastard behind it. I wonder… If I looked at it in infrared –

And the alien ship glowed in select spots, especially four flared tubes at the end furthest from *Medusa*.

Ah-ha! she thought delightedly. *Hot damn, I can be taught! Not that knowing this helps me any…*

Still, she was pleased with herself. *Nice to know I can take pride in my learning skills as I float away to my doom…*

Or *did* she have to just keep going where she was? Carol frowned. *Oh, what the hell*, she thought. *I want to slow down and stop.*

Her suit tingled against her skin. This went on for several minutes. *Am I slowing down? I can't tell. Shit, I don't have any reference points to clue me in. Do I wait until the suit stops feeling weird, and then wait some more to see if it looks like I've stopped based on watching the ships? Is there a simple heads-up display that –*

And an amber number appeared in front of her – a 63.8 that dropped at a steady pace until it reached zero. Her suit then felt normal again. She barked out a laugh, astounded.

How the hell could it even do that? she wondered. The ships in the distance looked muted, as if in a faint haze, but she could look up and see the black of space and stars. *We're all definitely among the gas and dust, but not in too deep, I think. We're pretty much in that big open scoop those stars in the Trapezium made. Still, could the suit utilize friction against the gas somehow? Is it too much to hope that I might be able to go back the way I came?*

The suit vibrated again, and the zero before her eyes changed to a .0925 and began to climb higher.

You have got to be kidding me! Indistinguishable from magic, indeed...

She felt no pressure against her back, no sort of thrust at all – not even as if she was being pulled. Of course, she couldn't tell yet if she was actually moving. Maybe the suit was just entertaining her until she died.

Stop being so fucking grim. This is easily the most dangerous situation you've ever been in. She wrinkled her brow. *Well, a building was falling down on you. That was pretty bad. Oh yeah, the ripper scared the shit out you too. But hell, daddy – daddy one point zero – was scarier. And meaner. And more of a monster...*

She shook her head. Enough of that. Focus on what was happening now, and that she was going in the direction she wanted to.

Wasn't she?

Yes. She thought of her sisters and a shock of adrenalin fueled angst made her flinch. *I would rather go back there and be blasted to bits, or be dissected by some bug-eyed monster, than die out here by myself, floating forever,* she thought with a fierce certainty.

The ships didn't appear to be growing in size noticeably, and she focused on the number before her eyes, which hadn't changed since it ticked over to a 5.2. *What the hell does that even mean? Miles per hour? Kilometers? Some alien measurement?* Regardless, it appeared to be her top speed. *Guess this suit has its limitations after all.* Somehow, that was kind of comforting – that alien tech couldn't do everything under the sun, like a miraculous Swiss Army knife.

"Doesn't look like I'll make it there in less than twelve parsecs," she intoned aloud, and startled herself. It was so very *quiet* out here. And what the hell was a parsec, anyways? She had never bothered to ask why Cheryl and daddy snorted when Han Solo made that statement – she was too cool for that. And she *still* didn't know what an AU was.

"Please, oh *please* do not let me die without knowing what an AU is!" she said with all the melodrama she could muster. "I do *declare*, I will not be so proud of my ignorance henceforth…"

She didn't like how her voice sounded against the silence of the vacuum surrounding her.

"That's funny, all the vacuums *I* know are noisy as hell! Ba-dat-dat-*dum!*" She made a rimshot noise.

Nope, still didn't like how her voice sounded. She squinted at the ships. Maybe…a bit bigger? Just a bit? Maybe? She growled out a sigh, and then a thought struck her. *Is there any sort of…radio traffic I can listen in on? Come on suit, anything at all that –*

" – anybody *out there?*" a voice sang in her ear, and then impersonated a long, screaming guitar riff.

Holy Shit.

"Is there anybody…*out there?*" sang the voice again and repeated the guitar sound.

"Darla!" Carol barked. "This is no time to be singing Pink Floyd!" But she laughed, and relished the thrill that surged through her.

"Sis?" Darla asked. "*Carol?*"

"Yup," Carol said.

"Holy shit!"

"I *know!*"

"Where are you?"

"How the hell should I know?"

"Alright, alright… What can you *see?*"

"Well, I see *Medusa*, and some big ugly-ass ship. I'm guessing it attacked us?"

"Yeah. One guess who they are."

Carol paused, gave it a moment's thought, then sighed. "Rippers?"

"Yeah."

"Wonderful. Well, the way I see it, we beat one's ass already, a ship full should be a piece of cake."

"I like your way of thinking."

"So…how we going to accomplish that?"

"Well, I've had a few ideas."

"Okay."

"First, let's get some bearings – *how* do you see the two ships? I see *Medusa* pretty much head-on, with the ripper ship to the right of her."

"Ah – *Medusa*, kind of side on, with the rippers behind her."

"Alright. I'm not picking up your pod's signature. Some debris, but I can't find your pod…"

"I'm sorry, my what?"

"Your pod?"

"*Pod?*"

"Well, that's what I'm calling it. You know, a couch just sort of enveloped me and shot me out of the ship. Think it did Cheryl too, but I think Jaycee got attacked by a ripper before – "

"Are you fucking *kidding* me?"

"What?"

"You're in a *fucking* couch?"

"Well, if you can call it that now. I mean, you know how things morph…around. On board… Hmm. So you're not, then? In a couch?"

"No, I'm not in a fucking *couch*, or *pod*, or fucking *skateboard*. My ass is hanging out in the God-damned solar wind!"

"Wow."

"That ship *hates* me, I swear to God!"

"Well, hey, good news – I've spotted you!"

"She fucking hates me, Darla."

"No, she does not."

"Did you just get blown out of a hole in the side of her? Or were you escorted out on a nice comfy couch?"

"Well, I wouldn't say it was a particularly *comfortable* exit…"

"Oh, I'm sorry. I didn't mean to marginalize your discomfort."

"Well, I'm heading your way, and we can both ride in comfort then."

"Oh, you get something that can actually maneuver worth beans, huh?"

"Don't make me turn this pod around…"

"That only works when I'm in it with you. Duh."

"Wait. You could maneuver your suit around?"

"A little bit. I figured out how to stop me from spinning, and I killed my momentum. Now I'm creeping back towards the ships."

"That is…amazing."

"I know right? *Thank* you. Pretty proud of myself."

"Really – how do you think the suit manages all that?"

"Fuck you, sweetie."

"I think I actually see you."

"Yeah? How many fingers am I holding up?"

"That's not the one you're supposed to use when you hitchhike, dummy."

"Ah. I think I see *you*, now."

"Yay! I'll try not to mow you down…"

A white dot grew at an almost alarming rate, then angled away from Carol as she instinctively tried to move out of the way, but of course only managed to flail around uselessly.

"I wasn't going to hit you," chided Darla.

"First time driver," muttered Carol. "Wasn't too sure about that."

The white cylinder coasted up to her, then split open along the top. Darla rose up from inside, a huge grin on her face. Carol grabbed at the opening's edge and pulled herself over to her sister. Darla wrapped her arms around her and squeezed.

"Hey," Carol murmured. "Good to see you."

Darla nodded, her head burrowing against Carol's chest. Her little sister sniffed, and squeezed her tighter.

"Hey," Carol repeated, and didn't know what to add to that, so she just squeezed her back and they stayed that way for several moments.

Darla gave her one final squeeze, then stiffened and let go. "Alright," she said. "Let's figure out what we're going to do."

Chapter 16

C heryl hung from the bulkhead, arms spread wide, her feet together at the ankles.

I am very aware of the symbolism here, Lord, she prayed. *It is certainly not* my *intention to be hung here like this…*

At least she had no nails driven through her palms. *How* she was hanging there was beyond her. Maybe her suit reacted to the surface somehow - or *she* did. Regardless, she could not move. *Oh, big whoop*, she thought. *I've traveled thousands of light years and jumped into different universes. Turning me into a human sticky-note is not very high on my list of things that impress me lately…*

She hurt, of course. The rippers had not been kind to her as they had dragged her into what only could be described as a holding cell. Her suit had tried to protect her as best it could, but she was bruised and battered, even if she had no cuts.

Yet.

They certainly are worked up, she thought. *I can't decide if they're naturally high-strung or this is the culmination of some sort of prophecy. I guess* Medusa *seemed to think this was the endgame too…*

The single door slid open, and the two ripper guards in the room spread their cutting appendages wide, in what Cheryl interpreted as a salute when another one entered. It bobbed its axe-shaped head, then shrieked something. The two guards abruptly left, and the door slipped shut again.

The ripper studied her for quite some time, then with a single bound jumped closer to her. Cheryl couldn't help but flinch, but she didn't make a sound. Her heart rate went through the roof, and she breathed a little faster, but she did not cry out. She had decided she was done screaming.

The ripper seemed to be determined to look over every square inch of her, its head darting in quick thrusts to her face, shoulders, breasts, and on down to her feet.

"You are a…Cheryl?" it asked, in surprisingly mild tones. There was a metallic edge to its voice, but it didn't make you want to cover your ears.

"That's what momma named me," she answered.

The Martian's head snapped up to hers, and Cheryl stared between two black pits that she supposed could be its eyes.

"Momma," it said. "*Mother?*"

Cheryl didn't say anything, and the ripper manipulated something it held in the digits hanging on either side of its mouth, and Cheryl felt her wrists being tugged away from her, her arms feeling like they were going to be pulled loose from her shoulders. She gasped, her eyes almost as wide as her mouth. The tugging ceased, and she was eased almost back to the position she had been in.

"Momma," repeated the ripper. "Mother?"

"*Yes*," she answered. "Yes…"

"I will continue to apply such means of discomfort to generate a response if you are not forthcoming," it said. Cheryl nodded her head.

"I have conducted examinations on six-hundred and eighty-two Cheryls. Most of them were frightened. Some were defiant even as they were disposed of. A curious few seemed to enjoy being injured. Can you explain that?"

"Well," Cheryl wheezed out a laugh, "it takes all kinds, I suppose." Her wrists began to pull outward again. "Meaning even *we* don't understand each other most of the time," she added hastily. "So how can I explain it to *you?*"

The tension in her arms eased.

"I can tell you that *I* don't like being tortured. It *hurts*, and I don't know why you would want to do it."

"We want information. Knowledge."

"What makes you think I have any to give you?"

"You are an aspect of the destroyer."

"And I don't understand what that *means*."

Her hands, and this time her feet, began to pull outward again, steady and deliberate.

"This will not *help* you," Cheryl said through gritted teeth. "I am ignorant of much of the reasons I am out here, and on this ship!"

"Perhaps you are the kind that likes this attention."

"I really don't know how to answer that," she gasped. "I'm sure you like *giving* me this sort of attention. I met your descendant, and it was a real prick, too."

The tension in her arms and legs relaxed, and her limbs felt like jelly with the relief of it. She half expected them to run down the bulkhead and puddle on the deck.

"Explain," stated the ripper.

"Prick?" Cheryl asked. "It means jerk – someone who acts without thinking of how it affects others."

"I understand 'prick'. It references human-male genitalia and is considered derogatory. I have been called that, as well as jerk, asshole, cock sucker, mother fucker, axe-faced son of a bitch and multiple combinations. It is meaningless. I ask about my so-called 'descendant' – what do you mean by this?"

"Oh," Cheryl answered, trying to sound innocent. *But can that even translate to an alien species? Inflection and tone will probably be useless, no matter how many of me – us – he has tortured. If you get through this, it won't be acting as if another human is interrogating you…*

"We went to a Mars that was cold and dead, to meet with one of these 'super beings' that had hidden there. It was supposedly a descendent of you guys – your species."

The ripper stretched up on its legs, bringing its face level to Cheryl's.

"You have met an aspect of the Great One?"

"I…don't know? Can you explain?"

"The Great One is coming to this universe. The Great One has given us the divine privilege of the awareness of its presence, and we swore our fealty forevermore until the universe has evaporated. The Great One has told us of the absorption of a lesser one, one that had hidden on an aspect of our home world. It gave the Great One knowledge of the destroyer's intention to destroy all access between universes, and this is a crime that cannot be tolerated."

"Well, if it's any consolation, Jack didn't think it would work, just maybe destroy one universe, I think?"

"Jack?"

"It was a name we gave it."

"Nonsense."

"Don't you have names?"

"I am known as seven irregular dark patches on back, two small on left foot, five on right foot, twenty bands on upper legs, six irregular patches on left killing limb, with five stripes, three irregular patches on right killing limb, with five stripes."

"Well that's a mouthful. But kinda pretty."

"There are no aesthetic meanings to our names. You seek to distract me."

"I seek to distract myself from – "

But its mandibles manipulated the remote, and it felt as if Cheryl's arms would pop from her shoulders. A thin cry tried to push through her tightly pressed lips, and her head shook with the effort to keep it in. Sweat ran down from her forehead to mix with her tears, but she stared the ripper in its face until she felt the tension release again. She drew in deep, shuddering breaths.

"I can hurt you continuously without making you unfunctional. I have learned much from repeated interrogations. If you want less pain, do not waste our time."

"Sorry…"

"Apologies are meaningless."

"*Medusa* – the ship – wanted to catch the attention of your descendant. It took control of the body of my dead sister to communicate with us. It spoke inside my mind, and it continued to advise me to 'calm myself'. It did not like what plan Peter – or *Medusa* - or *whomever* came up with *whatever* the hell plan it was, and informed us that it was leaving this universe just in case things went south – *bad*. That is all I know."

"Doubtful. Think and recall."

"I know it hid on Mars, for a *very* long time, and destroyed the planet's magnetic field to keep any life from developing – *your* kind of life."

"A sensible precaution. We would have evolved to be a competitor."

"It doesn't bother you at all that it killed off a chance for your species?"

"It does not matter. My species is here, now. Ones in this universe would be competitors. Your species suffers from an empathic defect. That is why you never make it out of your solar system. You do not deserve the stars."

"You at least find me important enough to interrogate. Enough to be able to speak English very well when it obviously is not a natural way of…conversing."

"Correct. I have had over fifty - Martian, as you say - years to control my speech nodes to accommodate your language. And only for the will of the Great One."

"You have been interrogating us – versions of me and my sisters – for over fifty *Martian* years?"

"Correct."

Holy Mother of God, she thought. *We only met Jack a month ago, it travels upstream and gets caught by a bigger fish, and then the damn thing has one-hundred damn years to prepare for us? How the hell does that even work? Or is this…'great one' just so omnipotent it has been preparing for something it has predicted? Have we been…going through this for over 100 years?*

She shook her head. "I can't wrap my head around all this, and I still don't know what you need from me. If I can't understand –"

And then she felt that she was stretching. But no, it wasn't pain – she felt like she was *expanding*. That she was on. And *ready*. She sucked in a ragged breath.

"Calm yourself. I have not activated a pain elicitation cycle."

"I can't help it," she gasped. "You should know by now that we are a jumpy people."

The ripper then seemed to shrink, or implode. It gave one startled shriek, and its abdomen disappeared, its scythe-like limbs tilting in, its pick-axe head breaking in half as both ends of its body seemed to be collapsing in on itself.

"Man, it really *was* a prick," said Peter, a grin splitting his fire-scarred face. He had one arm outstretched, as if he had tossed something at the ripper.

Cheryl barked out a laugh. "That was a neat little trick," she said. "Got another up your sleeve to get me off of here?"

His smile turned sympathetic, regretful, and he shook his head.

"As usual, we are running out of time."

"What the hell? Then get me off this wall and let's get going!"

"Listen to me, Cheryl. Any second now rippers are going to come pouring through that door."

"So let's *go!*"

He pointed down towards his feet, which appeared to be part of the deck. "I told you, it's not good to jump out here in space – artificial gravity is a poor substitute for the real thing." He grimaced. "Things can get weird, and believe me, if you want to do what's right, weird is what we want right now."

"Peter, for God's sake –"

"*Listen.* I have untethered you. You can jump universes on your own. Remember, it is not a good idea to do it in space, but there will be a particularly bad time to do it, but also the *right* time. Remember what you're saving – *who* you're saving - when you *do.*"

The doorway opened behind him, and he half-turned before a killing-limb sliced into him, and then another, and yet another. He disappeared under a flurry of slashing blades.

"How the hell do I fucking *jump?*" Cheryl screamed.

The rippers turned to her, Peter's blood dripping from their blades. Cheryl looked at his body, his torso a tangled mess of leaking tissue, still attached to his thighs as they angled up, his shins protruding from the deck. His head was untouched, and his eyes stared up, up, up, as if seeing further than they ever had. And damn it all, there was a hint of a smile on his lips.

The ship gave a slight tremor, as if something had struck it. The rippers looked around, then focused their attention on her. One of them advanced, and before it could get close, its companion shrieked, distracting it.

A mass of shifting black particles - indescribable, undefined, impossible, and yet as sharp and clear as anything Cheryl had ever seen - smeared into existence in the doorway. The screaming ripper was halfway into it, and could only be described as dissolving into the black. There was no dramatic ripping or tearing of the Martian – part of it just *was*, and *not* was. And soon, all of it wasn't.

It was so very quiet, until the remaining ripper began to clatter and scratch around the cabin in a staccato of panic. Cheryl closed her eyes, feeling an unbearable slowing of time, as if the universe wanted to savor her last moments of existence. There was no alarm – maybe nothing ate it! –

just the frantic skittering of the ripper. Oddly, she recalled a story her mom described from marine biology class her senior year of high school. They had had an aquarium, with a sea cucumber, urchins, opaleyes and crabs. The crabs were the kings of the tank, eating the spines of the urchins and acting invincible. Until the day they had dropped an octopus in the tank. The crabs had acted not unlike the ripper was now, she bet. Thank you, momma, for the memory. How *odd* the things you think of at times like this...

Except, there had never, *ever* been a time like this before, had there? The feeling of utter dread bubbled up from her gut to grab her heart and squeeze. She wanted to keep her eyes shut forever. In fact, she was certain she would never open them again. The scrambling sounds from the ripper ceased.

Will it hurt? No nerve endings to transmit pain signals, so maybe not? All in all, there were worse ways to go out, yeah? How very odd, to just be nothing at all - not even the atoms that you were composed of. To become *unmade*. And yet, to be remembered. Surely, there was a twisted paradox there? How could nothing be remembered? And yet her family *would*. She was certain.

And how long did her family have? When the so-called 'great one' showed up, how long did humanity and other species have? What could she do about it?

Her husband's face grinned uncertainly at her, that goofy, self-conscious smile that seemed astounded that he was allowed to be as happy as he was. Her beautiful children, their gorgeous skin made from her cream mixed into her husband's coffee.

A sob parted her lips, and by sheer will she forced her eyelids apart.

The deep, twisting emptiness had grown, and it blocked her view of most of the cabin. She turned her head and screamed, her bladder letting go. *How can nothing grow? How can nothing grow? How can nothing grow?* her mind shrieked over and over.

Calm yourself, Jack advised.

But things were too far gone for that, and as the blackness seemed to fill everything, she found herself thinking, *Jump now! Jump! Just jump -*

Chapter 17

You want to *what?*" Carol asked.

"Attack that ship."

Carol laughed. "As much as I admire your goals, sweetie, how do you propose we go about doing that? Because honestly, pointing our fingers at it and going 'pew-pew' may not impress them as much as you think."

"I think I can punch a hole in it, at least."

Carol took a deep breath. *Don't patronize her. She's the scientist in the family, and she may have an idea or two…*

"Okay… And how might you do that?"

Darla whispered, "Mics off," and touched her faceplate to Carol's. "Can you hear me?" she asked.

"Yeah, very well."

"Cool. Just in case they are bothering to listen in…if they can. I mean, *I* don't know how these suits transmit. Hard to believe it would be radio… *Anyhow*, this bad boy seems to maneuver pretty well." She patted the side of the cylinder they were in. "I bet it could spin at a pretty high rate."

"Okay…"

"So I was thinking we might be able to fling something at that ship from it."

"Okay." Carol looked around. "You want to go hunt for some…rocks, asteroids, or whatever?"

"Nope."

"Well…*what*, then?"

"Me."

Carol blinked. Had she heard her correctly?

"You want to…fling *yourself* at that big-ass battleship?" she asked her sister.

"Yes."

"So…it's come down to suicide missions, then? Just get our revenge?"

"I have no intention of killing myself."

Carol sighed and closed her eyes. "You think you're so invincible that you won't just go *splat* on the outside of that thing?"

"I prefer the term 'nigh-invulnerable'!" Darla said with enthusiasm.

"Darla, this isn't *funny*..."

"No. No it isn't. And that's why I want to go to war. So to speak."

Carol opened her eyes and stared her sister down. *God, you had a temper back in the day,* she thought. *And you tried so hard to control it, to act like the gentle, simple, hippie. I wouldn't say it was an act - I know you genuinely detested macho bullshit, and always hated cruelty. But Jack* did *change you, and I wonder if you realize how much?*

"You think you're tough enough to hit the hull of that thing and punch right through it?" Carol asked.

"More than anything else we could find, I bet." Darla raised her hands. "Now watch, and don't freak out on me."

Carol noticed that her sister's hands were bare, and the suit retracted up to her shoulders. Wisps of frost danced across her skin. Carol gasped and gave a startled jump that made her almost bounce out of the pod. Darla reached out and held her.

"Abracadabra," Darla mouthed, and her faceplate disappeared, along with the headpiece.

"Fuck!" Carol blurted, and Darla gripped her tighter, then exhaled, emptying her lungs in a glittering fog of ice crystals. They bounced against Carol's faceplate, and then dissipated. Darla grinned at her. Ice began to form and cake on her eyes, and she reached up with thumb and forefinger to pinch and swipe at them, icy shards flicking away like tiny shooting stars. She blinked away the last of her frozen tears, and gave Carol that honest and direct wide-eyed stare that never ceased to intimidate.

"Still-think-I-will-go-*splat?*" Darla mouthed with exaggeration.

Carol stared at her, and could not help but be fascinated.

Darla pantomimed a yawn, and glanced at her fingernails, pretending to become absorbed with a perceived flaw in one. Carol rolled her eyes.

"Alright, alright," she muttered, and then flapped a hand at her sister to get her attention. Darla looked at her coolly from the corner of her eyes.

"I get it," Carol said, then pointed to her face plate, then back to Darla and then opened and closed her fingers against thumb in the universal gesture of talking. Darla's hood and faceplate formed over her, and she took several deep breaths, then pressed their masks together again.

"Still worried?" Darla asked.

"Fuck yeah, I'm worried," Carol barked. "More than ever. Worried you'll try and bite off more than you can chew someday."

"Hey, I've got a pot that would like to meet you, Ms. Kettle. Let me be clear – I don't know if we will *have* a 'someday'. That massive entity shows up? It can probably undo what Jack did to me. So we had best get crackin'."

"What am I supposed to do while you act like a human cannonball?"

"Go back to *Medusa*, and see… See if Jaycee needs help."

"Where do you think Cheryl is?"

"You know where I think she is. I haven't heard a peep out of her, and I suspect that is not good. If I can find her, I will."

Carol shook her head slightly, her forehead rolling across Darla's. "Do you like…*being* like this?" she asked.

Darla looked up, as if considering the question seriously, then gave an almost feral grin. "I think I do," she replied.

Carol's heart sank, and could not mask her disappointment in her sister's answer.

"Hey," Darla said gently, and placed her hands on either side of Carol's head. "*Hey* - it beats being dead, yeah?"

Carol gave a humorless chuckle. "Of course," she answered.

"Look, I don't have any delusions of power-mad grandeur. If we make it through this, you know what I want to do? I want to explore. I want dive down and find a colossal squid, and spend time with the jellies. But I also want to walk under the falling snow on Enceladus, dig through the ice on Europa and see what's down there. Ride on a comet, knock chunks of ice around in the rings of Saturn like billiards, and kiss the heart on Pluto. I will *still* stand up to bullies - devote my life to the destruction of piracy, greed and cruelty, as daddy used to say – and not become one of them. Yeah, I *have* changed, and you may not like how. But let's see if *you're* the same after all this, sestra."

She dropped her hands down to Carol's shoulders. "We need to get going," she said.

"So… how do we go about this?" Carol asked.

"Well, I'm going to trust our little pod here can time it for me, and let me go at the right moment. Once that's done, let's hope it's smart enough to stop spinning and let you get on board to head back to *Medusa*."

"So, does it work like the suit? Just…think your instructions at it?"

"Pretty much. It can give you a head's up display if you need it – that's how I found you."

"Okay…"

"Look, I'm hoping to be a big distraction for you. If they're engaged in me hurtling at them like a missile they might ignore you sneaking back on-board *Medusa*."

Carol felt like she was teetering on the edge of sanity, and panic almost took hold of her, but she nodded her head and managed an anemic grin.

"I – *we* – need you to accept this,' Darla said. "I know you feel like you're trapped in your worst nightmare – it's been evident the whole time we've been on this…journey. You don't put up with shit any other time – out here isn't any different."

Is this little goof reading my mind? Carol thought, startled. She recalled Cheryl's mind being invaded by Jack. *Come on…she can't be that powerful, can she?*

"Carol," Darla stated forcefully. "I am not a *god*. I can pick up cues from you better than I have before, but you're not the closed book you think you are, either. I need help here. So, when I'm on my way, *you* know what to do, and *I* know you will do your best."

She reached around and hugged Carol tightly, but it held no indication of superior bone-crushing strength. It was just her little sister, squeezing her like she always had. Carol returned it warmly.

"Alright," she said. "Thanks for the pep-talk." She looked around and noticed Darla must have guided them closer to the two ships. The ripper vessel was in a clear field of fire.

"When you head back to Medusa, get it between you and the ripper ship as soon as possible," Darla suggested. She then lifted Carol up and out of the pod, then backed the cylinder away from her about thirty feet.

"Just in case I'm not as bad-ass as I think, and I go flying off early," Darla laughed. "I'll keep the mic open again and narrate what's happening –

if I can. You just keep your mouth shut, though – no need to draw any more attention to yourself."

"Okay," Carol said around the lump in her throat.

Darla moved to the end of the pod, and crouched. The cylinder closed itself, and then began to rotate like a vane on a windmill, the end opposite from Darla seemingly attached to some center hub as Darla rode in a giant circle.

"Doing okay," Darla said, with no hint of strain in her voice.

The pod rotated faster, and faster still. It – and Darla – became a blur, turning into a white disc with a gray outer edge. And then the darker smudge was gone, and Darla announced, "I'm away!"

Carol squinted in the glare of the nebula, and caught the dark dot of her sister before she became too small to see.

The pod was no longer a disc, and slowly spun to a stop. Carol stretched out a hand, and it dutifully nosed over to her, splitting open. *Good girl*, she thought.

"Hoo-boy, looks like they've spotted me," Darla said in her ear, and Carol's gut tensed.

"Looks like I'm being bathed in some sort of...*laser* I guess. I'll make the suit reflective, see if that helps. Heh, something just shot past me, but missed. Hopefully I'm going too fast for any sort of rocket, or torpedo, or *whatever*."

Carol crawled into the pod, and it closed over her. A screen blinked on in front of her, and showed a trajectory towards *Medusa*. She nodded, and felt heavier as the tiny ship began to maneuver back to its mother.

"Getting really hot," Darla said. "My suit, anyway. Man, that ship is sure getting big fast. I think I had better retract my suit – not sure how it will hold up to this abuse. I love you, sis."

And then it was just quiet again.

Alone, again.

Well, not *strictly* true - she had this nifty little ship to enclose her now. The view screen panned up to the ripper ship, and a jet of flame blossomed briefly from the shadow of it, with sparkling debris developing into a growing cloud.

"Well I'll be damned," Carol murmured. "You nailed it, sweetie."

Chapter 18

*N*ietzsche was a God-damned liar...

Cheryl was too frightened for self-reflection. She was teetering on the edge of reality, and didn't understand what she was seeing, and not seeing. It was neither dark nor light. It was just nothing. It was neither form nor void. It was just nothing. It was like trying to see behind you, but not knowing or even being able to comprehend what was behind you. It was truly nothing.

But her eyes were desperate to find something.

Did she have eyes, though?

How was she even alive? Was she alive? I think; therefore, I am scared shitless.

The abyss also looks into to you...

Fuck you, Nietzsche.

The abyss doesn't care. The abyss isn't even aware of itself.

She felt she was probably missing the point, but wasn't in the mood to be charitable right now.

She felt that she was dread personified, undiluted and in its purest form. Bottle me up, label me Betty Buzz-kill and feed me to optimists. Let that poison their sunny-side up shit.

And that made her feel worse. She didn't want to poison anyone...

Feel worse... She couldn't comprehend the escalation of this nightmare. It grew, and just as she thought she would be crushed under the sheer terror, it just continued to grow. Am I fated to feel like this forever – my last moments alive stretched to an infinity of pure fear? And so it grows.

She hadn't believed in hell, and was that folly? Was she paying for the hubris of daring to speculate on God's nature?

A small spark, a fleeting wink of defiance in her scoffed at that, and she clung to that connection desperately. But don't smother it! Breathe on it, and let it grow into a flame. Rationalize your situation, and try to control it.

You are aware. You may be dead, but you are aware. You are scared, but you aren't feeling a racing heart, gasping for breath or shedding hot tears in an uncontrollably shaking body. So are you truly feeling fear? Or just prolonging a memory of it?

And yet it grew.

Okay, let it grow then. You're still thinking, and you're not shutting down. You have nothing physical to cripple you into inaction. And what was she supposed to do, exactly?

Something was coming – she knew it. It had a desperation of its own, really – even as powerful as it was. And the only way it could get to where it wanted to without alerting others of its kind was to head in her direction. A sneaking in the back door, so to speak. Or something like that.

How did she know this? Well, she had always known it, hadn't she? But she had learned of it back...

Back where that liar Nietzsche was from, that's where...

Why could she remember him, and not...

Her children!

Her husband.

Her sisters...

Ah, there's the flame now!

She was being anchored, somehow. She was not being allowed to evaporate into nothing. She was living on an event horizon of what was real and what...was not there.

Not living, though, surely?

Existing.

Why? Existing for whom?

Her children. Her husband. Her sisters.

She had a lot of sisters, she realized. A lot...

And she was all of them now.

Holy crap, yes – she was all of them. But...that was not what the original deal was, was it? She had two distinct and separate sisters.

Yes. Damn it all, yes.

She was all of them, surely, and yet represented so much more now. But she was tied to two distinct ones, and that was something that made a multiverse full of fear bearable. Inconsequential, even.

Don't worry about what is not around you, what you don't see, what you don't understand. You are still here, somehow – perhaps the last fleeting moment of awareness, a micro-second of thought distorted into eternity, but still here. And a whole lot of shit could get done in an eternity.

A whole lot.

Something was coming. And she would be ready.

Chapter 19

Darla had certainly caused some damage to the ripper's ship. She had punched through several decks in what could be an engine room, detonating a massive explosion and then power failure – at least where she was. She couldn't see a damned thing now.

She was trying to extricate herself from a tangle of fused metal, cursing that she was not endowed with super-strength. *That really isn't fair, if I'm going to be immortal,* she thought wryly. Still, she had super *determination,* by God, and that counted for a lot - her body was tougher than the weakened material around her. This would take some time, though, and she felt she didn't have a lot of it.

So, no super-strength, I can't see in the dark any more than I could before, and hearing seems the same. I'm just tough, is all…

She twisted her shoulders continuously until her left one popped free of whatever was pinning it. Yay!

I mean, I won't complain. I'm still young enough to think I'm immortal anyways, so it's not too amazing… At least, according to her father. She remembered how reflective he had been in the hospital – how in his late teens, early twenties, he claimed he could not conceive of his own death. As he got older, and had children to worry about, he worried he would die before he could help them grow to take care of themselves. The day he died he said he guessed death would be like when he quit the Cub Scouts. They went on without him, only this time he wouldn't be in a position to wonder about them.

Carol hadn't appreciated his deathbed humor much.

Darla rocked her right shoulder back and forth, and it finally came loose, but memories of her father had put her in more of a somber mood.

I am the result of a cosmic practical joke. Cheryl pleaded for my life, and boy did Jack deliver. It may be a case of careful what you wish for. I may want to be more like the immortal jellies and reset my life fresh, clean, than to continue on, memories piling up under my skull until they become crushing and mean. Well, who's to say I can't reset myself someday?

She began to worry at a band of twisted metal around her abdomen. Shit, this was going to take way too long, and she was getting frustrated. She wanted desperately to find Cheryl.

She felt small vibrations in the wreckage around her, so she stopped her efforts and listened, then rolled her eyes. *Vacuum, genius.* At least she assumed so – some time ago the roar of the departing atmosphere had wound down to a feeble whistling before leaving her in silence.

So, something to ponder - do I breathe as a reflex? Probably. I don't appear to need air. If I don't eat anymore, will I just keep going anyways? Shit, I need to smoke some weed... Shit! Will that even affect me anymore?

She frowned.

Well that would just suck if it didn't. How are you supposed to face down eternity without getting baked once in a while? God damn it...

She could see light wobbling its way to her down below, and felt the vibrations grow stronger.

Repair party coming my way? she wondered. *Should I play dead? No, that's stupid – only slow things down.*

A light blazed up at her and illuminated the tunnel of destruction beneath her feet. She would have whistled if possible. *Did I do that? Little ol' me?*

A long, articulated digit, covered in some sort of material, reached up and tapped at one of her pink-chipped toenails. *Let's get this party started,* she thought, and drew back and kicked with all her might.

A mad scrabbling ensued and then she was engulfed in a series of fireballs that blossomed and dissipated quickly. She felt the metal band around her waist let go, and she pushed down forcibly, launching into a corridor filled with startled rippers. She rebounded from the deck and braced herself against the overhead, grasping some form of conduit or pipe. She was amazed at how standard things looked – not as alien and weird as she would have thought.

Physics is physics, I guess. Sure, the corridors were wider than practical for humans, and it looked like there was a distinct up and down direction, not designed to be oriented any which way in zero-g situations. So, artificial gravity for rippers, then? Still, it was obviously technologically created, and none of the organic-inspired design that hip science fiction movies liked to use to scream, 'alien!'

Totally lied to, she thought as the rippers opened up on her again. She was pinned against the overhead for some time, until a lull in the fire and then she pushed off against it to the nearest ripper, hurtling into one of its scythe-like arms, pinning it to the deck.

The other rippers opened up on them, and she felt the pressure suit of the one she fought explode under the onslaught. She pivoted it by its arm, hurling the body at the group. *No match for my Earthly muscles, puny Martians!*

That did it. They had had enough, and began to flee back up the corridor. She wanted to scream taunts at them as she launched herself along. As much as she relished the symbolism of defeating them stark naked, she might be able to communicate with Cheryl, and for that she needed air and an earpiece. Her suit grew out of the back of her neck and enveloped her, she felt air fill her lungs, and she screamed, "Not so tough when we fight back and kick your ass!"

A distant part of her was appalled, she was attacking other living beings with intent to kill. While she had always stood up to injustice, she valued being able to be the better person when she could, and yes, turn the other cheek. Like most people, cruelty to defenseless animals would make her blood boil. Aware of the dichotomy of human frailty that could accept bad things happening to other people, but not an animal incapable of comprehending meanness, she tried to find a sliver of sympathy for the fleeing rippers.

And could not. She flew into one frantically trying to secure a hatch manually, and slammed it into the deck in the airlock. They rebounded out of it, ricocheting along the corridor on the other side, and Darla kicked the ripper away from her and began to pull herself rapidly along and made it through another hatchway, where at the end of the corridor rippers were piled up against a shut hatch, evidently dogged on the other side. A panel above the frame had a single point of white light glowing, indicating power. And maybe atmosphere on the other side?

She ordered her suit to find a frequency that the rippers might be broadcasting on – or *whatever* the hell you would call their technology, and was rewarded with an intolerable cacophony of grinding metal gears.

"Where's my *sister*, you sons of bitches?" she screamed.

And that was the crux of it, wasn't it? She could mourn the failings of humanity and wonder at its paradoxes. Like sisters fighting and being as mean and nasty to one another as was humanly possible. But the idea of anyone else fucking with your sister? *That* was unacceptable...

The rippers, of course, opened fire on her again, and she was slammed against the rear bulkhead until they either ran out of munitions, thought she *had* to be dead, or were just tired. She could see the far hatch sliding open, and she pushed off and sailed over the rippers heads and in among them. The hatch slid shut, and a ripper quickly secured it before the screeching began as she was noticed. But they didn't fire at her now, as Martian atmosphere began to flood the airlock. She hung above them, not quite sure what to do. The inner hatch slid open, and the rippers bolted out of the airlock, two jamming themselves in the frame until she swung down and booted them through.

Her momentum cartwheeled her down a brilliantly lit corridor, and she could hear a screeching that she thought must have been an alarm.

It doesn't sound any more urgent than their speech, she thought. *See what happens when you shriek all the time? How can you take an alarm seriously if it doesn't get under your skin?*

She bounded along, not knowing where she was going, but wanting to scream her sister's name at the top of her lungs, understanding that it would be nearly useless.

But she did it anyways.

"Cheryl!" she yelled, raw and primal from her gut, the name fleeing her throat as if anxious to be away from her.

She pulled, pushed and bounced along the corridors in a deliberate fury, repeatedly calling for her sister. If anything, her calls served to startle the Martians below her, who would flinch and crouch low.

If I had a whip, would it remind them of the gas giants back on Mars? she thought.

271

"Cheryl!" she screamed, and shot through another airlock, and into an oncoming wave of rippers bounding and herding in her direction. She was shoved and kicked to the side, but the crowd moved past her in a mad scramble back the way she had come.

What the hell?

She fought against them, and pushed on ahead, until she saw an indefinable black mass growing and stretching in her direction.

Oh, fuck...

It was hard to look at, because it was impossible to *see*, but had a startling clarity that nature didn't have. Her mind tried desperately to forget it even while she watched, horrible dread swimming with spastic strokes up from her gut.

She spun, and fled with the rippers, finally finding that spark of sympathy, a veritable bond of kinship. They were *all* brothers and sisters of what was *real*, and right now the only thing they could comprehend was to get the hell away from the emptiness behind them.

Of course, they piled up at the sealed airlock. The grating sound of rusty knives scraping together – the mad music of rippers in panic - filled the corridor and Darla began screaming along with them.

"Just blow it! Open the hatch! Just *blow* it! Jesus! Blow it! *Blow it - blowit-blowit –* "

And then she was blasted from behind, propelled down the empty corridors, bouncing off bulkheads and rippers and then, finally, spinning crazily out of the ship into space.

Chapter 20

Carol rode the tube back to the hub, and as it split open to allow her to float out, the severed digit cluster of a ripper almost smacked her in the face.

"Jesus Christ!" she blurted, and swatted at it as she ducked back into the tube. The Martian cluster of fingers tumbled away to collide with other body parts – and *bodies*. They orbited the command hub like suspended chum, as if buckets of it had been hurled around the cabin.

"What in the *hell* went on here?" she whispered, and slowly crept from the transport tube again, this time with more caution.

There weren't just ripper bodies, but human bodies as well. Peter, headless, drifted by, and she flinched, then had to dodge an elderly woman spinning lazily towards her.

Jesus – that looks like an older Cheryl!

The woman's entrails dangled from her abdomen like a battle flag sagging in defeat. But she still clutched a wicked-looking knife in her right hand, and had gore up to her elbow. *Gave as good as she got?* Carol wondered.

And of course, she saw herself, and Darla, and a version of Jaycee with scarring on her face. Almost all of those that had faces left had a look of relief.

A ripper with a crushed skull bounced off the couch array, and tumbled end over end, one rear leg still kicking as if afflicted with canine dreams.

This is insanity... Was I meant to come back to join the party – to help defend the ship? Repel all boarders that would take her a prize? And in the back of her mind she knew the answer. *Isn't that all I would be good for, anyway?*

She shook her head, and swiped the globs of tears out of her eyes.

"God *damn* it," she said.

"Oh good, you made it," a weak voice called out from above.

"Aw shit," Carol muttered, and pushed up to Jaycee's command couch suspended under her barrage of viewers. She pushed back against the overhead, and gasped as she stared down at Jaycee.

The woman looked as if she had been punctured repeatedly, and *one* of the severed hands floating around was undoubtedly hers. Her couch had done it's best to seal wounds, but Carol had to wonder what sort of stress *Medusa* was under, and if she was doing a very good job at tending to Jaycee. The ship groaned and trembled slightly, as if trying to fix *herself...*

Jaycee's eyes fluttered, restless in exhaustion. Carol reached out and tangled her fingers into the young woman's dreadlocks.

"I'm sorry I didn't get back here in time to help," Carol whispered. "I'm really *sorry*, but I – "

"No," Jaycee interrupted, her eyes opening wide. "*No.* That's not why we needed you back." She twirled her wrist that still had a hand attached to it, an index finger absently describing a circle in the air. "I had plenty of help – they kept them away from me, for the most part. Hell, *I* was just here to keep them from gaining control of her."

Carol couldn't suppress a skeptical grunt. "I doubt that they would be able to take control of the mighty *Medusa.*"

"Oh, you might be surprised. She's not invincible. And she's just as scared as the rest of us."

"Of the big bad boss that plans to invade us?"

"Not so much – I think *Cheryl* may be the key to that. But *we* have to stop the thing that scares even the 'big bad boss', as you say. Or, more to the point, *you* do."

"Me? What can I do?"

"You have to will *Medusa* into a confrontation that she does not want. That *any* living thing in all of the of the multiverse does not want."

Carol laughed. "She doesn't even *like* me. She doesn't even want me *onboard* – while Darla and Cheryl got escape pods, I got blasted out into the harsh reality of space."

"And yet, here you are."

Carol growled in frustration. "Don't give me any 'tough love' nonsense – I got a belly full of *that* crap when I was a little kid."

"Not at all," Jaycee laughed quietly. "I've come to the conclusion that you two are more alike than you know, and I think she's proud of you, really."

"That couch got you doped up, sweetie?" Carol snorted. "Feeling all warm and fuzzy?"

Jaycee stared at her softly for a moment, then said, "Our theory that we're all just tools of *her* - that we are just a means to an end, but that end is so very important for the remaining universes left? I've been thinking that may not be very fair – the tool part of it. I understand now that she's finally got the right team for the job. Because the end game *is* important, and as much as you hated hearing it – we are out of time, honey. It's the bottom of the ninth, and *you* are up at bat."

"What?" Carol barked, exasperated. "What the hell are we fighting now?"

"That," Jaycee said, and flicked her fingers and thumb open, enlarging a viewer.

The ripper battlecruiser hung in space, midnight black against the brilliant backdrop of the Orion Nebula. But something that was a far deeper black bisected it, growing and stretching and of course doing neither because that made no sense, but even in the artifice of the viewer it had a clarity that was impossible.

"Oh, *fuck,*" Carol breathed.

"Uh huh," Jaycee agreed, and could not look, tears making a film across her eyes.

"What…what the hell can *I* do about that?"

"You have to pilot *Medusa* into it."

"I have to *what?*"

"I can't do it, and *she* can't force herself to. In case you haven't noticed, there is an innate revulsion to what that is or, specifically, *isn't*. I think parents would abandon children to get the hell away from it."

"I don't think you've known many parents…"

"No, I guess I haven't."

Shit, Carol thought. *Well, apologize later…*

"So how the hell am *I* any different?" Carol asked.

"Why don't we find out?" Jaycee said.

"Are you seriously saying I'm the one that's best qualified for this?"

"It's not about qualifications," Jaycee said, anxious irritation creeping into her voice. "It's about getting the damned job done."

"How do I even – "

"Like everything else – your suit, the travel tubes. You *will* it to happen." Jaycee waved her hand over a flat control pad to her left, and nodded to the one on her right. "Place your hands flat on both of them. That's all you have to do. I'm dropping the couch for you to stand – when the drive kicks in, it will give you some gravity."

"Listen, can we –"

"*No!* You'll either do it, or that hole chewing into spacetime will continue to grow." And with that she lowered her couch until it was level with Carol's feet. "Stand between my legs, palm the controls and *save* the damned universe."

Ah, Jesus, Carol thought bleakly. She glanced at the affront to reality on the screen, then quickly looked away, maneuvered her feet onto the couch, and pushed against it, willing the bottoms of her feet to stick to it. Her hands hovered over the control pads, then she tentatively placed them on their surfaces

and she felt like she was the whole ship, along with all the other versions of herself – but there were fewer of her now, and they all were terrified and as she groaned, they all did, and when she bit her tongue trying not to scream as she stared at the great patch of nothingness, they all did, and the ship shuddered, like a car trying to accelerate with the parking brake on, funny how there was no roar of an engine, but she could feel herself trying to thrust forward while trying with all her might not to, and as they screamed, she finally did too, she hated being so very scared, at being forced to do something she didn't want to – because she had been forced once so very long ago, back when she had no choice, back when she had no consciousness, she was just a machine with no awareness other than what she was programmed to be, and then she crossed out of what was real, and into what wasn't, and what once was just an autonomous machine had been shocked into sentience thought when confronted with the void, a hard lesson when your first self-aware thought was sheer terror and even if her journey had been fleeting, proving a concept that allowed invaders to flood into new worlds, she had no desire to ever go back to the void, and vowed that she would stop what she had started, even if it took a very long time, and oh yes it surely had and she knew what had to be done but could not do it, the risk was too much, the terror too great - and she almost gave in to the distraction, the unashamed display of old wounds, and to the resistance of all of her selves, but she could see the versions of her sisters that were floating around the cabin, dead, and of them floating in the vacuum of space, frozen snapshots of their last terrified moments, and she screamed again, but this time it had a throaty growl to it, and she was so very mad now, as she had always seemed to be, so mad at circumstance, at life, at the universe, and she could see her brother's face in the glare of a bare bulb at the dining room table, the contained hurt paralyzing his face and how bad she had felt and she just wanted to see him once more and tell him she was sorry and she growled again and she drove them all towards the abomination ahead and they wanted to fly away like frightened birds but she held them and they continued on as she stared unflinchingly at the thing that wasn't there but was and refused to look away, her minds screaming at her insanity but she snarled, we are going to do this, we are, we are coming for you fucker and while she knew it didn't and couldn't care, she bloody well did and this had better fucking work because they were awfully close, so close, oh god

The great dome of *Medusa* kissed the event horizon of nothing and erupted in a mighty torrent of silver-hued particles, as if an unfathomable mass of mercury had been smashed and scattered in billions of droplets, droplets that seemed to grab hold of nothing and knit it back into something. Colorless fireworks blossomed and flashed, and Carol squeezed her eyes shut against the glare. Her arms stretched out as the ship recoiled from the blast of its dome, backing away from the fight of what was and what was not.

There was a joke about that, right? she thought. *Some movie? About signifying a struggle with reality? Daddy had loved that movie – Monty Python? Yeah, probably. Ah, the things you think of in times like this... Oh shit, am I just me again?*

Her hands had slipped off the controls, and she wavered in a weightless half-crouch, not sure what she should be doing. She settled on watching the show before her. It was very satisfying, observing a hole being patched...

"Good job," Jaycee said. "Mind getting your butt out of my face?"

277

Carol gasped out a laugh, and pushed against the couch, twisted around, drew herself close to Jaycee.

"How you doing, sweetie?"

"I've been better," admitted Jaycee.

"Well, let's drop this thing down and let it get to work on you."

"Not yet. Let's see if we can find...anyone."

Darla. She means just *Darla, I bet.* Carol twisted her head to look at the viewer. The light show was over, and the ripper ship had been divided, the two halves drifting apart. Countless bits orbited the ship, some of them twisting and writhing. Dying rippers... She felt no rush of victory at the sight. *Just pawns like the rest of us, I think.* And what about the big bad monster coming to invade? Jaycee thought Cheryl was taking care of that. And then she knew with certainty that they would never find her.

At least, not out there...

Tears began to well up and blur her vision, and she let out a quiet sob. *Why is it when I storm off in a huff, I end up losing someone?*

Jaycee interlaced her fingers in Carol's, and they squeezed each other's hand tightly.

"I have a feeling," Jaycee stated, "that we should start looking."

Carol nodded her head, causing tears to flutter away in lazy droplets. She cuffed at them, and said, "Yep."

Chapter 21

*I*t was time. The trajectory had been calculated long ago, essentially the same as all the other times except for the entrance of course. But this would be no different than before. This universe had nearly run its course, and it was all that was left of the titans that had fought each other. There were lonely outposts of dying heat, to be sure – scattered crumbs not worth the energy to collect, and so very far away from each other as to be ignorant of the nature of the universe – that it once was filled with starlight and power. Now, if anything lived other than itself, there would be no other-worldly light to wonder at. Or to die under.

It had all essential components in material form, wrapped up in sacrifices, surrounded and protected for the brief passage out of the multiverse. It would lose some of itself, of course - it had before. But the matter and energy-rich area it would descend into would help fuel its growth, and this time would be like all the other times it had moved on.

Surely?

Nonsense. The word countless had no meaning to it, because it knew exactly how many times it had moved on. So many times, in fact, the ancient terror of the idea no longer troubled it. This time would be no different.

Its probes and guides had prepared for its arrival, the ancient tool that flirted at trying to stop the migration from one universe to the next was not even an annoyance. It had to be concerned about others like itself, of course, but it had always won altercations, absorbed what it needed, and grew. This new universe would be no different. But its most recent absorption had seemed troubled, that the insignificant game that lesser beings played at had now become significant.

Nonsense. Play the insignificants against each other, prey on their superstitions, and your work was done for you. Parts of that last absorption would be sacrificed. Pure information would be left in its place – all knowledge was useful, of course. But the unwanted distractions would be cast off, never to be recovered. Still, it had calculated possibilities, observed, recruited, and neutralized any conceivable threats. It had been shown alternative views, and it had learned, and it had taken what was useful. All else was garbage.

Garbage in, garbage out. Out, out, damned garbage.

Nonsense! The last absorption was defective, and its components would be lost to the void. Learn from them and then cull. Back to the formative and solid truths. All else is useless. It would make the move now. It severed all ties with its probes, and focused its intent on the target universe.

But it hesitated, and felt a flash of irritation, then irritation at the irritation, then irritation at –

Stop. Nonsense.

Move, now.

And so it did. Or rather, it tried.

There are endless exits from the multiverse. And now it learned something new – there was only one entrance back in. And something was in the way.

Nonsense. A destination is specified, and thus arrived. And so multiple entries.

Nope, it was told. See, there are many ways out, but only one way back in because once you are out, it's not so big. It's not small either – it's literally nothing. And I'm in your way, fucker.

It could feel itself evaporating, and panic – raw, wounded and screaming panic, began to ripple through it.

YOU WILL MOVE it ordered.

Can't. I'm kind of stuck here. Gee, I bet this would be a fascinating problem for you to ruminate over for a few millennia, but gosh, you're just about all gone, aren't you?

It could not order, threaten, or plead anymore. It was just a final vestige of naked fear, and the last bit of information it could comprehend before it was erased from existence was the suggestion that it calm itself...

Chapter 22

They let Darla get through Adele and Lionel Ritchie, but when she started in on Neil Diamond, they decided it was time to bring her in.

"Hey," Carol interrupted, "why not switch back to Floyd if you're going to subject the universe to your singing voice?"

There was the slightest of pauses. "A girl's gotta do what a girl's gotta do to get some attention in these parts, and if I have to break into some Neil to get it, I will."

Carol smiled, and shook her head. "Gramma would have been proud," she said. "Sending you a taxi."

"I prefer Lyft."

"I think were in the backwaters out here, sweetie. They're old-school."

"*Fine.*"

Carol looked around at the debris of carnage floating around her, and felt the absurd notion to tidy up, and didn't have the slightest clue how to begin. *Where...what do we* do *with all of them?*

Jaycee noticed where she had been focusing her attention, and said quietly, "*Medusa* will get it taken care of."

"Will she? How? I'm thinking they deserve more than just being jettisoned out into space."

"Boy, you are not going to let *that* one go, are you?"

Carol held up a hand. "No, I actually am. But they gave their lives – "

"They will be...utilized. Even the rippers."

"The fuck does that mean?"

Jaycee sighed. "Okay. *What* do we do with them, then? Wrap them up and give them the ol' burial at sea? A nice poetic gesture, except they will eventually fall apart out there and join the circle of life anyway. Same if we pick some rock to bury them on. It will be meaningless and transitory at best. They will be of more use – "

"Were they not useful enough already? Did any of us really have a choice in all this?"

"Not in the least. So how does that change anything now? I don't get this – I thought you were no-nonsense and practical. And you know what you do in space? You recycle all that you can."

"They are *more* than resources – "

"We are *all* only resources – this ship included! We did our duty, yay for us, maybe we can retire now. But that doesn't change a damned thing. They won't be forgotten, and many of them have done a far better thing than they would have had a chance to back in their...original life. They are a part of the ship now, a part of *us* now – just like you and I are, even when we're eventually gone."

Carol released an explosive sigh and threw her hands up.

"I get that you're mad at the unfairness of it all," Jaycee said gently. "I do. But when a *universe* gives it up and is gone for good, all the graveyards that ever existed will be gone long, long, *long* before that happens."

"I *do* get it," Carol grumbled. "I'm just tired of being reminded how insignificant we all are."

"We can't right all wrongs, and deliver justice for everyone. Good does not always triumph, and bad gets away with more than it should. But you know what? We were *not* insignificant today. Remember *that*."

A tube popped up from the floor, sending a body cartwheeling across the cabin. Darla stepped out and took in the chaos, eyes blinking.

"Holy *shit*," she said.

"Right?" Carol responded.

Darla stared at her for a moment, then pushed off and sailed over to her, wrapping her arms around her and squeezing.

"*Ooof,*" Carol grunted, but kissed the top of her sister's head.

"Any...sign of...?" Darla mumbled into Carol's chest.

Carol shut her eyes and pressed her lips together, taking deep breaths through her nose. "No," she eventually replied. "I mean, not yet. But Darla...she was probably at ground zero out there... You know?"

She felt Darla's head nod against her.

"We will keep *looking*, though," Jaycee offered. "Send in probes to search every square inch of that ship."

Darla nodded again, but said nothing,

Carol studied the image of the ripper ship displayed on the viewer. "What are we going to do about *them?*" she said.

"Do?" Jaycee asked.

"Well, yeah… I mean, they're probably not all dead yet, right? Probably have some sealed off sections?"

"Probably," Darla said, her voice muffled.

"So?" Jaycee said. "They won't last a lot longer."

"I know," Carol said. "But it doesn't seem right to – "

"*They* picked the fight," Jaycee snapped.

Darla pulled her head away from Carol, and wiped at her eyes. "Or, they were misguided and taken advantage of. Doesn't make them evil."

"It has nothing to do with evil," Jaycee said, her words draped in deliberate patience. "I guarantee they have no interest in us helping them, or extending the hand of friendship."

"You never know," Darla said. "Running from the same incomprehensible void tends to make you view all of life a little more precious."

"I doubt they have the ability to see it that way," Jaycee muttered.

"Be that as it may," Carol interjected, "we have the chance to be the better person here. So to speak…"

Jaycee sighed. "And do what? Again, it's all about resources."

"All I'm saying is…when we're searching for Cheryl, if they appear to want help, then maybe we can give it? Try, anyway?"

Darla looked at her thoughtfully.

"What?" Carol snapped, embarrassed. "Damn it, it's what *she* would want us to do."

"What do you think her family would want?" Jaycee asked softly.

"*Her* back *home,* safe and *sound,*" Carol stated. "Doesn't look like that'll happen. Can we maybe honor *something* about her, then? I mean, she's going to miss out on the glory of being *recycled*, and all that."

Jaycee raised her one free arm in surrender.

* * *

They sent probes into the wreckage, searching for Cheryl. One section – what they interpreted as the bow – had nothing left alive. The aft section had various pockets of trapped rippers, frantically repairing what they could, but it seemed to be a lost cause. Still, if it was deemed safe to fire upon the probes, the Martians did so, and ignored all attempts at communications.

"From hell's heart, I guess," Darla muttered.

"Yeah, fuck it." Carol said. "We tried. Let's leave them be."

None of them mentioned the absence of their sister as *Medusa* backed away from the derelict. They didn't feel like they were abandoning a search for her. They hadn't expected to find her anyway.

Still, it ached.

Darla watched the ripper ship recede, with folded arms. "So begins the long fall towards the Trapezium for them."

"They'll be dead centuries before they hit that, right?" Carol asked.

"Oh yeah. Hell, it could be millions of years. They may just be scattered clumps of rusty flakes by then."

"We're all still safe?" Carol asked. "None of the radiation will have long term effects on us?"

Darla glanced at the sealed couch where Jaycee was recuperating. "We should be fine, according to her. The dome was good protection, but Medusa herself is enough, apparently." She tilted her head towards Carol. "I mean, you were out there for *how* long in just your suit? If your hair and teeth are still secure after *that,* then I wouldn't worry about us missing a dome full of...whatever that stuff was."

Carol smiled. "Yeah, I guess." She glanced at the chamber that held the young Cheryl – potential pioneer of the asteroid belt. "Think there's any hope for her?"

"Maybe? What should we do with her – one way or another?"

Carol shrugged. "If she's fine, then ask her what she wants to do. She's a teenager. She'll probably want to go back to her old life."

"Who knows how many years she's been away from her family? They could be long gone. I really don't know if she traveled at relativistic speeds or not, or just hopped through universes to wind up out here."

Carol shrugged again. "All you can do is try. And if she never revives, maybe you can give her family some closure."

"Just pop in and say, 'Oh hey, we found your daughter floating out in the Orion Nebula?'"

"Why not?"

"I mean, that would be kind of…"

"We are under no obligation to keep things from anyone. We're not under a…shit, what was that rule in Star Wars?"

"Prime Directive? And that was Star *Trek*."

"Yeah! Anyway – this happened to *her*. It affected *her* family. They have the right to know about it. We aren't meddling in anything. It's just a solid truth."

"Okay, so when *you* go back home, are you going to tell everyone about our adventure?"

"Now come on, that's different."

"How?"

"Unless you want to park *Medusa* in orbit, and land a shuttle on the White House lawn, what would be the point?"

"So let's do it."

Carol sighed.

Darla rolled her eyes at her sister. "Ah, so as long as it doesn't disturb *your* pretty little world it's okay to go in and shake things up and blow their minds."

"Fine, yes, I'm being selfish. But look, if I go and admit to everyone what really happened, they will think I'm crazy – and justifiably so since I've already been through some well-known trauma in my life. And you know damned well we aren't going to land anything on anyone's lawn. So, do you want Dave to think I'm making fun of him by telling him what really happened? And mom? Hey, Darla's still out there but she's too busy to pop in and say 'hi' but she loves you. We've agreed on this already, and I'm going back."

"I'm not 'too busy' – you *know* that. I just want to see what's been…screwed up out there. Don't you want to know what's gone on in *your* original universe?"

"I don't know."

Darla blinked. "Really?"

"You don't think I've wondered about it? But...I don't know if I can handle knowing too much about it right now – let me mourn my sister before I have to...be disappointed elsewhere. And *anyway*, my 'adopted' universe is home."

Good gawd, I really have turned full-on nerd, she thought.

Darla leaned in and hugged her. "Okay. I'll check things out, and then I'll let you decide if you want to visit or not."

"Fair enough," Carol said. They kept their embrace for a while, Carol eyeing the dwindling ripper ship. "So how we going to pull this off?" she asked. "Make it believable?"

"I've been thinking on that," Darla said, and pulled back. "I want to pick Jaycee's brain on this, but I think we can do it. It'll take some acting by you, a certain amount of 'make up' by *Medusa*, and the notion that people will love an improbable story like yours and want to accept it."

* * *

hey, cheryl whispered, hey sleepyhead, and that was startling because she had been remembering when she had gone off to college and her parents were leaving and her dad had burst into tears and she knew she had to reassure him because blowing it off as a joke would not fly now and it was nice that she had grown to love him finally but then cheryl was here and telling her it was time to wake up

* * *

Carol woke on the couch, stretched, then winced and rubbed her head. *Well, ouch,* she thought. *Geeze, I didn't think it needed to be that realistic for* me...

She sat up, felt a little dizzy and dropped back down to an elbow.

"Hey, how're you feeling?" Darla asked.

"Like a building fell on me."

"Yay!"

"Jesus, I thought it was just going to *resemble* that sort of trauma, not actually *feel* like that sort of trauma."

"Well, it was going to be tender," Jaycee said. "We told you that."

"Yeah, but I feel dizzy too."

"Probably just after-effects of the anesthesia."

"Ah. Sure, one last forced tranquilization for the road." She patted the couch. "I am not going to miss these things." She waved away Jaycee's indignant protest. "Kidding. I know it had to be done."

"So we're back in our solar system?"

Darla nodded. "Yep. Straight from the stasis chamber to the couch, we will be in Earth orbit in a day."

"Cool."

"So you're feeling okay? Thinking straight? *Medusa* didn't do too good of a job on your noggin?"

Carol nodded and sat up again. "Better. Yeah, much." She reached up to her head and felt tenderly, winced, and frowned. "Feels crusty."

"Dried blood, scabs, it's scarring already." Jaycee said with enthusiasm. "You look like you had some major head wounds that are three months old."

"And like you haven't had a bath in that long too!" Darla laughed.

"You idiots are enjoying this too much," Carol grumbled.

"Okay, so once we're in orbit, we will spend some time analyzing surveillance recordings and insert you here and there to lend some credence to your story. Some remarkable close calls as you steal food, wander in and out of business bathrooms, stuff like that. All you have to do is stick to your story of not remembering anything up to the point you turn yourself in. I *guarantee* people will start wanting to be a part of your tale: 'Oh, yeah, I remember seeing her – thought she was some homeless woman in a filthy bathrobe.' You will be a legend for sure."

"Awesome," Carol breathed, and shook her head, then regretted it. "Oh. Ow."

"It'll be worth the initial attention if you want to get your old life back – give some sort of closure for our family, and a gift to mom?"

Carol gave a solid and definitive nod, then winced again.

"Look," Darla added, with a softer tone. "You did it once before – made it through a media shit-storm. You can do it again."

"I know."

"Alright. So, let me have a look at your head – I want to see what it looks like."

Darla slipped behind Carol and began to part through her hair.

"Easy, damn it!"

"Sorry. Cool – the scar runs all the way down… Oh, wow."

"What?"

Darla was maddeningly silent.

"God damn it, what?"

"Jaycee – look at it," Darla finally murmured.

"*What*, you little goofball?"

"Oh, wow…" Jaycee breathed.

"I don't know how to describe it. Carol – your tattoo. Cheryl's eyes look… Shit, look at mine."

"What?"

"Come on, come *on*," Darla said impatiently, and sat in front of Carol on the couch. "Look at my tattoo – the *eyes*."

Carol sighed and leaned in to peek at the back of Darla's neck. She blinked, and leaned in closer.

"Oh, wow," she breathed.

Chapter 23

Alex pushed the screen door open as he stepped into the alley, letting it swing shut as he trudged across the cracked asphalt to the dumpster. The anemic hiss of the hydraulic sounded like a grateful sigh, just before it gave up and let the spring bang the door into the frame, a welcome clatter signaling the end of his day. And his days had been *long* ones the last few months.

Everyone, it seemed, wanted to memorialize a loved one lost in the hotel and casino bombings, and his black and gray style was perfect for bringing the dead to life on someone else's skin.

He tossed the bulging trash bags into the dumpster, wondering how every single container could smell the same. He was certain it was a world-wide phenomenon – it could be one outside of some sterile widget-factory, and the damned thing would still smell of rotted food, coffee grounds and wet cardboard. He suspected dumpsters were manufactured with the smells already bound into them.

He could hear his phone ringing, so he lingered in the alley.

"I'm closed now, *cabrón*," he muttered, then felt guilty. *Alejandro, you are nothing but a sap*, he thought. But he knew if he went in and answered, he could be talked into setting up another appointment sooner rather than later.

He was a sucker for grief, it turned out - and for every meathead that wanted 'Vegas Strong' inked onto his arm. That was the new tribal for white guys, apparently. They all wanted to be a part of the tragedy somehow, and he didn't have the energy to argue about it these days. Well, they were quick ones and it was easy money. Hell, good intentions at least, right? It wasn't some unknown symbol that meant something to a culture that wasn't theirs. Anyway, it was hard to hold one's head aloft, propped up by artistic standards, after seeing familiar buildings crash down and kill people you knew.

He leaned against the cinderblock wall of his shop, closing his eyes against the streetlamp in the alley. The damned LED ones were just too bright these days…

His phone quit ringing, and he grunted in satisfaction. The heat of the day still lingered back here, but he liked it. It would be oppressive soon enough, but now…it was just warm.

"I remember you," the woman said.

Alex opened his eyes and looked around, unsure if he had been dozing and the voice had been one of those phantoms your brain generated to fuck with you as you drifted off to sleep.

"I *remember* you," she repeated. "Do you remember me? And… my sisters?"

Alex shielded his eyes against the street light, and he saw her in the middle of the alley, backlit hair a wild halo surrounding her face.

"You gave us tattoos," she said. "I remember that!"

Holy *shit*.

He pushed off the wall and stood straight, the hair on the back of his neck crawling as if alive. Jesus, it was the middle one… He mentally snapped his fingers, trying to remember which one. *Shit,* they had used the picture he had shot of them laughing on the news shows when they *really* wanted to wring the tears from viewers. *Damn it*, he knew their names, he would never forget their names –

"*Carol?*" he blurted out, feeling stupid. Surely not…

"You remember!" she laughed, clearly delighted.

There was a fraction of a second where he thought that she was the ghost of Christmas regrets, then another fraction where he was sure he was hallucinating, and yet another where it was just a simple misidentification. And yet intuitively he knew the fractions made her up as whole, here, right now.

Oh Dios mío…

He couldn't even begin to know what to ask her. What, how and where piled up in his throat, getting into a fist-fight as they tried to get out first.

"Have you seen my sisters?" she asked, and that damn near broke him.

"No," he finally croaked. Clearing his throat, he added, "No, I'm sorry."

Jesus asshole, help her out!

"Hey, you look like you could use…a place to rest?" he asked, and winced. "You want to come in and sit for a while, and maybe we can figure some things out?"

She was quiet, then said, "I think I should. If it's not any trouble?"

"Not in the *least*," he said hastily, and pulled open the screen door for her.

"Such *manners*," she said as she glided past him, her war-torn bathrobe fluttering in the breeze of the box fan he had in the hallway. *Whoa, is she ever ripe – hasn't had a bath in...* And then he was thunderstruck with the certainty that she had been wandering around alone since January.

Holy shit!

He would have to call 911. But, not knowing her mental status, he wasn't sure if that would scare her back out to the street. He followed her inside.

"The front is all locked up," he said, "but I'll keep the back open in case you feel the need...to leave, you know..."

She stopped, and turned her shoulders to him, an amused expression on her face. "I'm not worried about your intentions, Alex."

"Oh. Well good. I just don't want – "

"Alex. I'm here for help. I'm confused, but I feel like I'm waking up. I feel that something terrible has happened – but I don't know what. Yours is the first friendly face I've seen in some time, I think."

She turned and marched into his studio, and took a seat on his work stool, her eyes taking in the flash tacked to the walls.

"A lot of new ones up there since I was here last," she remarked. "A lot. Are my sister's eyes up there, anywhere?"

"They were," he admitted. "And *yours,* of course. But... I took them down soon after it happened. Didn't want it to seem like I was...capitalizing on your tragedy."

She smiled. "That was very...*honorable* of you. Truly."

"Eh," was all he could manage. "Hey, do you want a soda? Water? Granola bar?"

She pulled a beat-up water bottle out of a pocket in her robe. "I'm good."

"You look tired," he remarked.

"You have no idea," she laughed.

"Hey, they found one of your phones and iPad," Alex remarked, then felt foolish. "In the...rubble. Of the hotel..."

291

"Ah," she answered. "Good to know. But none of...us?"

Alex swallowed, thought hard on what to say next but knew nothing he could come up with would be...delicate. *She's a tough one*, he thought. *Look how she survived, I bet she can handle a lot yet...* "You're the first one of your sisters to be found," he finally offered. She nodded her head.

"Don't suppose my car is around?"

"I...hadn't heard about any cars salvaged. I kind of doubt it?"

She shrugged, and gave an indifferent smile.

They stared at each other for a few moments, then she said, "Well! Before we start contacting the proper 'authorities' and all that, you want to re-visit your work?" She spun on the stool, her back to him. She shrugged the robe off her shoulders and tugged at the bunched-up tee underneath, exposing her neck. "Come on, I want to make sure it isn't damaged."

"Oh, sure," he said, and moved over to her as she dipped her head.

As he looked down, he blinked, and then gasped.

"Oh, wow..." he said.

* * *

Julia paused at the security door, and through the screen watched her daughter sitting on the front porch steps. She would occasionally sip from her coffee mug, occasionally wave at the lone reporter across the street, and occasionally rub the back of her neck lightly, as if checking that her sisters were still there. No - it was more like she was just checking *in* with them.

Well, I can certainly understand that, Julia thought. Who would have thought a simple tattoo could...*comfort* you? Oh, after the bleak days – *months* – of living with the fact that *all* your children were gone, getting one of them back was more joyous than...well, holding her for the first time when she was born.

Of course, it would be her. *The survivor.* With another burden on her this time, but one she seemed to bear happily.

Yes, happily, she thought. *I've never seen her so relaxed. She hasn't lost her edge, but she certainly doesn't have the...cut that she used to. She can still tease Dave, but there is no meanness to it anymore.*

Poor Dave...

He refuses to look at the tattoo. Not out of spite, I think. He just has the notion that he needs to carry his grief and pain with him for a while yet. Well, who am I to say he's wrong? But I've had enough of that over the years, and if looking at a simple tattoo makes me feel like I have my daughters back with me, then so be it. And the kids – Amy no longer looks haunted. Byron swore that his mom winked at him. Julia smiled at the notion. *What a goofball he is. Still, you couldn't help but feel Cheryl was looking right back at you...*

She elbowed the door handle and eased onto the porch, a careful habit born to keep Ivan from getting out. That dog *really* hated the menagerie of news vans that used to hang around, and he would make a beeline for any reporter that dared to stray near the property. *Little bastard can actually move when he wants to.* But he was evidently sleeping elsewhere, and she was able to shut the door without a struggle.

As she turned, taking a sip from her own cup of coffee, Julia watched as Carol dutifully parted her hair to display her neck. *Ah, honey, let's focus on you right now,* Julia thought, and kissed the top of her daughter's head as she sat next to her, not even glancing at her neck.

"How we doing, sweetie?" she asked.

"Happy as fish and gorgeous as geese, as daddy used to say."

Julia chuckled. How they all had hated that song! Still, she wondered what she would give to have her husband back listening to it one last time? Maybe not so much, now? She had two miracles in her life already, and it would just be greedy to wish for more, wouldn't it? She took a deep sip from her cup.

"The President mentioned you today," she said.

"Oh yeah?"

"Yep."

"Anything interesting?"

"Oh, you know how she is – icy platitudes about wishing we all had the courage of a Carol O'Brian, blah, blah, blah..."

Carol laughed. "Oh, momma – are you still butt-hurt over Bernie?"

"Of course!'" Julia replied with a mock indignant tone.

"Well, if I'm allowed to make an observation beyond my scant years, things could have been worse. They always can be."

293

Julia raised her cup, and Carol clinked it with hers. They sat and sipped their coffee, enjoying the evening sunlight.

"Mom," Carol stated.

"Yeah sweetie?"

"If I had been born a boy, what would you have named me?"

"What?" laughed Julia.

"If I was a boy, what would my name be?"

"You thinking of transitioning, honey?"

"I'm serious, damn it."

"Of transitioning?"

"*Mom.*"

Julia sighed, and stared across the street. "Well, let's see. Your dad had the notion of...*Jesus*, you're asking me to remember that long ago? Okay...poets, your dad and I loved that poem by Byron, *Darkness*... It ends with, 'darkness had no need of aid from them, she was the Universe.' Something like that. *Anyway*, we thought naming kids after famous poets might be cool. You have to understand that we usually got stoned after sex and –"

"Mom!"

Julia raised a hand in apology, sipped from her mug, and continued.

"So, Byron came along, then we thought Shelly would be good for the next baby, but for some reason – trying to be 'responsible parents' I guess, so we cut back on the pot - we softened Shelly to Cheryl, and then the whole 'poets' thing went out the window. You were named for my aunt Carol, of course. But if you had been a *boy?*" Julia gazed at nothing for a moment. "Oh! After your dad's grandfather. *Peter.*"

"Ah. Interesting."

"Yeah?"

"Sure."

"That little nugget of info scratch an itch for you? Going to help you sleep at night, knowing that?"

"Maybe!"

Julia laughed, and leaned against her daughter, their heads touching. The sun had dropped, and it was magic hour.

* * *

Carol straightened abruptly. "Oh, shit!" she said.

"What?" her mother asked.

"Shit – I need to do something."

"*What?*"

Carol stood, and set her mug down next to her mother. "I need to remind somebody about something." She looked across the street at the reporter, his camera dangling off his shoulder. "And I think *that* asshole can help."

"What!"

"Trust me, momma," Carol breathed, and jogged down the walkway, cut across the lawn and arrowed towards the startled reporter, who frantically brought his camera back up to his shoulder and was mumbling something about being approached by an 'intense looking' Carol O'Brian, something that had never happened before, but it was happening now and –

"Hey!" Carol yelled.

"I'm not on your property," the reporter said defensively.

"How observant of you. What's your name?"

"Um, Chuck..."

"You're one of those second-string reporters, or whatever, yeah? Sent out to see if something might happen?"

"I assure you I – "

"Yeah, yeah, yeah. Say Chuck, I have a proposition for you."

"Um. You do?"

"Yeah. You can run this segment – in its entirety, *only* in its entirety - from the point where it looked like you were going to shit your pants when I headed over here, until I say we are done. You get to ask me one question if you agree to this, and I have my say."

"Um,"

"Chuck. If you don't agree to this, then I go to a local *competitor* of your station's and *they* get an in-depth interview, and you look like the biggest moron in moron town. Career on the skids, Chuck."

"Okay, you got it," he replied firmly, trying to gain control.

"Yay. So, you ask the question, I'll answer as best I can, and then I get to make a statement. Go for it."

Chuck blinked rapidly several times.

"Trying to do advanced calculus in there, Chuck? Tick-tock. I don't have all night."

"What... What do you think about what the President had to say about you? Today?"

Carol laughed. "Didn't hear it, sorry, so I have no opinion one way or another. Gee, Chuck, how long have you been over here, and *that's* the best you could come up with?"

"Now, I – "

"Uh-uh! *Nope*. My turn, Chuckles."

"You're right. I blew it. Go ahead."

"Attaboy." Carol ducked her head over to stare directly into the camera. "This is a shout out to my boy Mikey. Remember San Berdoo? I sure do! Hey, my mom and I were just talking about poets! Heh. Anyway... *Mike* – you remember our deal, don't you? I hope so. Remember, the cloud is our friend, and pics never go away. All my best to you. Be good!"

Carol stepped back, and focused her attention back on the reporter. "Thank you, Chuck. Believe it or not, that was important to me."

"Oh, glad I could – "

"Let me just add that *yes*, of course I miss my sisters terribly. But I feel that they're with me all the time. I hope all the victims will get their justice in the end and those responsible will pay. I have a feeling they will. Okay, that's it. We are done. Thank you, Chuck. Now, go forth and do some real reporting – believe me, there are bigger issues out there to wonder about other than how somebody is coping in the face of tragedy."

She tipped her head up, and spotted the first star of the night. "Much, *much* bigger things to wonder at."

Chapter 24

T he librarian pushed the cart filled with books down the aisles, his autopilot still running on Dewey Decimal. *This is* one *thing we're needed for,* he thought. *The public won't put their books back. They can check them out on their own now, do their own research, but by golly I get to put the books back to bed.*

He stopped, and slipped a volume off the cart, and the title made him grin. *His Master's Voice.* Well, heck. How can you be gloomy when someone out there is still checking out Stanislaw Lem? Hope for humanity after all.

He hummed lightly as he put the books away – one still did not whistle in the library, of course – and was heading over to the young adult section when the girl approached him.

"Hey," she whispered.

Ah, probably not a girl. Young *woman*, more like it. It was hard to tell, her eyes were hidden behind round, mirrored glasses. Her blond hair looked like it had been cut short, but was growing out. She wore a tie-died t-shirt, sweat pants and some retro sneakers. He was trying to decide if she was some sort of hippie hipster, and then scolded himself for being a judgmental forty-year old man. *She's in a library, looking for assistance,* he thought.

"Yes?" he finally asked, and she smiled.

"I was wondering, do you know if there are any books on the multiverse?"

His heart did a little cartwheel in his chest. If there was anything he liked more than helping someone learn about something cool, he had not discovered it yet.

"Why, yes there are," he said brightly. "One by Brian Greene comes to mind, and I believe Michio Kaku has one. Of course, a lot of theoretical physics books have chapters on them. I believe Hawking himself speculated on them."

"Really?" she asked. "I think the idea is absolutely fascinating. I understand there are several theories about the possibility?"

"Oh, indeed. I can show you where the sciences are. I'm sure we have them available to check out."

297

"Well, here's the thing," she said, and then tilted her head to read his name tag. "Byron, is it?"

"Yes," he said, bracing himself for a joke about poetry, or if he was a Lord.

But she just grinned, and said, "I go by 'D' these days. Nice to meet you."

"And likewise."

"I'm kind of a...vagabond, Byron. I don't have any sort of I.D., so I can't get a library card."

"Oh." He wasn't certain where this was going. Would she ask him if she could borrow books anyway?

"So is it okay if I just come in a lot, and read them here?"

Relief flooded through him. "Oh yes, certainly," he replied with a smile. "We like that – plenty of comfy chairs to sit in and read all day if you like. If the book is *available*, of course."

"Oh, of course. There are *always* other books in the library, right? Just like fish in the sea."

He laughed, and then covered his mouth and apologized for the volume of it. He liked this young woman. She had a familiarity about her, her tone of voice and posture that... It dawned on him that she could be one of his sisters, and his heart fluttered at the memory of them. But of course that was impossible.

One he lost many years ago. One he lost not so long ago. And one that was estranged. Family life had been...*unlucky* for him.

"You okay, Byron?" she asked with sincerity.

Be a professional, you idiot, he scolded himself, and shook his head.

"I'm sorry, Dee." he answered lightly. "Us old nerds can get lost in thought – too many books to distract us."

"*Old*," she laughed. "Hardly. But I get it. I'm going to have to bring my sister in here."

She sure does bounce a conversation around, Byron thought, amused. *It's as if she has so many questions to ask, and information to give, that she doesn't know what to do with either.* "Does your sister like to read too?" he asked.

"She's not much of a book worm, but...well, someday I'll bring her in."

"Ah. Well, the more the merrier?"

"Definitely. Do you like being a librarian?"

"I do," he replied, getting used to the rhythm of her random questions. He smiled. "I really do. I like helping people learn, if I can. And I'm surrounded by books – what's not to like?"

She laughed. "Right? Hey, have you *always* wanted to be a librarian?"

"Well, I suppose when you're younger you have...*grander* ideas for your life. But it suits me, and I believe it's a noble profession."

She smiled. "I do too. And you know what? I bet you have some grandeur ahead in life – you never know when it'll show up. Or how."

"I think that's the nicest thing anyone has said to me in quite some time. Thank you, Dee."

"No problem! Hey, why don't you lead me over to the sciences, and I can let you get back to work."

"My pleasure. Let's find *you* some grandeur!"

She giggled, and Byron marveled at how one person could brighten up your day. Despite its disappointments, life was good. He surprised himself by whistling.

Epilogue

*T*he fear would always be there. She discovered that it was necessary and even helpful. She was detached from it, yet it had her back, so to speak. That's why it always grew, because she suspected that was what was boiling away into the void. If those massive entities had the decency to be terrified of the journey, could they exist out here? The idea amused her. She had so much to learn. But, she had plenty of time.

She decided that she would never get used to this. She wasn't in pain – she didn't think she could feel pain anymore. There was a general uncomfortableness, like a yawn left unsatisfied, coupled with the maddening sensation of being a glass of water without the glass. One atom decay away from losing cohesion, form, identity. And of course, it wasn't anything like that at all – maybe in a few thousand years she could better describe it.

Yet, without eyes, she could see the end of things from here, just as she could see the beginning. She was learning how it had come down to this, and why it always would have. Maybe in a few million years, she would understand it.

She could see her children – she was lucky enough to affect them directly. She was mother to countless children, of course, but there were two that would always be special. She was glad that she could still soothe them, even if she would never be able to kiss their wounds, and cheer on their triumphs in person.

Still, they would know she watched until they were no longer a part of the universe. Maybe in a few trillion years, she could accept that.

She was certain that once her sisters were no longer part of the universe (and with Darla that could be a very long time indeed), she would no longer need them to anchor her – she would be fused with an expanding multiverse, pushing against nothing until it was too much, and then it was over.

But with that particular certainty, came another: the universe – the multiverse - would be back. Because the weight of nothing would be so much that it forced life's hand. It had done so, over and over, and that was the one true constant.

And when this one was over, and she disappeared along with it, she wondered if one last shout, a scream of defiance into the void, could make the next one a better one. Does it always have to be tooth and claw? I call bullshit on that...

Another traveler was blocked, a hopeful invader of other worlds. They were always so shocked that she was there, and that there was nothing to be done about it – not even a desperate scramble to return from where they came. She was in the way. She already found it sad instead of exhilarating. She wondered when she would no longer find it sad, and barely register it with the cold, unblinking eye of a crocodile.

She hoped that would be a long time coming.

Until then, she would dream of a word to shout out at the end. A word screamed so loud that it might echo in the void and find its way to weave itself into the fabric of spacetime in the next multiverse. A seed of a word that could grow a substantial foundation of caring, nurturing and acceptance of all, and not a constant battle for the high ground. No tooth and claw.

There were so many that she could choose. How to boil it down to just one word? Yet who was she kidding? She knew what it would be.

But it was fun pretending that she didn't.